Other Vampire Hunter D books published by Dark Horse Books

VAMPIRE HUNTER D

VOLUME 30
GOLD FIEND
PARTS ONE AND TWO

Written by
HIDEYUKI KIKUCHI

Illustrations by
YOSHITAKA AMANO

English translation by
KEVIN LEAHY

Dark Horse Books
Milwaukie

VAMPIRE HUNTER D 30: GOLD FIEND PARTS ONE AND TWO
© Hideyuki Kikuchi, 2020. Originally published in Japan in 2012 by ASAHI SONORAMA Co.
English translation copyright © 2020 by Dark Horse Books.

Cover art by Yoshitaka Amano
English translation by Kevin Leahy
Book design by Kristofer McRae

Published by
Dark Horse Books
A division of Dark Horse Comics LLC
10956 SE Main Street
Milwaukie, OR 97222
DarkHorse.com

First Dark Horse Books edition: July 2024
eBook ISBN 978-1-50672-080-7
ISBN 978-1-50672-079-1
10 9 8 7 6 5 4 3 2 1
Printed in the United States of America

Neil Hankerson Executive Vice President Tom Weddle Chief Financial Officer Dale LaFountain Chief Information Officer Tim Wiesch Vice President of Licensing Vanessa Todd-Holmes Vice President of Production and Scheduling Mark Bernardi Vice President of Book Trade and Digital Sales Randy Lahrman Vice President of Product Development and Sales Cara O'Neil Vice President of Marketing Dave Marshall Editor in Chief Davey Estrada Editorial Director Chris Warner Senior Books Editor Cary Grazzini Director of Specialty Projects Lia Ribacchi Creative Director Michael Gombos Senior Director of Licensed Publications Kari Yadro Director of Custom Programs Kari Torson Director of International Licensing Christina Niece Director of Scheduling

VAMPIRE HUNTER D

Gold Fiend

PART ONE

An Odd Employer

I

There was a knock. The darkness swallowed it. There was such a density to this darkness it was palpable. After ten more of the same, the sound became a voice.

"Hey, open up! A hell of a hotel you chose to hole up in. You gonna open up or what? If you don't, I've got dynamite with me. And I'm ready to use it, too. Nobody makes a fool of Old El, the all-purpose financier!"

The darkness responded.

"What do you want?"

"Oh me, oh my. Now, that's a step toward communicating. At any rate, do me a favor and open up this creepy old door. I got a sweet deal waiting for you out here!"

"Tell me."

"Wh-what? You wanna get me talking when you won't even show yourself, you little bastard? Sheesh, you're just a lousy dhampir—a half-baked failure of a vampire—so don't go acting like you're God or something. Ow! That hurts like a mother—"

Apparently he'd picked the wrong place to try and kick in the door.

Once his pained curses had expired, the man's voice continued in a tone not of anger but of naked pleading, "Oh, I'm real sorry about that. Us humans get up in years and we don't have much restraint anymore, and that ain't good. I figure it can't hurt to ask, but could I get you to protect me?"

"From whom?"

"Deadbeats trying to weasel out of paying their loans."

A silence ensued. The whole proposition probably sounded ridiculous.

"Hey! C'mon, don't fall asleep on me. This deadbeat I got, well, it's kinda special." Taking a breath, he continued, "It's a Noble."

This time, there was an immediate response.

"Fifty thousand dalas a day, and that ain't including expenses," a hoarse voice stated.

"Huh?" the speaker said, his eyes surely popping. The voice from the darkness had suddenly gone from a youthful ring to a hoarse croak. "What, you got your manager in there, do you? Well, no problem. So, will you take the job?"

"What's the Noble's name?"

"Marquis Verenis."

"Oh, he's a biggie," remarked the hoarse voice.

"Don't be daft. He's a liar and a scumbag and a disgrace to the whole Nobility. After getting antimatter circuitry from me worth over three hundred million dalas, he sends assassin duplicates of himself for me when it was time to pay up."

"Hmm. Was it due in a lump sum?" asked the hoarse voice.

"Nope. I was supposed to get it in twenty installments, each as a draft for sixteen and a half million dalas. And he stiffed me from the very first one."

"Hmm, that's definitely deadbeat behavior."

"I know, right? And I figured he'd run off, but no, he's still living in his castle, comfy as can be. Now that's what you call brass balls. I ain't about to let him get away with this."

"Didn't you have him put up any collateral?" the hoarse voice asked.

"His castle and his whole damned domain. He's so cantankerous, though, I can't seize the lousy property. I sent young fellas up there armed to the teeth to throw a scare into him, and not a one of 'em has made it back."

"Hmm, that's some blatantly premeditated action on his part. Which means he must've drawn up plans. And to have gone and gotten all aggressive with you, that's one nasty Nobleman!"

"I knew that when we inked the contract. That ship has sailed, though. What bothers me is what comes next. That bastard Verenis figures I'm coming to demand payment, naturally, so he'll have all kinds of assassins waiting along the way like as not. If it was just your garden-variety punks and warrior wannabes, I could handle that on my own, but when it comes to Noble-class killers, it puts me a tad on edge. Which is what brings me here to hire you. Now, I'd heard rumors, but you really do have a weird voice, don't you?"

"Keep your smart remarks to yourself. So, when are you headed out?"

"Right away."

"Good enough."

"What?" Old El said, his voice ringing hollow in his amazement. "You'll really do it?"

"You think I'm lying or something?" the hoarse voice said with a hint of menace.

"No, I'm all set to go. We'll set out straight away! Now hurry up and get outta that grave."

A few seconds passed.

A streak of light split the darkness vertically. Little by little it grew thicker, and the light increased.

Old El watched with loathing and trepidation as the bronze door opened right in front of him. For all the years he'd seen, his fear of the Nobility hadn't vanished. *I'm just your average human, I guess,* the old man thought to himself.

His right hand naturally tightened on the grip of his automatic stake gun. The safety was off, and the roller-bearing bolt was pulled back, leaving the first shot in firing position. A little more than a pound of pressure on the trigger, and compressed gas would propel a ten-ounce stake through a Noble's heart at a range of a hundred yards. If they didn't dodge it, that is.

Rust flaking from it here and there, the door finally finished opening. On the other side stood a figure in black. As the face beneath his wide-brimmed traveler's hat drew closer, Old El couldn't move a muscle.

"Hey," the hoarse voice called to the old man, snapping him back to his senses. A feeling of vertigo swept over him. Reeling, he reached for the granite tombstone beside him just to keep from falling over. When he looked at the face of the man in black, Old El's expression melted in rapture, and he actually seemed to be fighting back tears.

"So . . . handsome . . . Who knew . . . there were guys like this . . ."

"You'd better get yourself some sunglasses right quick," the hoarse voice told the old man, finally bringing him back to reality.

"So, you're D? I'm Old El. I work as an all-purpose financier."

"So I heard."

"Huh?!"

The old man got a shaft of steel down his spine. For the young man had finally answered in a voice befitting his appearance. Generally, the difference between that and the earlier voice was so great that most were left unable to respond for some time, so in that respect the old man was pretty resilient.

Madly scrutinizing their surroundings, Old El asked, "Do all you dhampirs rest in empty crypts?" The sun was still high in the sky. He continued, "I came running as soon as I heard you were in this here village, but then you weren't at the hotel. Weren't in any of the vacant houses, neither. When I heard you were out here, I didn't believe it at first."

"Depends on how we feel," the Hunter replied, his voice changing back once more, plunging the old man into confusion. "Graveyards echo with the voices of the dead. Their thoughts get woven into clumps of trees and pool between the tombstones. Apparently, they like to listen to them from time to time."

I guess dhampirs really do lean more toward the dead side, Old El thought.

"You can do the job okay, though, right? I can't have you off gossiping with ghosts when I need you the most!"

"First off, you'd best watch *your* step unless you want us talking with your ghost. Noble assassins are serious business!"

Old El was at a loss for words there.

The handsome figure casually walked right past the old man and down the dirt path toward the exit from the graveyard.

Heading after him in a fluster, Old El said, "Oh, I almost forgot. I was hoping to see just how good you are. Cut something for me."

"And if you don't like what you see, you'll reconsider hiring me? Just so you know, I never listen to the same job offer twice."

"Uh-huh," the hoarse voice concurred.

The two figures with three voices were approaching the graveyard's exit. One section of the stone wall, which was strictly ornamental, had an iron gate that was also purely for show.

D halted. He looked straight ahead.

In the lazy afternoon sunlight, a clump of trees was moaning. It was the wind.

The village lay directly in front of them. With a population of about three hundred, it was the kind of village you'd find anywhere in the western Frontier. Still, the roofs were painted red, blue, orange, or green. Even on the Frontier, people were mindful of staying fashionable.

From somewhere among those roofs, a silvery object was headed their way.

"Take cover," D commanded in a low voice. Soft and calm though it was, it had a power that would brook no debate.

Old El quickly assayed his surroundings, then made a dash for the largest tombstone.

D didn't move. For this young man, anywhere could be a battlefield. And anytime was a good time to fight.

The thing had the shape of one of the oldest flying objects. The body of it was reminiscent of an oversized walnut, with two six-foot-long rectangular wings projecting from the bottom of it, one to either side. Seemingly set with glass, those wings, as well as the tail fins, made minor adjustments to their angles, which in turn seemed to change the direction of flight.

A bird flying into the wind, it halted at a spot about three feet in front of D. The front of it had been carefully painted with a pair of eyes and a mouth. The eyes had a hard gleam to them. That was probably due to the compact camera lenses they contained.

The broadside of the wings turned to face D.

D's right hand made the faintest of movements.

Suddenly, the bird started a steep climb, as if it'd had a change of heart.

"Here we go!" said the hoarse voice.

The shape of the bird dissolved against the sun.

D dashed to the right.

The sun seemed to explode. Stark white light enveloped the world. Centered around the gate, the ground in a thirty-foot radius boiled and bubbled. Iron, stone, and soil all melted, eventually turning into a glassy substance.

At a spot about thirty feet from the outer edge of the blistering hellhole, D's eyes sought out Old El.

"Did they get him?" asked the Hunter.

"He hopped in the shower," the hoarse voice replied.

Eleven hundred feet above the surface, the murderous flying machine was preparing for its next assault. Exposing the energy-absorbing side of its heat beam panels to the sun, it waited five seconds. Since the cameras were in a fixed position, the machine had to be pointed nearly straight down to acquire a target.

Though the twin lenses detected an object rising from the ground at terrific speed, the person controlling the flying machine couldn't tell exactly what it was. And before the controller could grow concerned enough to move the machine, the object became a stark wooden stake that pierced the faux bird.

A blossom of electromagnetic waves flowered in midair. That, in turn, was swallowed up by an even more massive blossom of white.

"You did it!" the hoarse voice exclaimed without a trace of surprise. In light of the miraculous way a wooden stake weighing less than an ounce had fought its way through crosswinds and risen eleven hundred feet to penetrate a metallic target, foil or not, such a response might've been something of an outrage.

"Oh, nicely done. Very nice, indeed."

This pleasant praise from the old man sounded slightly distorted.

Beyond the heat shimmer, a vestige of the blistering flare, there stood something silvery and vaguely cylindrical. It resembled the kind of portable shower tents used by long-term expeditionary parties. The surface of it split vertically, and Old El appeared. Touching his hand to the cylinder's surface, he quickly pulled it back again with a yelp about the heat, adding, "I don't know just what it was you threw, but to score a bull's-eye on an enemy flying way up there with just one shot, damn, that's really something. That had to be a thousand feet!"

"That wasn't Marquis Verenis, was it?"

"Oh, you could tell, could you? There's only one person who'd use a rig like that. A killer who goes by the name of Machete. He was hired by Julas-Han Toba—another deadbeat bastard. I'd heard rumors he was gunning for me, but it looks like he's finally making his move."

"How many defaulters do you have?" D asked in his own voice.

"At the moment, four. That's including the marquis, just so you know."

"I can't cover the other three."

"Why not?" asked Old El.

"They've got nothing to do with the Nobility."

"You—you can't be serious. They're gunning for me while I go to collect from a Noble. That there's plenty to do with the Nobility!"

"The deal is off."

"H-hey! Wait just minute, please!" the old man plaintively pleaded with D from behind as the Hunter started to walk away, avoiding the gate still withering from the blast of heat.

It was a heartbeat later that his cries bore unexpected fruit.

He shouted, "I met the Sacred Ancestor, you know!"

D halted and looked back.

The instant the old man saw his expression, he felt like he'd been stranded in a wintry wasteland.

II

"When and where?" D inquired.

And if I don't answer—That thought filled the old man's mind with terror.

"It was better than fifty years ago," said Old El, "back when I first got into the business, and we met at this old castle in the eastern Frontier. Back then, who'd have ever thought I'd run into the man known as D someday?"

"What did you discuss?"

"That's a secret. I'll tell you if you finish this job out with me."

"Fine. But it's four times the usual rate on account of all them humans to contend with," said the hoarse voice.

"That your negotiating voice?" the old man cried out in rage. D ignored him.

"If you don't like it, call it off."

"I could say the same to you. Don't you care what the Sacred Ancestor had to say about you?"

"Who's to say whether you ever even met him or not?" the hoarse voice protested.

"Oh, you still doubt me? Okay, I'll show you proof, then. I mean, I'll *tell* you it."

"Oh, yeah? Well, speak away. Come on! What've you got?"

"*Success.*"

The air froze. The speaker fell flat on his ass. Cradling his own head, Old El bit down on his finger, trembling like he'd been in a major earthquake. He was certain that saying that one word was the worst mistake of his life.

"You've got a deal," D said.

"Huh?" the old man replied, thinking, *I ain't sure my ticker can take this.* "And your wages?"

"My regular rate will be fine. But in return, you'd better not lie to me at all."

"O-o-o-of course not," he stammered. *How the hell could I? You'd probably rip me limb from limb,* Old El thought as he looked through a rain of fearful sweat drops at the young man of unearthly beauty before him. He wasn't even sure whether his trembling was due to fear or how gorgeous the Hunter's face was.

The old man's wagon was parked a short way from the graveyard. It was a cargo wagon drawn by a team of four cyborg horses. The wagon was divided into a living compartment and a cargo compartment, and in total it was about fifty feet long and more than ten feet high. By its side, D whistled. A cyborg horse came galloping over like a black gale.

Once one man was up in the driver's seat and the other in the saddle, the hoarse voice asked, "What was that cylinder thing earlier?"

"A 'personal fortress,'" the old man replied. "They say it was developed using Noble technology. There was this broke scientist who couldn't pay back the five hundred dalas he borrowed to cure his wife of a real bad ailment, but I tell you, he sure knew his stuff."

Having cooled from the heat, the cylinder had been quickly folded up and stored on the back of Old El's belt.

The old man swished the reins and the horses broke into a run, and soon after that he turned to D, riding right alongside the wagon, and said, "I got something I'd like to ask you, too. What were the dead back in that crypt talking about?"

"The things you'd want to talk about."

Old El didn't know what to say to that.

"Living or dead, it makes no difference. Life ends, death comes around—they want to talk about things like that."

The old man said nothing more. When he talked to the young man, everything he saw seemed to take on a new appearance. And that was a truly horrifying thought.

The two of them didn't return to the village, but rather continued straight on to the highway that headed south.

Before long, the highway ushered the wagon and the cyborg horse onto the plains. The washed-out brown hue of the ground extended as far as the eye could see, and from time to time, semitransparent shapes resembling the sails of ships would form. They were clouds of dust.

There was a sound like a beast somewhere letting out a bass growl or echoes of a drum.

"There's a storm getting close. Just like the weather bureau predicted. Better haul ass to the next way station," Old El murmured, looking up at the heavens glumly. But he glanced over at D, galloping right alongside him to his immediate right and said, "You mean to tell me it don't make no difference to you either way, storm or shine? Nothing matters to you except killing Nobles—no, strike that, you ain't interested in the Nobility either. Just what is it you see?"

Still, the old man got no reply.

Flustered that he was ready to strike and with no one to lash out at, the old man continued again, "We're heading into a mess of killing, and you don't even ask me about who we'll be up against—though I reckon I should fill you in."

He waited a bit for some response, but wasn't prompted for more information. With a shake of his head, Old El said, "I'll give 'em to you from oldest to most recent. First up, there's Galkis Thomas. He's the boss of a mob of flying bandits called Quetzalcoatl, and he came to borrow money for repairs on the airship they use as their main base of operations. Three million dalas. When I went to collect, though, he took off right in front of me and flew away. So in return, I found out where Galkis's mistress lived and started putting the screws to her for info. Hell, I started out with the light stuff, and she went and bugged her eyes and keeled over then and there! Had a bad ticker, don't you know. That got the son of a bitch all pissed off at me in turn, meaning he sends killers after me wherever I go! And they're a bugger to deal with, coming at me from above. Plus, they use these artificial wings, huge aircraft, long-range fighters, and a crew that's the cream of the crop. I got no problem with him sending 'em after me, but the least he could do is pay me back my damn money!" the old man said with a hint of rage, and then he shut his eyes. He was calming his mind.

Soon, Old El continued, saying, "The second one's Julas-Han Toba, from earlier. He's a beastmaster. Uses hypnotism to control monsters and supernatural critters. He was bringing ice beasts back from the Frozen Wastes beyond the northern Frontier sectors when an accident left him unable to use that hypnotism of his, so I sprung for his transport costs. And like the rest, he acted like he didn't owe me a thing. I hit the storage facility where he keeps his beasts out of the blue and moved 'em all somewhere else as collateral. In other words, he'd have to pay me to get 'em back. Well, apparently that hit the bastard where it hurt, and he sent word he'd pay back the money, only this murderous virus ran through the place I'd stashed his beasties, killing the lot of 'em. Seems he went to a hell of a lot of trouble training 'em, so the bastard tells me he's gonna get me and hires Machete. Now, Machete can't control beasts, but he uses a lot of gadgets. Like that flying machine earlier, or a runaway train, or a submersible craft that fires torpedoes from underwater. Almost did me in a couple of times. I was relaxing this one time with a smoke because the only thing around was a kid playing with a toy, and then the damn kid exploded. His stuffed bear had a bomb stuck in it.

Thanks to that, I had the kid's parents and all his relatives after me, too, for a good stretch!"

"Sounds like real trouble," D said. It was probably enough to leave anyone stunned.

Old El went into overdrive. "The third one is a puppet master. His name's Langen Tupperman. He came to me saying his wife and kids were starving and he wanted to borrow fifty thousand dalas, but he paid me back on the due date, sure enough. Or rather, it *looked* like he paid me. A month later, though, I realized they were just leaves with drawings like real money on 'em. That sly old fox! I searched high and low for him, finally tracking him down to a show he was doing at a club called Jealousy in the eastern Frontier. As luck would have it, he used his powers to turn the hostesses into dolls, and the lot of 'em kept me from getting him. They were fixing to kill me, so I busted up every last one of 'em, I did. It so happened one of 'em was Tupperman's girlfriend, though. And Tupperman swore he'd keep after me as long as I lived."

"They borrow money and default on their loans. Try to collect from 'em, and they hold a grudge without fail. These are the kind of scumbags you have to deal with in this job. They started making my hair go gray, I tell you!"

"Bet they'd say the same," the hoarse voice murmured.

"What'd you say?"

"The lightning's getting closer," D said, streaks of blue still reflected in his dark eyes. "It's a thunder beast. Ground yourself."

No sooner had the old man pulled back on the reins than D dismounted and got his horse to lie on its side. Taking a black protective cover out of one of his coat pockets, he placed it over the steed. As cyborg horses were electronic devices, there was some concern that electrical discharge could cause them to malfunction.

In addition to radar, there was a veritable forest of sensors and antennae on the roof of the wagon, but now it was time for the lightning rod to come into play. A cord was connected to the ground, and then the preparations for dissipating discharges from the electrical lifeform were complete.

Viewed dispassionately, it was no more than a black cloud floating a scant fifty yards off the ground. Every few seconds the entire thing was lit from within by a prismatic glow, and then nearly a hundred bolts of lightning would hammer the ground. Many were the poets who loved that glow to a fault.

"Here it comes!" the old man bellowed into a microphone, watching an image from the surveillance camera from beneath his shielding. His shout reached D through a speaker mounted outside.

Darkness and light covered the two of them. A high-voltage discharge of half a million volts scored direct hits on their respective shields.

The hoarse voice immediately remarked, "Persistent sucker."

A normal thunder beast would discharge electricity over and over again as it moved along. There was no chance of it stopping anywhere. But over ten seconds had passed since D had come under fire. Fire spouted from the shields. D twitched from head to toe. He'd taken a direct hit to the head from one of the electrical blasts.

"What's this—one of the assassins after the old man?" the hoarse voice mused.

Apparently D had the same thought. He raised his slightly twitching body from the ground.

"Don't be crazy! I don't care who you are, you'll be in real trouble if you keep getting electrocuted!"

D raised the shield before he'd heard everything the old man had to say. He stood there like a wrathful guardian deity, his body wrapped in rain and wind and light. Lightning lashed his form without pause.

But a different kind of flash shot out in the opposite direction. Though he'd drawn it from the sheath on his back and shifted it to the other hand faster than the eye could follow, the Hunter had hurled his blade in the blink of an eye. It had literally been done with lightning speed.

Run through in a vital spot with remarkable skill, the monster quivered in midair. The foreign substance that'd been introduced into the thunder beast's body ravaged its electrical nervous system, preventing the transmission of information. It no longer had control of its bodily functions. Its ability to discharge electricity destroyed, it released the charge into its own body.

D didn't bother watching the black cloud as it headed in an unlikely direction, shooting lighting as it tore apart. Throwing off the flaming shield that covered it, he got his cyborg horse back up.

Just as the Hunter got in the saddle, Old El appeared in the driver's seat of the wagon.

"Damnation, you've gone and done it again! I'm mighty impressed, I tell you. Who'd have thought you'd take down a thunder beast?!" he said, with more than a few sighs mixed in. When his gaze shifted from D, it was to the electrical monster on the plains about a hundred yards away, now reduced to a small black cloud. There were occasional flashes of light within it, and electromagnetic waves filled the air, but it was clear that its showy display would soon be at an end.

"You said something about being an all-purpose financier," said the Hunter. "Taken any swords as collateral?"

"Oh, yeah. A whole bunch of 'em. I got more fine, classic swords than you can shake a stick at!" the old man replied, thumping his chest forcefully. That was followed by a fit of coughing.

III

Opening a door in the cargo wagon that had a scrap of paper scrawled with "Merchandise Storage" taped to it, D was greeted by an area about the size of a very small house, and indeed it was filled with merchandise. The first thing to catch his eye was a mountain of plastic containers with the word "clothes" written on the front.

Stacked all the way to the ceiling, one near the middle had its cover askew, giving a peek at its contents.

"What the hell's that?" the hoarse voice asked as the Hunter walked past it. D's left hand had happened to pass right over the one with the cover partially open.

With a grin from ear to ear that said, *I'm glad you asked,* Old El thrust a meaty paw into the container and pulled out a fistful of tiny, flat vinyl packets. They were two inches square, and couldn't have been even a tenth of an inch thick.

"Those supposed to be clothes?" the hoarse voice inquired.

"Yeah, the latest development from the Capital, a little something they call 'compressed wear.' Don't matter whether it's synthetic fibers or real silk, they can compress anything from ladies' underthings to dresses down to this size. Man, the traveling show folks love this stuff. And since they basically take up no storage space at all, housewives living in cramped little places dream about something this size. Gets 'em damp no matter how it looks on 'em!"

Taking one of the packets, the old man pressed his finger down on one corner. There was the whistle of rushing air, and then a crimson evening dress filled his hand.

"As you can see, not a wrinkle on it. And the effect is guaranteed for a hundred years. There are more orders for women's and children's clothing and household supplies than anything else on the Frontier. They keep coming up with inventions like this, and it'll revolutionize trade between the Capital and the Frontier by leaps and bounds."

"As I recall, the Nobility had a miniaturization method using molecular dynamics," the hoarse voice remarked.

"You mean the one they came up with for the OSB War? They could take any cannon or missile or base, no matter how huge it was, and make it fit into a leather satchel—some folks say they could make things small enough to carry around in your breast pocket. Humans haven't got as far as that yet."

Returning the packets to the container, the old man led D further into the back. To the weapons corner.

Mixed in with the big stuff—things like atomic destructo-beams and laser cannons the Nobility had handed down to the humans—were a wide assortment of old-fashioned arms like gunpowder rifles and pistols, crossbows, and more. One corner was packed with nothing but swords.

"Choose any one you like. They're all high-quality pieces from ancient times."

Not giving so much as a glance to all the blades as straight as walking sticks, D took it upon himself to walk on a little further, grabbing one wrapped in gold brocade that rested on a gorgeous rack fashioned from animal horns. Untying the cords and taking off the dazzling fabric revealed the black sheath and black handle of a sword so impressive it would give most who saw it goosebumps. The Hunter grabbed the sheath and handle, drawing it just the tiniest bit, and that made the old man adjust the front of his coat without a word, his forehead covered with sweat.

The hoarse voice had let out a low groan. The alluring glint of the blade reflected a face of unearthly beauty, and that beauty drank up the glint.

Suddenly, the battle of the exquisite ended. Returning the blade to its sheath, D said, "A hundred thousand dalas."

For that amount, you could purchase a small village, lock, stock, and barrel.

Old El made an expression somewhere between smiling and weeping. He wasn't sure exactly how to react.

"S-s-s-sure. That little gem comes from an island country they say existed in the far east long, long ago. Ordinarily, I'd ask for twice that price, but seeing how good you are with one of them things, I'll let you have it at half price."

"What are you talking about, you lousy con man? The bag's got a sticker on it right here that says it's ten grand!"

"Whaaaat?!"

"Ha ha ha! I'm just messing with you," the hoarse voice guffawed.

Glaring at D, the old man bared his teeth, saying, "That's a sick little hobby you've got there." He thought D was doing some kind of ventriloquism.

"That thunder beast was being manipulated," D said, taking the sword in hand. "I suppose you can imagine who was behind that. Your enemies are one step ahead of you. Better watch yourself."

And having said that, the Hunter left the storage area without a sound.

After midnight, the wind and the rain only grew fiercer.

"This is too much for me now," said Old El. "About six miles from here, there's the ruins of a Noble base from back during the OSB War. We can wait out the dawn there."

D had only one thing to say in regard to the old man's suggestion. "Give me the reins," he said, moving over to the driver's seat.

"Hey—what do you think you're doing?"

"Get some sleep. I'll keep them moving."

With that, it dawned on the old man that the worlds they lived in were reversed. As a dhampir with the blood of the Nobility in his veins, the Hunter was heading into the very best time to be active. That being the case, Old El was quick enough to change gears.

"Okay, it's all yours," he replied, promptly taking the passage down from the driver's seat to the interior, as that was sure to make things easier for D, too.

The whip snarled viciously through wind and rain, and the wagon picked up speed. D's cyborg horse followed along without complaint.

"Wow, this is incredible!" the old man practically screamed with joy, strapping himself into his seat. "At the rate you're going, forget about hitting the next way station tomorrow, you'll get us there tonight! This is great—huh?!"

His body jerked forward. The restraints dug into his belly, nearly squeezing the life out the old man.

As soon as the jolt of forward momentum had passed, Old El popped his head up by the driver's seat, still wheezing for breath.

"Wh-what's going on?" he stammered.

"We're going to the base," D replied, staring straight ahead.

The old man's eyes followed suit, but they saw nothing save darkness. Instead, he heard a sound, though. Water splashing. It continued endlessly.

"Is that what I think?" the old man asked.

"There's a river about twenty yards away."

"Th-there sure as hell shouldn't be! There's nothing but plains out here for the next sixty miles!"

"It's probably a trap."

"What? It's an illusion, then?"

"No, it's real. We'll have to throw a bridge down to get across. But there's probably something in the water."

"Better to do it tomorrow, then, eh?" Old El suggested.

"Now's best for me. But we don't have any material for a bridge. The ruins of the fort had some building materials."

"Er, okay," the old man replied with a nod, thinking all the while, *This guy's really scary. Them dhampirs are something else!*

During the OSB War, to defend from their foe's old-fashioned aerial attacks, the Noble side had built an equally analog fort defended by anti-aircraft guns. Though there were as many theories as there were stars in the sky for why these two civilizations, which even among interstellar races probably ranked as the top two in the history of the universe, would choose to engage in such archaic warfare, not a single one of them was conclusive, but ultimately speculations settled on the theory there was an almost inescapable longing for the days of yore coded in the DNA of both species.

"You know, I hear this plain once had a plant for manufacturing synthetic blood," said Old El.

Now, little more than dusty remains were left on the wild plain, and despite the Nobility's attempts to protect the place, no amount of scrutiny could uncover anything more than heaps of stone and concrete. One part remained that was reminiscent of a dome, and though the floors and stairways still held their shape, the machines of war that'd filled the place had either been disposed of on their destruction, or else carried off by humans who'd come through later. What was left stood in the driving rain, an empty husk that'd been stripped of its soul.

Parking the wagon behind the cover of the dome, D climbed onto the back of his cyborg horse and galloped off. Whoever made this river was undoubtedly a foe after Old El. If their plan was to throw up a roadblock and strike while the old man was still figuring out what to do, they'd probably be coming soon. If they were thinking of striking after daybreak, then the old man and D should get back out on the wasteland, where they'd have freedom to maneuver, before then.

Before he'd gone a hundred yards, D was greeted by a large cluster of trees. Branches bent and leaves cried out in tiny voices. From the rain's bombardment.

Climbing down from his cyborg steed, D walked over to a trunk that was twice as large as his arms would fit around and made a casual swing of his sword. The blade cleaved the trunk like it was slicing butter, cutting clean through it. Before the crash from the toppling of the gigantic tree had even subsided, D had a second one lying at his feet. Walking exactly twenty yards from the end he'd cut, D lopped off the rest. Half of the branches he'd taken off on the way up there, and by the time he came back again the trunk was bare. Without a moment's respite, D put his blade against the first cut he'd made and slowly walked the length of the trunk. What followed was a miracle born of an expertly crafted sword from that eastern country and D's skill coming together flawlessly. For he'd split the twenty-yard-long trunk lengthwise without pausing for a second.

After repeating the procedure on the second tree, he loaded one split log on his right shoulder and the other on his left, then left the woods. The wind assailed him, as if that were the very moment it'd been waiting for. Though the tree trunks swayed, D didn't.

Wood or not, each of those halves weighed more than three tons. Shouldering a total of twelve tons, he headed in the direction of the splashing sounds.

Four shadowy figures stood up, one to either side of him, one to the front, and one to the rear. All of them had been lying on the ground.

The sound of the running water echoed off freshly drawn blades.

"Who put you up to this?" the hoarse voice asked. D had either hand resting on the logs on his shoulders. And the voice had come from the vicinity of his left one.

"We don't know, either," said the figure in front of the Hunter. "But we do know this—you've got your hands full, D!"

Swords came at him from all sides. At the center of the swings and thrusts, D had already drawn his sword, and still holding on to the wood, he brought his weapon into play. The trunk that rolled off his shoulder made the attacker on his right stop in his tracks, while the foes coming at him from the front and back slipped under the trunk on his left shoulder, though a half turn of his blade was enough to bisect them both horizontally and then impale the opponent to his left.

Not one of their blades had reached D.

Leaping over the tree trunk, the last one had his sword held high over his head. It sank into the flat side of the split trunk, while another blade came from below, piercing the trunk and attacker alike and jutting from the back of the latter.

"Oh, what do we have here? Golems?"

As the hoarse voice said that, the four attackers turned into eight-inch-tall dolls, and the way they dissolved in the pounding rain was a testimony to the fact that they were made of mud.

"Langen Tupperman," said the hoarse voice. "But golems don't die when they're stabbed. Anybody who can put them down with one blow is a man to be feared."

The voice flowed along with D as he crouched down to collect the second trunk from the ground and put it back on his shoulder, then continued on toward the riverbank.

When he arrived at the river's edge, D bent his knees slightly and straightened them again. The two split tree trunks were laid across the river, flat sides up. After another two were down, even the old man's merchandise-laden wagon would be able to cross them.

As the Hunter turned around to head back to the woods, a terrific explosion rang out from the direction of the ruins, and flames shot up toward the darkened sky. Anyone would've felt that the wind and rain had been peaceful by comparison.

Stealthy Approach
of the Shadow Warriors

CHAPTER 2

I

On charging into the dome, what D saw was the infuriated cyborg horses, a still-burning mass beside the wagon, and the toppled mud dolls in and around the flames.

"Survived, did you?" Old El remarked, his head popping up by the driver's seat. "When things get like this, there ain't a chance in hell of me going out there. That's the safest bet. Which is why they came at me in human form. They started swinging their steel all of a sudden, but they couldn't even put a dent in the wagon. And then—"

The old man was trying to say one of them had pulled out a bomb.

"Not even my wagon could've stood up to a blast from that up close. So I let 'em have it with a missile before they could unload on me. That took care of 'em!"

"Who put them up to it?" asked D.

"Tupperman, like as not."

"And where does he live?"

"A town called Gimmicklin about a hundred and twenty miles from here."

"Is that a fact?" the hoarse voice remarked. "I've heard that's an awful weird town. Seems travelers passing through there come out dead broke or not at all."

"Aw, that's nothing! Just so long as I can get him to pay up," the old man said, his voice invested with strength. "But before we get there, we gotta pass through the towns of Chiriki, Dynemaely, Timothy, Sekatae, and Amanly. And you can bet your sweet ass Galkis Thomas and Julas-Han Toba will be lying in wait in at least one of 'em. I'll be counting on you!"

"By first light, we'll have a bridge down," said the hoarse voice.

"You'll do what?!" the old man exclaimed maniacally. Then his eyes shifted to D's left hand and he began to laugh out loud. "Oh, you're too much. To start work on a bridge, you'd need about thirty times our numbers and a hundred tons of machinery. That's the bare minimum for even the simplest kind. You gonna do that alone? There ain't but an hour till dawn. You gonna put out a call for workmen now or something? Bwahahaha!"

The next morning, the old man wore a stupefied expression as he crossed D's "bridge."

It was more than three hours later that Old El squinted his eyes with suspicion, saying, "What's that out there?"

"Someone wearing a flight device," D replied. Apparently the Hunter had long since spotted him. He couldn't have been more than a mile and a quarter away. The wide-spread wings and the figure beneath them was slowly drawing closer. He must've been after a covered wagon that was racing down the highway.

"Quetzalcoatl?" asked D.

"Don't rightly know—but yeah, probably," the old man replied, squinting even harder. "What the hell?!"

The winged individual—or birdman—had suddenly started to descend. A cylinder that tapered to a point slid from the oblong box that hung from his wings, then disgorged flames in midair.

The birdman began a rapid climb. Still trailing flames, the cylinder sank into the back end of the wagon as it raced across the ground. More than the fiery gout of black and orange, it was the shockwave that flipped the covered wagon forward end-over-end.

"That's Quetzalcoatl for sure," the old man said, raising his whip. "What's the plan?"

"Go out there and help them. That's only right."

D raced forward. He quickly covered the distance to the covered wagon.

His climb now finished, the birdman must've spotted D, because he once more went into a descent. Whether D noticed this or not, his eyes remained directly in front of him. The tube under the wings spat fire. A split second before the airborne explosive detonated, the hem of D's coat swished backward. To the birdman, it may have looked as if a black and ominous bird had suddenly appeared. Easily sailing over the blistering death of the fireball, the Hunter hurled a streak of white.

The birdman was gripped by a vision of his own death. Though he worked the cables to change direction, his body moved no more as it began to climb. A terrible pain pierced his heart, and forgetting to even beat the wings over which he no longer had control, the birdman plummeted headfirst back to earth.

Not even bothering to confirm that his stake had done its work, D went over to the covered wagon. A red-haired girl grabbed the hand of a man—apparently her father—and attempted to pull him from the driver's seat of the inverted vehicle. When D approached, the girl called out for help, never letting go of that hand.

Grabbing the man's hand, D pulled him free, setting him down on the ground not far away. He knew the man wouldn't last long. Every breath he took brought bright blood spilling from his nose and mouth. Broken ribs had punctured his lungs.

"Take my daughter—my Lydia . . . to Amanly . . . Her Uncle Scob . . . lives there . . ."

The man's hand seized the hem of D's coat. His eyes, already muddying with the hue of death, pierced D with a momentary gleam. Most likely that had been the last of his strength. Though the man closed his eyes, his hand didn't let go.

Pulling free of it, D stood up and looked at the girl, who stood stunned behind him.

The hoarse voice said, "Bury him, at least."

At that point, the transport wagon pulled up and Old El ran over. Surveying the scene around the man's remains, he grimaced and said, "A hell of a thing this is. The poor thing."

To which the hoarse voice replied, "With you around, the corpses are just gonna keep piling up."

"What are you talking about? That Quetzalcoatl thug had nothing to do with me."

"He was probably out here to get rid of you. Too bad about the girl and her dad, eh?"

Lydia was staring at Old El. Her face a crumpled mess of grief and anger, she said, "We—we were your collateral damage?" She threw the question at him like a knife. "So, Papa died on account of you? That guy who came out of the sky was really after you, wasn't he?"

"N-no, you've got it all wrong," the old man stammered. "I had nothing to do with this. Who the hell are you to say a thing like that?!"

"You're awful!" Lydia groaned, hiding her face in her hands. "We were just minding our own business, then we get attacked out of the blue and Papa gets killed—but we're collateral damage—and it's all just a joke to you."

"We don't know whether you were collateral damage or not."

The girl's expression melted in rapture, even the death of her own father forgotten. His was just such a voice.

Quietly gazing at the now speechless girl, D then asked, "Where are you from?"

"Ipswich . . ." Her tone was hollow, as if she were under a spell.

It was one of the coldest villages in the northern Frontier. The region was terribly impoverished, and there was no end of people trying to emigrate to anyplace else. Lydia and her father must've numbered among them.

"What takes you to Amanly?"

"The frost damage in Ipswich was really bad this year . . . Wiped out all our crops. So Papa said we'd go ask my uncle with his own business in Amanly to help us out."

"Your father have any distinguishing marks on him?" asked the hoarse voice.

"Excuse me?" the girl said, not surprisingly blinking her eyes.

"What do you mean by that?" Old El asked, shooting D a surprised look. "Hey, just a second, there. Don't tell me you don't believe her?"

"Not her or her father," said the hoarse voice.

"What do you mean?" asked the only one there who still didn't understand.

"How about birthmarks?" D added.

"Birthmarks? Any birthmarks? Oh, that's right—he's got a little one on his left calf."

D went over to the man's corpse and checked.

"We taking her with us?" the Hunter asked the old man.

"Should be okay," the old man replied with a nod. "But she's your responsibility."

"Understood."

"Okay, missy—seems a waste to leave all your baggage lying out here. I'll just load it into my ride!" Old El suggested.

Turning her eyes toward the ground, with a sad look on her face the girl replied, "Okay—we don't have anything, though."

However, the old man returned in good spirits, saying, "A pair of rifles, three pistols, and crafting gear. Your father an engineer?"

"He was a blacksmith by trade."

"Even so, these weapons have all been converted from single shot to repeating action. Mounted another tube under the rifle barrels, that's a magazine right there, and you slide this lever forward again

to chamber the rounds—is that right?" the old man asked, noisily working the weapon, but Lydia ignored him.

Beside them, D had just finished digging a grave for her father. The rule was those who passed away out on the road were buried out on the road. The girl climbed down into the hole with D, and the two of them laid out the corpse before climbing out and covering him with dirt.

"Will you read a prayer over him?" D asked the old man.

"Don't recall a single one!"

"O good person," Lydia said, almost in a mumble.

D and the old man stared at the girl.

"Tarry not in the town of grief. Thou goest to the town of the joyous dead. The requiem comes to the living. Nevertheless, rejoice! Rejoice!"

Not once did the girl's voice catch. A girl of seventeen, she remembered the prayer for the dead. In order to travel on the Frontier.

On returning to the wagon, Old El said, "Better push on as far as we can while the sun's still high."

"The wind's picked up. Gonna be a cold one," the old man said after they'd driven a while. "By the way, you still got your suspicions?" he asked D, who rode alongside the wagon.

"A member of Quetzalcoatl out flying alone attacks a wagon. Right before our very eyes."

"Her father—well, a man died."

"That might've been an unexpected accident," the Hunter replied.

"What about the part where he asked you to take care of his daughter?"

"A pro would do that."

It occurred to the old man that this gorgeous young man would never trust a single person as long as he lived.

"If that's the case, we've brought a snake to our bosom. Knowing that, you'd give the okay for her to come with us?"

"If we didn't, they'd only hit us harder."

"I see," the old man said, vigor flooding into his face. "So, she's like a hostage, then? You dhampirs don't miss a trick, no sirree!"

The unearthly beauty of the young man's visage absorbed the financier's spiteful cynicism without a problem.

"I didn't sign on for merchandise control," D reminded him. "Be careful."

As if struck by lightning, the old man whipped around in the driver's seat and peered down into the wagon. For he'd finally realized this was the prime example of troubles at home and abroad.

II

They reached the town of Chiriki around dusk. A white haze blurred the neon lights of the saloon and the painted signs of shops. It was a fog arising from a lake twelve miles away. Chiriki was also known as "Fog Town."

When they went into the hotel, they were told all the rooms were taken.

"You're telling me this boondock hotel is booked solid?! Don't give me that bullshit. Who put you up to this?"

Despite Old El's intimidation, the hotel clerk politely insisted that every room was full nevertheless, adding, "However, on the next street over to the south, there is a hotel that was used for isolating victims of the Nobility. It's a sturdy building, and it still has beds for the staff that were stationed there. What's more, it's free of charge. Might that not serve you?"

"You've gotta be kidding me," the old man growled, reaching for the pistol on his belt until D stopped him.

"That'll make it easier for friends to drop in on us," said the Hunter.

Enraged though he was, the old man soon digested the meaning of D's words and stiffened. "I see. Fine, then. But what'll we do about the girl?"

"It'd probably be best not to let her out of our sight."

Quickly grasping the implications of that remark as well, Old El replied, "Okay. I didn't wanna stay in a cheap rat trap like this hotel anyway. You'd best take care nobody sets fire to the place, you know." And having snarled that at the person at the front desk, he went back outside.

A minute or so after the creaking of wagon wheels was heard, they reached the former hospital-cum-asylum.

"It ain't often you find something like this smack in the middle of town," the old man remarked, tilting his head quizzically as he stood in front of the two-story wooden building that, indeed, looked rather sturdy.

"Used to be a lot in the old days. All of 'em must've been moved to the edge of town on account of trouble," a hoarse voice replied, making Lydia's eyes go wide.

The old man was about to hand D an electronic lantern when the Hunter stopped him by remarking simply, "I can see." There wasn't an iota of amiability to his words.

The doors were shut with heavy chains with a lock on them.

"Shit, that bastard at the hotel left out at least one important detail," Old El groused, but as he glared at the chains there was a flash of light right before his eyes. Even after D's longsword clicked back into the sheath on his back, the old man remained in a daze. It had happened faster than his eyes could follow.

"Jeez!" he groaned when the chain he gripped split in two and went slack. Lydia couldn't say a thing, either.

"Stick with me," D said, pushing through the doors.

"How awful!" Lydia was the first to moan.

Forty feet wide and twenty feet high, the space was occupied by a narrow corridor with iron cages set to either side of it. For those bitten by Nobility and fated to join their ranks, this was actually one of the kinder treatments. For both the victims and those to whom they were entrusted, nothing cut so deep as the fear of a faux Nobility—a creature that was neither Noble nor human. If they were the living dead, they could be granted death and that would be the end of it.

But what could be done with those who sobbed for forgiveness even as they sought blood, neither Noble nor human?

Seeking a medical or psychological solution, people locked the victims in iron cages, with their family visiting to give them blood, but that wouldn't last long. The victims would plead for death even as they reached out for the pale necks of their family, seeking blood. No longer able to bear the vile faces of these ravenous lunatics, many families would kill the victims before taking their own lives. How had the victims and their families felt in those long hours in this dark asylum, where the skylights were covered and the curtains still drawn over the windows?

Though there were no pale victims' faces behind the bars, their maddening hunger and sadness seemed to shout pathetically at the trio from the old beds and chairs and still darker corners of the cells. If there was someone there who could see the formless or hear the inaudible voices, they might've nodded to themselves and acknowledged that the trio was not alone in this vast space. In fact, Lydia said, "It's cold in here," hugging her own shoulders.

"Hell of a place that bastard at the front desk sent us. Tomorrow, I'm gonna put him out of his misery," the old man remarked menacingly as he surveyed their surroundings. "You two oughta go ahead and find some staff beds so you can get some rest. I'm gonna go procure myself a little sleeping potion."

Lydia turned a bewildered expression toward D, then melted in rapture.

"Booze," the hoarse voice informed her.

"I know my way around saloons," Old El assured the Hunter. "You stick with the girl."

"I was hired to protect you," said D.

"Bars are just nests of trouble!"

The second, hoarser remark also seemed like it must've come from D, leaving Lydia blinking stupidly.

"This has nothing to do with the girl. My job is keeping you safe. I'll go with you."

"And I'm your employer! Talk about bars—I've been to 'Hell's Crucible' three times, and come back safe each and every time."

"I'll be damned," said the hoarse voice.

The Gomorrah Belt, the worst red-light district on the entire Frontier, was a crime-ridden area where outsiders were said to have only a fifty percent chance of surviving. If he'd been to that bar three times and come back safely, his chances of surviving tonight were a hundred percent.

"And as your employer, I'm giving you an order. Stay here with the girl."

The old man immediately headed off, and after D had watched him go, he turned to Lydia and said, "Sleep in the wagon."

"Yes, sir," Lydia replied. As far as she was concerned, nothing could've made her happier. No way did she want to spend the night in that creepy place.

After watching to make sure the girl went into the wagon, D headed off after the old man.

"That geezer is nothing but headaches," the hoarse voice murmured, causing a pair of men passing by to turn in surprise. They thought D had said that.

Though saloons traditionally had swinging doors, this one had regular glass doors to keep the fog from coming in. Naturally, the place also doubled as a casino. Aside from the bar, people were free to play cards at their tables, and high-stakes card games and roulette were available in another room.

Old El ordered a whiskey at the bar. Though the bartender responded with the unsociability shown to outsiders, after seeing the old man order and down three whiskeys in rapid succession with complete composure, he said to Old El, "You sure can handle your liquor."

In keeping with the people who lived in that harsh environment, Frontier liquor had to be cheap and provide a powerful stimulation. Pickling the head of a desert viper in alcohol was one of the tamer serving suggestions, while some of the worst bars were all too happy to announce they mixed black tarantula venom into their drinks.

The liquor in this saloon was strong enough that downing a drink in one swig would put a normal man flat on his back—and the old man had downed three of them.

"Looks like you're used to the hard stuff, but why not go for some of the pricey good stuff for a change? We've got Noble wine."

"To hell with that. See, I'm on my way to go make a collection from a Noble."

"A collection?"

"Yeah. He owes me money."

"A Noble borrowed money from you? That's incredible!"

"Bastard's trying to bilk me. So the last thing I'd want is any of the crap those clowns drink. Hey, gimme another one," he said, smacking the counter.

At that point, a man said to him, "You're in good spirits, old-timer."

At a glance it was clear the man in the flashy coat and soft hat was a gambler.

Skillfully fanning the cards in his hand, he continued, "What do you say to a game?"

"Put a sock in it, and go bug somebody else."

"Such a warm greeting," the gambler replied. Still, he smirked and continued, "Not a fan of gambling? How about a test of skill, then?"

"A test of skill?" Old El asked, his eyes alight.

"Yeah, like this!"

The gambler's left hand shot up. The cards flew straight up. Every one of them was spaced exactly the same from the next. When the gambler's right hand moved, it seemed to stroke the top of the falling cards. A cork dartboard hung on the wall by the door. Three of the cards were imbedded in it.

Once the ruckus from the customers who'd see this died down, the old man said with a grin, "Oh, made of steel, are they?"

"Yeah, and I could lop the head off a desert cobra with one!"

"I don't suppose a person's melon would fare much better, eh?"

"So, how about it? The bet's a thousand dalas," the gambler pressed, judging from Old El's expression that he was game. The cards in his hand bent like they were made of paper, bouncing from one palm to the other and back again.

"Okay, I suppose."

"That's what I like to hear! Hey, Catherine."

The big-boned beauty who'd been sitting at the table next to the gambler was in the process of putting a piece of steak so rare it dripped blood into her mouth, and she looked dazedly in his direction. There was something terribly untamed about her, and she had an air of fearlessness to match any man.

"I've finally found a player. Go stand by the wall."

The woman—Catherine—rose from her chair without a word, wove between the tables, and stood against the wall with her side to them. Her movements were so smooth, Old El let out an appreciative gasp.

"Pardon me," Catherine said, pulling a fat cigar from the breast pocket of a man seated at a nearby table who looked to be a wealthy merchant and holding it between her crimson lips.

"That's the target. Whichever of us cuts it closest to her lips wins," the gambler explained.

"Good enough," said Old El, getting down off his stool.

The gambler pulled another deck of cards from his pocket, broke the seal, and handed them to the old man. They had a substantial heft to them. Handling them like they were paper must've taken inhuman skill.

"I'll go first," said the gambler, drawing a card and throwing it without even taking aim.

It sliced through the cigar scant hundredths of an inch from Catherine's lips and stuck in the wall.

"What do you think of that?" he asked Old El, his beaming face overflowing with confidence.

III

The woman took another cigar from the same man's pocket and put it between her lips.

"Hmm, no way I can cut it any closer than that," the old man said, seeming to easily concede defeat, but then he gazed at the target with a smile even more confident than the gambler's. He had a lewd look on his face. "So, is it okay if I get some laughs with my own style of throwing? First, a little playing around."

However, the way he chose one card and took aim was so prudent it seemed to be anything but playing around.

"There!"

Released with a throw utterly lacking in confidence, the card flopped through the air so weakly you'd want to cover your eyes, sinking into the wall about four inches shy of the end of the cigar.

Laughter rocked the saloon.

"Pull yourself together, old-timer!"

"The next one's gonna hit the moon!"

At the center of those jibes and jeers, the old man scratched his head.

"I wanna get in on this, too! Fifty dalas on Buckley."

"I'm in for thirty."

"Ditto for me for a hundred and ten."

Apparently Buckley was the gambler's name.

In no time at all every single customer was involved, and the total was in excess of two thousand dalas. Add to that Buckley's thousand dalas, and it totaled three thousand—enough to build a house.

Not surprisingly, Buckley was in a bad position, saying, "Hold up, this won't make a proper wager. Isn't there anyone willing to bet on the old-timer?"

His answer came as a hard clatter on the table. All eyes were drawn to it, and all of them bugged out at what they saw. A glitter of gold that put their ten dalas and hundred dalas coins to shame.

"Five thousand dalas on the old man."

They turned toward the door, and once again their eyes bugged. Several of them lost their footing, and the cigar dropped right out of Catherine's mouth. The hostesses sitting on customers' knees rose to their feet as if pulled on a string. For their sense of beauty had forced them to reject those uncouth men.

"Go on," D urged him.

The woman hastily retrieved the cigar and put it in her mouth.

"All right," Old El said, taking a card and making a nonchalant throw.

It was unclear just how many people were paying attention to him. However, their ears caught the whoosh of something knifing through the air. The instant the second card stuck in the wall less than a fifth of an inch behind it, the first card went flying like a shot out of a gun. It skimmed past the woman's lips, and when it landed right on top of the cards the old man held in his hands, it drew a clamor from the people, who strained their eyes and fell silent a heartbeat later.

The cleanly cut cigar had fallen to the floor.

"So—which one's the winner?"

Old El gave a nod to the middle-aged man coming out of the gambling room who'd posed the question. A sheriff's badge glittered on his chest. After all, given the paucity of recreation on the Frontier, gambling wasn't regarded as a bad thing.

"Got something to say, Buckley?"

At the sheriff's query, the gambler smacked his soft hat against his thigh, called out to Catherine, and left. As the beauty followed after him, the last thing her eyes glimpsed as she went through the door was the young man in black. And then that cloying look of lust vanished out the door.

Quickly gathering up the mound of cash, the old man said, "Setting aside your five thousand and my thousand, there's two thousand total to split right down the middle."

And with that he pushed six thousand dalas worth of coins toward D.

"That's not enough," said D.

"What?"

"You didn't put up a thousand dalas. My share is half of three thousand."

"Maybe you'd better consider your position, eh? I'm your employer!"

"I'll quit if I have to. Seems like you could be trouble later."

"Damn it, all right, then. I'd heard dhampirs weren't particular about gold, but you've gotta be an exception. Lousy skinflint."

"Where'd you hear that?"

"S-s-shut up, already. Okay, there's the other five hundred. Take it and get the hell out."

"Then our contract's at an end? Good enough."

Old El jumped to his feet, saying, "No, no, no. Just go back where you were!"

"You're not coming?" D asked.

"Not in the mood. Gonna have myself another drink before I go back."

"I'll join you."

"You the kind of dhampir that likes pissing people off? Get outta here!" the old man shouted, his body trembling. "That creepy hospital's the perfect place for you!"

Once in the wagon, the girl had made a little space between the mountains of merchandise. And the instant she laid down, she fell fast asleep.

Deep in the darkness, a voice called out her name. Something cold stroked her forehead and cheeks. A finger, she thought.

She opened her eyes. And saw pale faces. There were a number of them. She couldn't tell if they were male or female, but the faces of all of them were intently staring down at her.

"Nooo!" she cried, managing to choke out that single word.

She opened her eyes.

There were no faces.

Relief wiped the sweat from her body.

Sitting up in bed, Lydia dazedly stared ahead. And then her blood froze. She wasn't in the wagon. In the darkness though she was, that much was clear to her. It was that hospital—the old asylum. But when had that happened?

Overtaken by fear, she looked all around her. There were seemingly endless rows of beds and chairs and cages. The one Lydia was in was on the right-hand side facing the back of the hospital—a cell about halfway down the corridor.

"What's all this? Nobody said anything about this."

Standing, the girl pushed against the door. It didn't budge an inch. It wasn't locked. And yet, it wouldn't move, as if some unseen hand had reached out to hold it fast. What was going on? And what was going to happen next? What were the intentions of whomever had brought her here?

Going back to the wall opposite the door, Lydia charged back against it shoulder-first.

Having sent D back first, the old man had downed three more whiskeys and was finally beginning to feel a buzz. Leaving a tip, Old El exited the saloon only to be sheathed in darkness and fog. With a surprisingly steady gait he set out on foot, humming a folk song as he did.

The black shadows that clung to the roof to his right looked to be more drawn to the old man's singing voice than his movements.

> Shadows fall on the pale plains, and the sun sets
> Can't soothe the endless sorrows in my heart
> But there's a road
> And long though it be, your village is at the end
> I can't go, and down you go
> The years pass, piling up on me

Up ahead, the silhouette of the wagon and the asylum came into view.

The shadow flew at the old man. Skimming his neck, it landed ten feet to one side of him, and as it did, Old El turned to see a black quadruped.

The old man reeled.

The beast loosed a threatening roar, but it carried puzzlement as well. Its long, sharp claws should've cut halfway through the old man's neck as it passed him. And sure enough, Old El had his left hand pressed to his neck.

"You can tell from the feel of it, can't you? My neck's got a thick covering of synthetic skin. Got it as collateral on a loan to the guy that patented it, and them claws of yours couldn't cut through even a fraction of an inch of it."

Bending all four of its limbs, the beast poised to attack. The animosity that rolled across the ground seemed fit to freeze even the mist.

"Kinda hard to make you out in this fog, but you're that woman from back in the saloon, ain't you? Take off, Catherine. Just leave me with pleasant recollections," the old man pleaded somewhat morosely, and then a gorgeous sound rang out behind him.

The figure in black who'd appeared from behind a row of houses had batted away a flying implement of death. What's more, a masculine cry of pain rang out from the direction the weapon had come.

The old man asked the figure who stood in the moonlight with sword in hand, "That you, D? Was that other one the gambler?"

D nodded.

It had to be Buckley. From the look of it, he left the killing to Catherine, who'd transformed into a leopardess, but had come to see how she was doing.

The leopardess bounded without a sound. The darkness some thirty feet away swallowed her up, and even the sound of her footfalls vanished.

"Don't!" the old man cried out to D. He was afraid the Hunter would go after the woman. He knew that no matter how good she

might be at transforming herself into a stealthy, death-dealing leopardess, where D was concerned she was no more than a slovenly pig.

Sheathing his sword, D said, "She'll be back."

"Well, that's fine. But I wish that looker would at least come at me in human form."

"Have it your way, then," a hoarse voice remarked, stunning the otherwise nonchalant victim while D started walking ahead of him.

"Hey, what about the guy—Buckley?"

"He won't be back," a hoarse voice replied, and given the young man that was involved, Old El could accept that.

The gambler known as Buckley was found at the end an alley to the left of that street with one of his beloved iron cards stuck in his heart and having breathed his last, but only after the one who'd dealt him that death had departed town.

When they returned to the wagon, Lydia was back where she'd been, snoring peacefully.

"Looks like she was fine," Old El said, seeming to breathe a sigh of relief.

D gave no reply, but turned to face the hospital. Only the chill of night filled its gravely still interior.

"They're one shy," said the hoarse voice. "Seven of 'em—looking over here from way in the back. But before we left, there were eight."

"Was she possessed?"

"I don't know—but probably, yeah. Taking her along is too dangerous!"

The air suddenly cooled.

"They're around us," D said, as he could also see them.

Less than three feet away, seven men and women had formed a circle. He was at the center. Pale-faced individuals, they wore blue pajamas. Their lips alone were vivid crimson, with fangs peeking from them. However, their expressions as they looked at D were so horribly starved, they weren't the haughty looks of Nobles but rather feeble ones. The "half-Nobled"—even now, they were still victims.

Their mouths all snapped open, baring their fangs. Once they attacked, D's hand went for the hilt of his blade. There was but a single sound of a slash through the air. His longsword clinked. The sound of it being sheathed. However, no one had seen him draw the weapon or slash with it. Or even what he'd slashed.

"They've passed over," the hoarse voice said, a slightly sentimental ring to it.

There was no reply. The young man of unearthly beauty didn't seem to have a mote of concern as to the fate of the foes who'd beset him.

"Seeking the blood of the living even after their destruction? There's no salvation," said the hoarse voice, but like the footsteps headed for the doorway, its words flowed off into the night air.

Refusing to Pay

CHAPTER 3

I

The trio passed the night until dawn in the hospital's beds. Old El said he wanted to sleep somewhere roomy, and D was forced to keep the old man safe, so Lydia got out of the wagon.

"I slept real well," the old man said, stretching his arms in the air.

On seeing that, the hoarse voice whispered, "Got plenty of nerve," at a level the financier wouldn't hear.

Even after D had dispelled the demons with his blow, ordinary people would never want to spend the night in there.

However, when they asked Lydia how she'd fared, she too had apparently slept soundly, and her expression was cheerful.

While Lydia was at the sink washing her face, Old El came over, elbowed D's arm, and said, "That'd be on account of you, stud."

"What would?"

"A scaredy-cat like that girl being able to sleep like a log in a creepy place like this. Because you were by her side. You dirty dog, you."

Stepping away from his teasing elbowing, D walked over toward the entrance. Halfway there, he stopped and said, "We've got company."

"Who?" Old El asked, at which point he realized it was a stupid question. After all, the door was still closed.

"A half-dozen riders. There's something grim about the way they handle the reins."

"Bandits?"

"No, probably not."

It turned out to be the sheriff and his men. A lawman would have two paid assistants at most, with the rest being volunteers. Constantly preyed upon by humans and worse, Frontier towns had no choice but to form vigilance committees to survive. The thought of eradicating dangers to their community was always foremost, and though it was a job they did at the risk of their lives, there was no shortage of volunteers whenever the call went out.

First, Old El stepped to the fore. As his protector, D took up a rear guard.

Verifying the name of the old man who stood before him, the sheriff said from the back of his steed, "Warrants for your arrest have been issued by the sheriffs of both Jidan and Ibus. You'll have to come with me."

"On what charges?"

"Extortion."

"Whaaat?!"

"According to the complaint, you charged two debtors usurious rates, and threatened to kill them if they didn't pay—but you can offer your defense in the circuit court."

"Hey, I was just collecting on a debt! Ain't no way around using language that's a tad coercive."

"Be that as it may, since we've got this request from the sheriffs' offices, I've no choice but to arrest you. Come with me."

"The hell I will!" Old El shouted with every ounce of his strength.

The sheriff raised his right hand. Having already dismounted, his men reached for their swords and guns.

D glided between the two sides.

The men's hands—and the rest of their bodies—stiffened.

"You his bodyguard, then? What's your name?" the sheriff inquired, his voice carrying an undisguisable tremble.

"D."

Frost seemed to form solely around the half-dozen men.

"Never thought I'd see you here," the sheriff groaned. "But I don't care if you're the greatest Hunter of Nobility on the Frontier, I still have to uphold the law. Interfere with this arrest, and we'll haul you in right along with him."

"Think you can?" Old El jeered. "One flash of his sword, and the lot of you will be lacking heads. Just stay out of my way, okay? I've got deadbeats to track down."

"What'd you say?" asked the sheriff, swallowing hard. He'd steeled himself to see this through. His men also adjusted their grip on their weapons.

"Are you in a hurry?" D suddenly asked the old man.

"What do you mean?"

"This collection. The one who owes you money isn't exactly the sort to run off."

"Well, I suppose not, at that."

"Then take the stand."

"What?! You're supposed to be protecting me, but, what, now you're fixing to turn on me?"

"Extortion hardly counts as a crime on the Frontier. You'll get off with a hundred dalas fine."

"Don't make me laugh! I'm supposed to pay a hundred dalas over a measly threat?!"

"Or you can always do ten days hard labor."

"Exactly," said the sheriff, breathing a sigh of relief as he wiped the sweat from his brow. He saw now that D didn't stand against them. "You can choose whatever court you like."

"Shit!" Old El cried, baring his teeth as he looked by turns at the faces of both D and the sheriff—one unearthly in its beauty, the other rough as stone.

The trial was scheduled to be held from twelve noon in a hall at the community center. However, the judge didn't come. An hour passed, then two, but still he hadn't arrived.

"What the hell's going on here, sheriff?" Old El asked, glaring at the lawman in the waiting room.

With a glum look, the sheriff replied, "It happens a lot. Just keep your pants on. I'll ask the judge to take this time off your sentence." Then his eyes shifted to D, standing by the entrance.

Due not only to the beauty of his face but also the fact that his entire form was practically perfect, the Hunter looked like a statue of unearthly beauty—a work of art. What's more, that work of art gave off an indescribably eerie aura, like the guardian spirit of this hall or some kind of devil, freezing not only the flesh of all who looked upon him but their very souls as well.

However, the sheriff's attention wasn't focused on D, but rather on the hall window that faced the courtyard. Ever since D had entered, women had flocked there, trying to peer in. Naturally, there were girls from good families, but also married women, saloon girls, and even prostitutes, all jostling to be first and apparently sparking a few skirmishes. They had no interest in the trial of the man accused of extortion. They were there for D. It was a constantly changing lineup at the window, because those at the head of the line kept fainting dead away. The lawman had quickly sent an assistant to fetch a doctor, but the ladies kept pressing forward, one after another, so they'd never be in time. An hour earlier, he'd started to worry that every woman and girl in town would be in the hospital by the time the judge got there.

Naturally, Old El also noticed this, commenting, "Hey, you sure this is what you want? The ladies ain't gonna give a second glance to any man in town at this rate!"

And no sooner had he made that cutting remark than the judge finally arrived.

Circuit courts loaded a judge, a secretary, and all the necessary equipment into a wagon that traveled around to towns and villages and dispensed legal solutions to their troubles. They generally visited larger towns and villages about once a month, traveling in a radius of one hundred and twenty miles to preside over cases over what should've been a week, but actually residents flocked in from a six-hundred-mile radius, making it an arduous job with little to no sleep or time off. Add to that the fact that they were risking their lives. This was the Frontier, after all.

Taking a seat behind his large desk, the judge pounded his gavel and declared the court to be in session. Since people had been gathering for this for the last three days, Old El's case was number thirty on the docket.

"I sentence you to three months hard labor."

"The verdict is not guilty."

"I sentence you to four months and ten days in the Gargo Valley mines."

"You are hereby sentenced to a fine of a hundred thousand dalas or one year hard labor."

Circuit courts characteristically wasted no time. Once the plaintiff read out the charges, the defendant had one chance to address each of them, and then came a closing statement. The judge passed sentence promptly after the closing statement.

If things weren't handled this way, they could never get through the entire docket.

As they were waiting in an antechamber, gunfire could be heard. There were three shots, then silence. Everyone turned that way instinctively, but on realizing it was probably nothing, they quickly went back to whatever they'd been doing. A plaintiff or defendant unhappy with the verdict had let loose. Sometimes it was merely a threat, other times they were actually aiming at someone, but that wouldn't change the verdict.

There were restless footsteps in the corridor, and someone said, "Hurry up and get him to the doctor's."

"You shot me full of buckshot, you bastard!"

"Count your blessings it wasn't a grenade."

The unsettling discourse faded down the corridor.

It was past noon when Old El was called into court. D stood by the door to the rear, and the old man sat in the defendant's seat, but when the plaintiffs came in shortly thereafter, Old El took one look at them and was stunned.

"You sons of bitches—you've got your nerve coming here!"

Coldly looking the other way as they seated themselves was a pair of what looked to be affluent merchants with an added touch of avarice. One was quite portly, and the other thin as a wire.

"Hedva and David—finally showed yourselves, eh?" Jabbing a gnarled finger at them, the old man continued, "Hear me out, folks. These clowns got no right charging me with anything. The fat one's Hedva Totty, and the skinny one's David Hamnick—fatty borrowed a hundred thousand and skinny eighty thousand to be paid back over ten installments, and they took off without even paying me once."

Though the old man's voice echoed across the courtroom, the two plaintiffs merely sat there with mocking smiles.

"You bastards!" Old El growled, and he seemed ready to pounce on them until the sheriff held him back. He was serving as the bailiff, and his deputy was taking care of the plaintiffs.

"Keep your mouth shut, and get your hands off me!"

Unable to restrain the old man in his rage, the sheriff was just reaching for his gun when the side door opened and the judge came in. Old El immediately settled down. He was afraid to get on the wrong side of the person who'd preside over his trial. The judge took his seat, and a stolid-looking man sat on a chair in front of the desk. His role was that of security. And it was he who'd defended the judge in the shootout earlier.

Pounding his gavel, the judged declared court to be in session. The left shoulder of his coat was ripped, and something red was seeping into it. Blood.

"First of all, we'll hear the complaint—sheriff," the judge said in a deep, grave voice.

The sheriff stood up, approached the witness stand, and started to say, "The Nobility—" He quickly caught himself, continuing, "The complaint was filed by these two plaintiffs—Hedva Totty and David Hamnick. The charges are usury and extortion."

And two winters ago, the plaintiffs Hedva and David had borrowed a hundred thousand dalas and eighty thousand dalas, respectively, learning when the contract was drawn up that interest was set at eight percent per month, a rate beyond the pale, and they were threatened that if their payment was even a day late, it would be the last day of their lives, the plaintiffs purported.

"The emotional trauma of that had psychologically damaged the plaintiffs, plunging them into a severe neurosis that left them unable to work. They were unable to sleep at night, and were forced to relocate for medical treatment. Attached are the contract with the usurious interest rate, a recording disk that captured the threatening language, and an explanation from their physician. They request half a million dalas from the defendant or a sentence of three years hard labor."

Once the sheriff's closing arguments were concluded, the judge asked for the defense to present theirs.

II

"All right, then," Old El said, getting to his feet. "Every bit of that pair's testimony is false. They headed for the hills without paying me even once."

"That's because we were forced to seek medical treatment on account of your threats!" the fat one—Hedva—shouted.

"It's all documented in the evidence. See the writing on the wall and pay the fine, or do your time!" bellowed the slim one—David.

"Order!" the judge cried, pounding his gavel. "Does either side have anything to add?"

"I do not," Old El said in a strangely composed tone.

"Nothing for us, either," the two plaintiffs chimed in.

"Wow, doesn't have a snowball's chance in hell, does he?" a hoarse voice remarked from the vicinity of the left hand of the gorgeous figure standing by the door.

A low voice, heavy as steel, replied, "I don't know about that."

"And now, for the verdict," the judge declared after less than ten seconds had passed.

The security officer pulled the shotgun resting across his knees a little closer.

Fatty and skinny smirked.

"I find the defendant not guilty—case dismissed."

He didn't explain the reasons for his verdicts not because they were clear, but because it would hold up the next case. However, the plaintiffs were furious.

"This is completely unlawful!"

"I'd bet my eye teeth he bought the judge! We'll bring a fresh suit against you!"

"Put a sock in it! You lost!" Old El shouted. "But don't go far. I'm gonna file a case on the loans you ran out on. Just you wait and see."

"Court is adjourned!" the judge declared, his words overlaid by the sound of his gavel.

"What a surprise. There's no way this is remotely legal!" said the hoarse voice.

"This is the Frontier," D replied. "Reason steps aside when unreasonableness passes by."

"You can say that again."

As soon as they stepped outside, clouds of war were brewing between the old man and the pair that evening in front of the community center.

"Shoulda paid what you owed in the first place, you idiots. Now you'll have the law breathing down your necks!" Old El blustered.

One of the pair shot back, "Shut up. You're flat out of luck, running into us here. Don't think you're leaving town alive. We've already seen to that."

"And I'll carve the words 'filthy loan shark' into your tombstone!" said the other, but then they turned their backs without saying another word. Because the sheriff and his men were nearby.

"Looks like they hired themselves a killer or a warrior. Better watch your back!" the hoarse voice said to the old man when he came back.

"That's why I've got you, isn't it? No, they're the ones who're shit out of luck running into me here. I'll wring every last dalas out of 'em!"

"We don't do collections," the hoarse voice reminded him.

"You won't have to. I got everything I need for the job from collections I've already made. Speaking of which—that girl, she's getting off in this town! I ain't about to keep her kicking around forever, eating me out of house and home."

When they got back to the wagon, there was no sign of Lydia.

"What, did somebody grab her?!"

"No, there's no sign of a struggle. She left on her own," D said after inspecting the interior.

"Is that a fact? I hope she don't come back. Well, I'm off to go meet with them two. Come with me."

"Where are we going?"

"There's a hotel here, ain't there? They're bound to be in its bar having a drink."

"And they'll figure you're coming, too."

"Hmm," Old El said, reaching for his combat belt and checking how it was set.

If they knew he was coming, they were bound to be armed, too. And they'd undoubtedly hired warriors or killers. They might've brought some with them, but the town also had no shortage of drifters. Spread around enough money, and some of them were bound to bid a fond farewell to their honest lives and hire on as killers.

"I know that full well. You're coming along, ain't you?"

"It's my job."

"All righty. Shall we get going, then? You might be nigh-on immortal, but there's no saying what kinda trap's waiting for us. Make sure my safety's your first concern."

"Understood."

"Well, wait outside for a little bit, then."

And saying that, the old man went into the cargo compartment as soon as D had left and began noisily rummaging around for something.

It was some twenty minutes later that he joined D where he waited outside. The main difference was that he now had a total of four metal cylinders eight inches in diameter and about twenty inches long strapped to either hip and on his back.

"What the hell are those?" the hoarse voice inquired.

"Just a little insurance. Collateral on a loan I made to a scientist in the Capital. I don't wanna use 'em, but it can't be helped."

The hotel bar was awfully crowded. It was the sole form of recreation in this countrified town, after all. There were more drifters there than townsfolk. The bar's hostesses doubled as prostitutes, but there was still quite a large number of them for a town this size. When merchant parties or tourist groups were in town, or on weekends after the townsfolk got paid, they'd send some fast horses to neighboring towns to bring in more girls. That was probably the case now.

When Old El opened the door, everyone who looked in that direction froze. From the way their expressions melted in bliss, it was perfectly clear the old man wasn't the cause. Those who noticed the change in the others and looked in the same direction fell under the very same spell.

Old El spotted the pair at a big table toward the back. Like the other patrons and the women, they were drunkenly staring in the old man's direction. Including the pair in question, there were seven people at that table. All the others were drifters.

"Okay, looks like we've got something else to talk about, eh?"

When they remained in their daze, Old El suddenly banged on the table, shouting, "We've got us some talking to do! Some talking!"

That finally brought them back to life.

"Oh, son of a bitch—when the hell did you get here?!" Hedva said, getting to his feet. Surprisingly enough, his chair was still stuck to his ass. Apparently, he'd really squeezed himself into it.

"What, you gone blind or something, you lousy deadbeat?" Old El bellowed, his fury stoked by having been ignored. "You've got nerve, though, not bolting outta town. I suppose you're ready to pay now, ain't you?"

"Yeah, we're ready, all right," the fat one—Hedva—said, throwing away the cards he'd still held and reaching for the gun on his right hip.

"We'll pay you in lead slugs!" shouted David, who was also on his feet now, his words licking out like flames.

The other five people turned pale and moved away from the table. Apparently, they weren't hired muscle.

A captivating swirl of color stepped between them. In a dress embroidered with beads, the woman had both a figure and a face that were incredibly alluring.

"What the hell do you want?" Old El said, hoping to be intimidating, but there was no power at all left in his expression.

"I'm Alma. And I'll thank you not to get rough in here. Say, why don't you buy me a drink so we can enjoy ourselves?" she said, looping a pale, exposed arm around the old man's neck. Her eyes shifted to D, and she continued, "Well, if you're not so . . . beautiful . . . for a man . . . But . . . oh, what a man . . ." The tone of her voice changed. "Shouldn't have . . . looked at you . . . Me . . . Alma . . . I'm gonna . . . lose my mind . . . Oh, no . . . Somebody . . . help me . . ."

Her shouts growing particularly shrill, the woman turned around. She extended her hands, as if seeking help.

A stark flash of light split her head from the crown to the jaw. But it wasn't bright blood that gushed from her bisected face. It was blue light—electromagnetic waves.

The automaton that had called herself Alma was about to give up the ghost.

"Bea-bea-beautiful man . . . ma-ma-man," she exclaimed as she slumped forward.

Electromagnetic waves tinged her twitching form with blue, then faded unexpectedly. And at the same time her movements ceased.

"What are you doing?" Old El asked dumbfoundedly. Though he understood she was an automaton, cutting her down without so much as a single word was crazy.

D indicated her right hand with the tip of his sword.

People noticed that her small palm was wrapped around a little weapon.

"A heat gun," one drifter murmured. "Seen one before. Freaking small enough to palm, but it could take down an armored beast with one blast."

"You sons of bitches hired an automaton to kill me," Old El bellowed, and when he turned with a look of rage on his face, the pair was frozen.

A stark blade had made a horizontal thrust right under their noses. D's sword. Hedva groaned something, but didn't quite form any words.

From a table at the other end of the room, a man walked over, saying, "I saw the whole thing." On his chest he wore a lawman's badge. Pointing to it for the old man's benefit, he continued, "I'm Heisler. Let's go report this to the sheriff."

The instant his right hand moved from the badge to his hip, a bare wooden needle pierced his throat. Groaning, Heisler reached for the needle and pulled it out. The other customers saw threads of gore shoot from the wound. But it was a black liquid.

His right hand still gripping a pistol, Heisler dropped knees-first and moved no more.

"A bio-man?" Old El groaned. "That's a lot more human than an automaton. They say it's impossible to tell the difference, so how'd you know?"

Indicating the two debtors with the tip of his blade, D replied, "They started to smile. They did it both times one of them showed up."

"Oh, I get it. Couldn't tell he wasn't perfectly human, but it was easy for you to read the humans, eh?" Old El gave a satisfied nod, then circled behind the pair who'd collapsed into their chairs, clapping them on the shoulders as if they were old friends. "Okay, the game's up. You gonna pay me my money?"

The pair bared their teeth.

D pulled his sword away.

"Hey—what do you think you're doing?" Old El snarled.

"Collections are your job."

Sheathing his sword with a *ching!*, D looked all around the room.

The spectators hurriedly started back to their own seats, still in a daze. This time it wasn't from D's beauty, but from his unearthly aura.

"Hmm," the Hunter's left hand groaned faintly.

"What is it?" D asked in a voice no one else would hear. It was like the conversation between the two of them was at an ultrasonic frequency.

"I'm sure you must know it, too. And have since we came in, right?"

At those words from his left hand, D turned toward Old El.

After listening to such excuses as "We don't have any damned money," and "Blew it all on those two right there," the old man fell silent for a little while before saying, "All right, then. We'll just go collect your collateral."

"Don't have any of that, either. We're flat broke."

"We hired those two to kill your ass dead. Like we said, we blew all our money on that!"

Old El twisted his lips, but his anger was soon replaced by something else. His lips formed a sly grin, and he said, "Good enough. Then I'll have to take payment in something other than cash."

"Whaaat?!" exclaimed Hedva, knitting his brow.

David did the same, but his eyes were laughing.

"I don't know, but it looks like this ain't settled yet!"

"What? Spare me your sour grapes," Old El replied intimidatingly, and just then his debtors fell flat on their backs.

They'd intentionally kicked off the floor to knock their chairs backward. All that remained was their cry of "Kill him!"

III

The place shook as every customer in the bar went into action. They'd all just stood up.

"You're kidding me," the old man murmured, staring at the people dumbfoundedly. "They're pulling the strings on all these people?"

The people leveled the pistols, rivet guns, and nail shooters they already gripped.

This was the time for his bodyguard. However, the old man shouted to him, "Keep outta this!" and pressed a button on the remote controller he held in his right hand.

The world was filled with the sound of a motor that was like the beating of an insect's wings. The customers staggered in unison. All of them held their heads and reeled, looking like some ceremony for a weird religious cult.

"That field generator sends vibrations directly into their brains," Old El remarked proudly. "It's a little old-fashioned, so I needed the four transmitters in different directions to set up the field. Okay, let's go."

His final command wasn't directed at D, but rather at the pair of debtors.

Having hired nearly fifty automatons and bio-men, there was no way they had any money left to give him. But the old man led the way to the door, seemingly determined to get something from the two of them. His debtors followed after him, leaving behind them only writhing assassins and their moans.

Once the pair was inside, the wagon immediately sped away. There was no point in hanging around any longer.

Leaving town, Old El ordered D, who was up in the driver's seat, to stop out in the wilderness more than a half mile away.

Dragging the two debtors outside and shoving them to the ground, the old man pointed his finger at Hedva and said, "A hundred thousand dalas from you." And to David he said, "Eighty thousand dalas from you."

"So, what of it?" Hedva shot back, but he had none of his former swagger.

"Since you don't have any money, you'll have to fulfill the contract with something else."

Old El pointed the same remote control he'd used to activate the field generator at the wagon. The transport vehicle door opened, and a silvery form that was clearly a robot skillfully walked over on two legs, halting right beside Hedva.

The old man simply commanded it, "Cut that guy's arms and legs off right at the joint."

"Oh, wow," the hoarse voice remarked, sounding impressed, while Lydia, who'd just stepped down from the wagon, let out a little scream.

"Wait—what are you doing?" she cried, and the look she turned toward the old man made it seem as if she were dealing with the devil himself.

"I ain't being unreasonable here. It's just payment on their debts."

"I know that, but cutting off his arms and legs—couldn't you just settle for an ear or something?"

Even that was a pretty harsh thing for the girl to suggest so casually.

Her words fell on deaf ears where the old man was concerned, and he replied, "Ears won't get me squat. What I need is limbs, brains, or organs. And a hundred and eighty thousand dalas just happens to be the going rate for two pairs of arms and legs."

"Please, don't!" Hedva shouted, but his body was pinned to the ground by the robot's steel arms.

"Get back in the wagon, or go somewhere else so you don't have to see this," Old El told Lydia

"No. Stop what you're doing. It's just horrible!"

"Don't worry. I'll give 'em artificial arms and legs. And electronic ones at that. They're a hundred times handier than their original arms! Hey, get cutting."

The robot raised its arm. A blade more than three feet long rasped from the end of the tubular appendage.

Oddly enough, the pair didn't scream but remained silent.

"Shot 'em full of anesthesia, eh? All right, then."

"Stop him, D!" the girl cried, clinging to the Hunter's arm, but he easily pulled free.

"Old El was owed the money they tried to get out of paying, and they tried to kill him—he's well within his rights."

"He's even using anesthetic."

Just as Lydia's eyes bugged again at the hoarse voice's comment, the air whistled with the falling blade.

"Damn you!"

"Don't think we're gonna forget this!"

Apparently still under the effects of the anesthesia, the pair slurred their threats, their limbs now giving off a metallic gleam.

It was around evening time. The sterilization, reconnecting and suturing of nerves, and freezing of the amputated limbs by the surgical device had taken that long.

"Spare me your grumbling. If you don't hurry back to town, the man-eating ants will be on the prowl!" the old man yelled down from the driver's seat of the wagon, giving the cyborg horses a crack of the whip.

After they raced away, Old El soon said, "Ah, that was a sweet little deal! The brains and guts of clowns like those would be half-pickled with booze, and that drives the prices down. There's always demand for arms and legs, though. I'll make a bundle selling 'em to some hospital in the sticks!" Old El chortled. His mood was so good, he even said, "See, D? In this world, it all comes down to money! If you've got the coin, you can buy somebody's soul. Whoever came up with the idea for currency was the smartest person in the world."

"Can you buy a verdict with it, too?" said D.

"Oh, you were wise to that? Well, that judge hit me up for a loan of a thousand dalas about twenty years ago."

"And he ran out on it?"

"Yep. And he's got the nerve to ride around as a circuit court judge. What a joke. The second he recognized me, I'm sure he knew what he had to do. Now, I wanna make it perfectly clear I didn't put any pressure on him! Enough about that, though—what's the story with you? I could see it happening to humans, but what makes you so good-looking even automatons go soft in the head?"

The old man had only to look at the Hunter to know. But he didn't look at him. He couldn't. If he learned the answer, he'd wind up just like that automaton.

D asked simply, "Weren't you going to leave Lydia at the last town?"

An incomprehensible grumble from the old man.

"Or did you forget?"

"I forgot," Old El replied, shutting his eyes. His thoughts were summarized by the fist he smacked against his thigh. "Shit! Now I'm stuck feeding her again."

The old man ground his teeth. And though it should've been charged with anger, the air around the driver's seat was strangely tranquil.

"Only an hour until the sun's down completely. Let's gain all the ground we can before that!"

"I thought you said you weren't in a hurry on this trip?"

"This is a whole other kettle of fish. It'd be a shame to dilly-dally on the way there."

Lashing the cyborg horses time and again, the old man managed to cover forty miles before stopping the wagon.

They made camp. Lydia used chemical fuel to start a fire, then cooked bacon and eggs over it. Though there weren't supposed to be any dangerous beasts in the area, there were still plenty of things that description didn't cover. In the skies, in the trees, on the ground or under it, the Frontier was always sharpening its claws and baring its fangs, just waiting for some stupid humans to come along.

They finished eating. Old El let out a satisfied burp as he headed back to the wagon. D stood there like a statue in black, and Lydia came over to him after washing the dishes. Out on the plains, they used sand instead of soap and water to clean their plates and utensils. Coarse and arid, sand proved extremely effective at cleaning off grease.

"Aren't you going to sleep?" the girl asked.

"Nope," the hoarse voice replied.

But Lydia wasn't surprised. She had a lot more nerve than the old man.

"I don't know who you are," said the girl, "but it looks to me like you're D's spokesman. Aren't you sleepy?"

"Nope."

"I have a question."

"What would that be?"

"What's going to become of me?"

"The old man said we'll leave you at the next town, didn't he? After that, I have no idea."

"You're a cold one, aren't you?"

"Hey, this is the Frontier. Nobody wants to get involved with somebody they don't know from a bump in the road, do they?"

Lydia let out a sigh. "I suppose that's true. And it's not like we could stay together forever. How long will you be traveling with him?"

"Until he's done making his collection."

"I've never heard of a Noble borrowing money!"

"The world's a hard place to live in. Nobles can't just go around draining humans of their blood whenever they feel like it and making threats like they used to."

"Do they have to pay people to let them drink their blood?"

"Good question," the hoarse voice said, its tone carrying laughter. Lydia's words had conjured an amusing image of a Noble debtor. "Anyway, to be perfectly honest, we've still got our doubts about you."

"I sense that. You think Papa's death was all an act, and I'm an assassin out to kill the old man or something, don't you? That would be the role of a lifetime. That, or a prostitute."

She hazarded a glance at D, but his heavenly beauty remained silently trained on a single point in the darkness.

"That's about all I can do if I get tossed out of here. Maybe it won't be as bad as you'd think, right?"

"You've got an uncle or something in Amanly, don't you? Why don't you try and finagle a ride that far. Lift that skirt of yours and give the old man a gander, and quick as that, he'll—gaaah?!"

Lydia gave a puzzled look to the Hunter's clenched left fist. As she gazed in rapture at the Hunter's profile, a pinhole of sense seemed to have opened, and the girl said in a steady voice, "I want you to—"

Her next words were trampled by the hoofbeats of approaching horses.

"Who is it at this hour—travelers?" Lydia asked, her brow furrowed.

The hoarse voice replied, "Nope. Too far out for them to be going anywhere. Anybody in their right mind would've made camp by now. Probably bandits or outlaws. Get back in the wagon."

Old El had jumped down to take her place. He and D walked about five yards from the wagon before a trio of steeds and riders appeared from the highway, halting in front of the pair.

"Sorry, but could we trouble you for some water?" the lead rider called down from high in the saddle.

"I think we can manage that," the old man replied easily.

It was a rule of the Frontier that even when complete strangers met, they had to be prepared to make some sacrifices.

Old El then added, "That'll run ya one damon a skin."

"Hey, this old-timer's just full of surprises," the leader said, looking back at the other two. "Looks like he figures to charge us for water!"

"You're not a merchant, are you?!"

"It's just lousy water!" the leader growled with an evil scowl, every bit as angry as the two behind him.

"See, I'm in the loan business," Old El said impassively. He must've been well accustomed to such exchanges. "Whatever you want, I need something as security. Be it goods or cash."

"We ain't gonna ask you again!" said the leader, running his eyes quickly over D.

D was staring straight ahead, so his face wasn't visible from above.

"Well, if you're a lender, that's just perfect! We happen to need money. In fact, we came here to make you hand over your water and your money!"

The leader's lips twisted into a grin. His right hand went for the oversized rivet gun on his left hip with no particular urgency. But something stopped it.

Moving only their eyes, the three riders stared at their other prey. And all of them realized the mistake they'd made.

They were the prey.

"Heh heh heh!" Old El guffawed, his shoulders rising and falling with the effort. "Underestimated my bodyguard, didn't you? Okay, now this is where I'd tell you to get the hell outta here—only you were fixing to kill me, and I can't abide that. Oh, I've got it. In exchange for me not telling the sheriff, each of you is gonna leave a thousand dalas with me. How's that sound?"

"Screw that!" one in the back cried in a rage.

The instant his right hand went for his rivet gun, a stark white needle pierced his shoulder. And although it was his left shoulder, his right hand was immobilized.

Mushroom Town

CHAPTER 4

I

"The next one will be through your throat," D said softly.

The trio were straitjacketed by an unearthly air. And just like that, the thugs lost their will to fight.

On seeing that, Old El smacked his hands together, saying, "All right, then, a thousand dalas! Let's see a thousand dalas!"

"We don't have that kind of money," the leader groaned. "We got taken for everything. That's why we couldn't even buy water."

"And how was that?" the old man asked, eyes gleaming. As soon as he heard the phrase "got taken," he knew money was involved.

"Thirty miles down the road, they built a town called Marcel. You know it?"

"Never heard of the place. The next town's supposed to be Dynemaely."

"Well, in a spot about two-thirds of the way there, they found an energy deposit eight days ago. So, before the jokers from the Capital could lay claim to it, prospectors and miners from nearby towns moved in, and the town was put up a week ago to capitalize on 'em. That's where we got fleeced!"

"I see. Sounds like a fun place," Old El said, smiling with satisfaction. "Okay, boys, I'll cancel your debt in exchange for some information."

The trio's eyes lit up.

"Sure thing. Go ahead and ask us anything."

"I take it there's a pretty good gambler at the casino, am I right?"

"Yeah. A real good one. Looked to me like him and the bookie—who runs the casino—were in cahoots."

"C'mon, we're talking about a bookie in a hick town thrown up a couple of days ago and a vagabond gambler. Just watch. I'll show you they're snot-nosed kids compared to Old El." Furrowing his brow, he continued, "They *were* in cahoots? You saying they parted ways already?"

The trio exchanged glances.

"No, somebody caught him cheating. Once the shooting started, the bookie stepped in and apologized, gave back the guy's money, and the guy who'd picked the fight went away happy as a pig in shit. It was the next morning they found just the gambler's head at the entrance to town. They knew some huge beast chewed him up, but not exactly what it was."

"Hmm. That'd be a beastmaster's doing," the old man murmured, nodding time and again. "Say, there ain't a place you could water animals near town, is there?" he asked.

"There sure is!" one in the back promptly replied. "There's an old swamp about three-quarters of a mile to the east."

"Hmm. Came after all, did he?"

The old man seemed to be taking all this in when the hoarse voice asked him, "Toba?"

"That's right. Julas-Han Toba, beastmaster," Old El said, his shoulders trembling a little. "It'd be the water beast he controls that killed that gambler. Matches another case I know of perfectly. Finally showed yourself, you greedy bastard. I won't let you get away with this! I'll fix you good, just mark my words. This is a fight for justice."

A little whistle issued from the vicinity of D's left hand. Apparently misinterpreting it, the entire trio turned frightened eyes toward D.

"I'll do it!" Old El cried, looking up at the heavens.

The hoarse voice spat, "Fight for justice my ass," but fortunately the old man's ears couldn't hear it.

After the trio had been disarmed and the one injured man had been treated, they were immediately released.

The next day, the group set out with the coming of dawn.

When they arrived in the town of Marcel, the sun was high, and people were working vigorously out in the stark light. Though most of the buildings were prefabricated units, some "balloon houses" with inflated bags of metal leaf swayed here and there. They were safe enough when filled with the proper expandable gas, but cheap ones making use of hydrogen could explode from a slight shock or flame. Still, they were used if for no other reason than these balloon houses were convenient to transport.

There was a chain of firework explosions in the blue sky, perhaps intended to set a festive mood.

"There's a mess of bars, but they're all still closed. Guess nobody here wants to make any money," Old El remarked.

"Where will we go?" the hoarse voice inquired.

"The mine!"

"What for? The casino's not open yet."

"Mines are worked in shifts. Those who've come outta the hole usually got nothing to pass the time but gambling."

"Good point."

They continued on for five minutes, at which point the main street faded away and a craggy gray mountain drew nearer.

In twenty minutes, they'd reached it.

A mine shaft in the face of the rock yawned like a black maw that disgorged a pair of rails onto the ground. The tracks for handcars carrying ore. The place was a sort of square where muscle-bound men could be seen lounging here and there or amusing themselves with card games.

Halting the wagon, the two men climbed down and hitched the cyborg horses to a post. But there were three people now.

"What are you doing? Get back inside!"

Lydia stood impassively in the face of Old El's bluster, the collar of her blouse turned up. In seconds, there would be a storm of whistles and lewd catcalls—but they never came. For a wind called beauty had blown through the rough men. Unearthly was the only word to describe it, and it was accented by an eerie aura.

"It ain't you that's got 'em all smitten," the old man said to Lydia.

"I'm well aware of that. But thank you for feeling the need to point it out anyway!"

"Just thought it'd be easier on you to get that ironed out."

"Enough already!" the girl said, and she was about to stomp her feet in anger, but restrained herself. She was too far out of her league.

"What'd you come out here for?" asked the old man.

"I wanted to get a breath of fresh air."

"Well, you've had your fill of that, I wager. Back inside."

"I want to see all kinds of things. No way am I going back in there."

Old El broke off the exchange there. He was so angry, he thought he might as well let her get a taste of some danger. The fact that D was there if worst came to worst figured into his calculations.

Quickly opening the door to the closest barracks, the old man called out loudly to the group of ten or so miners gathered around the table, "Anybody here in need of some funds for gambling? Your savior has arrived!"

Not one of them reacted. For all of them had seen D.

Quickly realizing that, Old El said, "Hmm, this is no good. I've got it. Hey, here's a little token of friendship."

Pulling something from his coat pocket, he threw it up into the air.

It was a shower of gold that fell on the heads of the enraptured men. Dropping to the floor with a mellifluous sound, it resolved itself into several gold coins. And yet, the old man's customers still wore entranced looks on their faces. Though some among them had looked down at the gold coins, all they could do was stare dumbly at them.

Not surprisingly, Old El folded his arms and gave a groan, but just then—

A gunshot suddenly rang out.

"Holy shit!"

With cries of astonishment, some jumped out of bed, others cradled their heads, still others ran for the hammers leaning against the far wall or got ready to use the big knives they wore on their belts—pandemonium had broken out.

Looking for the cause, their eyes focused on a smoking pistol—and went wide. From both the sight of the gun and the one who held it.

"That's right, everybody—if we could have your attention, please."

It was Lydia, and she gestured to Old El with her free hand.

"When the hell'd you pick that up?" the old man asked distractedly.

"Oh. I borrowed it for self-protection," the girl answered honestly if somewhat sheepishly.

"Don't ever dip into any of my stuff again without my say-so, am I clear?"

"Yessir!" she replied in a manner that didn't seem the least bit remorseful. She followed it up by crying out, "Okay, everybody, gold coins! And they belong to whoever snatches them up!"

That cry finally broke the spell that beauty had cast over the men, and this time it was shouts of greed they let fly as they dove for the gold coins that glittered at their feet.

II

"Got it!"

Here and there, hands were raised gripping the little glimmers.

"You bastard, that was mine!" someone else spat, though it was unclear whether that was the truth or a lie.

In no time at all, the fairly spacious barracks became a wrestling ring.

The trio watched this for just a few seconds. But in that time, there was a cacophony that included the sound of breaking bones, beastly howls, and groans that were close to a death rattle, and then they suddenly stopped. The matter of ownership had been decided.

"You sure are a generous coot, ain't you?" said one of the men.

"Sorry, but if I've got this hundred dalas coin, I don't need to borrow anything more!" exclaimed another. "Guess you're a day late and a hundred dalas short."

Coarse laughter erupted. But it stopped suddenly.

The old man had raised his right hand up to his face. Between his fingers he held a gold coin. With a grin, Old El bit down on it and twisted as hard as he could. With a little squeal, the gold coin snapped in two.

Throwing it down at the men's feet, the old man asked, "You were saying? They're all fakes!"

In unison, they began biting down on the coins, throwing the pieces to the floor before standing as one.

"You son of a bitch!"

"I hope you're ready for a whupping."

"Okay, hem 'em in!"

The floor creaked loudly, and the trio moved to the center of the closing net. There were nearly fifty men, all armed with knives, shovels, or other tools, and they boiled with a thirst for blood.

"Listen up," Old El said, spreading his arms. "I'm a moneylender. And I've come to help you with your gambling. What you just saw is but a tantalizing taste."

"Shut your pie hole. You screwed us over."

"We can take all the money we need for gambling off your corpse!"

"And we'll take the woman, too."

Even as these hot winds of terrible hatred and lust drove Old El backward, he grinned. "I'm afraid not. You've seen that me and the girl are hardly the only ones here, right? So, why don't you look at that fella? Why go to so much trouble, then take your your eyes off of him? Just so we're clear, he's my bodyguard. And he's got more going for him than just a pretty face!"

"Shut up! We can gang up on 'em. There's only one of him. Kill the lot of 'em and bury 'em and nobody'll ever need to know."

The man who shouted that had pieces of metal jutting from either shoulder. He'd been cybernetically augmented. Of course, he was a daunting presence, charging at D with the pickaxe in his hands raised to strike, and the power behind it when he brought it down seared the air, causing a hot wind to strike the old man and Lydia on the cheeks.

Cries of surprise rang out.

The tip of the pickaxe was embedded in the floor at D's feet. Just before that, the people had seen a momentary flash of light.

"Hyaaah!" the man grunted, raising the pickaxe again.

D didn't move.

"Die!"

When he brought it down again, it was with such speed the man himself let out a confused groan. Spinning in almost a full circle, the man ended up slamming himself against the floor.

Desperately raising his pickaxe, he looked at it. The top half of it had been lopped off.

"It's behind you," Lydia whispered.

Turning, the man had the wind knocked out of him.

The tip of the pickaxe was stuck in the floor. It'd been cut off. But when had that happened? There'd been a stark flash of light before he raised the pickaxe again. But it didn't appear as if D's sword had ever left its sheath.

Given the circumstance, the man stood there befuddled, but he snarled to his compatriots, "Get him!"

His compatriots must've been ready to do that even before he gave the word. However, not a single one of them could move a muscle. It wasn't just that they'd seen that momentary flash of light. In that split second, the eerie aura given off by the one who wielded that blade had frozen their blood and their hearts. Fifty tough men, all of whom were no strangers to violence—and all of them were defeated by a flash of light from a solitary young man. They were up against someone who wasn't human.

"Okay, folks," Old El called out, "there can't be anything to do for fun in a bunkhouse like this except gambling. Then do it up in style. Now, I know your income is limited, folks. So, why not take me up on my kind offer? However, I will need some collateral, don't you know."

"Coal-ladder-what?" a miner with a western Frontier accent asked. "None of us got anything like that!"

"No, you do. Anybody who can't pay back the money can give me their left arm."

"Couldn't do our damn job if you did that! We'd be outta work for life!" a different miner shouted.

"Like hell you would. A set-up like this is bound to have cyborg arms and legs to replace any lost in accidents, or even artificial organs. When all the ore's been dug up here, the company'll just move on to the next territory. Go with 'em. You'll be able to earn a living as a miner all your days. If you don't wanna do that, just run off with the replacement limbs they give you."

The men fell silent at Old El's words. But they drew a reaction soon enough.

"I'll take a loan! Gimme ten thousand dalas."

"Me, too!"

"Twenty thousand dalas!"

"That'll cost you both arms," the old man replied.

"Fine by me."

"Anybody else?"

Almost everyone raised their hands.

"All right, then, form a line, single file. Sign on the dotted line, and I'll loan you ten thousand dalas for an arm."

In no time at all, a line had formed, twisting around beds and desks like a snake's tail.

Seeing Old El take bills and silver and gold coins from the bag on his hip, Lydia turned in D's direction. The figure of beauty was just slipping out the door. Lydia followed after him. The old man didn't seem to notice at all.

D was standing by the door. Perhaps he was looking at the scenery by daylight, but it might have been that he wasn't looking at anything at all.

After letting the sight of him burn itself into her eyes for a moment, the girl faced the same direction as D and said, "Funny, isn't it?"

D didn't respond at all.

Unfazed, Lydia continued, "I was certain the sunlight wouldn't suit you at all, but now that I look at you, the light seems to change just to suit you. It's so bright out, yet it seems like a winter's day locked behind the snow. Why would someone like you sign on to guard a loan shark on a collection run?"

There was no reply. Lydia's question was a matter for a world that had no connection to D.

"Is it the Noble you're after? I seem to remember Old El saying something like that. So, your aim is to kill that Noble?"

"The term is 'destroy.'"

The hoarse voice surprised Lydia.

"Okay, let me rephrase that. *Destroying* that Noble's your aim, is it?"

"Why do you want to know?"

Once again, Lydia was surprised, but relief spread across her face. That response had been in D's voice.

"It has nothing to do with your way of life," the Hunter continued. "Or your *human* way of life, that is."

"Oh, dear," said Lydia, her eyes going wide. And then she got a somewhat sad little smile on her lips and looked at D. Oddly enough, she wasn't enraptured. "You—I happen to be human."

Nothing from the Hunter.

"I'm no different from Old El. Don't go putting on airs!"

"What should I say?" asked the hoarse voice.

"That doesn't surprise me anymore. So why don't you just knock it off with the ventriloquism?"

"I suppose you have a point there."

There was no response to what he said. Lydia was just staring at that figure of beauty, her mouth hanging open.

"Say," she said to him a few seconds later. Her voice was nearly as hoarse as his. "Now, unless my eyes were playing tricks on me, did you smile just now?"

Nothing from the Hunter.

"Yeah, you did, didn't you?"

Not a word.

"What, are you being bashful?"

But the girl quickly realized that wasn't it.

At least five men were coming from a hut in the direction D was facing. Each wore a pair of pistols on their belt and carried a rifle in their hands. On closer inspection, one of them had a pair of what looked to be tin-plated cylinders on his back, with a rubber hose running from them to the gun he held in his hands.

"D?" the girl said, her voice nearly crushed by an imposing presence that was different from that of the miners.

"These'd be the mine's enforcers," the hoarse voice replied. "Finally took notice, did they? There's gonna be trouble for sure! Will he have to take 'em down by force, or will he cut 'em in on the action?"

"Force, I'd say. And he'll ask D to do it," said Lydia.

"I second that. Huh? Wait a second—"

D's eyes were following the men, but they halted further down the rails—at the entrance to the mine shaft.

"Something happened inside, eh?" said the hoarse voice, and just then, a miner staggered from the black hole, advancing about a dozen paces before he tumbled to the ground. Not only the enforcers but everyone in the area raced over to him, all of them calling out to ask him if he was okay.

Seeming to be about thirty years old, give or take a bit, the man had white hair, and his face was slick with sweat and still looking upward as he extended his right hand and pointed toward the hole.

"There's . . . something . . . down . . . there."

As soon as he finished wheezing out those words, he lost consciousness.

At that point, Old El walked over to the man who'd come up behind the enforcers and seemed to be the site foreman, asking him, "Are there still miners down below?"

"Yeah, one team—there's a good fifteen men in there. An alarm went off in my office. Hey, somebody get him to the lounge!"

"Ain't you gonna have a doctor look at him?"

"There's not a damn mark on him," the foreman countered. "He's not bleeding, either. Hell, we'll let him get some rest and he'll be better in no time."

"You figuring to just let your guys down below take a rest, too?"

The foreman glared at Old El, but apparently understanding the gravity of the situation, he looked up at the enforcers and said, "I want you to come with me."

The five men nodded. Apparently used to such things, they didn't seem at all frightened.

Just then, the miner who'd gotten up again and had a compatriot on either side to hold him steady whispered something in a fragmented tone.

In that instant, the rough but otherwise ordinary mining town became something else.

"Sa . . . cred . . . An . . . cest . . . or . . ."

III

It was an accursed name usually sealed away beneath a subconscious boulder in the depths of the human psyche. However, the instant they heard it, the boulder popped like a soap bubble, and the words bounded to the forefront of their minds with a scream of liberation.

How fragile, the human psyche! A number of people fainted. Even rough men like these miners fell flat on their asses—or rather, the reverberations of the words that even now still hung in the air made them back up and try to get away, while only a few people like Old El barely managed to cling to their inherent strength and pride.

The miner was lying on the ground. He'd fallen there along with the compatriots who'd hoisted him to his feet. And each and every one of them could think of nothing save fleeing from the epicenter of this fear.

Just then, a pale shadow fell across the miner. But the thinness of it didn't seem to register with anyone. However, in the present state of extreme mental chaos, in the midst of the violent collapse of human values that reduced even the rule of thumb to junk, here was something that brought hope.

Confronting this fear was someone who knew no fear. Though they might even be described as sensitive, it was clear at a glance that D's fingers were as hard as steel, and he placed those fingers and the palm of his hand on the miner's brow.

The miner opened his eyes. Perhaps it was due to the Hunter's palm that he didn't melt away in rapture.

"You said 'Sacred Ancestor,' didn't you? Did you see him?" D asked the miner, peering into the man's face.

The miner nodded.

"Just . . . his outline . . . But I could tell from that . . ."

"What happened down there?"

"We were in Number 7—down in the deepest shaft, and digging our way forward. Then, all of a sudden the rock the pneumatic drill was planted in collapsed, and this huge hole just opened up. Inside, it was just incredibly deep, filled with what looked like ruins and such."

At that time, the men who were ready to flee were listening raptly to what the miner had to say, but no one reacted to his words more strongly than the foreman and the five enforcers.

Ruins. There were only two places that word could lead: "Nobility" or "OSB." Though in the case of the latter, they were more correctly termed "bases." However, if the form of the Sacred Ancestor lingered there, it was safe to assume it was the former.

"Everybody was just bowled over. I'm the biggest scaredy-cat around, so getting outta there was the first thing I thought of. So, I went back to where the tram was and sounded the alarm. But all the rest of them, they went right on in. I could see it all from the tram. Right away—no, it might've been a minute later. It might've been an hour later. A terrible scream rang out. Just look at me—my hair's bone white, isn't it? My hands are so wrinkled you'd think I was some hundred-year-old coot. And it's all on account of that scream. The scream broke off right away. I thought my whole body might've turned to stone. I couldn't lift a damn finger. Couldn't even shut my eyes. And that's why—"

The miner's voice suddenly became a tiny ball of iron.

"—that's why I had no choice but to keep looking. At that hole. A black shadow slowly appeared from it . . . At first, it was the size of a man . . . And yet . . . it was so . . . so freaking huge. It plugged the hole with pitch black . . . The whole tunnel . . . Oh, man, it's coming this way . . . Toward me . . . No . . . Stay baaaaaaaack!"

Extending his hands, the miner clawed at the air in front of D's face. Everyone understood that fear alone could drive that kind of strength and action. Suddenly, the movement stopped and his arms fell limply to the ground.

And a hoarse voice from the vicinity of the Hunter's left hand made everyone around him bug their eyes by declaring, "He's dead."

D stood up. Looking at the hole and confirming that the tram was there, he said, "I'd like some time."

His words were addressed toward Old El.

"Are you gonna meet with the S-Sacred Ancestor?"

From beside him, Lydia asked, "What do you hope to gain by seeing him?" She had just rushed over. There was no chance she'd heard the miner say that name. And though she didn't understand even after seeing D on the move, she'd followed after him and finally managed to piece it together.

"If these are Noble ruins, there could be treasure down there," said D.

That was true. The value of gold and silver treasures went without saying, but rumors of a farmer who'd brought an unknown mechanical device to scientists in the Capital and became a billionaire echoed across the entire Frontier.

It was only natural that the old man gave a hearty nod to that notion.

"Though you're still under contract, I'll allow you this special exception."

"Wait just a minute!" the foreman protested. Which was also only natural. "This here is a mining site of the Matilda Mining Company. We're not about to give you the run of the place!"

He made eye contact with the others. The five enforcers split up, surrounding D.

"Heh heh, this should be good," Old El chortled. "Gonna try and stop him by force? Not a problem, but you could have a thousand of these punks and not get the better of that demon with a sword!"

"Punks?!" one of the enforcers shouted, mouth going wide. "Oh, you've gone and made my day with that. What are you trying to say, that pretty boy here is a freaking Noble or something?!"

"I'd like you to let me through," D said to the foreman.

The Hunter's beauty and unearthly aura had already writhed their way into the very bones of the man who managed these roughnecks.

"N-n-no, I can't do that. We'll check it out first. After, we can discuss it." In a pinch, the foreman asked the crowd, "Anyone want to head down?"

There were Noble ruins down below. If it were just that, there'd have been no shortage of greed-blinded volunteers. The compatriots of the deceased miner were that way—and even though he'd died, when a Noble treasure was involved, it was probably worth far more than any gold. That was something worth risking your life. But if the form of the Sacred Ancestor lurked there—

"We'll go!" said the giant of a man who was the apparent leader of the enforcers. "But there'd damn well better be a special bonus in it for us."

"Okay, okay. First of all, get rid of this interference."

The five men grinned at the foreman's instructions. Their lust for gold and spilling blood blew through the fog of rapture.

"If you wanna go dig around, you'll have to go through us first. Or we can talk it over if you like!"

The man with the metal cylinders on his back stepped forward, the end of his gun pointed toward D. The other men held guns at the ready.

"So, what'll it be, pretty boy?" the foreman said triumphantly, giving his belly a slap.

A stark blade was thrust right at his throat. The foreman stopped breathing. The enforcers bugged their eyes—as did everyone else in the vicinity. The sword was D's. But when had he reached for the hilt, and when had he drawn it?

"I'm going below, okay?"

The question was so quiet and beautiful and utterly unsettling.

"S-sure," the foreman replied with a nod. His eyes were focused on the Hunter's blade.

A gleaming arc was limned in the air. And it took a strange course. What made people think so was because the tip of the blade had sunk into the heart of the dead miner.

The world froze. Had the young man just killed the dead miner a second time? Could it be—that he might rise from the dead? But at present, sunlight was still pouring down on them.

The blade was sheathed with the faintest of sounds. D had already started walking toward the tram.

"Hold up. We ain't about to let you hog all the glory," said the leader of the enforcers. "You're bringing us along with you!"

The foreman once again nodded his agreement to their request.

The five of them followed after the Hunter, and behind them, Old El and Lydia followed along as well.

"Me, too."

"And me."

As soon as he'd climbed into the front of the tram, D realized it was ready to depart. The dead miner hadn't even bothered to turn off the engine. When the Hunter reached for the safety lever, there was a thud behind him. The other seven people narrowly managed to climb aboard. D didn't even wait for them to pull the safety bars down in front of their chests. With screams still onboard, the tram began a fearless dash into the pitch-black depths.

When they arrived at the bottom of the more than half-mile deep mine shaft, all of the passengers seemed half dead. D hadn't applied the brakes until the last hundred yards or so. The tram's free fall down the nearly vertical shaft had robbed the other seven of their nerve.

"Damn freak!"

"One of these days I'm gonna kill you."

"This ain't over!"

Behind the men grumbling curses, Old El rubbed his temples and said, "I sure hired a real winner in him."

"But it was incredible! We got here in no time at all," Lydia exclaimed, unable to contain herself. "Ordinarily, throwing the brakes that close wouldn't have cut it. See, I used to do some mining, so I'd know. The lot of us should've been splattered against the wall at the end of the tracks. So, how'd he manage to stop us?"

"Only he'd know that, dhampir that he is."

Not exhibiting the slightest interest in the rearguard, D gazed down the tunnel before them and said, "Wait here."

Not waiting for the other seven to make of that what they would, the figure in black surrendered himself to a world of swaying shadows and light created by the lantern.

"Wait just a goddamned minute!"

The five enforcers hustled after the Hunter, but when Old El and Lydia tried to get even closer, two of them came back.

"What do you want?" asked the old man.

"Not a damn thing from you. But something from her."

"A hostage to use against D, eh?"

"Bingo. Okay, come with us and don't give us no trouble."

A gleaming longsword was thrust beneath the noses of the old man and the girl.

"Okay, okay. Take her already."

Old El gave in so easily, Lydia was too stunned to even get angry as she looked at him and said, "Hold on—you're terrible, you know that?"

"Sure is," one of the enforcers concurred. "I don't know squat about why you're with this old codger, but the sooner you part ways with him, the better! Come with us!"

"You've got to be joking. Stop it!" Knocking away one of the man's hands when it reached for her, the girl had nerve enough to follow it up with a slap to his cheek.

For a second, bloodlust blazed in the enforcer's eyes, but it immediately faded, and the man smiled.

"I'm liking you more every minute! Lucky for us, everybody else's gone on ahead. All that leaves is my buddy and the old man, so what do you say to getting a little nasty, sister?"

The man pulled her close.

"Stop it!"

"Why don't you leave her alone?" Old El said, trying to get between them, but the barrel of a gun was shoved in his face.

"Just pretend you didn't see nothing. After him, it's my turn. We'll give you a crack, too!"

"You damn fool!"

There was no trace of his earlier heartless comment, and the old man indignantly pushed the gun barrel aside—no, he actually tried to, but it was pushed against his forehead, wresting hand and all, and pierced by a great, booming gunshot and flames.

Lydia let out a scream. Her hands were pressed back against the hard floor of the tunnel.

"Did he kick the bucket?" the other asked.

There was no answer.

"What the hell?" the man said, turning for a look, and his blood stopped cold in his veins.

When they heard the gunshot, the group was near the end of the tunnel—more than a hundred yards from the borehole. Before them they could see clearly enough—a gaping blackness. The three enforcers turned and looked back, mixed emotions on their faces.

It was the leader who'd given the order for them to capture Lydia to exert some control over D. However, there'd been trouble. When the young man in black learned it involved his employer and the girl travelling with them, what kind of action would he take?

He did nothing. The Hunter just pushed onward, never halting.

Look at this freaking guy, the enforcers thought to themselves, something cold running down their spines. *Doesn't he give a shit about the old guy and the girl? His blood's gotta be colder than ice, I just know it.*

D halted in front of the hole. The men saw him stick his left hand out. He remained that way for several seconds.

"An experimental facility, eh?"

The hoarse voice that flowed from the palm of D's hand astounded the hardened men.

"But it was soon abandoned. Partway through construction. My guess is it wasn't used even once. The reason has less to do with the energy deposit and more to do with destruction by the OSB. The OSB's unique energy still lingers here."

"So—what about *him?*"

"Hmm, it's probably—"

That was when it happened.

The air became a gust of wind. It blew from the depths of that enormous hole.

The enforcers were like dead men. Heads blocked all stimuli. Hearts stopped beating. Blood wouldn't circulate. Nerves forgot to

transmit electrical pulses. All of that was commanded by the black form that gushed from the massive hole. Over sixteen feet tall, it practically scraped the ceiling. It had substance. However, it was a shadow.

Deep beneath the Frontier, something that couldn't exist did.

The shadow raised its foot over D's head. It intended to trample him.

Screams rang out—and died. The shadow had faded away. But just before it did, the men had seen a stark flash of light between the bounding D and the shadow.

Raising his head ever so slightly, D asked, "Well?"

The hoarse voice replied, "I learned what it was when your blade made contact. Though he's left the facility, an impression of his presence remains here in the form of a mass of energy."

"*He* doesn't attack humans for no reason."

"It wasn't him. In a manner of speaking, it was an image of him. Worse yet, it doesn't have his thoughts or discernment. It's just an impression of his presence. When those miners were killed earlier, it wasn't because he wanted to do it, but simply from making contact. It was like they touched the blazing sun."

It was unclear what D intended to do after hearing that. But his course was decided by the sudden, intense shock and rumbling that assailed them.

The Vermilion Brink

CHAPTER 5

I

Unable to remain standing, the enforcers collapsed, the color draining from them as they saw cracks racing through the walls and ceiling. "Run for it!" was all one could manage to say. Down on all fours, they began to creep backward.

"It's because this abandoned facility was held together by a physical force charged by *his* energy down in this pit," the hoarse voice told the Hunter. "Now that you've cut that off, it's all turning back to dust."

D started back the way he'd come. Showing no signs of offering a helping hand to the men crawling back beside him, he made it back to the tram.

"Are you okay?"

Old El and Lydia were waiting for him. The pair of enforcers lay at their feet, foaming at the mouth.

"What happened?" the hoarse voice inquired with apparent glee.

"Bad enough they tried to get fresh with her, but they went and threatened me, too," the old man replied. "So I slammed 'em against the rock wall!"

"Yeah, what kind of move was that? You scared the life out of me," Lydia said, her cheeks flushed with genuine excitement.

"Get in. This place is collapsing," D said, taking a place in the driver's seat.

Old El and Lydia jumped aboard, and the other three enforcers barely got there in time with their two unconscious compatriots before the tram pulled away.

When they reached the surface, the first thing Old El did was to exclaim, "What have we here?" And the second thing he did was to follow that up with a puzzled "Him?"

No doubt he was referring to one man who stood with nearly a dozen others beside the expired miner, who'd been left lying in exactly the same spot. Wearing a long coat that outshone all the others in style and character, he was talking with the foreman.

The group had arrived a few minutes earlier in a thundering cloud of cyborg horses. As he'd inquired what had happened from the foreman who met them, the man's eyes had been riveted on the corpse.

"Jonas," he'd said.

They dismounted in unison, and the man immediately dashed over to the dead miner.

"I thought I'd finally found you, and you had to go and die, did you? Always the shirker. Who killed him?"

He asked that in a tone so haughty, the foreman answered, "Damned if I know."

The foreman was just turning away when sharp pains shot through both his cheeks. The hand he ran across them was covered with fresh blood.

Softly tapping the chest of his puffed-up coat, the man said, "That's the work of my 'little kitty.'" With an unsettling grin on his lips, he continued, "It's not as patient as I am, unfortunately. You wouldn't believe the headaches I have paying compensation for those that end up dead. Still, I'm not about to part with it, no sirree."

The foreman began to tremble. His eyes couldn't make out any kitten, or any other creature, for that matter. With this man calling the shots, and the rest of his party armed to the teeth with rapid-fire rifles and more, the lowly mine foreman couldn't do a blessed thing. And his trusted enforcers were down in the mine.

"Who killed him?" the man asked once again.

"Who the hell are you?" the foreman replied, pressing his hand to his forehead. Blood dripped from between his fingers and his brow.

"I'm the one asking questions here."

"Okay, okay—he died of shock."

"The hell he did!" the man countered with a quiet smile. That was frightening.

"There's a stab mark on his chest. Made by an expert. Not the kind of person who'd be at a mine like this. So where—"

That was as far as the man got before he turned and looked, as if he'd just been given a jolt of electricity.

D had just emerged from the depths of the mine.

"Run for your lives!" Lydia shouted as she ran alongside the Hunter. "The tunnel collapsed. You're all in danger here, too!"

Panic ensued. Miners who hadn't flinched while watching the tense exchange between the man and the foreman ran away letting out shrieks that were far from manly. The ground shook. And the foreman joined those who were taking flight. Only the man remained standing there, staring at D as he calmly walked that way.

"You the one that stabbed my younger brother, then?" the man asked. "He's Jonas Happiness. And I'm his brother—Kilco Happiness."

"D."

The man's expression changed.

"You're . . . I see. In that case, it's little surprise my brother's dead, then. Was it a duel?" he asked.

"He died of shock. I ran him through as a finishing touch. Just in case."

"Just in case? Was he bitten by a Noble or something?"

"Dead doesn't necessarily mean safe."

"Are you trying to say my brother might come back? Even though he wasn't bitten?"

"The place is collapsing," said D, both those words and the Hunter himself passing by the man's right side.

"Oh shit!" the man exclaimed, leaping away.

When he landed some thirty feet back, the ground had begun to subside dramatically, swallowing up the mine and his brother's corpse. Everyone managed to flee to the entrance to the work site, and it bordered on the miraculous that the sinking stopped just before it got that far. Fatalities were limited to Kilco's brother and the fourteen miners who'd died far below.

The rumbling of the earth subsided, and after the long silence that followed it, the first words to be uttered came from Old El, who said, "So, we meet again at last." He was addressing Kilco Happiness.

Glaring at the old man for a little while, the man finally got a look of revelation on his face. "What the hell are you doing here, you bastard?" he asked.

"Here, there, or anywhere, you're shit out of luck running into me. Okay, hand over my money, and be quick about it. Kilco Happiness—that's a hell of an alias you've got there. Your name's Julas-Han Toba. Your younger brother's Cornelius Toba. So, where's Machete?"

"He and I parted company. Most amicably, of course. And I can't pay you back your money."

"What?!" Old El exclaimed, rolling up his sleeves.

"The newly deceased Cornelius ran off with all the money I'd earned in the last decade. Fifty million dalas! I spent five years chasing him, all the while hearing nothing but stories about how he'd given money to women, or gambled from dusk till dawn. And the amounts we're talking about were outrageous! I had to catch him as fast as I could, and when I finally do catch up with him, look how I find him. So as a result, I can't pay back your damn money."

"Then I'll take your collateral."

"Oh?"

"By which I mean both your arms. Looks to me like the mysterious power you got to control beasts is tied to those arms of yours."

"These?!" said Toba, grabbing his left arm with his right hand "Well, I really can't let you have these babies without a fight. If you want them, just try and take them!"

There was a succession of clicking gears from all around the old man. Toba's underlings had cocked the hammers of their guns.

At that point, the foreman said, "Hey, I can't have you starting any trouble on my work site!" Behind him were the five enforcers, their weapons also cocked and the barrels trained unerringly on Toba and his men.

Toba grasped the situation immediately.

"Unexpected reinforcements. I see. Guess I'll call it a day, then. I'll be staying at the hotel, old-timer. I'm leaving first thing in the morning, but let's get this talked out before then. I'll be waiting."

And he left, along with his men.

"What the hell? The whole place sank into the earth?! Fifty thousand years from now, I bet humans still won't be able to hold a damn candle to the power of the Nobility," Old El cursed.

"What're you doing tonight?" the hoarse voice inquired.

"Going to the hotel, of course. A lousy beastmaster's no match for a financier. I'll take those arms of his off at the shoulder."

"Good luck, then."

"Huh?" Old El exclaimed, staring at D.

"I won't be coming along. You see, something else concerns me."

"Something concerns you? What? And does it involve making money in any way?"

"No. But good luck with your work."

II

Night fell. But it was a gloomy night, with no starlight, and even the moon didn't show itself. The miners had worked almost until nightfall straightening up the thoroughly devastated work site, returning to the hotel the company had arranged for them and falling asleep covered in dirt instead of taking a shower.

Around that time, at the rim of that great subsidence a voice said, "Run off already, has he? Back to town, then!" It was a voice so cold it seemed it would turn all who heard it to ice, human and inhuman alike.

The enforcers had a two-room suite. The leader and one of the others claimed the beds, while the other three elected to sleep on the sofa or in chairs. And in the middle of the night—someone rapped on the window. Since it sounded like the timid rapping of a spineless youth on his ladylove's window, the occupants of the room didn't even acknowledge it, even on a subconscious level. Had it at least stirred their subconscious, they might've noticed the fact that the sound was a regular succession of taps, and that a man's voice could be heard murmuring something in time to the noise. The pattering was intended to put all who heard it to sleep through certain principles, while the voice was instructions to gain hypnotic command over someone.

How much time had passed since the strange disturbance to their sleep had begun?

One of the enforcers muttered, "Hitting the head," as he got up.

However, he didn't go into the bathroom. Standing before the windowpane where the rapping continued, he gazed out through glass that seemed spattered with darkness.

A face appeared. It was that of Cornelius Toba.

"Open up, if you don't mind," he was heard to say between raps.

The enforcer didn't hesitate. Opening the window, he backed away a step. A glowing fog flowed in. Cornelius's face floated in the center of that fog. Of course, the fog showed no hesitation at all as it flowed toward the rough men sleeping there.

Even the hotel bar was quiet. If there were any customers, they seemed likely to naturally drift off to sleep. But there were no other customers. Julas-Han Toba and his men occupied two tables.

On entering the hotel, Old El went straight into the bar.

Toba showed his pearly teeth.

"Nice of you to come. Even though it just means you've come to die like a man."

"So, are you ready to come up with my collateral?" Old El asked, reaching his right hand back over the collar of his coat and grabbing a wooden hilt. Slowly drawing it, he embedded the two-foot-long, six-inch-wide machete in the table. "Got one just like that old buddy of yours. You're well past the payback date. Hurry up and put your arms out!"

"Don't be so full of yourself without D here," Toba said, showing him a cruel grin. "Boys, it's about time we throw him some lead!"

All around him, there was the sound of hammers cocking again. If these were confident and skilled warriors, there'd be no way for the old man to escape.

The doors burst open, and there was the sound of a number of people walking in. Those footsteps took the form of the five enforcers from the mine, who formed another ring around the table.

"What the hell do you guys want?" Toba inquired. His tone was a composed one.

"Your brother put us up to this. See, we're going from mine enforcers to killers," said the leader.

Giving him a good, long look, Toba groaned, "You folks got bit, didn't you?"

The second those words were out, the man who lurched in from the leader's flank turned the nozzle of his hose-based weapon toward Toba. It wasn't bullets that it disgorged. It was ten-thousand-degree flames. They enveloped Toba, and the man swung the nozzle from side to side, turning four men into human torches.

Suddenly, long, savage screams erupted from the mouth of the victims. They weren't those of anything human. Rather, they were the howls of some unknown beast of peerless brutality.

The burning masses suddenly collapsed. At the same time, someone leapt from the flames, landing on the floor. Toba's underlings. Their faces were shrouded in flames. Their hands beat them out. Hands that were covered with hair. And not just their hands, but their bodies were hirsute as well. With a few small flames still on them, the men were undergoing a rapid change in appearance. Their skulls shrank, and their eye sockets protruded. Like bubbles forming atop the water, fur began covering the surface of their bodies. Their bodies leaned forward precipitously, and when they went down on all fours, they were finally ready to rend something with tooth and claw.

They were beast men.

Behind the counter, the bartender reached for the emergency buzzer directly linked to the sheriff's office. That action was followed by a streak of red. The bartender's head went flying. A fountain of blood sprayed vermilion everywhere.

The streak returned to one of the men's mouths. It was his tongue. Capable of shooting out dozens of yards and tough enough to shatter even bone, his tongue was a weapon.

"Oh, 'tongue-slippers,' eh?" said the enforcer, stopping his flame-thrower and grinning wickedly. Even knowing the true form of his opponent, he wasn't scared.

Giving a look of suspicion to the enforcer's strangely pale profile, Old El murmured, "Looks like the beastmaster is still alive and kicking. But he's got some pretty nasty competition!" And having said that, he crouched down and scurried under a round table.

The tongue of another underling skimmed right overhead, wrapping around the necks of two of the enforcers and quickly strangling them.

"Huh?" Toba exclaimed, knitting his brow.

The enforcers whose heads had been taken off had caught them in their hands and placed them back on the stumps of their necks.

Toba's eyes went wide.

The color faded from the gash, and it disappeared.

A tongue whipped around, slashing through the necks from the opposite direction. The enforcers grabbed it and actually bit down on it. The tongue-slipper writhed in agony. As if drawing in a net, the two enforcers then went on to pull that lethal weapon of a tongue right out by the roots.

"Stab the bastards through the heart—they're 'half-Nobled'!" Toba shouted.

An enormous figure flew over his head. The leader of the enforcers. A pair of fangs jutted from his lips—the mark of the Nobility.

The leader had a machete raised to strike, but he halted in midair. Four tongues with points as sharp as awls had impaled him from below. Fresh blood scattering like a rain of crimson petals, the enforcer leader groaned. One of the tongues had pierced him right through the heart. However—

The leader's machete flashed out. All of the tongues were lopped off, and the leader dropped onto a table. Landing lightly, he gathered the tongues running through him into a bunch and pulled them out with both hands.

"So, you can't destroy the heart of a Noble, even a faux Noble, with anything but a wooden stake or iron sword?" Toba mused.

The beastmaster got up. In front of him, there was the sound of rending flesh and agonized screams. The last of his underlings had just been beheaded by an enforcer's machete. What good were the beast men's fearsome combat abilities in the face of indestructible Nobles?

And that wasn't all. Look. Several of those who'd expired from being slashed and shot were swayingly rising to their feet, as if drawn by invisible strings. Their eyes opened. And those eyes were the color of blood. They had died after being bitten by the enforcers. It was supposed to take a full day for those bitten by the "half-Nobled" to return as one of their kind. The reason they alone immediately completed the change into Nobility was a result of their beast man nature accelerating the "transformation of life" process that change entailed.

"Guhuhuhu!"

It wasn't a groan. It was a laugh.

Ten of Toba's underlings had perished in no time flat, and, worse yet, they had become "half-Nobled" and joined the opposition. Given the circumstances, his defeat was all but assured, but Toba leaned back and laughed. And the aura of confidence that tinged him from head to toe testified that this was no bluff or hollow threat. Fifteen foes surrounded him. All of them were "half-Nobled." So what gave the man such whole-hearted confidence in such a situation?

"Charge!" shouted the leader of the enforcers—and Toba shouted it as well.

Baring their fangs and raising their machetes, the "half-Nobled" rushed forward. Just as the claws of the one at their vanguard was about to tear into the man's throat, something shot out from Toba's chest. The throat of the "half-Nobled" split open, and blood sprayed out unexpectedly.

Look. Fresh blood is gushing from the throats of all fifteen, and they're reeling!

"What . . . ? How . . . ?"

And saying that, the enforcer leader fell at length. His head dropped to the floor.

Not one of them moved. A cold wind blew across the room.

Fifteen "half-Nobled" had had their heads cleanly removed from their bodies and now lay on the floor of the bar.

"Come on out," Toba said, knocking on the table with one hand.

Old El appeared.

"I saw it all from down there, and, wow, it was incredible. You gotta have ice water in your veins."

"That's rich, coming from a loan shark," Toba replied, glaring at him.

Old El continued nonchalantly, "Damn, you made short work of the same 'half-Nobled' who had no trouble taking down your tongue-slippers. Was it a familiar?"

The old man was referring to the kind of supernatural creatures that served witches. They generally assumed the form of an animal, with crows and black cats being prime examples.

"Don't use that pedestrian phrase. You're talking about my little kitty."

The old man looked to the heavens and shuddered. "So, how does this little kitty of yours kill vampires?"

"I replaced its teeth and claws with steel."

"I see," Old El remarked, crestfallen because the mystery had been solved so simply. "Who turned them enforcers into Nobles, though?"

Toba said nothing.

"And how come they were after you?"

"Well, we never were on very good terms, you see."

It took just over a second for the old man's eyes to bug. "Your kid brother? It can't be! Anyway, he sank into that fissure in the ground, and . . ."

"Who else would it be?"

"Well, you got a point there—But, D ran your kid brother through the heart!"

"Then someone with a power greater than D's sword must've bitten him or possessed him or whatever."

"But that's . . . impossible. Who's ever heard of a 'half-Nobled' that Vampire Hunter D's sword couldn't destroy . . ."

"But such is the case, dear brother."

Those words rained down on them.

Stunned, Toba and Old El turned in that direction—and looked up the staircase.

Both hands resting on the second-floor banister, the miner who'd been stabbed through the heart by D's blade was staring down at the two of them with a smirk on his face.

"Cornelius!"

"How'd you get in here?"

The miner turned his face toward the ceiling. There was a skylight. And it was open. That was where the cold wind had come from.

"I see. So, you really have turned into a 'half-Nobled,' then. But, you were—"

"Stabbed by D? Very true. However, apparently the power of the one who possessed me surpasses even that! To be perfectly frank, in all the wide Frontier, I am the only one who can slay D."

The eerie aura that billowed from every inch of the miner made the two of them believe that was no lie.

"Try it," someone said.

III

This time, it was Cornelius who was clearly astonished. The voice had come from behind him, but he hadn't noticed the speaker's approach. However, he didn't seem rattled at all as he slowly pulled back from the railing and looked at the speaker.

"D, is it? Came in the back door, did you? Sorry to say it, but I ain't dead!"

"I have business with the thing that's possessing you. Leave that man."

"You've gotta be joking," Cornelius laughed. But his smile froze.

D had turned his left palm toward him. Though blurry at first, the surface of it had a human face that gradually took more definite shape.

"You son of a bitch . . ."

Cornelius writhed, and though he raised his right hand high to strike, there it halted.

The face that'd risen on the Hunter's palm opened its mouth, and a terrible blast of wind slammed the former miner against the back wall, and moreover, he remained immobilized as if nailed to it. Cornelius shouted something. Perhaps it was a curse, though it might've been a spell to extricate himself from his dire situation. However, it was crushed by the howling of the wind, the words never taking shape.

D drew his blade. Cornelius could only watch as it slowly sank into his own heart. Gouts of blood sprayed from Cornelius's mouth, splattering the floor. While that was happening, he fell flat on his face and ceased moving.

"That was easier than expected," the left hand murmured, not sounding entirely convinced.

Saying nothing, D grabbed Cornelius by the collar and pulled him up, throwing him over his shoulder. When D had slowly descended the staircase, Toba and Old El were there to greet him. Neither of them could say a word. D walked right between them and exited the hotel. Walking to where the wagon was parked on the edge of town, he set Cornelius's corpse down on the ground about twenty yards from the vehicle. His left hand rose.

"Burn it," D commanded.

A single tongue of flame stretched from the palm of his hand, enveloping the miner's corpse. It was no ordinary flame. The burly body quickly crumbled, melted, and turned to ash in less than five seconds.

Once the blast halted, D walked over to the pile of ashes that were still giving off white flames and scattered them with his feet.

"Just to be sure, eh? Good idea."

As soon as the face in the palm of his hand had finished saying that, its tiny eyes shifted in the direction of town. There was the sound of iron-shod hooves approaching. A quartet of cyborg horses. The sheriff and his men soon took shape.

"There was trouble at the hotel. You're gonna have to tell me all about it."

The right hand of each man was ready to go for his gun.

Coming nose to nose with the Hunter, the sheriff continued, "Did you just burn someone up? You know, we don't take too kindly to that!"

"Have you been to the hotel?" asked D.

"Yeah. Nothing but stiffs there. Killed the way a 'half-Nobled' does it. This is a rough-and-tumble town, but that's too brutal even by our standards. Wouldn't happen to know who did it, would you?"

Turning to the still-smoldering ashes, D said, "He's right there."

"What, you burned up the culprit?"

The sheriff gave a toss of his chin, and two of his deputies got off their horses and ran over to the ashes, looking down at them for a while before one of them called out, "Ain't nothing left. Just ash."

A look of distress plain even in the gloom of night rose on the sheriff's face. He knew to the very marrow of his bones that this situation was far beyond their abilities. All he knew was that he had to bring this gorgeous young man back to his office for questioning. He cursed ever hearing testimony from a passerby who'd seen the young man leaving when he'd ridden up to the hotel.

But it was the sound of two sets of hoofbeats that settled the situation. Toba and Old El had rushed to the scene. And there was one other person, as well. It was the foreman from the mine, who was riding double with Old El on his cyborg horse. Apparently the sleeping man had been dragged from his bed, and he had his pants on backward. He testified that the suspect in these murders was a miner who'd been bitten by a vampire down in the mine, had in turn preyed on the enforcers, and was trying to kill the brother who was pursuing him when he was killed in the ensuing battle.

To that, Toba added, "See, that young fella right there protected me. I'm the one that took care of them. He didn't slay but one of their number. That clears him of any guilt, doesn't it? Burning's the best way to deal with a blood-crazed 'half-Nobled'!"

No, the sheriff thought to himself, *just drive a stake through its heart or lop off its head,* but he was prevented from saying as much by the foreman's next words.

"The mine collapsed, but a survey team will come out for the company, and who knows, maybe they'll find another deposit. If that happens, this town'll be booming again. It'd be better if there weren't any nasty rumors going around, wouldn't it?"

And better for your job security, too. As long as the town keeps going.

"Okay, okay. But we've gotta write up some reports. You'll have to come back to my office, Mr. Foreman."

"Sounds perfect," Toba said, clapping the foreman on the shoulder. "That ties everything up nice and tidy. Just get it all down on paper, sheriff. Right?"

His last remark was directed at the foreman. The foreman gave him a somewhat grave nod. And that was the end of it.

Once the foreman had left with the sheriff, the hoarse voice inquired, "How'd you get the foreman on board?"

"Money, of course. Money! See, I heard from one of the miners that the foreman needed cash. So I slipped him a thousand dalas! And with that, all's well that ends well. Whenever you go somewhere, it's just common sense to get something you can hold over two or three people with power in the community. There ain't nothing better when something goes wrong."

"Hmm. That's good. But why—"

"Why did you help me?"

In an instant, the Hunter's voice had gone from being one that seemed centuries old to a youthful iron tone.

Understandably surprised, it took Toba a little while to reply, "I want your help with something." Pointing at Old El, he continued, "See, this geezer won't shut up about getting his money back. Fortunately, I want money, too. It takes a fair amount of cash to keep beast men. So, I decided to go get that money somewhere. To be honest, I don't feel right about just the two of us trying it. Come on!"

"No," D said in his own voice.

"Don't say that. Your boss has already given me his okay! Haven't you?"

"That's right," the old man conceded. "I told him he was screwed running into me here and demanded he pay up, and all he can tell me is how he ain't got the money. Well, that crap don't pay the bills. After some bickering, he came clean with me about a Noble treasure that's supposed to be buried just sixty miles from here. So, money's money, but this is Noble treasure we're talking about. Who says everything don't work out in the end? We need you on this."

"If there are Nobles, then it's a job for me," said the Hunter. "But treasure hunting isn't part of the job description."

"Well, the truth is, it's kinda fuzzy in that regard," said Toba, furrowing his brow. "The Noble who owned the treasure's supposed to have croaked more than five hundred years ago, but rumor has it he still guards it. Just in case, we'll be counting on you."

"Okay, I suppose."

D's answer brought gasps of disbelief from the two men. They'd anticipated an ironclad refusal from him. They'd asked him only because it couldn't hurt to try.

"Well, that's just peachy! Glad to have you on board!" Toba exclaimed, rubbing his hands together.

"That clown's coming, too?" the hoarse voice inquired.

Toba gave a sarcastic smile, saying, "Don't worry about me. I'm coming along out of my own self-interest. I may be unwanted, but without me, you won't know where to find the damn treasure."

The night wind swept ashes past his feet.

It was early the next morning that they left. And true to his word, Toba rode alongside the wagon on a cyborg horse.

Galloping along on the opposite side of the vehicle, D heard repeated low groans from his left hand.

"What is it?"

"It's just got me worried. Hmmm."

"What has?"

"No—it's nothing. Hmmm."

This went on for a while, and after a dozen repeats, D asked simply, "Is it Cornelius?"

Apparently the Hunter had hit the mark, and the hoarse voice fell silent.

"Back at the hotel, it was disappointingly easy for us to defeat him," it finally said. "I don't get it. I know you must've thought the same thing. Otherwise, there'd have been no need to turn his body to ashes."

"We can't do any more than that," said D. His forelock swayed in the wind. "If what you fear is true, there's only one thing he'll do." His heavenly beauty turned ever so slightly to the left.

"Give chase," said the hoarse voice. "But will he be after *him* or *you*?" By *him* he meant Toba. And *you* was D. But pursuing them—what could inspire such tenacity?

"Deep in the ground, that miner was possessed by *his* spirit—or by the air. The fact that your little jab through the heart wasn't the end of him is proof of that. And if that's the case, it's kind of a problem. Hatred toward his brother, and hatred toward you—that's more than enough cause to rise again."

D had turned his gaze ahead once more. The straight road cut across a vast plain of red clay. He was bound for the end of it. Did the gorgeous young man not know what awaited him there? But whether or not such thoughts occurred to him, his beauty glimmered in the breeze, overshadowing even the sunlight. Perhaps beauty was the true measure of immortality.

The Hunter turned his face toward the driver's seat of the wagon. Old El held the reins, but he had his upper body ducked into the wagon for a look.

"What's wrong?" Toba asked the financier.

Not answering him, the old man wrapped the reins around the auto-pilot and hurriedly slipped down into the wagon. When he returned less than twenty seconds later, his expression was a bit perplexed. Looking at the riders to either side of his wagon, Old El said in a somewhat unpleasant tone, "It's the girl—she's got a bad fever. And I don't know that the medicine I got will do her any good."

D's ears alone could make out the pained gasps that escaped from the vehicle.

What Waits in the Temple

CHAPTER 6

I

T he wagon drove on for three days. The reddish-brown plain gave way to a distant mountain range, and the road became a steep climb along its ridge line. Each and every traveler or farmer they passed intoned either local prayers or those of their homes, and they made signs to unnamed gods. On the left-hand side of the road was a waterfall that was miles long, and it took all their skill to get the wagon behind that curtain of water, to say nothing of D's and Toba's respective cyborg steeds. The road to the waterfall's basin was barely wide enough for the wagon's wheels, with less than four inches to spare. But the biggest problem was the mountain creatures and the mountain folk.

Giant lizards and carnivorous spiders that deftly crawled the sheer walls to assail those on the road, and two-headed eagles that silently dove from the sky with deadly talons ready were only a few of the documented threats, while others' existence had yet to be confirmed by survey party guides, but more unknown creatures were said to definitely exist there.

In lands that no amount of searching by day might discover, the mountain folk conducted their weird rituals, attacking people not to dine on them, but rather to impale them as offerings to their gods, a practice that made them the object of absolute terror among travelers. They built kites to ride the winds, or else summoned the gods of wind, firing arrows and throwing nets from heights and angles unrivaled even by the monsters.

Here winds blustered, rains tempted the rock walls to collapse, lightning struck those who ventured out, snow froze their very hearts, and volcanoes and lava swallowed them up alive—and in order to survive the mountains' dreaded elements, the inhabitants were forced to become exceedingly cruel. Even now, it was said that only half of those who crossed the mountains reached the lands on the other side, with the other half falling into the hands of the mountain folk and being sacrificed to their gods.

Soon after entering the mountains, the wagon and the pair of cyborg steeds became the focus of countless eyes. And yet, looking all around, there was no sign of anyone, nor a single voice to be heard. The only sound was that of ordinary birds, ringing from the trees and the air. That alone would've been enough to fray nerves, but in truth, they were beset with troubles both within and without— the condition of Lydia, who lay in bed, only continued to worsen.

They were all to blame. When they were racing across the plain toward the mountains, not one of them had suggested bringing Lydia to a town or village out there. Old El and Toba were both blinded by greed, while Lydia's sickness was surely a trivial matter where D was concerned. Though the wagon's suspension performed reasonably well, when the road itself became rocky, the invalid was tossed about brutally, and it seemed that none of the medicine in the vehicle's first aid kit had any effect at all. Her fever wouldn't subside, and for the last three days, Lydia hadn't eaten so much as a piece of bread or a bowl of gruel.

The cause became known on the first day. D had held his left hand to her sweaty brow, and the hoarse voice declared, "She's possessed."

"By what? And since when?"

Old El and Toba both wanted to know the same things.

"I don't know. Ordinarily, whatever was possessing her would try to keep its existence a secret until it'd achieved its ends. It's not often one manifests like this."

"What's that supposed to mean?" asked the old man, the color draining from his complexion. They were off to make some money, so all this talk about possession was outside his scope. Especially when they didn't even know what was possessing her.

"Something's sparked whatever's possessing her, making it go nuts. But I don't know what that is," said the hoarse voice.

"Then she'd have to be possessed by two different things!" Old El exclaimed, furrowing his brow. "Hey, Toba, are you sure that Noble treasure you mentioned is really there?"

"Would I have come all the way out here if it wasn't?" the beast-master jeered, the whereabouts of the treasure still unshared. As he put it, "There's nothing to keep you from killing me once I've told you," and there was certainly something to that. "Unless I miss my guess, we'll be there in another two days. I just have to last that long. Once I get my hands on the treasure, I don't care whether I live or die, but—" At that point, he seemed to remember something. "Come to think of it, the dying pilgrim who told me about the treasure said there was a mirror in it that could cure just about any possession!"

"Why, with that—" The old man broke off there, saying, "I've heard of 'em, too. A mirror like that can reflect any spirits taking possession. And it's also supposed to tell you how to get rid of them or something like that. So, if we bring her to it, it'll clear everything up nice and tidy! Say, D, how many days you figure she'll last?"

"Barely two, I suppose," the hoarse voice replied.

Though they knew it wasn't D's, it still put them in an undeniably strange mood.

"Good enough. Full speed ahead!" Old El declared to D and Toba.

"Seems a little dangerous just leaving her like that, though," said the hoarse voice. "No telling what the girl will do if one of the powers battling inside her wins out. Even if the fight isn't settled one way or the other, there's no saying all that power won't drive her crazy. Both the things possessing her are powerful. What do you think

would happen if the energy of both was unleashed? It could reduce a mountain or two to dust!"

"What are we supposed to do, then?"

"*We'll* keep watch over her. You two focus on driving the wagon."

"But, I—" the old man protested.

"We're talking about the kind of power to reduce a mountain to dust. What do you think either of you could do about that?"

Ultimately, it was decided that D would watch over Lydia, and Old El and Toba would man the driver's seat.

It was the next morning—the fourth day of their journey—that the mountain bared its fangs. The wagon was zipping through the valley at the outrageous speed of forty miles per hour when Old El pulled back on the reins without warning.

"What the hell is that?" the dumbfounded Toba asked from where he sat beside him.

"An egg, I think," the old man responded as if he didn't believe his own words.

Even at ten feet wide and almost thirty feet high, it would've been hard for anyone to take it as anything but an egg.

"What kind of egg?"

"How the hell should I know?" Old El replied, no strength in his voice.

Fortunately, it wasn't directly in front of them, but rather was affixed to the sheer cliff to their left.

"Any way, time's a-wasting. And time is money," the old man said. "Let's go."

"Wait," said, D, who'd just come up from the wagon's interior.

"Why are you stopping us? We've gotta get to the treasure as fast as we can. How's the girl?"

"There's no change in her condition," the hoarse voice replied.

"Then that's all the more reason to—"

"Look at the surface of the eggshell," the hoarse voice told them. "It's crisscrossed with black cracks, right?"

Straining their eyes as they might, neither of the other two could see anything.

"Try speeding along another two seconds with the sound of these wagon wheels hitting the ground. It'll break that shell to pieces. And what do you think's gonna come out of it?"

"Damned if I know. What are we supposed to do, then?"

"Pass by it nice and easy. There's no other way to do it."

"Wait, what if it cracks?" the old man protested.

"Okay. Let's go," Toba said, taking the reins in his left hand. D's hand came down on his shoulder. "What are you—"

"No sudden moves."

Toba was about to argue, but held his tongue. He'd noticed D's voice was lower than ever before. His eyes weren't turned toward Toba.

The beastmaster turned his head in the same direction.

Something white was sliding down the egg's surface.

"A piece of the shell. It felt your movement just now."

"Not a chance," Toba replied, his voice even lower than D's.

"Slow the wagon as much as you possibly can, and don't say a word. Even a fly landing on it might be enough to crumble it. Old El, cut loose the cargo compartment."

"What are you talking about, you—you—"

No doubt to Old El, the gorgeous young man must've seemed insane.

Turning to Toba, D asked, "Is there really a Noble treasure up ahead?"

Although it was the quietest of questions, Toba thought he could hear the blood stopping in his own veins.

"O-of course so."

D's eyes shot to the old man. "In that case, you can lose that cargo and still come out ahead of the game. Any complaints?"

"Yeah, what are you gonna do if he's blowing sunshine up our skirts? We've got no guarantee there's any Noble treasure!"

D countered the old man's protests impassively, saying, "You'll just have to take that gamble. If you don't cut the cargo compartment loose, you won't get past the egg. The way I see it, the creaking of that car will be more than it could take. If we go another twenty yards, the whole shell will crumble."

If this were anyone but D, the old man would've ignored even the most logical of arguments and pushed onward out of sheer obstinacy. However, the words of the gorgeous young man carried a weight that crushed the financier's own powerful ego.

"All right." That was the only answer he could give.

The linkage between the compartments was uncoupled in less than a minute. Before doing that, D had asked Old El if the cargo compartment had an independent locomotion system, and the old man had replied that it did. After replying, Old El had thought about asking D to wait a minute. Sure enough, once the uncoupling was complete D got in the cargo compartment without saying a word, and as the old man and Toba watched, backed up over a hundred yards before cutting the wheel hard so the vehicle plunged off a cliff into the valley below. Old El cursed the Hunter, who'd barely leapt out in time, but D merely said, "It would've been blocking the road."

That silenced the old man.

The Hunter continued, "Let's go."

That simple phrase probably had the greatest effect of all.

"Try not to breathe if you can."

D took the reins.

On seeing the Hunter work them, even Old El in the foul mood he was in had his breath taken away. With D at the reins, the cyborg horses' hooves didn't make a sound. The road was bare rock. Yet the iron-shod hooves didn't ring out at all. What's more, the wagon wheels didn't even creak.

Who the hell is this guy? There's a limit to what even a dhampir can do!

The wagon reached the egg without incident. The two men had climbed down from the vehicle and were following it cautiously. Both of them were barefoot. The wagon went past the egg. It was followed by Toba, and then Old El.

Something struck the old man on the shoulder. He barely restrained himself from flying into a panic.

Another piece of the shell had broken off.

Old El narrowly managed to catch the fragment as it fell from his shoulder. With the bare minimum of movement. His blood ran cold. The piece of shell was nearly an inch thick. His started to ponder the size of whatever was inside it, but quickly stopped himself.

The old man's breathing was pained. Every time the soles of his feet touched the ground, it felt like they caused a roar of thunder. His legs were like taffy. He had to wonder if he was even moving forward.

The strength drained from the pair's bodies when they'd gone an extra ten yards past the egg. Toba and Old El clambered up onto the wagon and climbed inside, where they were finally able to breathe a sigh of relief.

At that moment, a scream rang out. But what was Lydia, who lay on a cot, screaming about?!

II

"What the hell are you doing?!" Toba cried, diving for her and covering her mouth with both hands.

She grabbed both his wrists with one dainty hand. Toba could hear his bones creaking. *Is she gonna break them?!* he thought, but at that very instant he was slammed back against the wall, striking his head and being rendered unconscious.

"Lydia, you're . . ." the old man stammered, reaching for the stake gun on his hip.

Lydia—or rather, this woman—had eyes that glowed crimson. His gun half drawn, Old El stopped what he was doing. Whatever was sitting up on the cot now was something other than Lydia. The woman with blood pooled in her eye sockets slowly got off the cot and approached the old man. He was about to call for D, but no sound came from him. His vocal cords were paralyzed.

"What's possessing you? What stirred it up?" he groaned, a bead of sweat rolling past the corner of his mouth. It looked for all the world like he was going to die without getting an answer to his questions.

An impact changed everything. Lydia was thrown backward, with Old El following suit. While he sailed through the air, his heart lightened at the notion that his situation looked to be changing, at least.

The instant Lydia let out her scream, D tried to get the cyborg horses going, but they wouldn't budge. They instinctively knew what was happening. They knew enough to fear what was assailing them from the skies. The beating of colossal wings could be heard from the section of road they'd just passed. The wind blowing at them shook the ten-ton vehicle and uprooted trees completely. And yet, the horses remained as motionless as stone statues.

The next change was that darkness descended. It covered the sky. But there were breaks in the darkness, and in them the beating of countless wings could be heard. Tens of thousands of black birds had gathered in the air. Their numbers made them a cloud. And they were diving straight for the wagon. The birds had black bodies with eyes as red as blood but black beaks and talons.

D's sword flashed out, each slash cutting down nearly ten of them, but the rest mobbed the cyborg horses. Their skin had a protective coating that could stop the fangs of a sabretooth beast. However, under the relentless assault of thousands of beaks and talons, fresh blood finally gushed from the cyborg horses.

"Hyah!" D shouted, cracking the reins. He believed their pain had broken the spell the enemy had cast over them.

The cyborg horses started to gallop, with monstrous birds still swarming them.

It was at that very moment that Old El was in mortal danger inside the wagon.

As he cut down the pursuing monstrous birds, D raised his left hand.

"Haven't consumed anything but air and soil lately. I won't last long," the hoarse voice said with apparent dissatisfaction.

"Do it!"

"Whatever you say, you lousy slave-driver."

Perhaps the birds' red eyes made out the tiny mouth that rose in the palm of the Hunter's hand. Black smoke gushed from it. But it was no ordinary smoke. Somewhere in the palm of his hand, it had done something to the air and earth that resulted in nerve gas. The fearsome birds dropped one after another, while the rest turned away. And as they did, the wagon gained more ground at a reckless speed.

Now more than two hundred yards from the flock, they were still speeding away when Old El poked his head up by the driver's seat.

"Did you subdue her?" D asked.

"You knew what was happening?" the old man asked in disbelief.

"I heard the sounds."

"You don't mean to tell me that sudden start back there was to save my skin, do you? No, I mean, was it to knock Lydia out? She whacked her head something fierce. Of course, that also saved me and Toba's necks. She's sleeping now."

"She'll be back to normal soon. As in, back to being a peaceful woman who doesn't remember the ghost that possessed her."

"You don't say. What the hell got into her, anyway?"

"Probably the spirit of a 'half-Nobled' from back at that asylum."

"And you mean to tell me you knew about that and didn't do squat about it? Ain't you Mister Happy-go-lucky!"

"If you don't handle it right, the host will die when the spirit leaves."

"Damn. So, that's why you did it that way?"

"Well, being possessed isn't necessarily always a bad thing, either."

"What?" Old El exclaimed, staring at D in spite of himself—and just as he started to melt with rapture, he hurriedly looked away again.

"As far as the possessing spirit is concerned, the host is a base that allows them to keep living in this world," said the Hunter. "They have to take good care of it."

"Take good care of it? Then, what about that scream back there? She almost brought the damn bird down on us!"

"Just as some things can become too much of a strain for us to bear, the spirit possessing her reacted to the supernatural aura given off by the egg. Those two aren't strapped in, are they?"

"Strapped in? Nah. They're just lying on the cot and on the floor."

"Better tie yourself down with something fast—here it comes!"

"Huh?" the flustered old man cried, quickly looking all around them.

Everything was darkened. Something had blotted out the sunlight. The terrible sound of beating wings and a wind enveloped the two of them and the wagon. What Old El saw a heartbeat later was enormous talons descending at them from the sky.

"Oh shiiiiiiit!"

A powerful shove was delivered to his chest, sending the financier sailing back-first into the wagon. Fortunately, he didn't hit his head. Fighting through the pain, he ran over to Toba on the floor and Lydia on the cot.

Terrific power raised the wagon.

Too late? the old man wondered.

The instant the approaching talons were within striking distance, D made a horizontal slash with his left hand. The bird's two feet had a total of six talons, and all of them were lopped off. The Hunter's blade came around again. A foot was taken off at the ankle. Blood gushed out for the first time. A shriek rang out in the darkness above.

"Take over!" D called out from midair.

Old El heard him, having just dragged Toba up to the driver's seat with him, but he saw no sign of the man in black anywhere. Even now, the wagon raced on. There was a curve visible up ahead. They were going to go flying right over the edge, without a doubt.

"Shiiiiiit!" Old El shouted, grabbing the reins.

"Keep outta my way!" cried the hoarse voice.

"Huh?" the old man exclaimed in spite of himself, somewhat taken aback. His eyes darted around restlessly, finally locating something gorgeous attached to the reins. D's left hand.

"Get your mitts off the reins!" the hoarse voice barked. "Go cower inside or something!"

Oh, so when D said to take over, it'd been directed at his own left hand.

It was the jolting wagon and the rapidly approaching curve that made up the mind of the thoroughly confused old man.

"It's all yours!" he cried out, jumping back down into the vehicle.

Fifty yards to go. The left hand pulled on the reins as hard as it could.

Just then, there was once again the shriek of the monster descending from the distant sky.

D's eyes had gleaned the true nature of their foe. He'd entrusted the wagon to his left hand. All he had to do was focus on the opponent before him. Longsword grasped between his teeth, D climbed up the bird's leg with just his right hand. It wasn't feathers that covered the bird's body. It was a pliant skin. He could tell the bird was frantic because of the erratic way it was flying. If he allowed it to live, it was certain to come after them again.

Just then, the bird turned in his direction. The world was overwhelmed by a beak that seemed like iron hooks. Descending almost vertically from its nostrils, the beak looked hard enough and strong enough to bite through iron plating with one shake of its head. In addition to the eyes on either side of its head, the creature had a third open just above where its beak protruded. While the other two were ablaze with crimson, the third eye glowed azure.

Even before D became aware of the light burning itself into his retinas, he drove his blade through the beak, reaching the brain. An unearthly shriek came from the monstrous bird as it began to plummet, and without a hand to cling to it, D also dropped like a stone. Not toward the road. Rather, he fell toward the unknown blackness of the depths of the valley.

Even as it listened to the monstrous bird's shrieks, the left hand's handling of the reins was perfect. Rapidly decelerating just before the curve, it then lashed the horses' flanks once they were on a straightaway again. The vehicle had climbed the steep incline faster than it could've under either Old El's or D's control.

"Hey, shouldn't you stop or something? What about D?" the old man inquired, his peace of mind finally returned.

"He'll be back soon enough," the left hand replied impassively.

"Well, if you say so—"

Old El thought Nobles and dhampirs had the same abilities. Surprisingly enough, that was the common perception among many Frontier folk familiar with both.

Suddenly, the wagon tilted. With the way the left hand was working the reins, the problem wasn't the horses.

The ground had collapsed.

"Aaah!"

"That's not good."

Shrill cries and a composed analysis of the present situation intertwined, and the wagon, along with its three passengers and single severed appendage, dropped from the cliff toward the abyss.

"Shiiiiiiiiiiiiii—" Old El shrieked, and he would probably continue to do so for as long as he remained conscious. However, he stopped before they'd fallen ten yards.

"What the hell?"

Opening his eyes, the old man was shocked.

The wagon had stopped. Of course, it was still in midair. There were sheer cliffs to either side of it. Their benefactors were ahead of them—floating above the cyborg horses, which were still working their legs. But it wasn't the giant monkeys' arms and legs that kept them aloft, but rather the pairs of wings that grew from their backs. The powerful beating of wings reverberated from all sides of the wagon. There could be no doubt that an army of giant winged monkeys had arrived at the last second and were now supporting the wagon and its horses. A number of them clung to the cyborg horses and began working with their hands and feet.

"Wh-what the hell are they up to? Are these the 'mountain folk'?" Old El inquired in a low voice.

"Yep. They may have saved us, but watch yourself. You don't get such large numbers of a creature like this in nature by accident. The Nobility have been at play. They'll be every bit as cruel as any monster out there!" the left hand replied, and its tone was also a little tense.

"What are they fixing to do?"

"Look at the fire in their eyes. They're so hungry it's driving 'em crazy. Look at those fangs and claws, and how they're slavering. I bet they'd love to tear us to pieces and fill their bellies with us."

"Why don't they come after us, then?" asked Old El.

"The mountain folk are a superstitious lot. They've got something that resembles a religion."

"For goddamned winged chimps?"

The old man thought he'd murmured that remark, but his disbelief might've amplified it a bit, because one of the monkeys in front of them bared its fangs.

"What the hell?"

"Simmer down," the hoarse voice told him. "They're probably gonna bring us to their god now."

"And what happens then?"

"Oh, they'll sacrifice us to it, for sure."

"What the hell?!"

"Shh. Would you rather they let go of us right now, or set us down on the ground?"

"Well, the ground'd be better."

"Good enough, then."

Suddenly, the cyborg horses whinnied. It was a scream.

Old El could only watch in amazement as all four of the animals dropped toward the valley below.

III

"Wh-what the hell are those bastards doing?! Without them horses—"

"That's only a problem for us," the hoarse voice said in a reassuring tone. "For things that can fly, those animals would just be in the way. Oh—"

The wagon flew up even higher into the growing darkness of the night sky.

Old El went inside.

"What's going on?" Toba asked. He gripped a rifle in his right hand.

The old man gave him a brief explanation of their situation.

"Oh, hell. If D were here, things might be all right, but we're in some serious trouble!"

"Yeah, I know," Old El replied, and he was about to go over to the door in the back when he finally realized something. The way he just sat himself down right on the spot, he looked like he was folding up. "—I got nothing. D was the only thing that could've kept us safe. We're truly screwed."

"Of course we are," Toba spat, turning away in a snit.

What was the left hand doing? Undoubtedly there was nothing it could do.

Before long, the wagon was back down on the ground, and the giant monkeys had disarmed the two men, leading them and Lydia outside, but there was no sign of the left hand anywhere.

The trio was surrounded by giant monkeys. Their weapons were spears. Though primitive, consisting merely of tree branches with sharpened stone heads tied in place with vines, in the hands of these creatures they would probably be brutally effective.

A strange elation seemed to rule the night air.

"Oh, they're gonna sacrifice us for sure," Old El said to Toba, who was walking alongside him. Lydia was behind them—and in midair. A pair of giant monkeys had grabbed her by the shoulders and feet and were carrying her.

"Let's do something, then!" said Toba, his reply carrying a force that stunned the old man.

"You don't mean to tell me—*this* is the place?"

"Yeah. And it's not too far up ahead," said the beastmaster. "He stashed it in some ancient ruins while trying to get away from his pursuers, and there were offerings of bird meat at a weird stone statue. I figure that's their shrine."

"That's a hell of a place he chose to hide it. Why didn't he stash it someplace safer?"

"Well, there's no use bitching about it now."

Rows of stone pillars supporting a stone dome took shape. Judging from the foundation sunk into the ground, the facility was quite enormous. Flames burned here and there.

On seeing an ape-man holding a torch, Toba said with unveiled contempt, "These goddamned beasts use fire?"

"Humans used to be like this way back, too. But where the hell is D?" Old El mused, not quite abandoning hope yet.

"Hell, he's run off with his tail between his legs."

Before they knew it, countless ape-men had gathered around the pair. Though their grunts were those of beasts, mixed in the clamor were what seemed to be a few human words, much to the old man's surprise. Beside the pillars and above the dome, shadowy figures with torches in hand had halted. Beyond the row of pillars, a statue of some sort towered beneath the dome. It stood over sixteen feet tall—and it was hewn from stone. Though pieces were missing here and there and it was cracked, it had a face with eyes and a nose worn off in a testament to ages spent exposed to the elements, and that weathered face peered down at the pair disturbingly.

Once they'd been brought before the statue, the two men were ordered to kneel. Lydia was set down there as well.

Peering up at the statue, Toba said, "Looks to me like this thing didn't have anything to do with these creeps. It's wearing a necklace and bracelets."

"That's what makes it a god. Where's the Noble treasure at?"

"There's an opening at the base of the statue, right? In there."

"Hmmm. Say, where's that 'kitty' of yours, anyway?"

"It took off. After I whacked my head, it probably got out the hatch up to the driver's seat."

"You're freaking worthless," Old El told the man.

A giant monkey stood before the trio. He wore a number of stone ornaments on straps around his neck, and his face had a dignity that resembled that of a human.

"This their chief?" Toba asked, sounding unsettled.

"Their shaman, most likely," Old El replied.

"What are they fixing to do?"

"First, he'll address his underlings, then pray to their god, and finally slit our throats, I'm guessing."

"And you're just gonna let them do it?"

"You got a play?"

"That's what I'm asking you!" Toba replied, his expression understandably grim.

Death was plodding ever closer.

Suddenly the giant monkey looked around at his compatriots and began to screech something. From time to time, he would drum his fists against his chest. And every time he did, the others cheered, whipped into even greater excitement. Before long, his speech was finished, and the giant monkey gave a satisfied nod before turning to face the stone statue. Swinging his arms, he squatted and began turning to and fro. It was the kind of dance that might break out at any time normally, but as far as the two men were concerned, it marked the approach of something ghastly. And then it, too, ended.

The bloodlust emanating from the mob around them bound the two men tightly. The giant ape pointed at the pair—and at Lydia—and screeched. The monkeys at the forefront readied their spears. Their actions were repeated by almost a dozen more overhead. Old El shielded Lydia with his own body. Even he had a hard time believing what he was doing.

The spears flew. Though the monkeys may have been lacking in intelligence, they certainly had strength. More than a dozen spears went right through Old El and Lydia both. They then melted away like dissolving paint.

Toba was impaled as well. In hellish torment he grabbed the spear, but it and his pain both suddenly vanished.

"Wh-what the hell is all this?"

The only other person who might've asked that question was the monkeys. But no sooner did it occur to their undeveloped minds than they, too, disappeared. Not only that, but Old El, Lydia, and Toba all vanished, as well. Now in these ruins where not even a single flame burned, the moonlight alone shone down as a stark spotlight.

"Upsadaisy!" a voice seemed to grumble from beneath the stone statue— in the vicinity of its base, to be precise. Like a veritable spring, a pale shape shot from the hole Toba had indicated, resolving into the left hand before saying, "Oh, that's not good. Not good at all. I've zapped 'em all away. Better bring 'em back quick."

And greatly agitated, the hand bounded back into the hole. When it emerged again, Old El and Toba were back where they'd been, puzzled looks on their faces as they rubbed their chests and sides. Lydia lay flat on her back.

"What the hell, I felt kinda dizzy, and then—where'd the damn monkeys go?"

"To another world," replied a voice from down at the financier's feet, drawing a sudden and surprised look.

"Where the hell have you been?!" the old man asked in a rage.

"Don't give me that when I just saved your lives!" the left hand blustered back.

"Y-you did that?"

"Well, the Noble treasure did it, technically."

"Wh-what?!" Toba exclaimed, lunging forward.

Jeeringly, the left hand said, "Yeah, that machine—well, it's made of an ultra alloy that looks just like gold, so I can see where somebody could make that mistake. But bring it to a Noble researcher in the Capital, and you're looking at a hundred million dalas or a billion dalas—you could name your price."

Nothing from the men.

"It's a Noble weapon, something called a dimensional transporter. All them winged monkeys got sent to another world. So did you. Well, that was a lovable little goof on my part, though."

A ferocious look skimmed across Toba's face. However, it was instantly effaced by one of barefaced greed.

"It's in there?"

"Er, yeah."

It wasn't the most emphatic reply, but Toba didn't care, and he was about to dash into the hole—and then he hit the ground face first.

Pulling back the leg he'd used to trip the other man, Old El dashed into action. Toba grabbed his ankle and wrenched, and soon the two of them were tussling for their lives—for an instant, before a blue light bathed their bodies. It was from electromagnetic waves shooting from the hole in the statue's pedestal.

Both men were speechless.

"So—who told you about that thing?" the left hand inquired.

"Well, I heard about it from a merchant who was dying out in the desert. Said he was high up in Quetzalcoatl. Seems they found it in the castle of a Noble who got destroyed. And apparently they made off with it a good long time ago."

"That's not the story we heard before. Not that it matters now. It's garbage."

"Garbage?!" Toba and Old El exclaimed in unison.

"That's right. I could tell as soon as I started working it. Got it to work twice, but then it was shot. As you can see."

The blue light was already fading.

"So, you're saying I risked my life for some Noble's trash?" Toba said absent-mindedly.

Old El grabbed him by his lapels and shook him, saying, "Damn fool! You were gonna palm some garbage off on me? Well, I've had it with you! Where's my money? Gimme my money!"

Just then—

A black shooting star fell beside the two men, then took the shape of a primitive spear. A dozen more spears stuck in the ground in rapid succession, and more continued to fall.

"Maybe I missed a few?" the left hand groaned.

"We'll make a break for it in the wagon," said the old man.

"We don't have any damn horses!" Toba shouted.

"It's got a gas engine for just such occasions. Has a tough time going up hills, but from here, it's all downhill. Hurry up!"

With Lydia under one arm, Old El sprinted into action. But suddenly, he stumbled forward. Clucking his tongue, Toba raced over, put Lydia over his shoulder, and started running.

"Don't plan on leaving me here, do you, you bastard?" the old man bellowed.

The left hand was just scuttling by his face at terrific speed when it stopped.

"Huh?" the old man exclaimed.

"Don't give up now, loan shark."

And then the five fingers kicked off the ground, and the hand was soon out of sight.

"Shit, screw the lot of you! All I'm doing is engaging in an economic activity based on legal commercial transactions."

Just shy of his nose, another spear jabbed into the ground, and there was the sound of wings beating in descent, of all things.

"Oh shit!" Old El cried, scampering like a scared bunny for the wagon, climbing into the driver's seat, and hitting the ignition button under the seat.

The engine caught on the first try.

"Here we go!"

Weaving around the spears that continued to rain down or having them bounce off it, the horseless wagon raced out of the ruins at a terrific speed.

The Rigged Town

CHAPTER 7

I

On the tilted sign at the entrance to town, the words "Welcome to Gimmicklin" had been scrawled in red paint. It was noon of the following day. The sun was high, and on account of that the world was full of light.

"You say that bastard Putterson or whatever his name is lives here?" Toba jeered from his spot by the old man.

"It's Tupperman. Langen Tupperman—and he's a whole lotta trouble!" Old El replied while working the steering wheel attached to the vehicle. They were up in the driver's seat. D's left hand was with Lydia.

"And just why's he so much trouble?"

"I got more than a few ways to deal with simpletons like you who solve everything with violence. But that don't work with the puppeteer."

"Oh, screw you," Toba retorted, but then he added, "Something's not right," his expression distorting as he peered at the row of houses ahead of them. It looked like an ordinary hick town on the Frontier. However—

"Yeah, something ain't right," the old man concurred. "That row of buildings—blacksmith, grocer's, saloon, stables, hotel, and the sheriff's office. Nothing strange at all. First thing I was gonna do was get us some weapons and food. Something's off about this, though."

"Yeah. But I don't know what it is. It's like a derelict in a tuxedo—it just doesn't add up."

"At any rate, let's get going." And with that, Old El stepped on the gas and the wagon rolled into town.

The two men looked at each other. The sun had suddenly dimmed. On looking up, they found the heavens shrouded in leaden gray clouds that looked like they'd been there for a century.

"What the hell is this?" said Old El.

As they were looking around, a fat woman appeared from a building on the right side of the street, the hem of her skirt gathered up as she headed toward them. She had a notepad in her right hand. And a pencil had been tucked inside the cover of the notepad.

"Welcome to Gimmicklin," she said, standing in front of the wagon so they had no choice but to stop. A reckless woman. Reaching up with a hand like a bunch of plump caterpillars, she shook Toba's hand, saying, "I'm editor-in-chief of the *Gimmicklin Journal*. Emma Piggle's the name. It's been a while since we had any travelers through here, so would you mind if I interviewed you?"

"Sorry, but we're looking for somebody," the old man said, turning away.

"Well, in that case, I can be of service," Emma declared, striking her ample bosom.

"We're fine. I'll just ask at the weapons dealer over there."

Old El brought the wagon over by the wood-planked sidewalk, and then he and Toba climbed down without another look at the woman reporter, heading toward a shop in the row of buildings to their left. It had a sign with pictures of a rifle and a knife, and the words "Ishii's Weapons."

As they pushed against the door, there was a sound like a twig snapping behind them. Turning for a look back, the two men were taken aback. Half a pencil protruded from the thick, almost amphibian lips of the woman. The other half quaked in her right hand. An intense look of anger on her face, Emma Piggle trembled from the most intense emotion a human being could feel.

On opening the door, the two men were assailed by a fresh incongruity. There wasn't a single customer in the fairly large shop, and the well-past-middle-aged man who sat behind the counter greeted them with a smile. It just wasn't possible. A weapons shop with only one employee was practically begging someone to kill them. Shops of this kind would keep at least one enforcer around. Because they had to be prepared for the worst if they were rushed by more than one person. Rifles, bows and arrows, swords, and spears on the wall and in showcases caught Toba's eye.

Old El said to the shopkeeper, "I tell ya, as soon as we got into town, it clouded over all of a sudden. Strange little town you got here, eh?"

"Is that a fact? It's been that way ever since my great-grandfather's days. You ever seen any other kind of weather?"

"Hell, set foot outside town and it's sunny as all get-out!"

The shopkeeper gave the old man an odd look, saying, "I wouldn't know about that. See, I haven't been outside town a day in my life. No one in town has!"

Whether that was the truth or a lie was unclear.

Old El rightly remarked, "Pretty strange place, you know? By any chance you familiar with a fella by the name of Langen Tupperman?"

"Sure, everyone knows him. Take that street out there and head toward the end of town, and you'll know the place straight away."

"You don't say."

In the end, Old El and Toba ended up buying two rifles, two pistols, four longswords, four bows, four spears, and two hundred arrows, then got enough bread and ham to feed three people for ten days at the grocer's next door.

When they stepped outside, Toba gave the bag he carried a shake and asked, "We gonna be able to eat this?"

"Damned if I know."

"There was somebody in there ahead of us, and a woman came in after us, but something isn't right, you know?" said the beastmaster.

"Yeah, I don't know how to put it, but it seems kinda staged. Like they learned how to go shopping just for this."

"You'd better shake the money out of that puppet master or whatever he is as soon as you can so we can get the hell out of here!"

"Listen to you run your deadbeat mouth when that Noble treasure of yours was a big, fat fraud."

"Well, you know, I really couldn't do anything about that. Besides, everyone's entitled to make one mistake in life."

"You're entitled to pay me back once in your life, and then you can go right to hell!"

"Sheesh!"

"Talking straight here, how you figure on paying me back, anyhow?" asked the financier. "I sure as hell ain't letting you get away!"

"Don't make me laugh. The only reason I'm with you, you old fart, is because it's more convenient that way. If I wanted to, I could take off any time I liked, you'll see!"

"Well, I got something for you to see, too," Old El said, skillfully shifting the paper bags and pulling a red capsule from his pocket.

"What the hell's that?"

"It's the kind of medicine we give to nasty little lowlifes and scumbag debtors like you who probably still wet the bed. It's full of liquid gunpowder."

The color seemed to audibly drain from Toba's face. He realized the old man wasn't bluffing.

"The capsule dissolves the instant it hits your stomach acid, and the gunpowder mixes with your blood. It ain't poison or nothing on its own, but with the right electrical signal it'll go ka-boom. Every one of your blood vessels just explodes, you know? No chance of surviving that."

"But I—I don't remember swallowing one of them things!" Toba protested.

"The capsules also dissolve in alcohol. And it don't change the effect none. The day you boarded my wagon, I slipped one into that bottle of whiskey you like so much. Now, I haven't seen you drinking it since then, but I don't think you've sworn off the stuff, either."

"You son of a bitch!"

"Don't go dropping that bag, now. The detonator's set in one of my molars. If I bite down real hard—ka-boom. The signal's good for a hundred and twenty mile radius. Okay, go ahead and run now."

"You-you-you bastard," was all the debtor said, but he could do little but grind his teeth together as Old El shot him a faint grin.

"Square your debt off nicely, and I'll give you a drug that'll break down the liquid gunpowder. So you'd best get to thinking how you're gonna pay me back. Bwa ha ha!"

Old El's laughter continued until he returned to the wagon and noticed the left hand and Lydia had disappeared.

They did, indeed, spot Langen Tupperman's residence soon enough. As the two men watched, the house kept changing shape before their very eyes. The roof subsided and one with an entirely different shape popped up in its place, windows spun around, and eaves rolled back so that new and different ones could jut out to replace them. Dumbfounded though they were, the pair opened the door to find yet another door. Ultimately, they wound up opening twenty in a row, cursing all the while. Toward the end, they were getting desperate.

"Damned fool!" Old El cried, kicking one open and falling into the space beyond, where the interior of the house became visible.

In a hall inconceivably roomy from the outside dimensions of the house stood a young man wearing a purple robe.

"We meet at last, Tupperman. I'm here to collect!"

"How good to see you again, Mister El. You look as fit as ever. Gold is the key to your life and longevity, isn't it?"

"I didn't come out here to listen to you flap your gums. And just because this is the Frontier, don't think you can pay me off in counterfeit cash. On top of everything, you went and turned your damned girlfriend into a doll and had her attack me, then got mad at me for gunning her down. How many times have you tried to cook my goose, you bastard?"

"When you put it like that, I'm not sure I feel entirely comfortable answering, but on four occasions or so."

"I wasn't looking for a straight answer, puppet-boy. Know how much I've had to spend on shooting up your goddamned hired killers? Want I should tack that on to what you already owe me?"

"That's probably illegal."

"And I suppose skipping out on your debt and hiring killers *is* legal?" Old El countered.

"I suppose different people have differing views on that matter."

"Oh, you think somebody has that view? Pay up already," Old El said, pointing his newly purchased rifle at the man.

"Oh my, don't tell me that item's something you purchased at the local weapons store."

"You're damn straight it is."

"In that case—please, fire away. I can't repay my debt."

"The contract said, 'If a single payment is even one day late, the entire amount is due immediately. If you have no money, you can have no objection to losing your life.' You remember that little clause, don't you?"

"Of course I do."

"Then, die!"

That was a Frontier collector for you. No doubt the old man figured he'd be able to take the man's arms once he'd killed him.

Old El suddenly started blasting. There was a click, and then the old man's eyes went wide. The gun barrel he'd pointed at Tupperman was now pointed at himself. But when had it got turned around? No, there was no way that had happened. The gun itself had changed. It'd transformed to point in the opposite direction!

"Everything he sells there he got wholesale from me," Tupperman stated, puffing his chest.

"That's some tricky shit you sold him. Hey, Toba, shoot him dead."

"You've got to be joking. You think I'd kill someone when there's not a lousy dint in it for me? Do it your damn self."

"Ten thousand dalas."

"A hundred thousand," said the beastmaster.

"Thirty."

"Eighty."

"Oh, all right, all right."

"You've got a deal," Toba said, pulling the trigger.

A bullet came out. The barrel of the gun jumped up from the force, and in return Tupperman's head was blown away.

"Search the house!" Old El said, ignoring the headless body of the puppet master that still stood there. He headed for a door to the back half of the house.

"Okay," said Toba, merrily following along after him until someone grabbed him by the collar. When the beastmaster looked over his shoulder, his face was expressionless. Powerful surprise and fear had wiped the emotion right off it.

"The back door leads to the lockup. That door over there goes to the sheriff's office, and that one leads to the town-run beast-breeding facility."

Those were the words of a headless torso.

"Don't let him fool you, Toba. That's a puppet. Onward!" Old El exclaimed, running straight forward. And Toba followed after him. Being addressed by a headless human and things of that kind were all in a day's work for them.

Turning the door knob, the old man shouldered his way through the door. Toba followed him.

"What the hell?"

The two of them stood stunned in a narrow space surrounded by stone walls and iron bars, and beyond the bars Tupperman sat at a desk wearing a sheriff's badge and looking right at them. They were in jail.

II

"Son of a bitch, you're the sheriff?! What the hell's going on here? Hey, Toba, shoot the lock."

"Sure thing," said Toba.

But from his gun belched no flames. The two men looked down in disbelief as his neatly disassembled weapon fell in pieces to the floor.

Their jailor's words rang in their ears as he said, "Well, the charge against you is threatening Sheriff Tupperman, which would be me. I guess I'll make you the centerpiece of our local festival."

"Local festival?"

"Centerpiece?"

The pair exchanged glances, but that brought them no closer to understanding or agreement. The town that seemed to slumber under cloudy skies hadn't looked the least bit like it was going to have a festival.

Then his deputies gathered, wearing badges, and with rifles and stake guns at the ready they cowed the two men and pulled them out of the cell. The instant they left the office with Sheriff Tupperman at the fore, their eardrums were rocked by a gaudy blast of music.

"When the hell did they organize this?" Old El asked, his eyes filled with the radiance of the lights that now decorated the streets and the sight of smiling people making their way down the street. The glow of the fireworks they carried or luminescent hoops they wore flowed beautifully beneath the day's cloudy sky. The day's cloudy sky? No.

"Hey, it's evening already," Toba remarked, looking up at the sky.

"I know. I have no idea what the hell's going on anymore."

"You said he's some kinda puppeteer and gadget whiz, didn't you? You think maybe this is one of his tricks, too?"

"Think you can change the weather any time you like with tricks? Ain't you a little old for believing stuff like that?"

"Well, how do you explain it, then?"

"How the hell should I know?"

As the men grumbled back and forth, they entered the line of people and headed toward the edge of town. The first thing that caught their eye was a strangely immense tree. Its massive branches

jutted out in all directions like unsettling arms, and a number of human forms dangled from them. Thick ropes linked the figures' necks and the branches.

"Hey, were those all lynchings?" Toba whispered.

"You think anybody's stupid enough to string up that many? And on top of that—they're women!" Old El replied, swallowing hard. "But, they're—they're all Lydia!"

That left Toba at a loss for words, too. Straining his eyes, he groaned, "Ten . . . twenty . . . thirty . . . all Lydia. Damn it all, what the hell happened to that freaking left hand?"

"Hey, Tupperman," Old El said, glaring at the puppet master who turned and looked at him from the roots at the base of the tree. "Those are puppets, aren't they? You trying to scare us? It ain't gonna work!"

"Oh, those are just to liven things up. That's not your friend. Take a better look, if you will," Tupperman said, his right hand rising.

"What the hell?!" the old man exclaimed.

One of the hanging Lydias had just dropped right beside him. And she stood there, having landed on her feet. But the face that smiled at Old El wasn't Lydia's.

"B-but you're . . . ?!"

With streaks of vermilion running across her pale skin from lips even more devoid of color, the woman extended a hand toward the old man, who madly struggled to elude it as his eyes bugged.

"It's my girlfriend, who you killed, believing her to be a puppet."

Old El and Toba were surrounded by a succession of thuds. Ghostly women with pale faces dripping streams of blood—and every face was the same as it gazed at the old man resentfully.

"I didn't know. And it was all your fault for turning your girlfriend into a killer in the first place."

"Yes, quite right," Tupperman said with a laugh. It was cold, horrible laughter. "To be honest, I'd grown tired of her. So I forced her to join a group of assassins. Whichever of you died, it would've suited me just fine."

"Then why threaten me with these handiworks of yours?"

"Why not? You're going to die anyway."

"Hey, all I'm saying is to pay back my damn money!"

"Not a chance," said Tupperman. "I don't intend to pay you a stinking dint. If everyone paid back what they borrowed, the world's economy would be terribly stifled!"

"You're talking rubbish. Of all the travelers who come to town, I hear there ain't a one who didn't come out a pauper. I know you've gotta be knocking them off and swiping anything worth any coin. Use that to pay me."

"That goes to the cost of maintaining the town."

"The town? Are you the freaking mayor?"

"Why, I'm insulted. I'm its creator."

"Oh, so you're God, then? That's proof you've socked away money."

"Hold your tongue."

"The two of us aside, what about the girl in the wagon? Let her live, damn it."

"The girl? She went off somewhere, I suppose."

Toba was the first to react to Tupperman's bitter remark, saying, "Went off somewhere? More like you carried her off somewhere, you bastard."

"You're wrong. I went over to the wagon as soon as the two of you left it, but there was nobody there."

"Come again?" said Old El.

"Well, not that it'll matter much to you. Okay, string them both up."

His deputies put ropes around the men's necks. The other ends were tossed over a thick branch, then given a sudden pull.

"You son of a bitch!"

"Gaaah!"

Before his voice became groans, Old El reached out toward Tupperman and shouted, "You bastard! Gimme my moneeeeeeeey!" He looked like the devil.

His voice trailed off, rapidly growing thinner. Blackness was swallowing the old man's consciousness—and then he felt the soles of his feet hit something.

He'd fallen to the ground.

He immediately opened his eyes. All the folks from town and the ghostly women were backing away. Someone stood right by his head. And looking up—he found Lydia.

"Well, I'll be—she's possessed, isn't she?" said Tupperman, the only one who hadn't fled, gazing at the girl through narrowed eyes. "And by no ordinary spirit, at that, it appears. Hmm. Eyes that burn like hot coals, and slightly tapered cuspids. With skin that's nigh translucent—it's the evil spirit of a Noble inside her. Get her!"

The women, his deputies, and even the townsfolk charged forward. The festival lights reflected off the blades of their longswords.

Lydia turned herself around. The wind howled. Pale hands flashed out in vicious chops. All they touched were sent flying, knocked flat on the ground or slammed back against the enormous tree trunk. On seeing the attackers quickly turn into small dolls that lacked eyes or a nose, Toba let out a surprised grunt.

"That's the brute strength of a Noble for you. No, I mean a 'half-Nobled'—a fake Noble," Old El groaned.

"That's a hell of a friend you brought with you," Tupperman laughed, his expression dour. Before his very eyes, Lydia had revealed the true nature of every one of her challengers. Where fighting ability was concerned, his puppets were no match for a "half-Nobled."

Tupperman sighed deeply. "And after all the trouble I went to, creating this town—well, guess I'll be going now."

He spun around and started to run off. A mass of black skimmed across his throat from right to left. The puppet master fell flat on his back without a sound, however—

"He was a puppet, too!" Toba exclaimed, his mouth hanging open. The one who'd slain the puppet sat on his shoulder. "Kitty! You're still alive?!"

The beastmaster's cry of joy was nearly drowned out by a squeal of terror. It was Old El. A shadow fell at his feet. And it was clear that the naked blade stuck in the nape of its neck was held by none other than D.

"Wh-what's all this? All our saviors popping up at the same time?"

"Help me!" cried the old man's shadow, which still had D's blade stuck in it. The blade sprang upward, sending the black cloth-like object on it flying and revealing a young man cowering beneath it.

"You son of a bitch—"

"It's Tupperman."

"A minute ago, I thought the other one was the real you. How can I be sure you're really the real thing?"

"Rest assured, I am."

"Oh, shut up. I don't care how you disguise yourself, you're gonna pay me my money!"

"I don't have anything anymore. I poured it all into this town. What are you going to do, renovate it and turn it into an amusement park?"

"Don't give me any of your smart mouth!" Old El replied, getting closer and delivering a kick to Tupperman's face. Blood went flying.

"Oh, you're just terrible," the young man said, his face covered with blood as he spat out a broken tooth.

"Shut your pie hole, you lousy murderer. Just so you know, you ain't gonna wind up in court or nothing. I'll get rid of you right now," Old El said, grabbing a rock as big as a baby's head from the ground near his feet and raising it high.

"Noooo!" Tupperman wailed, shielding his head, but he soon looked up. "Kill me," he said, "and you won't get whatever you might've gotten out of me."

"Already said you ain't got nothing, didn't you? So, I'll take your life as revenge."

"Please, just wait a second. There is a way."

It probably hadn't occurred to the puppet master before now, but this was a good idea—or so his face seemed to say, staying the old man's hand from further violence.

Stone still raised high, Old El said, "And just what might that be?"

"Do you know Marquis Verenis? Um, what in the world—?" the young man said, breaking off there due to the unsettling silence that had fallen over the others as he looked around at them.

Dropping to one knee, Old El laughed, "Yeah, we're best buddies."

"Excellent," said Tupperman, eyeing the still-raised rock. "Tomorrow, I have to repay a loan to the marquis. Please, lend me your aid. We can dispose of him. Then, we can claim all the loot in his castle, raze the place for an empty lot, and sell everything to some collector of Nobility paraphernalia in the Capital—"

"Wait a sec. You mean to tell me you borrowed money from the marquis? As in, that the freaking marquis has been going around loaning out money?"

"That's right."

"How much did you borrow?"

"A modicum, enough to get this town built—roughly five million dalas. And I was one of the smaller loans, from what I hear."

"Don't give me none of that 'from what I hear.' How much would the bigger ones be?"

"He said loans of a hundred to two hundred million were fairly common."

"That son of a bitch, he's got the nerve to stiff me on my loan when he's making out like a bandit? Well, the bastard ain't getting away with it!"

Hurled with all Old El's might, the rock sank into the ground just shy of Tupperman's nose, drawing a cry from the man.

"And you said he's coming tomorrow?" the old man asked.

"Yes."

"I see. D, tomorrow night's the fight for all the marbles. He'll bring bodyguards, I'm sure. You'll get a chance to show us what you've got!"

D's head moved subtly. He'd nodded.

"Great! We'll nab that bastard Verenis and take him for all the money he's got. So, where's the cash you're paying him back with?"

"I don't have any," Tupperman replied.

"Whaaat?! Then, just how'd you figure on—? You weren't gonna skip out on another debt, were you?"

"Don't be ridiculous. I'm an honest man." Relegating the bug-eyed old man and Toba to his peripheral vision, Tupperman continued,

"And if I had the money this time, I'd have paid it back. However, you can't wring blood from a stone. My payment to the marquis is this town."

"This town?"

Old El and Toba exchanged glances.

"Originally, I borrowed money from the marquis to fund an expansion of the town. And he also happens to be quite fond of the town's contents."

"Hmm—and what time's he coming?"

"Seven tomorrow evening. Except, I'm going to him."

"Huh?"

This remark made even D turn and look.

Seeing that no one could comprehend what he was saying, Tupperman proudly explained, "The whole town is going. To the marquis's castle, that is. It's about a hundred and twenty-five miles west of here. I'd say it'll take, say, four hours?"

"How are you getting there?"

"You'll see soon enough. Get out of town immediately."

"Afraid I can't do that. He might've loaned *you* money, but *I* loaned money to *him*. I was gonna kick in his door after settling matters with you, but this is even better. I'll go with you."

"Huh? That sounds like trouble. You can't put me in that predicament."

"Can you pay me right now, then? Well, can you?"

"Very well. You may accompany me. And in return, you'll be kind enough to cancel my debt, I assume?"

"Don't make me laugh!"

Having listened up to that point, Toba smirked and ventured, "I've got a good plan for this."

III

"What is it? And don't even start if it's some half-baked notion. You and I ain't squared yet!"

"Yeah, I know that, chief." Shooting a glance at D, Toba lowered his voice and continued, "That's what I wanted to talk about. You know, we could bust in on Marquis What's-his-face and do him in."

"What?"

"Judging from what I've heard so far, he's got absolutely no freaking intention of paying you back. Bust in there, and he'll try to wipe the slate clean by force. In which case, you'll have just cause. That's where your beautiful bodyguard comes in. Once the Noble's disposed of, all you have to do is put his castle and domain in your name. I don't know how he'd be set for cash, but scholars in the Capital would slobber at the thought of a Noble's castle and lands. That right there is something where the sky's the limit. Isn't that something that'd repay his debt to you a hundred times over with money to spare?"

Old El eyed the man as if he were looking at a common thug and clucked his tongue, but before long, he said, "I see. What then?"

Oh, he's in, all right, Toba must've thought, lowering his voice even further and continuing, "You just have to rewrite ol' Puppetman's contract so the town is collateral for his loan. And do it right away, right?"

"Wh-why would we do that?" Tupperman inquired anxiously. "You're planning on killing both the marquis and Old El, aren't you?"

"What?! Preposterous. That's an entirely groundless supposition."

"Is that a fact? At times like this, everybody's got the same thing on their mind, but have it your way. Killing the old man'll be a touch difficult with that bodyguard around. At any rate, if you don't put the town up as collateral, there's no saying he won't have you snuffed with a single word. Just have to guard against that, you know?"

"But that would put it under contract to two different people," Tupperman protested.

"Well, we're gonna get rid of the marquis, anyway. Might as well break that contract."

"You're a true scoundrel, aren't you?" Tupperman said pensively.

"Oh, shut up. How does that strike you, old man?"

"Sounds good." As Old El gave a hearty nod, there wasn't a trace of any feeling of guilt on his face. From the start, the marquis's castle and lands had been collateral, but he had a feeling it'd be impossible to acquire them by direct means.

"You're gonna help out, too," Toba said, glaring at Tupperman. "The three of us together should be able to swing it, Noble or not. Plus, we've got that strong freaking bodyguard on our side, right?"

"Yeah, about that," Old El said, clearing his throat.

"What the hell is it now?"

"He won't give me any help making collections."

"Why not?"

"That's the kind of contract we've got."

"I believe I'd like to bow out as well," Tupperman said, but another glaring look silenced him.

"Do what you have to get him onboard," Toba coaxed in his lowest voice.

"No, you know who I'm dealing with here."

"There's no way he of all people would agree to guard you on this job in the first place. Don't tell me you've got him working off a debt, too?"

"Nope. At any rate, he won't help me collect. So, forget that."

"There's still one way to do it, though."

"What?"

"Just leave it to me. We're going to the Nobleman's castle anyway, right? I'll make my move on the way," Toba said, his lips curling in a true scoundrel's smile.

At that point an icy cold female voice flowed over him, saying, "I wonder if it'll go as well as you think."

It was Lydia. Until this very moment, the girl had been silently at D's side, but what kind of mental change did this signify? She'd left D, staring at the three men with eyes that called to mind arrows of ice.

"Wh-why the hell not, bitch?" Toba quickly growled back, but it was clear at a glance it was a hollow show of power. He was up against a Noble's kin hiding inside a girl's skin.

"Nobles aren't as gullible as all that," she said, her pale hand pointing into space.

Old El looked up in spite of himself, but there wasn't a single star to be seen. Because this was the sky Tupperman had made. Turning back to her, the old man asked, "What's that supposed to mean?"

At the same time, Lydia collapsed.

"Hey, don't go fainting on me whenever you like! What the—?"

Five languidly twitching fingers poked from the collar of the fallen Lydia, and then a human left hand from the wrist down appeared.

"What, it's you?!"

"She's possessed by a ghost but sleeping nicely," said the left hand. "I steered her out of the wagon. But I'm exhausted now. Can't push it any further."

"You don't say. I might as well ask, what've you been doing all this time?" Old El inquired, his gaze turned toward D.

"Getting filled in by him," said the left hand. "There was a river at the bottom of that valley. He flowed along, finally snagging on a rock at dawn. Strange part of it was, a monster cat snagged on the same rock—your precious little 'kitty.'"

Toba pressed down on the chest of the coat where the beast lurked.

Old El shut his eyes and deliberated, and apparently it finally sank into him, because he took a breath and said, "So, what was that pointing bit just now all about?"

"Right above us, there should be a geostationary satellite the Nobles launched ten thousand years ago for surveillance. It's under Marquis Verenis's control. A Noble satellite could pinpoint a single ant and pick up the sound it makes. Probably got all the info he wants on us. He'll be ready and waiting when we come."

"Oh, we should be fine on that account," Tupperman said, his comment leaving him swimming in the attention of all. He was still down on all fours. "Uh, at present, the sky above this town is covered by my mechanical clouds," he continued. "They render all forms of Noble sensors useless—no, I jest, they actually make them detect something else rather than the sight and sound of us."

"Such as?" Old El inquired.

"The sensors should detect a group of young people eating pizza and commiserating about their teacher and parents."

"Hell of a gadget you got there. Another one of your gimmicks?" Toba exclaimed, making no effort to hide how impressed he was. The way he saw it, there'd be a way to turn a tidy profit with that.

"You see, I had all the money I could ever need," Tupperman laughed.

"You mean *my* money, you bastard."

"No. The marquis's money. He was kind enough to invest in my talent. Though it pains me to say it, the pittance you provided couldn't have even—"

The old man finally hit his boiling point. Mouth gaping wide, he bellowed, "Sorry it was just a pittance, you lousy charlatan! And what do you mean, I 'provided' it?! Nobody gifted you that damn money, fucker!"

"Now, violence won't solve anything, sir. Kindly save that for the marquis."

"He's right," Toba said, catching hold of Old El's shoulder. "Let's get headed toward the marquis's castle as soon as we can. No telling what might happen along the way. So, let's get cracking."

Everyone was ready to set out. But before they could, the earth shook.

"The town's moving!" Toba cried out in surprise.

"That's the way it was built," said Tupperman. It goes without saying that he stated this with immense pride.

"This darkness is bugging the hell out of me," said the left hand. "How about dropping the sky cover?"

"Kindly wait a little longer. I'm preparing to do so now."

"Take the cover off?"

"You'll see soon enough," Tupperman replied. "Everyone, if you'd be so good as to retire to the hotel. Hospitality will await you there."

Nevertheless, nobody made a move to leave.

"Go," D suggested. "I'll watch him to make sure he doesn't try anything."

"Much appreciated. It's like having a million men backing me up. What about the girl?"

"Take care of her. And don't try anything."

Seeing the cold look he got for good measure, the old man felt dizzy. Out of pure fear.

"Y-y-yeah, I know."

The group left the square.

"Excuse me—do I have to stay down here?" Tupperman asked, still down on the ground.

"You can't be trusted. You'll stay there until we reach the castle."

"That's absurd."

The rhythm of a cha-cha-cha flowed through the air.

"It's coming from the hotel bar," said the left hand. "Carefree bastards."

"You can say that again," Tupperman replied. "However, the marquis isn't as gullible as they take him to be."

"Oh, you don't say."

"If he were, I'd have fled a long time ago."

"Good point."

"Did you know the marquis was one of those the Sacred Ancestor held dear?"

"Yeah, I know all about that," said the hoarse voice.

"If so, going to slay the marquis is the very definition of madness. Why not turn back now?"

"Don't try to do us any favors."

"You have nerve, I'll give you that. And on account of that, I have a favor to ask," said Tupperman.

"What's that?"

"I've prepared measures to eliminate the marquis's eye and ear in the sky. I'd like to ask for your assistance."

"Doing what?"

The puppet master explained, "There's a package behind you. Kindly throw it as far as you can. It doesn't matter which direction. As long as it's outside town, it'll be fine. The weight should be fine for a dhampir."

D turned around slowly. A metal cylinder just over three feet tall and eight inches in diameter stood there. Until a moment ago, there'd been no sign of it.

"What have you got up your sleeve?" the left hand asked suspiciously.

"Don't be ridiculous. I swear by every power on heaven and earth, it's nothing."

"Then, why—?"

At that point, D went into action. Lifting the cylinder with both hands, he threw it with all his might. It flew over the rows of houses as if it were a pebble and was swallowed up by the darkness.

"Only five seconds more," said Tupperman. "Three . . . two . . . one . . ."

"A missile?" the hoarse voice ventured.

"Right you are."

"If you put it together, it could probably take out the marquis's satellite. But he won't sit idly by after that!"

The darkness cleared unexpectedly. The barrier over the town had been removed. Outside, it was early evening. The missile had accomplished its purpose.

The ground shook. The town had sped up.

A single streak of light from the sky sank into the ground at the spot where the missile had seemed to originate just a few seconds later. The fireball was a bluish-gray hue.

The marquis's retaliation.

"The marquis has many enemies. Their bases are scattered around this area, in particular. Verenis will believe one of them blinded his eye."

"A criminal genius," the left hand groaned. "But don't underestimate anybody the Sacred Ancestor held dear. Payback will be coming."

"Well, we shall cross that bridge when we come to it."

And with those words from Tupperman, silence finally descended.

D gazed at the massive tree. Enormous branches jutted from it like the legs of some colossal spider, and beneath it stood a figure in black.

"Is this your doing?" D inquired.

"N-n-n-no . . ." the gimmick-maker replied, his voice hoarse with fear. For he knew. He knew who that shadowy figure really was.

A terrible, eerie aura blustered from it. And it was cut down by a stark white gleam. D didn't launch a second attack. The shadowy figure was fading away.

"*Him*—will *he* be waiting at Verenis's castle?" the Hunter's left hand said in a hoarse voice that shredded in the wind.

The stars were out. And beneath them, the mechanical town raced on and on, bearing the thoughts of its living occupants.

Gold Fiend

PART TWO

Lydia's Fear

I

T heir journey continued without incident until dawn began to brighten the eastern sky.

"Another three hours, and we should reach the marquis's castle."

Old El, the all-purpose financier, sat in the wagon's driver's seat with reins in hand, and beside him sat Langen Tupperman, who gestured with one hand, saying, "I think it best we charge right in and capture the marquis. We can then torture him later."

"Who said anything about torture?" Old El replied, glaring at him. "I just want my money back plus interest. If you wanna skin the marquis, pluck his eyes out and use 'em for your dolls, it'll have to be after that."

"I don't believe he's the sort to just meekly pay it back. I think you should hurt him first. That's what I'd do."

"You goddamned sadist," the old man snarled. "You'd do that to somebody who went and lent you money? In case it slipped your mind, you owe money to me, too!"

"And if we seize the marquis's estate, my share will soon vanish in the mists of memory, isn't that right? I hear obsessing over money is the leading cause of cancer in people."

"You'd better shape up, or else," the old man said, grabbing the puppet master by the front of his shirt with his free hand.

"What are you doing? So, you feel some sort of solidarity with a fellow lender, do you?"

"Shut your trap!"

Old El was about to give a jerk with his wrist, but he quickly let go of the man.

Further down the road, a town had begun to take shape.

"What the hell is that? Is there supposed to be a town out here?"

"No. But it's not all that strange, really," said Tupperman, his expression composed as he looked to either side of them. Though they were up in the driver's seat, the wagon wasn't moving. The cyborg horses were standing in the road just killing time. But the town of Gimmicklin was still racing across the ground at a speed of about thirty miles per hour.

Indeed, it wasn't all that surprising that a town might be blocking the way forward. The two of them were on the northern edge of town—in other words, at the very front of Gimmicklin.

"This ain't another of your tricky gadgets, is it?" Old El asked, probing as ever.

The puppet master shook his head firmly.

"Well, that's good. We've got a town that can run along the ground, and another that appeared all of a sudden—could be a good showdown, eh? Can we go around it?"

"We can, but if we stray from the road, we'll lose our stealth capabilities. The town is rather delicate."

"I don't wanna hear 'delicate' from a fella who was about to string some folks up. We're gonna have us a little talk when this is settled."

"At any rate, I'll stop the town. It wouldn't do to crash into them and damage it."

"So we stop, and then what?"

"We have no choice but to get rid of them. Have them get out of the way, or blow them sky high. I've never dealt with this before. It'll probably come down to the latter."

"You've gotta be joking, you freaking terrorist," the old man spat.

At that point, D rode up on his cyborg horse.

"Perfect timing," Old El said to the Hunter. "We're gonna stop the town. Go hash things out with that town up ahead."

"My job is dealing with the Nobility," D replied curtly.

"I see. Hey," the old man said to the puppet master, "go call Toba, then."

"Yes, sir. Anything you say, sir," Tupperman answered snidely, climbing down from the driver's seat and running into the central part of town.

"Best be careful," commented the hoarse voice that came from where D's left hand gripped his steed's reins.

"Like I need you to tell me that," the old man replied.

"Oh, feeling a little mouthy, are we? Gaaah!"

D squeezed his left hand into a tight fist, and a short time later, Tupperman returned with Toba.

"Gonna go scout out the town up ahead. You're coming along," Old El informed the beastmaster.

This one-sided declaration naturally drew a protest.

"Why the hell do I have to go?" Toba asked, teeth bared. "I only came along to help you collect from the marquis. I'm not sticking my nose into any other trouble, okay?"

Old El wasn't about to sit still for that. Glaring at the two of them, he bellowed, "Verenis, you, him—you're all a bunch of lousy deadbeats, and don't you ever forget it! If you got any complaints about what I told you to do, save 'em till after you've paid me back. Scumbags! And to think you call yourselves a beastmaster and a puppet master!"

Toba turned away in a snit, a sour look on his face, while Tupperman shrugged his shoulders and started to whistle a tune.

Smirking, the old man said to them, "Not ready to hit the road? Tell you what I'm gonna do. Every time you do what I tell you, I'll knock a hundredth of a percent off your loan. How's that strike you?"

The two men exchanged glances, then looked at Old El.

"For real?" Toba inquired, a fierce gleam in his eye.

"I'll take you at your word," Tupperman replied cheerily, unable to hide his excitement.

"Of course," said the old man, nodding decisively.

Halting Gimmicklin about fifty yards from what seemed to be the edge of the other town, the four men entered it. Old El accompanied the pair—so D was forced to, as well.

"Why are we even here? We could just go around it, simple as that," the hoarse voice groused to the old man.

"The way Tupperman tells it, it looks like we'd lose our stealth abilities. And the detour would cost us about an hour. If we came under attack then, the first shot would take us out. But if this here's a ghost town, we can do like Tupperman said and blow it all to hell with a lithium warhead," Old El replied gleefully, but D ignored him. He probably thought they were all just as bad.

The four of them advanced down the town's main street.

"Nobody here, eh?" the old man said, putting one hand to the tube running out of his ear. It was connected to something in his coat pocket. "Just the sound of the wind—no, hold on."

"The sound of meat cooking?" said the hoarse voice, making the old man's eyes go wide.

"Y-you wearing a sound detector, too?" Old El stammered.

Giving no reply to that, the hoarse voice continued, "The hotel restaurant, and the town diner. Hey, get a move on!"

What the four of them found there was a charred black steak noisily sizzling on an iron grill. Coffee boiled over from a pot that had been left over the flames.

"Strange situation, eh?" Old El said on entering the kitchen after the others, tilting his head to one side.

"What took you so long?" Toba asked sharply.

"Had a look-see at the restaurant. There were still half-eaten plates on the tables, cups of coffee and glasses of juice just sitting there half drunk. A lit cigar was still burning in an ashtray. It's almost like up until now—like just a couple minutes ago—there were customers there or something."

"There probably were," Tupperman remarked, running his hand back through his hair. "This is no gadget, no trick. This actually happened."

"Where the hell did everybody in town go?"

"They didn't go. They were probably taken," said Tupperman, heaving a sigh. Even he was frightened.

"Anyway, let's poke around a little more," Old El told the others.

"No point in it," the hoarse voice protested. "There's not a living soul in this whole town. Nothing's moving but the wind."

And that was when it happened. The wind stopped.

"Oh. That get gobbled up or something?" the hoarse voice said tensely.

D's right hand flashed out.

Something had definitely squirmed in a space where there was nothing. Waves of pain struck all four of them in the face. Only one of them was affected.

Toba's form twisted around. Old El and the puppet master could only watch dumbfoundedly as his body swiftly grew transparent. Toba's face distorted. The miraculous disappearance was a painful experience. His fingers, too, twisted, as if seeking aid, and even the two hardened men had to look away. When they quickly looked back again, there wasn't the faintest trace of Toba.

After the span of a breath, the old man glared at Tupperman and asked, "That your doing?"

"Don't be absurd. That's far beyond what any of my gadgets could do. Yes, indeed."

"It was the work of whoever took the town's residents," said D, his cool tone calming the other two.

"Oh, you're still here? So, did that fool Toba get himself eaten up or something? Down in the 'Fire Zone' in the southern Frontier, I recall seeing an invisible man-eater beasty at work from a good distance, but is that what this was?"

"No, it's something else," the hoarse voice replied, making the two men snap to attention. "Toba wasn't eaten. It'd be more correct to say he was abducted."

"Then, he could come back?" Tupperman asked, furrowing his delicate brow.

"Possibly," said a cold voice that had a beautiful ring in the men's ears. "But what kind of shape will he come back in?"

"That's the problem, isn't it?"

That hoarse remark caused the other two men to look at each other, questioning exactly who was talking to whom there.

"W-well, he's already disappeared, right?" Tupperman inquired somewhat angrily, just to be sure.

"He ain't here."

"What the hell is this thing?" Old El mused, giving the heavens an uncanny look. Apparently, when human imagination failed, people had no choice but to implore God. However, no aid would be forthcoming. The actions of the human race were of no concern to those in the heavens. Not even if the latter had made them to begin with.

"It's probably some kind of combat creature the Nobility created," said the hoarse voice. "This town might've just been a proving ground for its effectiveness."

"That's a hell of a thing to do, isn't it?" Tupperman said with naked anger.

Old El asked him, "You really pissed off?"

"No, just acting that way for the sake of convenience, you know?"

"Appreciate your candor."

"Sure."

"No point hanging around here anymore. They've all disappeared, down to the last kitten and flea—so, back to Gimmicklin it is. Move it, move it!" said the hoarse voice, but it ended with a choked groan. D had made a fist.

Turning his eyes to the far end of the road, the Hunter immediately kicked off the ground. His coat spread out around him. That in itself was a beautiful sight.

Tupperman moaned, "Exquisite."

And Old El grunted back, "Yup," frozen in his tracks.

Neither of them had the faintest idea what D might've seen or heard.

The figure in black vanished into the alley between a bar and the general store. There wasn't the slightest hesitation, though D must've given the action due consideration.

The still-enraptured pair watched as D quickly re-emerged from the entrance to the alley—with his left arm cradling a boy of five or six.

"Someone made it out alive, I see," Tupperman whispered softly. There was no affection or relief for the youthful survivor in it. His words sprang from distrust and misgivings.

"Best be on our guards," Old El replied in the same tone.

You could hardly say the pair was thrilled that someone had survived this disaster. Their attitude was completely justified as people who lived out on the Frontier. For there were any number of supernatural creatures that could take a child's shape.

They soon understood why the Hunter held him to his chest. There was a handkerchief wrapped around the boy's right foot. He'd probably sprained it.

"What happened?" asked Tupperman.

"The child was crying," D replied curtly.

"That kid—is he okay?" the old man asked, his grip tightening on the pistol on his right hip.

"For what it's worth, I checked him out," the hoarse voice suddenly stated.

With no other outlet for their psychological turbulence, the two men were left blinking stupidly.

"Nothing outta sorts. Might as well leave him be."

"A splendid idea," said the puppet master, nodding his complete agreement.

Giving him a glare that said, *You little ass-kisser*, Old El asked, "So, we taking him with us?"

"It's not like we'll be at his castle as soon as we enter his domain," remarked the hoarse voice. "We should come across a couple of farmhouses. Let's leave him at one of 'em."

"Why not leave him aboard Gimmicklin?" Tupperman suggested. "With my creations to defend him, he'd be safer than at a farmhouse. And the stealth shield will hide him from surveillance systems. No one will ever see him."

Spitting loudly, the old man said, "And we're supposed to trust these gadgets of yours? Besides, we're gonna have to abandon your town pretty soon."

"Ridiculous! Going there in Gimmicklin is definitely safer."

"Maybe that holds true for the highway, but there's forests and rivers up ahead. Even if they can't see the town itself, they'd find us by the trees and farmhouses we plowed through."

"Hmmm. Then, I shall wait here," the puppet master declared.

"Like hell you will!"

Old El grabbed the man by the chest, and Tupperman looked sorely aggrieved.

"Oh!"

D had long since stepped away from the two men, and the Hunter was now headed toward the end of the road they'd come down.

"H-he just took off!"

The instant that dawned on them, the two men felt as if the air around them had become a frost. What's more, it was creeping down their collars and up their sleeves.

"Hey, wait up!"

"Don't leave us here!"

Crying out pitifully all the while, they chased after the figure in black as he swayed in the morning light like some enchanting heat shimmer.

II

As soon as he was passed to Lydia, the expressionless child smiled.

"He'll be a ladies' man someday for sure."

"Reckon we'll see his face on wanted posters at some point, eh?"

"Knock it off, you idiots," the hoarse voice spat at them.

"I'm D. I'm a Hunter. What happened in town?" the man with the inhumanly beautiful face asked the boy.

They were in the lounge of the hotel in Gimmicklin. There were four or five other guests in various seats. They, the hostesses, and the waiters bearing cups of coffee and plates of steak were all mechanical puppets.

"I don't know," the boy replied, and he immediately began crying his eyes out, but Lydia stroked his hair and he quickly smiled again.

Old El bared his teeth.

"What's your name, kid? Mine's Lydia."

"Didi."

"Oh, our names are a lot alike, aren't they? And I'm really happy to meet you, so you should cheer up, too. Okay?"

With Lydia's encouragement, the boy told them how he and two of his friends were kicking stones around that alley when they heard cries of pain from places all over town. And as he stood there in shock, he heard it close by, too. Both his friends clawed at their throats as they turned transparent, with Didi staring on dumbfounded.

"Bim reached out to me. His lips were saying, 'Help!' But he didn't make a sound. I was so scared. I couldn't move my arms or legs. And I couldn't close my eyes, which is why I watched the two of them disappearing—right up to the very end!"

Didi clung to the girl's arm.

His family had a photography studio. The boy had returned home in tears, but neither his father nor mother was there. A frugal breakfast was laid out on the table, and a bit had been taken out of his father's slice of bread. Judging from the fried egg and plate that had fallen just shy of the table, that was undoubtedly where his mother had faded away. Having raced upstairs, Didi was disappointedly on his way back down when he missed a step. Though he'd twisted his ankle awfully, there was no one there to take care of it. Wrapping it with his own handkerchief, the boy had headed back to the alley. He didn't know exactly why. And there, he'd encountered D.

"Hmmm. Gotta wonder why this kid was the only one left behind, eh?" Old El mused with arms folded, while Tupperman had his eyes shut in deep contemplation. Behind them, the room echoed with the laughter of the mechanized hostesses.

"The first thing that springs to mind is that he's probably a weaponized survivor," Tupperman said, eyes still shut. In other words, Didi was a booby trap left to kill them all. An assassin in the shape of a young boy.

"We talking mechanical, synthetic organism, or a case of possession?" said the old man, but Didi denied it all in a quavering voice.

"At any rate, he's just a plain kid right now," said the hoarse voice. "Shouldn't harm anybody. Look after him, missy."

"The name's Lydia," the young lady said curtly.

"Yeah, whatever."

"About a half mile from here we hit the marquis's domain," Old El informed them. "We ditch Gimmicklin there. Then, we continue on by wagon and on horseback. Park the girl and kid at some farmhouse. Anti-Noble sentiment's pretty strong in this area. Think I know just the place for 'em."

"And they'll just wait there?"

"We don't have much choice. Relax. So long as we pay 'em, they'll keep 'em safe as long as need be."

"And who exactly will be paying for this?" Tupperman inquired.

"You, of course. Just sell some gadgets from this town of yours to come up with the money."

"Sell them where?"

"Hmmm," Old El grunted, crossing his arms.

"Looks like you've got no choice but to pay for it," the hoarse voice declared with apparent delight.

"Okay. Here's what I'll do: I'll loan it to you!" And having said that to Tupperman, the old man turned his eyes to Lydia.

The lovely girl looked at him and shook her head vehemently. "I want to go with you. Bring me along."

"Can't do that. You'd only be in the way," Old El replied, also shaking his head.

"Looks like it can't be helped, then. If you would be so kind as to front the costs of leaving the girl with someone," Tupperman said with a sharp and subservient bow, but he stuck his red tongue out.

Though the matter was largely settled, Old El still had his eyes closed and arms folded as he entered a state of deep contemplation.

"Sore loser. We're talking about, what, half a dalas here?"

Before the hoarse voice had finished ribbing the financier, there was a brisk *whap!* of a pair of hands being clapped together. By Old El. The face he turned toward D with eyes still closed was etched with a world-beating smile.

"Heh heh heh," he chortled. "I thought of a great plan. Hey, come on over here," he said, taking Lydia by the hand, leaving Didi behind as he led the girl over to the counter, brought his lips up to her ear, and cupped his right hand beside his mouth.

"What?"

That single groaned word was brimming with terror. It came from Lydia. She looked at D. And both her face and her eyes, one misstep shy of certain madness, were tinged with fear. Her lips silently formed the words *It can't be.*

"What's that clown up to?" the Hunter's left hand murmured, making it clear it hadn't caught whatever was whispered.

"Lydia?!" Didi cried out, ready to run into action as the pale girl fell to the floor like a white blossom. Though the boy shook her by the shoulders, the eyes she'd shut didn't open, nor did the color show any signs of returning to her paled face.

His youthful face turned toward the old man, pelting him with arrows of hate from tear-drenched eyes as he shouted, "Bring her back!"

Smiling, Old El replied, "When she heard what I had to say, the shock of it made her faint dead away. No need to worry, though.

She'll come around soon enough. Hey, Tupperman, have 'em bring us some real brandy!"

"Very well," said the puppet master. "Hey, brandy and two glasses here," he called to the bartender, at which point one of the hostesses who'd been flirting with a guest got a crystal decanter and some glasses from the bartender, put them on a tray, and brought them over. To all appearances, she was a human being. Focusing on her pale arms and ample bosom, Old El smirked at Tupperman, who he saw shaking his head. Taking Lydia from Didi, the hostess raised the girl's head and poured a little brandy between her slightly purplish lips. The flush returned to her cheeks, and Lydia opened her eyes.

"Great," the old man said with a nod, but D took hold of his arm and dragged him over to a corner of the lounge.

"What are you doing?"

"I ain't gonna do anything," the hoarse voice replied.

"Tell me what you said to Lydia." The request came from D.

"Oh, that? Well, it's not really all that easy to say, you know?" the old man replied, turning his smug face away in a snit. Suddenly, his whole body stiffened. The eyes set in his face, which had vitality swiftly draining from it, had locked on D. "Th-that your . . . weird aura?" said the old man, his voice hoarser than the left hand's.

"What did you tell her?" D asked, his query like a still night in winter.

"I . . . I . . . What the Sacred Ancestor said. What I told her . . . was the very same words . . . I heard. But . . . I won't tell you . . . what that was. Try to force me . . . and I'll bite my tongue off."

The old man's body suddenly relaxed.

"No!" said a fearful voice that rose from the floor. It came from Lydia, still slumped there. "I'll . . . I'll stay here. No way . . . that I'd go with you. Not with . . . with someone like that!"

It was clear who she meant by "someone like that." Everyone—including the mechanical puppet people—trained their eyes on D.

"Find a farmhouse," the Hunter said. He then told Tupperman, "Leave three of your automatons to guard them." And as soon as he'd said that, he left the hotel.

III

The town of Gimmicklin halted its advance about two hours later. It had come to the outskirts of a small village. Bordered by forests on three sides, the region had a mix of farmhouses of assorted sizes in the light of day, the buildings' only saving grace their sturdy construction. The smoke rising from their chimneys spoke of preparations for an early lunch. Old El and Tupperman brought the two of them to the village, asked directions to the mayor's house, then went there so he could introduce someone to take care of Didi and Lydia. At a large farmhouse, a couple agreed to take care of the pair for ten dalas a day. Though the old man bid them farewell, Lydia didn't ask him to hurry back. She was scared. Of D.

As the farmhouse and its closed door fell further and further behind them, the Hunter's left hand murmured, "Wonder what she heard?"

D didn't reply. And Old El was looking smug. That was the effect the words of the Sacred Ancestor had on those two men.

"Let's move," Old El said, giving a lash to the cyborg horses. Both his expression and his movements were charged with fighting spirit. "Let's go get every last dalas I'm owed!"

Tupperman shrugged his shoulders and D was expressionless as the air echoed with the sound of the cyborg horses tearing up the ground—and they departed en masse.

Up ahead was a hill like the back of a fire dragon, and the outlines of the castle that loomed at its summit came into view.

"Verenis's castle," said Old El, pulling back on the reins and halting his steed.

"Oh, I'd figured him for some impoverished, countrified Noble, but that's quite a residence he has, isn't it?" Tupperman remarked.

And as he'd let slip, there were easily more than twelve miles of towering walls around the hilltop castle, the structure they defended not only a castle but also an opulent western-styled residence, a dome equipped with parabolic antennae and a teleporter tower, and more, all on dozens of peaks and waiting in the moonlight. It seemed unlikely any castle in the Capital could rival it.

"See, for generations, Marquis Verenis's clan was in charge of transporting rare elements and minerals to Earth from the other planets in the solar system and divvying 'em up to the other great families. A perk of being so beloved by the Sacred Ancestor, don't ya know. Which is how they made so much money."

When the old man said that, Tupperman gave him a cold stare, saying, "I don't care how affluent they were in bygone days; now, he's reduced to getting a collection call from the likes of you, and the day that castle goes on the auction block can't be far off." And then the puppet master laughed.

Apparently, Old El took exception to that. "The likes of me? What the hell do you mean by the likes of me?"

Now I've done it, the puppet master thought to himself, but he quickly disguised his alarm with a smile, saying, "Oh, there must be something wrong with your ears. You're hearing things, I'm sure. Just hearing things. Look, how many fingers am I holding up?"

Tupperman held his right hand with three fingers extended.

"If I'm hearing things, why are you checking my eyes? You damn fool!" the old man bellowed. He looked like the devil. "Hey, don't forget you're a deadbeat just like the flat-broke Noble. Toba might've vanished, but no matter what shape he takes, I'm gonna get every last dint out of him, just see if I don't!"

"What if he's dead?" asked the hoarse voice.

"Er, well, uh, I guess I'll have the bastard's grandkids pay it off. Or else his distant relatives, his friends, his mistresses—and I'll keep after 'em until somebody gets me my money!"

The old man was so whipped up, he started twitching in the saddle.

"Calm yourself," Tupperman told him, shooting D a look that said he really didn't have any other choice.

"Leave him be. He'll settle down soon enough," the hoarse voice replied, and Tupperman's expression became one of utter curiosity.

"For a while now I've been wondering just what kind of gadget that is. I hear the voice coming out of your left hand. As gadgets go, that could be achieved by even the most elementary of means, but I really don't think that's what this is."

"Bwa ha ha," the hoarse voice laughed, while nearby, Old El was patting his hair back down.

"Might I have a look at how it works sometime? Naturally, I'd offer a token of my appreciation."

"Sure thing," said the hoarse voice. "Once this whole thing's over. Only, I don't come cheap."

"I never thought you did."

"What are you two blathering about?" Old El said with a glare. "We're about to shake down a deadbeat. No telling what kinda evil shit he's got waiting for us. Stay sharp."

The group galloped right up the slope that led from the plains to the castle, coming to the castle gates.

The Noble castle stood quietly in the abundant light of afternoon. It called to mind a corpse lying in state. Light and the Nobility—the one thing they always led to was death.

"Don't reckon the gates are gonna open," said Old El with a dour expression.

"Of course not," Tupperman replied with a nod. "We'll have to invite ourselves in. Looks like we'll be going in by force."

"How about ropes to climb over the walls?"

To that, the hoarse voice replied, "The Nobility has no greater foe than daylight visitors, but since on occasion their own kind might flee here from human pursuers, they have to be able to be reached. Let's try that."

"Try what?"

"Announcing yourself in a loud voice, what else?"

"Let's go with the ropes."

"And then he can call you intruders, which gives him an excuse to kill you!"

"Hmmm," Old El mused, his firm mouth tugged down at the corners as he glared at the massive gates. Taking a deep breath, he called out, "Marquis Verenis, you remember me, don't you? El, the all-purpose financier. I'm here about the three hundred million dalas in anti-matter circuitry you got at twenty percent. Repayment is long past overdue. So, with interest it comes to six hundred million dalas—will you be paying that back in full now? If not, I'll take your castle and domain, plus interest. Need I remind you, that was our contract."

Here was a true professional. There was no sign of weakness and no flattery as the old man made his request forcefully, but with an anxious expression Tupperman said, "No one knows about the dealing between you and the marquis, do they? In which case, what did you plan on doing if he decides at this point to bring down a nuclear warhead on you?"

"No need to worry. See, I sent a copy of our contract off somewhere. I got it to somebody with no connection to me, somebody who could get it to the person it needs to get to without even knowing it. If a week goes by without any word from me, this person who knows nothing about it sends the contract to a Noble who doesn't know anything, either. Somebody who's a pretty big deal in Noble circles, but nothing compared to Verenis when it comes to power and authority. I wrote in the contract that I transfer all right to collect on this debt free of charge. You reckon there's any Noble out there so kind-hearted he wouldn't collect money from one of their own?"

"Absolutely not. They could be ready to drain the blood from a beauty and race off to collect instead. The Nobility live to suck the life from things in more ways than one."

Examples of the Nobility's parsimony were too numerous to mention. Throughout the peak of their prosperity, the Nobility would invite beautiful women from their domains, or pressure them to answer their summons, or force their way into homes and slake their thirst whenever they liked, but as their society declined, it occurred to them to use contracts to fulfill their hunger. In other words, in exchange for loaning money to the impoverished residents of their domain, they demanded that family's blood in exchange. When this was done, the debtor's blood would first be put into a glass or other receptacle before it was offered up, since there was concern about creating pseudo-Nobles or faux Nobility. And the debtor could get through the transaction without suffering any of the disadvantages of having their blood sucked directly.

Of course, that was the ideal. The Nobility viewed humans as on par with insects, so there was no chance of them honoring a contract with them as if they were equals, and they used the weather controllers to wipe out the crops in their domain and hired bandits to plunder the fields, then loaned the humans money or new species of crops at exorbitant rates. And that wasn't the worst of it, as some Nobles used sorcery to rob humans of their free will and compel them to steal valuables from their castles, then demanded their life blood as compensation. Of course, it was guaranteed that the Nobles wouldn't drink from them directly. Yet there were almost no records of anyone invited to their castles as "collateral" returning unharmed.

And what of Nobles' dealings with their fellow Nobility? Long years of research had shed light onto that, as well. In the case of the Nobility, exchanges were more often of technology rather than money, with those of rank itself being even more common. For Nobility, pedigree and the social standing that brought wasn't their pride and joy, nor was it a cause for melancholy. The Sacred Ancestor occupied the Nobility's highest rank, a solitary being with no dependents, and the Greater Nobles just below him were direct descendants of ancient and honorable families from the days of antiquity when humanity still ruled the world. Some said those families numbered ten in all, others twenty, but the exact number remained unknown. The Sacred Ancestor was venerated, and more than a few recalcitrant Nobles faked their pedigree and demanded a place among the Greater

Nobility, but despite the fact that all of them were purged, even now there was no end to the number of pretenders due to the tremendous advantages higher rank gave in Noble society. Still, the humans knew of no concrete case of this at present. All that was known was this— that a Noble's rank was incredibly valuable. So it should come as some surprise that there were those who would transfer their rank in secrecy, as a form of collateral. According to records of receipts and disbursements left by a Noble who dwelt in the northern Frontier, a Greater Noble in the eastern Frontier agreed to adopt him into their family in exchange for permission to feed on half of the women in his domain between the ages of fourteen and twenty-five. Going just from that record, it can be seen that Nobles considered fresh human blood—particularly that of women—as a treasure worth ceding their position for.

When converting money into blood, three hundred million dalas would probably buy enough young ladies to satisfy a Noble's hunger for a few years. And the Noble who received that contract would undoubtedly employ measures far beyond anything Old El could do to collect what was due from Marquis Verenis.

"And I let that deadbeat marquis know it, too. No way he's gonna try and do me in."

"But if he has no money to pay back, he'll have no choice but to kill the collector, right?"

"Doing that ain't gonna do him no good. Right about now, he's probably trying to come up with something else, I bet."

"Something else? Worth three hundred million dalas?"

"It's not like he's got a choice, right?"

"I don't know," Tupperman replied, ready to keep right on arguing, but just then the gates before them began to open with a grave creaking sound.

"See? Here we go!" said the old man.

Enter and be welcome. The lord of the castle awaits you, a charming masculine voice told him.

"Looks like he didn't make a run for it," Tupperman whispered.

The lord of the castle neither runs nor hides.

"Oh my!"

"Anyway, let's get going," said Old El. "Hey, show us the way," he arrogantly ordered the source of that voice. "Noble action soon. I'm counting on you!" the old man told D with a nod.

Marquis Verenis's Financial Situation

CHAPTER 2

I

O nce the group had passed through the gates, the voice directed them toward their destination.

"We been down three corridors already! Who the hell does that snooty voice think he is, anyway?!" Old El cursed from the back of his steed.

"Just as I thought," the hoarse voice said pensively.

"What's just as you thought?"

"It looks like Marquis Verenis's finances must be in pretty dire straits. I mean, he can't even send an android or holographic guide to show us the way."

"If he's still a full-blown Noble, couldn't he do some element conversion and turn rocks into gold or something, though?"

"You've got some mistaken notions about the Nobility," said the hoarse voice. "Converting elements is an elaborate and difficult bit of physics even for Nobles. It requires ridiculously large machines and a huge facility. You think every Noble and his brother's got that kicking around?"

"You don't say. So, Marquis Verenis doesn't have that equipment, then?"

"I don't know, but judging from how sparse this place is looking, nope."

"Interesting," Tupperman remarked, his tone clearly one of scorn.

Turn left there. You'll soon come to the main castle, the latest directions informed them.

To either side were ramparts that looked to be over six hundred feet high. If the group were attacked there, they wouldn't last long. Actually, they could see rows of windows and arrow loops, as well as a number of holes that looked to be used for dropping rocks.

"Pretty old-fashioned, huh? These folks could manage interstellar travel, so why'd they design their castles and equipment to be so antiquated?" Tupperman remarked with disgust.

"Nobility have a kind of 'homesickness' for the good ol' days built into their DNA," Old El replied. "These guys had the smarts to conquer time and space to some degree. While the inner workings might be a different matter, they were all too happy to build anachronistic castles with outward appearances that didn't make a lick of sense, though the reason was a mystery even to the Nobles themselves. The latest research has finally got to the bottom of it, though."

"Were the old days all that good?"

"You'd have to ask a Noble. Damned if I know. Humans have a limited shelf life. There ain't time to be looking back. When you live forever, though, you probably think back on lots of stuff."

"Ah."

D was silent.

In no time, the three steeds had passed through the main castle's gates. They came to a square. Dismounting there, the riders had just tethered their horses' reins to the hitching post when they were told, *Kindly enter this way.* The door was open.

They were greeted by a drab hall.

"Not a single painting hanging here. A dead broke Noble, just as I thought," the Hunter's left hand murmured.

"Enter, if you please," said a voice from the back, and it wasn't the same one that had guided them up to that point. A door was open there. Going through it, they walked down another long corridor, then entered a spacious drawing room.

"Interest, interest, interest," the old man muttered.

"What's this 'interest' you're getting?"

"His girl," Old El replied.

Tupperman froze in his tracks. As if that weren't enough, his mouth also hung open. "His girl—and she's a vampire, I take it?"

"I suppose. I dunno, maybe she's human. Nah, he'd have taken 'er for a wife in that case. Meaning, maybe she's his actual daughter. Hey, what do you think?" Old El asked, his query directed at D.

"We'll know soon enough," a steely voice replied.

Huh? Old El thought to himself, his body tensing from head to toe as his ears caught approaching footsteps from the vicinity of the door at the far end of the sparsely furnished room. The door opened, and a tall Nobleman in a wine-colored cape appeared.

"Welcome, and thank you for coming. Ah, it has been quite a while, hasn't it, Mister El and Mister Tupperman? As for your muscle— excuse me, your escort, I don't believe we've met. I am Marquis Verenis."

"D."

The eyes that glittered in the Nobleman's pale face snapped open wide. They were the eyes of a corpse. D's name had transformed the undead into a dead man.

"You're—D . . . A human and Noble half-breed who pursues the Nobility . . . Filth . . . But, no . . . How exquisite you are," the marquis groaned dumbfoundedly, his voice charged with sensual exhilaration.

"Hey, don't go blushing over the guy. Let's get straight down to business. You know why I'm here, don't you?"

"Only too well," Marquis Verenis replied with a fawning smile, advancing to the large table in the center of the room.

"Okay, three hundred million dalas—and figuring in the interest, that's six hundred million and then some. Now, since I'm no money-grub, I'll knock the 'then some' off to make it an even six hundred million. So, if you've got it, could I have you fork it over now?"

"Regrettably—I cannot repay it," the marquis said in a pained tone. "The truth is, the anti-matter circuitry I borrowed was destroyed. With it, I had intended to warp a black hole that was approaching Earth into the depths of space, but it didn't work. Which meant the honorarium I might have received from the Council of Greater Nobility for my efforts was also off the table. Ah, I was foiled at every turn."

"Maybe you think all you've gotta do is give me an excuse, but you think I'm just gonna eat a six hundred million loss? Do you?!" Old El barked.

"That—I fully understand," Verenis replied, nodding. "If you would but grant me an extension of three more days—no, even two will do. This I most humbly request."

He bowed. There was a thud, and the marquis reeled backward holding his forehead.

"Bang your head against the table all you like, I still ain't wiping your debt clean!" the old man said, giving the Nobleman a scornful look. "Knock off this pathetic act, all right? Can you pay me back or not? If you can't, I'll take the collateral from our contract plus interest!"

"Hmmm," the marquis groaned. His arms were folded and his eyes shut.

"Don't give me any of your 'Hmmm.' You only got two options open to you!"

And yet, for a full minute more the marquis continued to groan, "Hmmm," as if lost in another world before finally coming back.

"Very well, give me just tomorrow, one day," he said.

"No way. Pay me right now. If not, I'll get in touch with a big fish and give him the right to collect from you. And nothing I can do begins to compare to what he'll do to get it out of you!"

Letting out another "Hmmm," Verenis said, "The truth is, my daughter is bedridden."

"Whaaat?"

"Yesterday, she had a small quantity of blood from a young man in the village, but he suffered from an infirmity of the lungs. She has been left coughing in such a debilitated condition she can't get up. If you wish to see her, how would tomorrow evening suit you? The illnesses of the Nobility can be rather troublesome if contracted by a human."

"I know that," the old man replied with a sullen face, and now it was his turn to fold his arms.

Though the Nobility were ageless and immortal, they weren't completely indestructible. A stake of ash wood or steely sword through the heart could reduce them to dust, but germs in the air had no effect at all on them. They could breathe even the most lethal and corrosive of poison gases without suffering any ill effects. The sole exception was in cases when they partook of infected blood. Bacteria in the blood would become part of the Noble, causing them to manifest the same symptoms as a human being. The terrifying part was, the instant one cough or one drop of blood left the Noble's body, it became a plague a thousand or perhaps ten thousand times as bad for the human race.

"That reeks of an excuse, but there ain't much I can do. Tonight's all she needs to get over it, right?" Old El said, apparently well-versed in these matters, and Marquis Verenis broke into a smile at his words.

"But of course. Now, you have all night tonight and until noon tomorrow, so please rest from your wearying travels. Rooms have been prepared. We can continue this conversation in detail once you've rested a bit and supped—oh, Brendon!"

The marquis gestured, and a giant of a man dressed like a butler appeared, leading the group off to their rooms.

The rooms were all side-by-side on the second floor. Before a minute had passed, Tupperman paid a call on D and told the Hunter Old El wanted to see him.

All of the rooms were strangely spacious. Old El and Tupperman were seated on sofas, while D stood with his back to the wall.

"Let's see—we got a night and half a day's breathing room, looks like. What's your take on this, D?"

"He'll take his only way left to get out of this loan," said the Hunter, speaking cold truth in an equally cold tone.

"Hmmm," the old man said, accepting that.

Noon tomorrow was out of the question, so Verenis probably planned on doing away with the lot of them that night.

"That butler of his, Brendon, is clearly 'half-Nobled.' What's more, from what I see, he's a pretty rough customer," Old El said, extending his index finger and making a downward slash with it. "Think you can take him?"

"I don't know."

"You're a kinda surly one, ain't you? You've gotta have some idea how tough he is just from the look of him."

"I believe there's someone a lot more important than me right now."

"That's right!" the old man exclaimed, making a sharp turn to face the sofa across from him—and Tupperman. "As I recall, you said you'd borrowed five million dalas from the marquis, right? So how come Verenis didn't mention it at all? Hey, you gonna tell me why or what?!"

"I—I don't know why. Perhaps it slipped his mind?"

"Think a Nobleman would just up and forget loaning five million dalas to a human? C'mon, spill it!" the old man snarled, suddenly getting a stranglehold on Tupperman, whose eyes bugged.

"Gaaah!"

"Go ahead and spill your guts! Want me to kill you before the marquis gets a chance to suck the blood outta you?"

"Gah gaaah gaaaaah!"

"Ease up, or he'll kick the bucket for real!" said the hoarse voice, and Old El loosened his grip.

"Relax. I know exactly what I'm doing. Besides, this piece of crap's still gotta pay me back. The way he was so quick to say okay when I told him he was coming with us made me think something was up, though. You don't find that strange?"

"It certainly is, at that," the hoarse voice said malevolently. "So, give him the once-over?" the left hand said, putting its index finger against the base of Tupperman's neck.

The puppet master's knees buckled.

"Oh?!"

What lay at the two men's feet was a rough wooden puppet less than eight inches long. Its head and torso were carved from a single piece of wood to which arms and legs had been attached, but it had no eyes, nose, or fingers.

"Let's be respectful of my free will," Tupperman said, a wry smile rising to his lips as he stood in the doorway.

"Sonuvabitch," Old El growled, rolling up his sleeves.

"Not bad at all," said the hoarse voice.

"The sun's down," D remarked, his words halting all movement. "The living dead will be on the move." After pausing the space of a breath, he added, "And that includes the marquis's daughter."

"Yeah, about her—what's she like?" asked the financier.

Tupperman walked over, saying, "Well, I know her name, at least. It's Matilda."

Old El gazed out the window—and peered into the blue darkness. Because that's where the girl that bore that name would come from.

A stone-walled chamber deep, deep underground. Crushed under tens of thousands of tons, the darkness couldn't speak, and it was the darkness alone that would hear a groan here once or twice every thousand years. Now, the creak of hinges reverberated there.

If someone unfamiliar with the place were to see it, the vast chamber would've undoubtedly appeared to have been abandoned. A simple wooden coffin devoid of ornamentation sat square in the center of the chamber, having just given off a dazzling light.

"Brendon," said a young female voice.

"I am here," the butler replied, his voice issuing from the western corner of the vast chamber. The light didn't reach him. There was no light. There were only crushed black shadows.

"He has come, has he not?"

"If you are referring to the maker of gadgets, yes, he is already here."

"There shouldn't be anyone else."

"What will you do? Furthermore, this time someone even more troublesome has come calling."

"Oh, and who might he be?"

"His name—is D."

There was the sound of a sharply taken breath.

"Impossible!"

"He is up above. However, please rest assured. From appearances, he does not seem too taken with this job. Even the greatest Hunter on the Frontier is sure to present a weakness. And when he does, everything shall go just as we have planned."

"I see. At any rate, I shall make my move, just as you said. While we are still of a single mind—let us go!"

A dazzling figure walked off. There was no sound of footsteps. But that was only in keeping with the manners of a famous Noble house.

II

Though Old El thought it best the three of them stick together, Tupperman left, saying he'd sooner die then spend the night with two other men.

"He ain't right in the head," the old man groused to nobody in particular.

"Something's up," the hoarse voice said to him. "But he's not exactly the easiest nut to crack, on top of which we have no idea when we'll even have a chance to lay our hands on the real him. They're not joking when they call him a puppet master, you know?"

"Don't go fawning over him. I don't know about you, but I ain't about to let him get away. Fifty thousand dalas hang in the balance."

"You killed his freaking girlfriend. Why don't you just call it even?" the hoarse voice asked with apparent interest.

"Now you're talking nonsense. Fifty thousand dalas for one woman? All that aside, you said Verenis would take steps to kill us before sundown tomorrow, didn't you? Let's come up with a plan."

"I have one," the hoarse voice replied with utter confidence. "You'll wait here alone for a while. I'll go out on patrol. The sun just set. Even the marquis won't be on the move yet."

"How can you know that for sure? You're staying here."

"I have to defend you, money-grubber or not. This is part of that. Don't screw it up." Those were the words the financier heard a split second before the door D had used to leave shut behind him.

D returned to his own room. Chortling, his left hand said, "It'll serve a pigheaded guy like him right, having a little scare thrown into him. Leave him be till you hear a scream."

"Can you tell?" D asked, which seemed like an odd question.

"Yeah. Already on the move. Not sure where they're headed yet, though. Well, it's safe to say he's not gonna go after the freaking loan shark right off the bat. If he's gonna start any trouble, it'll be with one of the two who came with him."

Not saying a word, D shifted his gaze out the window. Unsettling bird cries resounded in the distance.

"That's a nighthawk," said the hoarse voice. "It wants souls. But is it yours it wants, or—"

D glided into action.

When the sun went down, human hearts filled with an almost incomprehensible shade of fear. But they knew the true nature of that shade. It was a hue called the Nobility. However, more than a millennium into their decline, fear of Nobles spread through hearts in the dead of every night—and the reason for this remained a mystery.

"Wonder if I'll be afraid of the night as long as I live," Lydia murmured softly to herself as she drew the curtain over the window.

A little voice rose from the corner of the room in song. It was Didi's. At his age, he was a boy soprano, but his singing voice was bolstered by a pathos and an exquisite sense of rhythm that left Lydia listening raptly in spite of herself.

"Nice voice," she said.

Didi closed up like a clamshell.

"Why'd you stop? Keep singing."

"Because I'm not very good."

"That's not true at all. Let me hear some more," Lydia said sweetly.

The boy hesitated briefly, then gave a small nod and closed his eyes, and a slow, soft melody began to stream from his lips.

Why can't we live happily?
Mountains, rivers, or plains
We just want to live there in peace
Why is the castle on the hill there
When I open my eyes in the morning?

And then—the song ended.

"What's wrong?"

"I can't sing anymore. That's a song I learned from my grandma. Mama was busy with work, so she never taught me any songs."

Lydia turned her gaze to the floor.

"But grandma disappeared before she could die. Just like Pa and Ma did earlier."

"Your grandma vanished, too? Why?"

"She borrowed money from the Nobility."

Lydia's eyes narrowed. This was about money, too?

"We were so poor, we were to the point where they said we'd all have to hang ourselves. But the night before we were gonna, grandma went up to the Noble's castle all alone and borrowed some money. She came back with it that very same day! And the very next morning, she was missing from her bed."

"Yeah, it was the Nobility's doing, wasn't it? But what happened this time—"

"I don't know. Maybe grandma wasn't the only security on the money she borrowed. Or maybe Pa and Ma took out a new loan. I don't know anythi—"

Didi's shoulders quaked. Before he could bring his hands up to his eyes and start crying, Lydia came over and wrapped her arms around his head.

"I—I'm so scared. Grandma and Papa and Mama all disappeared. Nobody's left but me. And I gotta wonder if I won't disappear soon, too."

"It's all right," said Lydia. She knew saying that wouldn't do any good, but she couldn't think of anything else to do.

"Lydia? Lydia?"

"What is it?"

"If I disappear, what happens to me then? Is it the same as dying, or is it different?"

"You're not gonna disappear."

The boy jumped up with terrific force, his head springing free of Lydia's arms, and he looked up at her and said, "Honest? You'll really save me?"

"Yeah," Lydia replied, and at that point she made up her mind. As a child, her parents had protected her. "I—I've always been the one being protected. But this time, I'll do the protecting. Don't you worry."

"Okay," said the boy, smiling.

Lydia cradled his head once more, drawing it close to her chest. Her eyes began to glow suspiciously. Glowing crimson. Apparently Lydia wasn't the only one who'd made a resolution.

There was a knock.

"Yes?" Lydia said, the eyes she turned toward the door back to normal.

"I brought your dinner," said the farmer's wife.

"Thank you. Just set it down out there, please."

"Sure thing," replied the farmer's wife, who'd seemed dubious at first but now left without asking any questions.

After eating more than their fill of dinner, Lydia said to the boy, "Sure ate a lot, didn't you? Not scared anymore, then?"

"No, I'm scared," Didi replied between sips of warm cocoa. "But when dinner comes, I eat it no matter what's going on. Because if I didn't, there was no telling when I might get to eat again."

"You were that—" Lydia was about to say *poor*, but decided to finish it in her heart instead.

The Noble who was lord of their domain would never hear the entreaties and rush to the aid of humans who could no longer bear their poverty. His grandmother herself had been the compensation for that. And his father and mother had both disappeared. The boy who'd been left behind feared it was his turn next.

"Sing a song with me," Lydia whispered to the boy. If he did, he might forget everything for a little while.

As they sang in perfect harmony, Didi's eyes went wide, and he looked up at the girl and said, "You're really good, Lydia!"

"Well, I did belong to the choir back home. Even won their Best Vocalist award."

"Where was that?"

"Ipswich."

"Where?!"

"That's the town where our house was."

Didi gushed, "And you were the best in town?"

"You have a problem with that?"

"Nope. You're good. The best in the whole Frontier!"

"Thank you. Shall we?"

Didi nodded, and the song flowed from their lips.

When their beautiful chorus ended, there was a knock at the door. Before Lydia had reached the door, the farmer and his wife came in. The eyes of both were damp.

"Cried like a couple of babies, we did. We didn't know we were putting up professional singers here," said the wife, dabbing her eyes with a handkerchief.

Her husband, with a face like a cracked rock, added, "My, but this is a surprise. We got a dog so mean it even snaps at me, but it drifted right off to sleep listening to the two of you singing."

The couple asked them to keep on singing before they left. Lydia and Didi looked at each other and laughed, and then the girl said, "Why not?"

They went on to sing five more songs they both knew, and then the house fell silent again.

Once they'd finished, Didi began nodding off. Putting him into bed, Lydia took an almost-yard-long stake of ash wood propped up by the pillow in hand and turned toward the doorway.

"Come on out. I know you're there!"

No sooner had she said those words than the creaking of the door's hinges could be heard. The darkness that choked the hallway took the form of a woman in a dress who entered the room. A young lady in a dazzling dress.

"Your name, if you please," said Lydia.

"It seems humans aren't familiar with courtesy. However, I shall give you my name. I am Matilda Verenis—the daughter of the marquis!"

"I'm Lydia. What do you want?"

"There is only one thing a Noble desires when they call on the house of a human. I'll have your blood."

"How did you know I was here?"

"Since the moment you entered this domain, all of your movements have been under our scrutiny. How long it has been since a man or woman came from the outside—and when I heard you were compatriots of Father's foe, I could not allow this opportunity to pass me by."

"Wasn't there anyone outside?"

"Three of them—not people, but pieces of rubbish."

Thinking of the fate of the bodyguards Tupperman had left there, Lydia felt her mood darken.

"We're only here to collect the money the marquis borrowed!"

Matilda laughed in a low voice. Her vermilion lips, the only color in the nigh-translucent paleness of her face, made a wicked grin that exposed stark white fangs.

"Do you think a Noble would pay back a loan from a human being? You shall learn what a cruel trick of fate it was, blundering out here."

As Matilda spoke, she walked. While she gazed straight ahead, her body naturally weaved around tables and chairs. And yet, in Lydia's eyes, it looked as if she were just walking straight ahead.

When the distance between the two of them had closed to about six feet, Lydia took a step forward and thrust out the wooden stake. Astoundingly accurate, it pierced Matilda's heart, poking out through her back.

"Yes!" the girl exclaimed in spite of herself, but right in front of her, the member of the living dead got a new smile on her face.

"Nicely done. However, I won't be destroyed by the likes of that."

"Why not?" Lydia asked, feeling all the strength draining from her body. Her legs fought desperately to keep from folding under her. "How could a stake through the heart not kill you?"

"It was for this very purpose that Father borrowed that filthy money from you lowly humans. As you can see, I will not die by being impaled with a stake, and I am free to walk in the light of the sun. However, it proved so costly, the procedure ended with me."

Taking hold of the stake, Matilda yanked it out. Her smile grew broader. Her pale hand rose. Lydia was unable to elude the woman's fingertips. Catching hold of the back of her hair, Matilda pulled the girl close and made her look up at her.

"Now that I've had a good look at you, you are quite the beauty. Ordinarily, I should find it repulsive to even take a human as a maidservant. I would tear their throat open and drink up all the blood that poured out, or, in the case of a woman like you, make a maid of her. Most unfortunate."

Matilda could probably make out the blue veins in the nape of Lydia's neck. The tip of a sinister claw of a nail pressed into Lydia's flesh.

Matilda turned around stunned, staring at the tall, shadowy figure standing in the same doorway.

"You're—" she groaned, a stark wooden needle jutting from her back that probably went all the way through her heart.

"D," the shadowy figure replied, bounding.

III

He flew up, and drifted down. The beauty of how the Hunter's coat spread like the wings of an ominous bird left Matilda standing dumbfounded.

A crimson line appeared on her from the top of her head down to the hem of her dress. Her look of astonishment became a smile. The red line faded without a sound, and Matilda pursed her vermilion lips.

She must've exhaled something that couldn't be seen.

D held his breath.

"Trouble!" his left hand groaned.

Something feverish invaded through every pore on his body, reaching all the way to his brain. D was aware of his brain burning. Thoughts fragmented and his motor center screamed, ordering him to collapse. He dropped to one knee.

"Oh, so you can take in my breath and still not fall? I wish I could say I should expect as much from a dhampir, but I have disposed of a number of your kind, and not a man among them weathered it as you did. What's more—"

Here she paused to catch her breath.

"What a gorgeous man you are. You're about to melt the very soul of me, you know." Indeed, the Noblewoman was rooted in place. Shaking her head fervently, she continued, "However, you are an interloper and must be destroyed. If left alone, you would become a foe to be feared."

Her dress glittering as she seemed to flow over toward D, Matilda crouched down and peered at his face. No matter what she'd intended to do, that was clearly a mistake. The woman's lovely face truly slackened with rapture. It was an instant later that a streak of red once again raced from the top of her head to the hem of her dress. The line instantly became a stain, spreading like a map of the world.

"But this is . . ." Matilda started to say, hiding her face in her hands. Her palms were stained with blood. ". . . my blood? Is this my blood I see? It cannot be . . . Such a thing is simply impossible . . . Blood has always meant the blood of others."

Even now, the Noblewoman's blood seemed intent on staining every inch of her red.

"Not merely gorgeous . . . Such a fearsome man . . . We shall meet again for certain. And when we do, I hope you take in my breath once more."

The woman ran to the door, and could soon be seen no longer.

"Are you okay?" Lydia inquired, also down on her knees but propping herself up. Her voice was tinged with more anxiety than concern. The words the old man had whispered to her still had an influence on her.

"Relax," the hoarse voice told her, and she didn't even bat an eyelash. It continued, "He's made of tougher stuff than the toughest. Give it a little time and he'll heal right up. But what she breathed out—didn't think it'd get to his head."

"That's why I'm so worried! When brain cells are destroyed, you don't go back to normal."

"Oh, you wouldn't happen to be the daughter of a scholar, would you?"

"Actually, my school choir had a physics and biology teacher in it."

"You don't say?"

"Is he really—" *okay?* she was going to ask, but D got to his feet before she could. His dignified movements didn't show the slightest trace of the effects of the deadly exhalation. For a fleeting moment, she forgot her fear of him.

"You saved me."

Having said that, the girl turned and looked over at the bed. Didi was still in the same pose—only his eyes were open. His lips didn't open until his eyes met D's.

"That was awesome. I saw the whole thing. Mister—you're great!"

Saying nothing, D gave a little nod. That was probably that young man's way of saying, "I'm glad you're okay."

"Back to sleep," Lydia told him, and the boy nodded, at which point the girl turned toward D as if she'd made up her mind, still keeping her eyes averted as she said to him, "That woman was watching us. But how'd you know she'd come here?"

"To clear his debt, the marquis only has from tonight until sundown tomorrow to get rid of the old man. The reasonable move would be to get rid of me, the bodyguard, first. But if they knew that'd be too much trouble, they'd probably try a more indirect approach. Such as making you one of them."

Though she listened to D's words in a state of enraptured bliss, Lydia soon repudiated that, saying, "That woman—Matilda—she said she'd kill me before she drank my blood. I don't think she was lying."

"A-ha," said the hoarse voice. "In that case, father and daughter might have very different intentions. If she killed Lydia here, it'd put the kibosh on negotiations without a doubt."

"That was probably her aim," said D. "In which case, what, the daughter wants us to take down her father?"

"We could always ask her."

Gazing at the speaker in spite of herself, Lydia forgot her fear and sank into the depths of rapture. D touched his left hand to her shoulder. The girl temporarily lost consciousness, and the Hunter scooped her up.

"When she wakes up now, her fear of you will have subsided. But it must've been a pretty shocking nugget the old man dropped on her. What was it?"

There was no reply from D. Perhaps it didn't matter to him in the least.

For Matilda, it felt good to dash along. The stillness of the dark of night infused every inch of her as she ran. And in the forest it was best of all. Such a bounty of life! The life of the trees, the life of the soil, the life of the moonlight—and the life of the creatures. Vitality filled her surroundings.

Everything is mine. Not a scrap of it would I give the lowly humans. But before I return to the castle, I must first go there.

Gathering the hem of her dress, she pressed on as if riding the wind, straying from the road to the castle to head into the depths of the forest. Before long she halted in front of the trunk of an oak so great it seemed it would take twenty grown men linking arms to encircle its girth. Towering more than a thousand feet high, the top of it seemed like it might stab right through the moon.

"My beloved Adam," Matilda said, rubbing her cheek against its black bark. "I have lived receiving life from you. Though the warm blood of the lowly humans sets my body afire, your life alone gives me quiet satisfaction. Why does so much life fill you?"

Matilda's dress glittered in the moonlight, her necklace and earrings set with jewels drinking up the glow for all eternity.

"Ah, this quiet, this cold. All I want is the life you give," she said in a voice that suited the word *rapture* more than anything else in the world. She was the very picture of a queen clinging to the chest of the man she loved—if the man were an enormous tree and this a sublime scene from a fairytale. Without any breeze, several leaves from the tree fell on the Noblewoman's back. Though Matilda didn't even glance at them, her gaze became sorrowful. But only for a moment.

"I intended to be with you always. Not for a thousand years, but ten thousand—nay, till the end of the world. Such was the life that dwelt within you. However—"

Her tone changed. As did the gleam in her eye.

"I, too, have changed," said Matilda. "And this evening is the last time I shall ever see you. Trunk of Life, no longer shall I call you so."

O night, what have you given this Noblewoman? When she turned her face to look down the road again, were her eyes not giving off bloodlight, her exposed fangs long and sharp, and her body brimming from head to toe with energy that warped the scenery around her?

Like silvery fish scales, the moonlight mixed with the wind and raced away, and for a moment the massive tree towered there exhibiting no change, but at length it began to tilt to the sound of snaps and cracks halfway up its height. The instant it rocked the ground, it was reduced to countless pieces, those shards breaking into even smaller pieces, and finally turning into dust. Look! The wind strips the bark from the remaining half, the wood crumbles, and in less than five minutes' time it has vanished from the face of the earth. The life that Matilda said would last ten thousand years had just ended. No, this was a ghastly show of decay, and that tree's life had undoubtedly ended long, long ago.

As she returned to the road to the castle, Matilda heard echoes approaching from the direction of the village. It was the iron-shod hooves of a cyborg horse.

"Impossible—and yet, such remarkable horsemanship could only be his doing. Such a fearsome man! And he is my pursuer."

As her face turned in the direction of the hoofbeats, she smirked in a way that overflowed with self-confidence.

"Oh, so fast—but that will be the death of you!"

Spinning herself around, Matilda dashed off toward the castle. As she ran, she plucked off five of the jewels embroidered to the waist of her dress. They were tiny dolls with jewels for heads. The fabric seemed terribly thin but cut out in the shape of people who were anything but, and they'd been sewn to her dress. Breathing on the heads of all of them, Matilda then cast them down at her feet. The five glittering jewels scattered across the road and were soon lost from sight.

"Jewel spirits who make a weapon of the moonlight," she laughed haughtily. "Prepare a reception for my beloved pursuer." And then she leapt off the road and took cover behind a cedar that towered to the right of it.

"Should be any time now," the Hunter's left hand said encouragingly. "But did you see that side path just now? All the plants were dried out, and even the bugs and critters had died out. The energy of the living dead's life force dished all that out. That woman's stronger than I thought!"

D's reply was: "She's here."

As he galloped along, five figures stood in a spot about fifty yards ahead of the Hunter. Their black limbs and the heads that hung above their chests gleamed like jewels.

"Her bodyguards, I take it. Those heads use light!" said the hoarse voice.

Streaks of stark light raced by D on the left and the right, above and below him. The distant trees and ground that they struck were enveloped by white radiance. And when it faded, the trees and ground were gone.

D bounded.

The light energy that pierced his body was moonlight. His foes' heads took the moonlight incessantly pouring down on them, altering it through energy lines within them and releasing it as blasts with terrific force.

D's form faded away.

The jewel men approached the remnants that fell to the ground. All that remained was fragments of black fabric. D had made the coat look like himself when he hurled it.

Five heads turned to follow the cyborg horse galloping away. And a black wind swept through them. That wind was the gust of a sword.

Without so much as a glance at his foes, now little jewels and the bodies that had lost them, D gave a low, sharp whistle. But rather than wait for his cyborg steed to return, he kicked off the ground and landed in the saddle a good thirty feet away, wheeling his horse around.

The Nobles' Accounting

CHAPTER 3

I

Feeling like she'd been staked through the heart anew, Matilda diverted her eyes from the battle that had taken mere seconds. That the soldiers she had breathed life into could be slain in an instant was something beyond her imagining. What a foe this was! Matilda's heart beat furiously. It was a rhythm of fear and surprise— and rapture. And it only grew in intensity.

When the foe she thought was going to ride away turned in her direction, she heard a hoarse voice say, "That heart's beating a little fast for one of the dead." But more than that, what turned Matilda to stone there behind the tree was the unearthly aura that was slowly approaching. He intended to dispose of the woman. How horrible! How cruel!

The unearthly aura—and the one it came from—entered into killing range.

The tree would serve as no shield at all. Matilda realized she was going to be destroyed. It was a feeling that lit a fire in her heart.

It was at that instant that she sensed a presence dropping down from above her. Not even knowing what the huge, shadowy shape was, the Noblewoman made a massive leap to the right. The instant the tip of the stark blade piercing the cedar's trunk appeared, the enormous shadowy shape filled Matilda's field of view. There was surprisingly little rumbling of the ground. In the blink of an eye, the trunk of a great oak more than six hundred feet tall was reduced to dust. Those flecks hid the world from prying eyes, and when they cleared a short time later, Matilda was fleeing through the woods a few hundred yards away in a gliding run.

D chased her no further.

Returning to the farm that'd been entrusted with Lydia and Didi, he purchased another horse there, put the two of them on it, and went back to the castle.

Even on entering the castle, no efforts were made to stop them.

"What's all this?"

"What happened?" Old El and Tupperman asked, their eyes bulging when D entered the room.

After the Hunter explained the situation to them, he declared, "The two of them will be joining us in the castle."

"That's crazy talk. You'd be serving 'em up on a silver platter!" said Old El.

"I should say so," Tupperman concurred. "They'll come and attack them in less than ten minutes' time!"

"The attacker was a Noblewoman who lives in this castle. Use her to extort him," said D.

"What are you talking about? Why, I'd never extort—" the old man bellowed, but then he said, "Hold on," and folded his arms. "Well, it certainly could be an advantageous situation. Okay, D. I'm gonna go negotiate. Come along with me."

"What about the girl and the kid?"

"Have 'em drink this and it'll be fine. I'll even post a guard."

Surely this was what they meant when they talked about strutting. Old El positively swaggered into the hall, and from the center of it he shouted, "Come on out, Verenis. That daughter of yours has made a real mess of things!"

Presently the marquis appeared, not seeming the least bit upset, inquiring, "What do you want at this hour?"

Smirking all the while, Old El recounted the incident as D had explained it to him.

"That was—most uncouth," the Nobleman replied, and the look of surprise that skimmed across his face was genuine.

"I'm supposed to think your daughter doesn't know the situation here? Fat chance of that!" the old man said, leaning over the marble table.

"I was certainly under the impression she grasped the situation."

"Call her in here!"

"Very well."

Less than a minute later, Matilda appeared.

"Oh, for the love of—" Old El gasped, reeling backward.

If she were human, her corpulent form would've tipped the scale at nearly four hundred and fifty pounds. The buttons on her dress looked like they might pop off at any minute.

"What the hell is this?!" asked the financier. "You buy her off a butcher or something?"

"This is my daughter Matilda."

"Of all the brazen—hey, if you screw with a creditor just trying to collect on a debt, you'll find yourself in a world of trouble!"

"Don't be ridiculous. She is my own flesh and blood."

"Hey, missy!"

"The name is Matilda," the girl said, still looking aggrieved, though she curtseyed gracefully in true Noble fashion.

"D, is that her?"

"No."

"What are you trying to pull, Verenis?!"

"Oh, but this is most vexing. Ah, I have it!" the Nobleman exclaimed, snapping his fingers. "Now that you mention it, I have heard tell of a woman calling herself Matilda prowling the villages in my domain in search of blood. I even dispatched a search party, but ultimately they failed to locate her. That must be it."

"What do you mean, 'That must be it'? Don't play stupid with me!" the old man snarled, glaring at the obese woman.

Her face looked ready to collapse under its own weight, but when she looked at D it started to melt in rapture. But her features suddenly stiffened. It looked as if her four hundred and fifty pounds had been condensed down to half that. Even the marquis and Old El had their breath taken away.

A terrible unearthly aura was filling the spacious hall.

The girl who called herself Matilda didn't even move a muscle when a stark streak of light was thrust at the tip of her nose.

"Stop it! What's the meaning of this?!" the marquis managed to croak.

The blade flicked away.

The obese woman clutched her right ear. Bright blood began to spill between fingers fat as grubs.

"Gaaaah, my ear!" the woman shrieked.

"What the hell?!" Old El shouted, but the instant he got to his feet, there was a stark gleam of light, and the marquis reeled backward while clutching the end of his nose.

The unearthly aura vanished in an instant.

The woman promptly turned herself around and dashed for the doorway that'd brought her there.

"Looks like she's not his daughter, eh?" D said, the hilt of his sword clicking against the scabbard on his back.

"You can say that again. She was all too happy to turn tail while you were cutting into her father. And he didn't bat an eyelash when his daughter's ear got lopped off. I was more surprised than he was," the old man said, letting out a deep breath. "I'll fix you for calling that creature in here and trying to pull a fast one on me. So, how do you intend to make this right?"

The marquis remained with his hand pressed to his nose, which was still dripping blood. A Noble's regenerative cells would make anything short of a lethal wound vanish in seconds. But they had no effect where the blade of the gorgeous young man was concerned.

"Where's your daughter?" D asked. Both hands hung naturally by his sides, quite some distance from the sword on his back. But when that stark blade flashed into action, no one even saw when it was drawn.

"Okay, hold on. Just hold your horses," Old El said, stepping between them. He was grinning. He'd come up with a way to profit off this. "Your daughter is interest on the loan. I can't have her getting all banged up. Don't bring her out again. D, you just simmer down. Verenis, how much is it worth to you to put this matter behind us?"

"How much?"

"Yeah, that's right. I'm a financier. There ain't but one solution to problems. And you're getting off easy buying your way out of it."

"But I—"

"—don't have any money. I know. And your lands were the collateral for your loan. So, here's what we're gonna do. There's that experiment or whatever you blew three hundred million dalas on. It was a success after all, though, wasn't it?"

There was an awkward silence from the marquis.

"Yeah, that's what I thought," Old El remarked with a nod to the speechless Verenis that seemed to say, *You don't have to say a thing.* "Let's just add that experiment to your tab to cover my inconvenience."

"But that's—" the marquis began to say, but he broke off, a frightening smile on his face. "Very well. I shall give you all the results of the experiment."

"Great. Might seem a tad steep to you, but it's your own fault for raising such a loose cannon. And don't let her pull anything funny again!"

"Understood," the Nobleman replied, his smile never fading as he bowed. "Well, I shall go rewrite our contract, then."

After he left still holding his nose, what remained was a ghastly scene. The floor was a sea of blood that had dripped from her ear and his nose—or if not a sea, at least a pond. And while he was the cause of all of this, D stood there a thing of beauty, with not so much as a drop of their blood splattered on him. When someone spoke of an exquisite scene from hell, this is precisely the kind of thing they were talking about.

"Damn marquis, trying to play dumb with me. Gonna have to go over that contract with a fine-tooth comb."

"No need for that," said the hoarse voice from D's left hand.

"Why not?"

"The smile on his face said none of that even matters. And since it doesn't matter anyway, he'll probably make up a proper one."

"That's great. But when you say it doesn't matter anyway—"

"Because he obviously has murder in mind. Yours and ours."

"Grrrr!"

"The girl might've been on her own when she pulled that stuff before, but this time the damned marquis really means business. You'd best stay on your toes," said the hoarse voice.

"You say that like it's none of your affair. Guarding me's your job. If you wanna know what the Sacred Ancestor said, see to it nobody lays a finger on me!"

"Yeah, yeah," the hoarse voice replied dismissively.

The old man was about to blow his top, and the veins in his forehead were about to burst, but one sideward glance at D made him melt away like a dotard.

"We've come to a critical juncture. I'm going to your room," D said, his gaze one that would pierce the depths of the darkness, and the old man nodded earnestly.

As he walked down a corridor where the candelabras' flames flickered, the marquis took his hand away from his nose. He wasn't bleeding. What's more, the tip of his nose that'd been lopped off was back in its original shape.

"It was no bluff when he said his name was D, it would seem."

Looking at an image floating in midair and the data beside it, Brendon wiped the sweat from his brow. Given that he had the metabolism of a "half-Nobled" rather than a human, that was a rare occurrence.

The image was one of Matilda in a coffin-shaped diagnostic case. The slim Matilda. The vermilion slash that had been depicted a few seconds earlier had now faded without a trace.

"Your DNA has been implanted with a regenerative factor even the blood of the Nobility lacks. I'll need more time to perfect the effects, but it should have been enough to easily fend off even wounds dealt by a Noble . . ." Pausing for the span of a breath, the butler continued, "He's a man to be feared. As it stands, the fortune the marquis spent on your enhancement procedures means nothing."

"You should sooner die than say that to Father. For he would kill you on the spot!"

"I know that."

"My body was not meant for battling that beautiful man. The true enemy is yet to come. And in order to prevail—"

Matilda's eyes burned vermilion in her transparent case.

"Very well," said Brendon, who'd been blankly staring at graphs of data, but his severe expression softened just a bit and he continued, "Now we can move on to the next level. A little time was lost, but we should still finish in time. But you mustn't squander your abilities in another futile battle."

"Understood."

"Now, I need you to go to sleep for a while. A blood sleep, for the sake of us both."

A switch was thrown somewhere. And the god Science commanded the undead's flesh to undergo new transformations.

II

As the night progressed, Tupperman became more and more unsettled. One reason was the five million dalas he owed Marquis Verenis. The money had been borrowed to build his town, Gimmicklin, and he had to put up collateral, of course. That was the town of Gimmicklin itself. He and Old El intended to steamroll that debt out of existence and even planned to dispose of the marquis himself, but Verenis hadn't shown the slightest hint of being ready to retaliate, treating him instead as a guest who'd traveled a long way. That in itself was frightening. The puppet master had no qualms at all about skipping out on a loan, but when face-to-face with the party he intended to stiff, it came as no surprise that things didn't sit quite right. Old El didn't worry him, but the Noble was another matter. Marquis Verenis wouldn't take that lying down. He had to be plotting something.

Pacing around his room and clutching at his head, Tupperman finally went out into the corridor. Quiet had settled once more over the castle's interior, which was filled with a weird air. This was after D had caused the obese woman and the marquis to leave. With stealthy steps he descended to the hall.

"What in the world?"

Though the puppet master believed he'd gone downstairs, he was clearly someplace else.

The darkness was deep.

"I'm underground. Master of gadgetry or not, it appears I've been taken in by one of marquis's gimmicks."

Turning back to the stairs he'd come down, Tupperman found a rusty iron door set in the stone wall, and that door looked to have been there for more than a millennium.

"Well, look at that," he remarked.

There was no other exit.

When he pushed against the iron door, it opened easily. The staircase continued downward.

"Wonder if I'll make it back up again," he said to himself, head tilted to one side, but it was a bold thing to say.

Tupperman went down the narrow stone staircase. The door shut behind him.

"Just wonderful."

These words, too, were the product of more than average self-confidence.

After descending more than fifty steps, Tupperman came to a wide corridor. Taking a right and continuing on, he came to a clearing as large as the hall above. Pillars decorated the perimeter as if hemming the area in, and all of them were chipped and laced with cracks. At their bases were a number of mounds that had formed from rubble flaking from the ceiling and walls.

The location of this place was anyone's guess, but filled with a darkness where light couldn't reach, ages of ruin had passed there.

"I suppose this is where you're waiting, is it?" he called out. It echoed for a while, and then there was a reply.

"Yes. I have been waiting for you. Welcome to my castle."

The speaker stood to Tupperman's right in a gorgeous dress. Matilda extended both hands toward the puppet master, who'd apparently forgotten how to speak. As if spellbound, Tupperman moved toward her with an unsteady gait. Matilda hugged him close, and the smile left her face. The tips of a pair of fangs slipped from behind her vermilion lips as they rose toward the nape of the puppet master's neck. The tips pressed against his flesh, sank into it, but the instant Matilda drove them in deep, her eyes went wide.

Tupperman had suddenly disappeared, and in his place was a little wooden doll that dropped at her feet.

"Over here."

Turning in astonishment to the voice behind her, she found Tupperman with a grin on his face.

"Feel like playing hide-and-seek until dawn?" he asked.

Matilda took an elegant step toward the grinning man, an angelic smile on her own lips.

Both Lydia and Didi felt the same fear. The incident at the farmhouse had left them wondering what was going to become of them, and now, all of a sudden, they'd come to a Noble's castle. Though D assured them they'd be okay, it counted for little when they were in the very heart of enemy territory. Fortunately, Didi fell asleep right away, with Lydia alone left bright-eyed as her sleep demons tussled with her fears. This was right about the time D and Old El were meeting with the marquis in the hall.

When she heard footsteps in the corridor, Lydia was taken aback. Footsteps shouldn't have been audible through the stone walls and heavy door.

What's going on with me? Lydia wondered, feeling like talons of anxiety were sinking into her heart as she kept her eyes trained on the door.

The footsteps halted right in front of the door.

"Who's there?"

The brass door knob turned. It was locked. After a few fruitless twists, it stopped.

"Didi," said a voice that wasn't Lydia's. It was the whispers of an older woman. But how had those whispers reached a room walled in with stone?

Behind Lydia, Didi got up.

"Ma?"

His voice was still slurred with sleep, but it quickly sharpened.

"It's my mother!"

Lydia barely managed to catch hold of the boy as he tried to slip right by her. The boy thrashed his limbs wildly.

"That's Ma's voice. She's come back. Let go of me!"

"We're in a Noble's castle. There's no way your mother would be here!"

"We're here, aren't we?! There's nothing strange about it!"

"Didi!"

A sharp pain shot through her arm. She'd been bitten. By the time Lydia regained her senses, his diminutive figure stood in front of the door.

"Don't do it!" Lydia shouted even as she heard it being unlocked.

A woman was standing in the doorway. Her black arms swallowed up the boy.

"Didi!" the girl cried. And with her cry, something else rose from the pit of her abdomen and shot forward.

The woman let out a scream. She was knocked away, leaving only Didi.

Running over, Lydia hugged the boy. Not even she really understood what had happened.

Pinned back against the door across from theirs, the woman shook her head as she moved forward. The middle-aged woman bore a strong resemblance to Didi. There could be no doubting she was his mother. However, she wasn't the mother Didi had known.

Lydia was just about to go back in their room when the door shut behind her. She turned, her eyes watchful. What was going to happen now?

Standing there looking at her with the door knob in hand was Julas-Han Toba, who they believed had disappeared.

"Are you—"

Friend or foe? The way they'd met, how he'd disappeared, and the fact that he'd showed up again all raced through her brain—and Lydia reached a conclusion.

"Long time no see, eh?"

His lips formed a smile, exposing stark fangs.

Foe.

Didi's mother came over and stood in front of Toba.

"Didi, take a good look at her. Is that your mother?" the girl asked, shaking the boy by his shoulders.

Peering at the woman's face, he shook his head and said, "No. She's not Ma."

The woman donned a look of feigned grief. "What are you saying, Didi? I'm your mother, aren't I? C'mon, come to me. You shouldn't be around a girl like that!"

The woman extended her hands again, walking toward the pair. Her eyes had begun to give off a red light.

"Come to me!"

She was just about to take a big step forward when Toba's hand grabbed hold of her neck from behind. Lydia had no idea when he'd moved. A split second later, five bloody fingers came straight out between the woman's breasts—from where her heart was—and she started twitching.

Having instantly killed the woman with a knife-like thrust of his hand, Toba tossed her body to the floor and smiled at the pair. From behind his stout form came low, beastly growls.

"Both she and I underwent reconstruction procedures beneath the castle. She was a half-assed piece of work, but I'm another matter. Come, Lydia. You and the kid will both be able to live a new kind of life!"

Toba's voice had a stirring tone of sincerity to it. He'd become a different man. However, Lydia backed away.

"Where are you going?"

"Wherever you're not!" she shot back.

"Not very smart, are you, girl? Kid, get over here."

"No way!" said Didi.

"Get over here."

Toba raised the hands he'd lowered and extended them as if pushing something. From behind him, a pair of black beasts on all fours appeared, halting at either side of him.

"You know I'm a beastmaster, right? I don't want to have to make them carry you. Come along quietly."

"Like hell we will!" Lydia shouted, scooping up the boy.

She turned and ran. For some reason, D didn't pop into her head. From behind her came the sounds of footsteps pursuing with savage speed. They were fast. She felt hot breath on the nape of her neck. A gaseous body swirled around Lydia from head to toe. It was far hotter than the beasts' breath.

"Begone!"

All sign of the dogs vanished, and something struck her back from behind. Lumps of dust.

"Are you—?!" Lydia heard Toba cry out in surprise even as she ran.

The next thing she knew, she was up on the roof. Moonlight rained down on her. There was nothing there. Surrounding her on all sides was nothing but towers and turrets basking in the moonlight.

"That's far enough!" said a voice to her right—Toba.

"Stay back!"

"After chasing you all the way up here? Give up already."

"Don't come near us," Lydia said, backing away, but her legs soon hit the top of a stone wall. There was nothing left for her to do but jump.

Toba's body quavered. His mouth was open, and something like black smoke poured from it, enveloping his body. It was an instant later that something flew diagonally from high in the air, piercing the left side of Toba's chest and his throat. Not saying a word, he grabbed the two iron stakes and pulled them out. The black smoke was tinged by fresh blood. The face the beastmaster turned toward the sky had the look of a devil emblazoned on it.

"You bastards—damned Quetzalcoatl!"

Another stake pierced him right between the eyes, and he staggered. Smoke trailing from him, Toba ran for the roof exit. A few more black glints pierced his body, but he vanished from sight without ever slowing down.

Several figures flew down from the sky, landing in front of the rooted and dumbfounded pair. Folding the wings that stretched to either side of them in no time at all, one of them said to Lydia, "Glad you're safe."

His face was familiar. She'd seen it on a wanted poster in a sheriff's office.

"Galkis Thomas," she remarked.

"None other," said the speaker, a man who seemed to be in his mid-thirties and wore a smile beneath his flight goggles. "Yes, I'm the boss of the Quetzalcoatl air bandits. And also the one who saved your lives. Possibly even your souls."

"You have our thanks. But how?"

"You mean, how'd we happen to be right here, right now to save you?" Looking to either side of him, Thomas continued, "You see, once upon a time, I loaned a guy some money. Since I heard he'd got his results, I raced here, and what do I find but the guy I'd borrowed money from has busted in here. So, for a while now, we've been watching how things play out from the skies. Twenty-four hours a day, I might add."

"Old El's gonna be so angry! He says he'll collect from you if it's the last thing he does."

"If he can reach me up in the skies, that is," Thomas replied, chest puffed out, but the next words he heard turned him to stone.

"Perfect. Can we have you take those two with you?"

The two new figures standing by the roof exit were D and Old El.

III

"This is a surprise. Nice that you noticed us up here," Thomas remarked, but Old El ignored him.

"Weren't in your room, so I wondered where you could've gone!" the old man said, glaring at Lydia. "Take our eyes off you for a second, and things go completely to hell. Never a minute's rest with you folks around. Tell me what happened."

Though Old El gripped pistols in either hand, the real reason he showed such bluster against five foes was because D was there.

"We were in our room and the kid's mother showed up. Toba was there, too. He chased us all the way up here, and that's when these folks saved us."

"Trying to make up for skipping out on your loan, Thomas?" the old man inquired sarcastically. "Well, I ain't knocking a stinking dint off it!"

"I know, I know," Thomas replied, scratching his head embarrassedly. People on the Frontier would tremble at the mere mention of the Quetzalcoatl flying bandits, yet their leader seemed a strangely affable man. "I live on the Frontier, too. I'd never even dream of trying to stiff the great financier Old El!"

"Say that again, you bastard."

"Okay, okay, lower your guns, please. Like I was just telling the girl, I came here because a loan I'd made finally got some results. I'll pay you back your money from what I make off that."

"What's this loan you're talking about? Probably something like making vampire dumplings from human blood and selling 'em for ten thousand dalas a bag, am I right?"

"Don't be ridiculous."

"What is it, then?"

"The know-how for flight via teleportation, actually. You know that's technology lost even to the Nobility, right? Well, a retired scientist living in these parts is working on it. When it's finished, Quetzalcoatl will go from being a threat on this one lousy little planet to one for the whole universe. Kinda exciting, right?"

"You idiot. Not bad enough you run out on your loans, now you've gone and got suckered by a con man. Teleportation flight? You met this fella and checked it out? No doubt you fell for this Frontier grifter and he swindled you outta *my* money. What was all that about repairing your airship, you damned fool? This is what you get for fixating on all this other stuff instead of on your banditry. Hell, that scientist of yours is already long gone."

At that, Thomas folded his arms. "Now that you mention it, there was a note stuck to the door of his lab saying he'd be gone for a couple of days."

Old El bared his teeth, saying, "All right, downstairs with me! We're gonna have us a little talk about collateral and interest, aren't we?"

That was the odd thing about the old man. No matter how you looked at it, the deadbeat Thomas had numbers on his side. What's more, his men were armed with stake guns and automatic firearms. If Old El were out of the way, those loans would be a distant memory. Yet he couldn't do that, not just because D was stopping him, but more due to a basic difference in intensity between the two men.

"Guess you got me," Thomas said with a wry grin.

With an evil smile, Old El brought his face closer, saying, "How'd you like to knock that interest down a bit?"

"Huh?"

"Do me a favor and take those two up top with you. A Noble castle's too freaking dangerous for 'em."

"Roger that. And in return?"

"A thousand dalas."

"Not even close. What about my collateral?"

"Aerial shots of the Capital taken from a stealth guard camera. With crystal-clear views of the major installations!"

"In that case, I need a little more."

"I'm offering a thousand dalas just to hold onto a girl and a little kid! That's an unprecedented deal. Just, unprecedented. You should be happy with that."

"We also saved the two of them."

"Eleven hundred," said the old man.

Heaving a sigh, Thomas replied, "Okay. I'll do it. But how about making that fifteen hundred?"

"Thirteen hundred."

"All right, all right."

Elated, Old El told Lydia and Didi, "So, that's the way it is. You're going up into the skies."

"You've got to be freaking kidding me!" said the girl. "These people are part of the bandit group that attacked Papa and me. No way am I going with them."

"It's safer than staying here," said a voice of iron. Its tone was so fierce and beautiful, all of them turned in spite of themselves toward the face they'd intentionally turned their backs to.

"But—" Lydia protested.

"Put up with them, just for tonight."

That made her hold her tongue.

"And in return, you're responsible for keeping them safe," D said, his eyes reflecting Thomas. It wasn't a threat. From the tone of it, it was just an ordinary instruction. However, even through the dark of night it was clear the color had drained from the face of Quetzalcoatl's leader. There was nothing his four men could do.

"Understood," Thomas replied, and with that the blood of the world started pumping again.

"Forget your baggage. Get going right away."

"You heard him. Let's go!" Thomas said with a toss of his chin, and his men took Lydia and Didi's arms over their shoulders, bowed, and spread their wings. Each wore a storage case the size of a small parachute on his back. There was a single sound of their wings beating as they rose easily one after another. They vanished into the depths of the night sky with considerable speed.

D could make out the black airship floating about six hundred feet above them. The color of its hull changed depending on the brightness and hue of its surroundings, normally keeping it hidden from sight. The only time it showed itself was to threaten people on the ground from up high.

"If I don't check out these loan results that bastard's talking about real quick, there's gonna be trouble!" the old man said as he walked toward the roof exit.

"Did you know he was gonna come?" asked the hoarse voice.

"Yeah, pretty much. Heard tell he used the money he borrowed for something else. Caught glimpses of him a few times in my travels, too. That was no accident. I was sure he was headed toward the marquis's place. And it was just as I thought."

"How'd you know to go out on the roof?" the hoarse voice inquired.

"The medicine we gave them two was an inducement drug I got as payment on a loan to a medicine peddler. It makes you wanna flee upward."

"And what'd you plan on doing if they were caught before they got out on the roof?"

"That was the gamble I was taking."

The hoarse voice fell silent.

The old man drew a breath to laugh, but it caught in his throat. A naked blade had been thrust under his nose.

"You said you'd post a guard on those two, didn't you?"

As a result, D had left their side.

"Um, well, what I meant was—"

"Do that again, and you're dead," D said, his icy tone reaching every capillary in the old man.

"Understood," Old El replied in a quavering voice. Thomas had answered the same. Perhaps "Understood" was all people could say when D told them anything.

"You'd better," the hoarse voice added gravely.

That son of a bitch, the old man thought, but there was nothing he could do about it. Instead, Old El directed his rage elsewhere. "Anyway, what're these results Thomas was yapping about?"

"I don't know. But we'll know soon enough. By tomorrow night, at least. That's when he'll come down from the sky, right?" said the hoarse voice.

The two of them went back into the castle.

"Just wanna check in," Old El said, knocking on Tupperman's door. After waiting several seconds, he mused, "What, is he out or something?"

Just as he furrowed his brow the door knob turned and Tupperman poked his head out. Rubbing his eyes, he asked, "Did something happen?"

"Not a thing. Just don't want you bolting on me is all."

"That's a delicate issue, isn't it? At any rate, I won't be fleeing."

"Still haven't told me why you were perfectly fine with coming out here. Until we get to the bottom of that, I ain't trusting you a bit!"

"Suit yourself," Tupperman replied, letting out a massive yawn. "I'll see you later, then." And with that he shut the door.

"Didn't have any holes in him, right?" Old El said, pointing to the nape of his neck.

"The neck's not the only place folks get bit. Best stay on guard," said the hoarse voice.

"At any rate, I only gotta keep patient a little longer. We'll clear everything up in the morning. Okay, let's head back!"

"You know, I don't have a good feeling about this," the old man said in an exhausted tone, sitting on the sofa. "Verenis is playing coy, and there's something more between him and Tupperman than just a loan. And all I can figure is that Toba is in cahoots with the marquis now that he's back. What do you say we go give the pot another stir?"

"Don't bother. You'll just get the runaround again," said the hoarse voice. "But some weird plot's been going on in this castle with your money for certain. Tupperman's loan and Didi's grandmother's too, most likely. Money makes it all happen."

"You got that right. Whether you're Noble or human, money's the foundation the world's built on. You'll see soon enough. Verenis, Tupperman, Thomas, and Toba—I'll have 'em all bowing at my feet after I've plucked 'em like a chicken!" the old man exclaimed, his excitement so great he raised his stout right arm high above his head.

"Dawn is still a long way off," said D. "It's going to be a long, dark night."

A New Creditor

CHAPTER 4

I

The farmer and his wife were utterly terrified. Taking in the girl and the little boy in exchange for a handsome sum hadn't been a problem, but both of the youngsters seemed to have their issues. However, their beautiful harmony had moved the couple, and just as they let their guard down for a minute, there'd been a scuffle with a Noble, and ultimately the children had left. But that was okay, because the couple had been paid more than enough gold.

However, if the Nobility were after those two, that was a different matter. No one could say just when or how the vengeance of the Nobility might be played out on this house. Ultimately, the couple had begun to argue about just which of them had agreed to lodge the children, and just as they were about to come to blows, someone knocked at their door. They were trembling so badly they couldn't move.

"I'm a traveling doctor of Qigong. I should like to rent a room," an elderly voice ventured breathily.

Looking out the peephole, they saw a gray-haired old woman leaning on a cane, hunched over at a right angle and wrapped in layer upon layer of fabric. That seeming fine enough, they invited her in, and she spilled through the doorway almost as if tripped and actually ended up falling flat on the floor.

After downing the brandy she'd asked for in a voice like a death rattle, she looked all around and suddenly stared at the two of them, saying, "You'd be Jean and Melcha Strohoy, wouldn't you?"

"Yes, we are, but . . ."

"Then have a look at this."

She raised her right hand, covered with veins and age spots, and brought it crashing down on the table. At some point, a yellowed parchment had been placed on it. Its surface was covered with rows of uncanny symbols and pictographs from what could only be some ancient alphabet.

"What's this?"

"Here is what it says. *I, Ezra Strohoy, hereby borrow the sum of ten thousand dalas from the Qigong doctor and financier Duchess Dorothea Marlingen. The repayment period, including twenty percent interest per month, is until sundown a year from the date on this contract, and in the event that repayment is delayed, the family of Ezra Strohoy will offer up their blood. This contract will be in effect without limit until repayment is complete or the collateral is expended.*"

On hearing the date at the end of the contract, the farmer bugged his eyes.

"That's over a thousand years old—and a contract with one of my ancestors? You don't really mean to tell me you're Duchess Marlingen . . . ?"

"None other," the old woman replied, letting out a ragged breath. "Due to certain circumstances, I was reduced to dust drifting through the air until today, but I have finally returned. So, I thought I would have you make good on this contract. Fortunately, it appears you still occupy the land owned by your ancestor. That was of immeasurable help."

"It can't be . . . After all this time . . . you want to collect on my ancestor's debt?!"

"This contract is ironclad!" Duchess Marlingen said, striking the table with both hands. The part they struck buckled, as did the couple's nerve. "There's no time limit on it. Now, I'll thank you to pay it back. Ten thousand dalas plus a thousand years' interest comes to two million, four hundred and ten thousand dalas. Can you repay that in full?"

"Wh-where would we get that kind of money?"

The couple looked at each other. Their expressions were already those of the dead.

"Of course you don't have it. Not in a hovel like this," the old lady said, looking all around her. "In which case, I have to take your collateral."

She grinned, and a pair of devilish fangs peeked from behind her purplish lips.

"Damn you!" the farmer's wife cried, as it was she who first got the fight back in her. "You say we've got a tab that's a thousand years old? Fine, I'll pay you back. Here's some precious metal for you!"

Grabbing the almost perfectly square cleaver that sat on the table beside some hard bread, she threw it at the old lady's head. Her aim was true, and it stuck in the woman's little face, splitting it down the middle.

"Grab the stake gun, dear!"

"Uh, yeah!" her husband replied, his wife's actions having finally broken the spell over him, and he dashed to the corner of the living room.

The cleaver that came whistling through the air sank into the back of his head, the force of it knocking the farmer forward in an almost perfectly upright position—leaning forward ever so slightly until he collided with the wall in front of him.

His wife was frozen in her tracks, an unpleasant and incomprehensible attempt at the word "dear" issuing from her throat. More than the death of her husband, the woman's consciousness was effaced by how bizarre this was—the old lady slowly circling around the table as the gaping wound in her forehead swiftly grew narrower, having completely vanished by the time she stood in front of the farmer's wife. Though she'd heard how indestructible the Nobility were, actually seeing it firsthand was a miracle to make your heart shrink.

"You needn't worry. I don't want your blood," the old lady said gently but with certain purpose. "However, I will take something else in exchange. Thank you for your hitherto pointless life."

Until her last instant, the wife had to stare at the tip of the cane that'd been thrust at the base of her throat.

With a scream that shook the spacious laboratory, Matilda jumped up. One of her hands thrust away the lid of the medical check case, which struck the unseen ceiling.

"What's wrong?" Brendon asked, rushing over, at which point the lid finally hit the floor. He looked at the console panel, adding, "We barely made it in time—more or less. What's wrong?"

"She's coming!" Matilda cried as her eyes swept her surroundings, never settling on one point. If someone had opened the woman's body up at that point, undoubtedly her insides would've been pitch black. That was the color of fear.

But what was having this effect on this Noblewoman, normally so haughty and cruel? Or rather, *who*?

"Who are you talking about?" Brendon inquired, his face not surprisingly tinged with a strong admixture of anxiety and tension.

Matilda gave a small but vehement shake of her head. "I do not know. But it is someone who has pursued me for a very long time!"

"Human?"

"I do not know."

"A Noble, surely?"

"Again, I do not know. Ask me no more. I still long for sleep. Even if only to glimpse nightmares. But if she ascertains this location, I shall have no more time for napping."

"Is she so great a threat?"

"Beyond a doubt," Matilda replied with a nod.

Just then, someone pushed against the iron door and entered. It was the marquis.

"How fare you, Father?"

"Such was my question for you. I had come below to fetch some wine and—Has something happened?"

"Not a thing. I merely had a bad dream is all."

"That and nothing more?" the marquis pressed.

"Yes."

"Having lived five centuries, such darkness can honeycomb your mind. Noble or not, such is inescapable. Very well. Continue your enhancements. Tomorrow night is the time. After that—I shall be counting on you!"

Eyes downturned, Matilda nodded, and as the marquis immediately turned around, she said to him, "Father, why did you not undergo the procedures yourself?"

"As you can see, I have marked two millennia of existence. You, only a little more than five centuries—and thus still capable of enduring some hardships, I warrant."

"You changed me into a weapon to lay claim to all the blood in the four Frontiers—that was your hope, was it not?"

"Yes, it is. Toward that end, I need strength enough to make all the other remaining Nobility bow before me. You are that strength. My glorious warrior! My heart swells with pride for you!" the Nobleman said, a smile covering his face.

"That gladdens me," the beaming Matilda replied, but there wasn't a trace of laughter in her eyes.

"Your lordship," Brendon said with some urgency, and the Greater Noble left them.

On confirming he was gone, Matilda gazed at the butler and asked, "Have some 'guards' been prepared, Brendon?"

"Yes, but there are less than ten of them."

"Is that not too few? Think of how many humans I have abducted."

"Yes, but there are limits to human vigor. Changing bones, melting flesh, replacing organs—these are procedures perhaps only one in a thousand can endure."

"Hmmm," Matilda replied, her expression growing bleak. "And what of them—can they slay D?"

"It should prove a good fight. But only if all of them beset him at once."

Shutting her eyes, Matilda chewed his words over one by one. "For one so gorgeous as that, you may be right. How badly does he desire to destroy himself, though?"

"D wishes to destroy himself?" the butler asked incredulously.

"Yes."

"Why is that?"

"Because of how gorgeous he is. All that remains after that is destruction."

Brendon didn't know what to say.

"For those at the pinnacle, there is naught save decline and decay. Such is the law of nature." A desolate shadow skimmed across Matilda's lovely face. "It may well be that the Hunter fights for his own destruction. In which case it would be a mercy to hasten his end. Brendon, I now have another purpose for this body in addition to Father's demands and my own desires."

Brendon couldn't conceal his anxiety at the Noblewoman's boastful laugh of superiority. "Lady Matilda, you must do your very best to avoid engaging the Hunter," he said.

"Oh, and all this time I imagined you feared nothing save me. It surprises me to find you such a coward at heart. Brendon, have you not made me the mightiest warrior in the history of the Nobility?"

"Beyond a doubt," the butler replied with a nod. "But the Hunter is an exception. He has an unearthly air about him unlike that of any Noble I have ever known. It torments not only those around him, but probably himself as well. I should not be surprised if the average Noble would rather die the instant they were born if such were their lot."

Cold sweat rolled down Brendon's cheeks. When he spoke about D, it felt as if he were chanting some forbidden spell.

"Enough. As for your proposal—I shall consider it."

Brendon was barely able to hold back the words *You mustn't do it!* He felt dizzy. A darkness called despair was spreading. In its depths shone the face of a young man of unearthly beauty. Perhaps those who gathered around him would be the first to die for his beauty.

Desperately recovering his footing, Brendon said, "I shall do away with the Hunter myself."

But can I really? he thought, the doubt running him through the heart.

The cries of the nighthawks grew even more intense.

"Shut up!" Old El spat, but they never relented. "We got no souls to give you! Back to the land of the dead with you already!"

"Expectations fill the castle now. The birds are just stating their own," the hoarse voice said, chortling. But there its tone changed, and it asked, "What's this now?"

"Their cries draw nearer," said D.

"What?!"

Two voices cried out in unison.

"Someone without a soul is coming," D continued. "And apparently not just passing by—they're outside the front gate now."

"Hey now," the old man said, pouncing on his bags. "This is what you need at night."

The black bat in his hands spread its wings. Old El threw it out the window. Falling at first, it soon beat its wings and vanished into the darkness. The old man already had a controller in hand with a screen in it, and he took a seat on the sofa with it. All the images the bat's electronic eyes saw were linked from the screen to his own vision, his every nerve in tune with the imitation nerves of the creature. Old El had now become the mechanical bat itself as it flew across the sky.

Looking at the screen, D groaned in his hoarse voice, "Uh-oh. That is one serious old lady. From the look of her, all around her's gotta be swirling with a weird aura. She doesn't look like any acquaintance of the old man."

D alone heard that voice.

"What's she here for?" it continued. "I know, why don't we go out to greet her?"

"Gaaah?!" Old El exclaimed, clutching his abdomen and reeling back.

"Heh heh," the hoarse voice chuckled, "what's the matter, get a bellyache?"

Swiftly growing paler, the old man shook his head. "The second that old hag pointed her cane at me . . . Oof! It was like a punch in the gut."

"A Qigong attack," D said softly, placing his left hand against the old man's solar plexus. Seconds passed, and Old El took a breath, his color returning.

"Shit, that's a weird kind of spell to use. Who is she, and what's she here for?"

"Probably a debt collector, right?" the hoarse voice said, its tone dripping with sarcasm.

"What do you mean by that?" Old El snarled, baring his teeth. "A debt collector? You got a problem with debt collectors? What's wrong with collecting the money you loaned out? It's a commercial transaction done in the light of day for all to see."

"Yeah, I know, I know. Oh, she's knocking on the door. Hey, can you still use that bat of yours?"

"It's shot now. I'll use another one."

"You got more?"

"Yeah, bet you didn't know yours truly had taken in such variety of stuff as collateral."

Exactly one minute later, Old El was back on the sofa, and D was watching his screen from over his shoulder.

II

It was Brendon who came to answer the door.

"I have come because it is clear from the hue and fabric of your raiment that you are a Noble. What is your business?"

While it seemed possible the old lady might flinch at the brusqueness of his response, she was heedless of it, pushing her way inside.

"Hey!" the butler cried.

The tip of the cane flashed up at the hand that sought to stop her. Although it only appeared to touch him gently, the butler clutched the limb as he dropped to one knee. Pain had exploded through his entire body.

"Oh, she's good," Old El remarked, his eyes aglitter. "That's a Qigong attack. But the speed of her cane—did you even see it?"

There was no reply. D remained gazing at the screen.

The butler didn't say a word, merely trembling as the old lady said to him, "Matilda Verenis is here, isn't she? Tell her Duchess Dorothea Marlingen has come across the ages to collect on her debt."

The low-ceilinged great hall was filled by dignity and a freezing aura.

"Kindly wait for the time being," Brendon said, and choking back a scream he got to his feet before leaving through the same doorway that had brought him there.

The old lady—Dorothea Marlingen—glanced down at the floor. Her eyes met D's. Or perhaps it would've been better to say they met Old El's. A smile adorned her face, which seemed ready to shed its wrinkled skin at any second, and she cooed, "Oh, look at that cute little black kitty. What a coincidence. I love cats. Come here."

The old lady's hands filled both men's field of view. In a second, they were replaced by her face. She'd picked up the cat. She had yellowed eyes that peeked from between thick eyelids, plenty of teeth missing, and horribly dried skin—yet she also had the undeniable grace of a Noblewoman.

"I really wish I could just set you down again," the old lady said, gently stroking the cat's nose. "But, you see, I really hate bats and all their friends!"

The instant he realized she'd lifted it up again, Old El clutched at his head. The impact of being dashed against the floor had just rocked it. It wasn't the real thing. However, Old El had become one with the spy gadget, and the effect was not unlike a hypnotic suggestion.

"Trashed it completely, eh?" D's left hand groaned.

"No," said D.

"Huh?" his left hand exclaimed in surprise when it was turned toward the screen.

It still had a picture. Although diagonal lines occasionally rolled through the image, the two eyes were looking up at Dorothea Marlingen.

"She didn't use Qigong—she's underestimated us."

Before the hoarse voice could finish saying that, Brendon returned. Marquis Verenis was with him.

"Your name is one we have heard before. It would seem you have business with my daughter. I shall entertain you in the living room."

"Fine. A hall like this without any chairs is hard for the elderly, you know."

The marquis walked out, and Dorothea followed after him. Halting after five steps, she looked down at her viewers and blew a kiss.

"Bye-bye, kitty. And this time, it's for good."

The tip of her cane rose.

Old El shut his eyes and cradled his head again, while D folded down the black screen.

"So, she was wise to us all along, eh? In this case, we just can't go without listening in! There's something going on with her. I'll go," the left hand volunteered.

Just then, someone knocked at the door.

"Who is it?" Old El asked, still clutching his head, his tone the very epitome of displeasure.

"It's me—Tupperman."

The old man opened the door, then closed it again.

The first thing out of the puppet master's mouth were the words, "Somebody interesting has shown up, huh?"

After looking cheerfully at the other two, he stared at the door. "You saw her?"

"Of course I did. You're not the only one who knows a thing or two about peeping."

"It ain't peeping," Old El said. "It's surveillance."

"Call it what you will. I rigged something up as well."

The old man was finally reminded what this man's stock in trade was.

"Please, leave this to me. I'll keep an eye on things the whole time."

"You don't think they'll find it?"

"They found yours, didn't they? Mine was fine."

The old man turned away in a snit.

"I'm following after them even now. Have a look at that screen, if you will," Tupperman told them. He held out his right hand, and an image of the three people going down a corridor appeared in the air about a foot in front of his face.

"I see. That's a lot newer than what he had," the hoarse voice remarked.

"Shut up," the old man said, this time baring his teeth. "Mine was a cat, but what's yours?"

"A rat."

"Why are you telling us this?" D inquired.

"Huh?" the puppet master replied, his mouth dropping open more from D's beauty than what the Hunter was asking.

"Information about that Noblewoman could have considerable value," D continued. "You didn't think to keep it all to yourself?"

"That's a crazy thing to say," Tupperman said, shaking his head from side to side to dislodge the image of D. "Are you trying to say I'd have been better served keeping it to myself rather than sharing it? I consider myself a compatriot in the very same boat as the rest of you. And that being the case—"

"The woman said she wants to see the girl I fought. That made you anxious."

"I'll thank you not to jump to conclusions like that," Tupperman replied, his whole body stiffening, bracing for a quarrel. "I don't know the young lady of the house. Though I've met with the marquis, not once did I meet his daughter. I knew he had one, and that she was incredibly rotund—according to rumors. I didn't even want to see her. Still, there's a dictum regarding women."

"You thought you'd bring us information so we could destroy that Noblewoman—or am I wrong?"

"Th-that's not true at all!"

"Hey, the two bigwigs are just about set to get down to brass tacks!" the old man informed them, as he'd been watching the broadcast in midair.

Tupperman and D turned their eyes toward the same scene.

"You say you are Duchess Dorothea Marlingen, and indeed, I have heard that she vanished without a trace at the height of her beauty about four millennia ago," the marquis said with a healthy dollop of sarcasm.

To this, the duchess replied menacingly, "Hmph, well, pardon me. Oh, I certainly did disappear. And ultimately I ended up with a body that shows my age. And it's all your daughter's fault."

"Matilda's? Why, that is utterly—" the marquis protested, his expression seeming to ask *What on earth do you mean?*

"Do you know a Noblewoman by the name of Desiree Penzolton?"

Thinking briefly, Marquis Verenis replied, "I recall hearing she was in the northern Frontier under the great Lord Greylancer, but that she soon enough earned his displeasure and was banished. That was a good four millennia ago."

"Four thousand, one hundred and two years ago," the duchess said pedantically. "She fled to the western Frontier, where she proceeded to ensnare a shameless Noble named Duke Riatro Marlingen. My husband."

The marquis fell silent, and Old El looked at D. The financier's expression was like he'd been struck by fate. There was something in the old Noblewoman's brusque tone that could sway the hearts of those who heard her.

"When a cunning and evil woman like that gets involved with a far-from-worldly boy, well, I suppose you can imagine what happens. After terrible mismanagement, the Central Government confiscated our lands and our property on Pluto, and Riatro was ultimately sentenced to death. But you see, that stupid husband of mine had even gone so far as to borrow money from human loan sharks to support her."

"Oops," Old El remarked, the wry grin on his face beggaring description.

"That is quite an ordeal," the marquis remarked, a look of disgust on his face. "But what has this to do with my daughter?"

"Hear me out to the very end," said the duchess, draining the glass of wine the marquis had offered her and turning the glass upside down. "A refill, if you please—yes, thank you. The only things that idiot husband of mine was good at were choosing wine and pouring it. In return, he was utterly lacking in common sense, and in the end he even tried to steal my jewelry. There were Garamon diamonds that'd come from our property on Pluto, something not even the Nobility's element conversion technology could produce. They must've been worth a hundred million dalas a gram. When I caught him in the act of stealing them, well, I laid down the law. 'I have no intention of giving my precious jewels to the likes of your whore,' I told him. 'If you want them, write me an IOU for them.' I thought he'd back down, but the damned fool put pen to paper. He agreed to borrow ten quadrillion dalas worth of jewels. With one year to repay it. I demanded collateral. That's simply basic moneylending. And what do you suppose he offered me?"

"I haven't the faintest idea."

"Not a clue."

"Damned if I know."

Those were the respective replies by the marquis, Old El, and the Hunter's left hand.

Gulping down half of a fresh glass of wine in one swig, the duchess continued, "Desiree Penzolton—his mistress."

Here, the strangest silence filled both the hall and the Hunter's room.

"The collateral on the money he was borrowing for his mistress was his mistress—I couldn't comprehend that at all. I thought he was trying to curry favor with me. He was a miserable enough man he might try it. But when it all ultimately collapsed, I went to his mistress to get my money back. However, it seemed she, too, had succumbed to despair. She suddenly drove a rough wooden stake through my heart from behind me, then staked herself as well."

It was a common enough story in the human world, too. On hearing it, a Noble's heart wouldn't be moved even a hair, but when the story involved their own domain, it wasn't surprising that it seeped into their bones, and a strange sense of emotion lingered about the marquis as he listened to her.

"Fortunately, the wound was the barest fraction of an inch shy of being fatal, so my life was spared, though when I came back some two weeks later, my face and body were as you see them now. Nothing I've tried can do anything about that. Of course, his mistress ran the stake right through the center of her own heart and was reduced to dust. But I couldn't rest with them running out on that debt. Think of it—this woman owes me ten quadrillion dalas. And those who are destroyed are reincarnated. So, I decided to wait until then, and then collect on the loan."

Crossing his arms, Marquis Verenis said with considerable admiration, "A grandiose plan, indeed."

Old El let out a deep breath.

"Now there's some tenacity," said the left hand, sounding kind of impressed.

Unfolding his arms, the marquis leaned forward and said, "You mean to say that my daughter, Matilda, is—"

The old woman nodded. "It was five hundred years ago that a certain prophet told me she'd been reincarnated, and I've been searching ever since. I finally went to Stephan Rye, said to be the greatest astrologer in the human and Noble worlds combined, and he was finally able to give me what I've wanted for four thousand years. You probably think this is a false accusation against your daughter. Your daughter, Matilda Verenis, is my idiot of a husband's tramp, Desiree Penzolton. Now, will you make good on that contract?"

III

"But, this is all so . . ." the marquis protested quite naturally.

"Can't say as I blame him. It's a real bolt out of the blue," Old El remarked sympathetically.

"You like talking out of both sides of your mouth, don't you? Trying to be the good guy just when it suits you," the Hunter's left hand spat.

"Money again," said D, the words slipping out uncharacteristically. He must've truly been disgusted by the situation. "Seems there's no difference between humans and Nobles there."

"True enough. After all, money makes the world go round. My father was a good-for-nothing traveling salesman, though he descended from a money lender with an iron will. Seems my ancestor made a ridiculous fortune out in the northern Frontier by helping both the Nobility and the OSB with their finances. And I aim to return our bloodline to that heyday," the old man declared excitedly, raising his fist high once more.

"Well, I'll be," said D.

"Oh, finally somebody else who gets me, eh? I'm a lucky soul to have a reasonable fella like you around, especially one who's such a good bodyguard. Huzzah!"

But no sooner had Old El raised both arms than Tupperman shushed him.

All eyes focused on the screen.

"I wonder which of us has time on their side?" said the marquis. "My daughter's past life may have been as you've described, but is it not preposterous to ask that she now honor that debt?"

What the Nobleman said made sense, but the old lady just smiled. From her threadbare bag she pulled a discolored and dried piece of parchment that had apparently been around for many years.

"These are ancient characters, but I'm sure someone like you can read them. This contract from your daughter's past life says it can be enforced even if she's reincarnated—it's all right here in writing. Or do we need to take this all the way to a notary public's office for the House of Lords or a court of law?"

Marquis Verenis groaned and closed his eyes. He was recalling the verdict in a similar case. Nobles recognized their connection to their past lives. And that applied to legal matters as well. If it went to trial, he had no chance of winning.

"At any rate, would you at least let me meet your daughter? We'll discuss it after she recovers her memories of her previous existence."

"Please give me a little time," said the marquis. "I must explain the situation to my daughter and get her consent, such as it is."

"You're not thinking to make tracks in the meantime, are you? Of course, no matter where you go, I'll run you down as long as you live."

The marquis laughed. "Ha, I would never—at any rate, please wait."

Rising with composure, Verenis vanished from the far end of the room, driving Brendon ahead of him. The butler was dragging one leg.

"Okay, now what's the old lady gonna do now that she's all by her lonesome?" Old El mused, his eyes narrowing with interest.

"What in the—?!" Tupperman exclaimed, his lower lip curling.

The old woman had stood up, put her hands on her hips, and had now begun twisting her upper body from side to side.

"Is this some sort of witchcraft?" Tupperman inquired, his eyes ablaze with curiosity. "She's chanting something. Oh, it's witchcraft, without a doubt."

Even Old El nodded his agreement, his features tense.

"No, it isn't," said D.

"What is it, then?"

"Listen carefully. That's *ichiniisanshi* she said."

"You're right. Oh, now she's twisted the other way, and again, *ichiniisanshi*."

"So, it's witchcraft after all, isn't it?"

"It's calisthenics," D said softly.

They were all dumbfounded.

"Follow the marquis," said D, but the screen immediately went completely white.

With a bitter look, Tupperman said, "We've been jammed. As I expected, the depths of the castle will be a problem." He glared at the screen.

"Nothing we can do about that," Old El remarked. "Go back to the old lady."

"Roger that. Huh? She's not there!"

The hall was vacant.

"Where the hell's she got to? Hey, D—?!" the old man said, turning, but just then he noticed that the gorgeous young man had also disappeared.

Duchess Dorothea Marlingen had decided to slip through the walls and do some sightseeing in the castle. That wasn't to say that it was possible for her to shift into another dimension. Standing in front of the wall, she put the tip of her cane against it. She then moved forward, and the stone wall buckled in like it was made of vinyl, the tip of her cane finally piercing it, at which point she was sucked into the interior of the stone. All she had to do then was move forward, and she took a few steps through the stone as if she were underwater, then passed through the opposite side. As far as resistance went, it was like wading through water.

She gave off an air that could change the substance of these enormous stones—or perhaps it would be better to call it her supernatural Qigong?

She stepped into the corridor. Passing through another wall, she entered a different chamber.

"In a castle laid out like this one, it should be about here," she said, jabbing her cane into the floor.

The surface of the floor sank like a mortar, swallowing up the old lady in a bizarre manner that called to mind an ant-lion pit.

Below her was another chamber. Duchess Marlingen came down from the ceiling. Or rather, she fell. It was a good thirty feet high. Slamming against the ground, her body was caught by the floor, which had become supple. Pulling the cane she'd stuck into it back out again, the old lady got to her feet.

"Well, I'll be."

A number of shadowy figures had appeared from the depths of the chamber and were drawing closer. Eight of them, male and female—and they were dressed like ordinary townspeople and villagers. All had bows or stakes or swords in hand, but more than that, it was the tips of fangs peeking from their tightly pursed lips that made their true nature clear.

"So, you'd get rough with an old woman like me? Well, you look to be more than just Noble wannabes. Did the marquis put you up to this?"

Instead of answering, the shadowy figures kicked off the ground en masse. They swung their weapons in midair. An ax and a stake sank into the top of the old lady's head and her chest, respectively. But no one had seen the tip of the wooden cane touch the end of their owner's right foot a split second before they made contact. Ax and stake alike bounced off her. It wasn't that the old lady's body had been transformed into something else. Rather, their steel had been changed into wax.

The wooden cane swept through the farmer who'd landed and the bartender who was still in midair. They split in two. They hadn't been cut. They were torn apart. And not a drop of blood spilled from the upper or lower halves of them that rolled across the floor.

Not surprisingly, the remaining attackers stopped in their tracks, and some of them even backed away.

"Put a scare into you, did I? By the look of things, you're humans who've undergone surgical upgrades, but stuff like that's been going on since my great-grandmother was a little girl. Better to not even try anymore, since they always fail, and the failures bust into human villages and cause a big ruckus, but it seems things go a little better. Well, have at me, anyway," Duchess Marlingen told them. "What, you're not coming? In that case, I'll come to you!" She then started counting them off, saying, "So, six of you left? What a pain. I'll try a proxy war."

The old lady drew a winged creature on the floor with the tip of her cane. All she did was accurately trace the outline, but the instant she took her cane away, a cloud of hundreds of bats exploded from that spot to assail the assassins. And they weren't ordinary bats. Their eyes gave off a vermilion glow, and every tooth in their heads was a fang. The biological weapons bit into the assassins' throats and faces, and began greedily sucking their blood.

"Vampire bats made from her Qi? Now, that is quite an accomplishment. Little wonder she has made it to such a ripe old age!"

"I would say that is merely the tip of the iceberg for someone who showed up demanding payment on a debt from four thousand years ago. Could it be that the lot of them shall meet their end without achieving anything?"

"Impossible."

However, the assassins were covered in blood. The bats that'd been made from the old woman's Qi were unhindered by their swords and spears. Every wound promptly closed, each severed piece and the one that'd lost it regenerated, so that one bat literally became two and two became four, swelling their ranks.

"Oh, such a waste," Duchess Marlingen laughed. "How many hundreds of millions of dalas did it take to make each one of you? Rather than spending so much, it would've been much cheaper to just come clean and pay me what I'm owed. Nobles still don't understand economics, do they? Well, I guess that's because they've still got the whole ageless and undying thing working for them."

Every living creature's actions are guided by "survival instincts." It's said that culture developed to fill that limited lifespan. And economic activity was a part of that. So, what would happen if that guiding principle were to vanish? At the very least, economic activity between Nobles didn't exist. This was due to the fact that they didn't need to labor or reap those benefits in order to live. Dealing with human beings was the sole exception to that.

When the Nobility took the stuff of life from the living, it was a special situation, and they needed money for that. In general, when Nobles became infatuated with humans, they inevitably needed someone to get information on a human if that person went into hiding, and money talks.

However, Nobles being Nobles, their use of money was rather cavalier from a human standpoint. It was to that the old lady was referring. Nonetheless, the chamber was stained red, as if to challenge economic principles.

One of the assassins trembled bodily, as if quavering, and became a figure of blistering heat. Perhaps that, too, was part of their weaponization, because he and his compatriots could radiate more than ten thousand degrees of heat from their bodies without any ill effects to themselves. Creatures of Qi or not, the bats had substance, so they were forced to comply with the laws of the physical world. In the blink of an eye the bats had been burnt away, not a single accursed cell of theirs remaining.

The flames assailed the duchess. The instant they touched her withered form, the flames stopped flickering. Maintaining the same color and shape, they had been turned into vermilion-hued crystals.

A swipe of the old lady's cane scattered thousands of autumn leaves across the floor.

"That was—really something."

"She is quite formidable. Better you should abandon Father's soldier conversions, pointless waste that they are, and study her powers instead. Have them retreat. I am what the woman seeks. Perhaps I shall go strike her down."

"You mustn't. If anything were to happen to you, our plans would all be for naught. What in the—?!"

"What is this?"

"Stand back," said a voice heard not only by the assassins but by the old lady as well. The new figure who appeared from the depths of the darkness approached Duchess Marlingen with an agile gait. There was something beastly about his voice.

It was Julas-Han Toba.

Fate of the Sacrifice

CHAPTER 5

I

"Quite a bit of pep you've got for an old bird," Toba said, a smile on his face. "You know, I like an old lady with some spirit to her. Killed mom and dad with my own two hands, but my granny was always good to me. That's why I cried a river when she died. Haven't cried since, though."

"My, how you blather on about yourself. If that's how you feel, be so good as to give me a hand here," said the duchess.

"It pains me to say it, but I can't do that, either. That'd just end with me in tears again."

"That's a fine way you have of honoring your grandmother!" the old lady scolded him. And just as she did, Toba stopped in his tracks.

Reaching both hands behind his back, he swung them forward again almost perfectly in unison. Two masses of dark brown fur flew at the old woman. It became clear that their half dozen stubby legs were only for ground use the instant broad wings spread from their backs. Gliding through the air for a heartbeat, the two of them then climbed steeply and were about to pass over Duchess Marlingen's head when they dropped something the same color as their bodies.

The old lady and her surroundings were bleached white. Glittering beads had filled the world. Surprisingly enough, the two climbing creatures were caught up in the silvery white waves. Losing speed, they began a steep dive, their bodies breaking into thousands of pieces and scattering in all directions.

"Ice demon eggs from the northern Frontier," Toba told her in a low tone that was almost a groan as he backed away, "The least I can do is give you a death that's like dropping off to sleep. Forgive me for not doing more, won't you?"

The white cryosphere that had halted suddenly faded before his very eyes.

"It can't be!" Toba exclaimed, tepid air blasting his face.

The old lady stood in her original position, staring at Toba.

"Did you think that half-hearted effort would slay me, big talker? If you like to fancy yourself some friend of the aged, do me a favor and die right here and now!"

Her cane rose. Toba was sent flying without a word, landing on the stone floor some thirty feet to his rear and sliding on his back. He writhed around, letting out unintelligible cries of pain.

"Serves you right," the old lady told him, but at the same time she collapsed. Her ordinarily pale face was nearly as white as the snow. For the enormous cost of passing through stone walls, transforming weapons, and dispersing an atmosphere that was nearly at absolute zero had come due.

It was Toba that got to his feet first. Covered in sweat, his face was nearly a death mask, looking like he'd aged a century all at once. He was coughing violently, retching, and wheezing for air as he gave the command, "Kill her!"

On seeing the six remaining assassins charge at Duchess Marlingen in all their blood-stained glory, Toba looked down and retched again. He knew the only reason he'd gotten off this lightly was because the old lady had been drained of her strength. His sense of horror still hadn't faded.

A scream shook his eardrums. And more than just one—at which point he looked up, and his half dozen underlings were all lying on the floor.

"D?!"

Indeed, it was none other than D who stood in front of the old lady, who lay on the floor just like Toba's compatriots.

"How did you . . . get here?" the duchess inquired, her words creeping along the floor.

"I followed you," D replied.

Once that was lodged in her head, she said, "And the stone . . . you passed right through it? Who could do that? Just who are you . . . ?"

"Don't you remember?"

"What?"

"I don't recall exactly when it was, but we met in the village of Garcia," said D.

"Huh?" The agony vanished from the old woman's face.

"An enemy had hit me with a bacterial attack and I was down. On the road."

The old lady sifted back through her memories, and recognition dawned on her face.

"Now that you mention it . . . It was you . . . that night . . . lying there in the darkness? As I recall . . . I tossed you a one dalas coin . . . and told you, 'That'll cover your funeral' . . ."

There was a hard clink on the floor by Duchess Marlingen's face. It was a ten-dalas coin.

"I've paid you back."

D had gone over to Toba.

The beastmaster barely got to his feet.

"We meet again," he said, his voice sounding as close to death as he looked.

"Why'd you come back?" asked D.

"We're weapons. For the lord of the castle to claim all the human blood on the Frontier as his own. It's a hell of a thing, though. Didn't think we'd all be killed so damned easily!"

"You're after her?"

"That's what we were told, at any rate. If it's okay with you, hold off a little. Then we'll be able to fight on an equal footing."

"Don't fall for that," said the old lady. "Just don't . . . Chop his head off . . . here and now."

D stood where he was.

"I'd heard you were ten thousand times as heartless as any Noble . . . but . . . you have my thanks!"

Toba stood there. Reaching into his coat with his left hand, he tossed something down at D's feet. A small bag that made a metallic jingle.

"That's the hundred thousand dalas I borrowed from Old El. I fleeced it out of the marquis as payment for undergoing the procedure. Pay the old man for me."

"Give it to him yourself," the Hunter replied.

Toba smiled. If they fought, D was certain to win. And D was the only one who didn't recognize that.

"I'll never forget your name or your face," he said, his smile never faltering. "And my kitty would like to say thanks, too!"

Toba's right hand touched the breast of his coat.

D's body dipped, and there was a flash of stark light. It intersected the black light shooting out in midair, forming a black and white cross.

Lopping off Toba's head with the return stroke, D turned toward the old lady.

An enormous cat-like beast had one of its forepaws pressed to the nape of Duchess Marlingen's neck.

"Bad kitty," the Hunter's left hand groaned.

Toba's pet cat radiated an aura of hatred toward D from its massive form, now nearly ten feet long. It gnashed its fully exposed fangs. The old lady groaned. The giant cat raised its other forepaw and made a horizontal swipe with it. And as it did, its weight was on her. The gesture was telling the Hunter to drop his sword.

"Think we can do that?" the left hand said with apparent interest.

D seemed to throw his sword down as hard as he could. It hit the floor, and just as planned the blade and hilt took the impact at exactly the right angle, flying straight at the gigantic cat. Changing direction in midair, the blade sliced off the paw that pinned the duchess, and then, as if this too had been planned, it sank into the creature's right rear leg. When it raised its head to howl with pain, a rough wooden needle went right through its windpipe and out the other side without a sound.

The huge beast leapt. Its remaining forepaw made a horizontal swipe at D. Narrowly dodging it, the Hunter moved over in front of the old lady and gazed at the gigantic cat. It had collapsed on top of Toba's corpse. And it looked as if it were hugging him. Letting out a single breath, it then moved no more.

D shifted his gaze to the duchess.

"Here," she said, extending a wrinkled hand. "Young fellas these days aren't particularly thoughtful, are you? Hurry up and give me a little help here."

"Are you pressing on?"

"Don't be ridiculous. I'm so run down I've got one foot in the grave. I'm heading back."

D turned toward the far end of the corridor.

The marquis and Brendon had just rushed in.

"I was wondering where you might have gone. Oh, however did you come to be in such a state?" Marquis Verenis asked, the color draining from his complexion.

"Well," the duchess replied, "I got myself into a fine mess when I took it upon myself to wander around a bit. We old folks are more curious than you'd think. This handsome young man and I got a little rough in here. I'm afraid I must apologize for putting down your servants."

"Yes, they were rather valued retainers."

"How can I make it up to you?"

"Well, consider my daughter's debt settled."

"Spare me. I'm supposed to write off ten quadrillion dalas for killing these nine grubby servants? You're dreaming. You'd be lucky to get ten thousand dalas for the nine of them in total."

"A hundred million dalas."

"What?" the old woman exclaimed, turning to see the speaker. Before her, D stood like an ice sculpture.

"Pay him," the Hunter said.

"Just a minute, you—" There, the old lady's voice failed her. Every bone in her body was telling her she'd lost her drive. "Your eyes . . . Only once have I seen their like . . . As if they were peering into a fate impossibly dark and deep . . . Knowing full well what awaits . . . without sadness or fear . . . Accepting that fate just as it is . . . But never . . . never at anyone's beck and call . . . Deeper and darker than the darkness into which they peer . . . And yet . . . oh, why must they be so clear and penetrating?"

Duchess Marlingen's knees buckled. She stood there, desperately clinging to the cane to support her aged frame.

"Very well . . . A hundred million dalas it is . . . I'd pay anything . . . any price named by a man . . . with eyes like those . . . like *the great one's* . . . Who could resist?"

It was the marquis and Brendon who furrowed their brows at that.

"Duchess . . . just who do you mean . . . by *the great one*? You don't mean to say . . ."

There was no reply. The old lady wasn't looking at anyone. Her interest was focused on what she had to do now. Her trembling right hand removed the ring she wore on the ring finger of her left hand. A large red jewel glittered on it. It was blindingly brilliant. It snagged on her knuckle, but she pulled it off without the slightest hesitation.

Unfazed by the torn flesh and the blood seeping out, the duchess tossed the ring to the marquis.

"Take that . . . And, if you would . . . have a room readied for me, so I can rest. Negotiations with your daughter . . . will come after that."

"Good enough," Marquis Verenis said with a nod, having finally regained his composure. Turning to Brendon, he ordered him, "Prepare a room."

The man acknowledged his command and went to make good on it, but from behind him the old lady said, "I'm going, too, so kindly

show me the way. Oh, what a thing to see in the castle of an impoverished bumpkin of a Noble . . . I wonder if I'll even . . . live to see
tomorrow's dusk . . ."

II

"You fools!"

Slaps reverberated from the cheeks of Brendon and Matilda once
the lord and his butler had returned to the lab where the Noblewoman
had remained. Marquis Verenis had removed his still-sheathed sword,
lashing out with lightning speed. Brendon's head had turned completely around, and Matilda's cheek had split open.

"What are you doing, Father?" Matilda asked, pressing down on
the wound. Bright blood dripped from it. Her tongue snaked out
and licked it off.

"Master, you mustn't raise your hand against your daughter," Brendon
added quickly. His head turned back toward the front with a sound
like grinding gears.

"Idiots," said the marquis, trembling from head to toe, his face pale
with anger. "What could that ancient crone do? Brendon, I believe
I told you to pretend you saw nothing!"

"It was I that gave the order to dispose of her," Matilda stated,
staring coolly at her father.

"Why?"

"As a test of the humans you reconfigured, Father, and for a glimpse
at the power of this woman who has business with my past self. I
wished to see just how tenacious she was after spending five centuries
searching for me. And, lastly—"

"Lastly what?"

"—it was about me."

The marquis didn't know what to say to that.

"I wished to see how I have been changed in accordance with your
will, Father. However, the opportunity did not present itself."

"Matilda."

"That is for the best, though," his lovely daughter continued, donning a smile that made him wonder if anything in the world could seem quite as terrifying. "Though I am well aware I am but a tool for fulfilling your lust for blood, Father, three foes have come to take your measure before we can do that."

Marquis Verenis softly muttered some figures to himself and nodded, but didn't fail to furrow his brow.

"Sooner or later, all of them will have to die both for your sake, Father, and my own. It will prove the perfect opportunity to test the power the conversion has given me."

"You have a future. The road ahead is one you must walk with me. And until that day comes, I cannot allow you to take such risks."

"Which is to say it would never do for me to die before I have served your purposes?"

"Matilda."

"Very well. However, all your other reconstructed humans have been laid to waste. There is no one save myself to stand against those three."

"There is me," the marquis replied.

"Oh, how could I forget!" she said, opening her eyes as wide as they would go in what could be taken as either a genuine show of surprise or mere mockery. "I hadn't realized that. Well, after I have been destroyed, there is still you, Father, which entirely puts my mind at ease."

"What are you saying? Just watch me get rid of the four pests here in our castle. All you need do is stay out of trouble."

Matilda smiled mysteriously. "Very well. I leave it in your hands, Father. I shall be waiting here quietly."

The look on her face and that in her eyes were so cold it hardly seemed possible from his own daughter, and it left the marquis sullen-faced.

Duchess Marlingen was probably at her noisiest close to death. With Brendon's guidance and both D's arm and her cane for support the old lady reached her room, where she fell at length on the bed and began a litany of complaints.

"My lower back is killing me. Rub it for me."

"You know, these kneecaps of mine haven't been right the last five hundred years."

"I used too much of my Qi. I'm dying, I tell you. Dying!"

When D placed his left hand against her, she remarked, "Oh, what's this, now? The stiffness in my shoulders and my lumbago both vanished, just like that! What an incredible technique you have there, eh? It's a miracle! A veritable miracle."

Now she was so raucous about how impressed she was that D stepped outside. It couldn't do any harm to ignore her for a while.

"I'm surprised she came here to collect!" Old El said to D when the Hunter returned, a troubled look on the financier's face.

"Given the situation, why don't we try to get along with her?" Tupperman suggested. "Old or not, she's a fully functioning Noble. Since our aims are the same, we could always join forces, couldn't we?"

"I leave that to you," said D.

"What?"

"Sounds good to me," Old El said, clapping his hands together. "Go get it done."

"Wait just a minute. None of this has anything to do with me!"

"You're here, so you're in the same boat with the rest of us. Nobody here can say they ain't involved."

"That's right. Plus, you've got the most upstanding face of the lot of 'em," the hoarse voice remarked with apparent pleasure. "Go offer the old lady an olive branch. Sleep with her if need be."

"P-p-please, send someone else," Tupperman replied, trembling.

"No, you're going. And if you do it, I'll knock ten thousand dalas off what you owe me."

"Make it twenty."

"Fifteen," Old El countered.

"Good enough."

"Oh, and I need you to leave your surveillance unit here. Can't have you spying on us, after all."

"You think I, of all people, would do something like that?" said the puppet master.

"Yeah, more than anybody."

"What's it worth to you?"

"Thirty."

"Fifty."

"Forty."

"You've got a deal."

Setting down a small surveillance unit, Tupperman headed off.

"It's a bitter pill to swallow, but hard knocks in your youth is like money in the bank," remarked the smirking old man.

"That's a pack of lies," said the hoarse voice. "All hard knocks do is leave a human filled with hatred and resentment. You suffer a hundred pains and not profit once. It's just poison, plain and simple. Oh, I can hear him now!"

Old El got up from his chair. Putting his ear to the wall that divided the old lady's room from his own, he got a look of terrible amusement on his face.

"Oh, she's saying how her shoulders ache and telling him to rub 'em," the financier whispered to D. "He's started doing it. 'Ow, that hurts. You're miserable at this.' She belted him and he's running around like crazy," the old man chortled. "'Help me! Help me!' he's saying. What a loser."

"The old lady's got a lot of pep," remarked the Hunter's left hand.

There was something tranquil about D's expression.

Now Old El was clutching his belly. "He ran out!" he guffawed. "The damned puppet master ran out of there. So fast you'd think his freaking tail was on fire—oh, and she went after him like a shot. Ha ha haa!"

From an altitude of more than fifteen hundred feet, it was difficult to describe the world below as anything but black. Still, tiny lights were visible here and there even though there was the danger they might advertise their habitations to the Nobility and supernatural creatures. They were undoubtedly the lamps of watchtowers that safeguarded the villagers' peaceful sleep or lights from a comparatively placid region.

In the cramped room they'd been given, Lydia felt her eyelids growing a little heavier as she looked at the face of the slumbering Didi, but she was strangely on edge and didn't feel sleepy. She was ready to try counting sheep when there was a knock at the door.

"Who is it?"

"The landlord," replied Galkis Thomas, head of the Quetzalcoatl flying bandits.

"What do you want?"

"I've got some wine I picked up in the Capital. How about a nightcap?"

"You'll wake up the kid."

"In that case, how about in my room?"

"I'll pass," said the girl.

"Okay, I'll just drink here, then. And you'll be in there. Sharing a drink through the door sounds pretty chic."

"Yeah, let's do that," Lydia said, going over to the door. "Pour me a glass."

"As you wish," Thomas replied, a wry humor mixed with his words.

"I'll open the door a crack. But if you come in any further than you need to, I'll shoot you!"

She had a repeating rifle she'd been given for self-protection when they were brought up to the airship.

"Yeah, yeah, I know."

Thomas kept his promise.

Closing the door and raising her glass, Lydia downed a mouthful. She'd started drinking to stave off the cold, but apparently she had a talent for it, and she'd quickly become a heavy drinker who could down it by the barrel. Her father had been no lightweight, but when he tried to keep pace with Lydia, he'd be out like a light in less than ten minutes.

"You can hold your own," the man told her, and that didn't bother her, but now, more than fifteen hundred feet off the ground with the mellow aroma of wine around her, the arrival of that first mouthful in her belly made her keenly aware that she was a drunkard.

"How is it?"

"Delicious," she replied in all honesty.

"Don't you wanna drink face to face?"

"No, thanks."

"Nothing ruins a body more than a woman's stubbornness, you know."

"I'll have you know my father was killed by one of your men. Who'd drink with you after that?"

"Really?"

After she told him the day and time as well as the name of the road where D and Old El had saved her, Thomas's voice was tinged with anger. "I was almost two hundred miles east when that happened. The guy who attacked you was a son of a bitch we kicked out for all the rotten shit he pulled."

"And bandits are in a position to judge sons of bitches and rotten shit?" the girl asked.

"Don't put it like that. Say what you will, but we've got a set way of doing things. We hardly ever kill anybody, and don't burn down towns or villages nearly as often as rumors make out. Hell, the only news that spreads on the Frontier is showy, evil stuff."

"You're making excuses for killing people and burning towns and villages! That's the stupidest thing ever."

"Still, hear me out. I'm sorry about what happened to you. C'mon, let me apologize to you in person"

"Screw your apology."

Her sparring partner fell silent.

Lydia questioned how she could even talk so casually with those responsible for her father's death. Though she had a down-to-earth character, life on the Frontier, where you witnessed human life and death on a daily basis, played a large part, too. For humans' most

profound and philosophical object was the world they had utter confidence in but never gave much thought to at all. On the Frontier, humans had to stand in the depths of hatred.

Humans.

Lydia got up. Undoing the lock without hesitation, she turned the door knob.

"Oof!"

Thomas fell flat on his back. Apparently he'd been leaning against the door. Ass over elbows, he looked up at Lydia. His cheeks were flushed. He didn't appear to be much of a drinker.

"Damn, you sure are sexy, you know that?" he said. "You look like somebody else entirely!"

"You like me?" Lydia said, aware of how terribly low her voice was.

"Yeah. You're great. Hey, give me a drink mouth-to-mouth."

"Sure!"

Emptying the contents of the glass she still had, Lydia planted her knees to either side of Thomas's head and used one hand to raise his upper body.

"Wow, you're freaking strong!"

"That's because I'm a country girl."

"Still, I don't know, your eyes are kinda red."

"Are my teeth pointed now, too?"

"Now that you mention it, a little, yeah. But you sure can talk well for somebody with a mouth full of booze."

"That's my special talent."

Lydia brought her own paler-than-usual countenance closer to the man's rough but still refreshing face. Their lips met without any emotion. Thomas's Adam's apple bobbed up and down as he swallowed the wine.

Pulling her strangely red lips away from his, Lydia pressed them against the nape of Thomas's neck. But the sudden roar of a klaxon pulled the two of them apart.

III

"Get in your room," Thomas told the girl, getting back to his feet. Pressing the trigger of a small pneumatic bow attached to his right arm, he loaded an iron arrow into the firing position.

The corridor branched off to the left and right at either end. Two members of Thomas's gang came flying in from the left side, hitting the floor face first—well, more like belly first, since they had no heads. What they did have was buckets of blood to spray everywhere.

Marquis Verenis and Brendon suddenly loomed there. From his hands, the marquis dangled a horrific cargo. A pair of severed heads dripping gore. Most likely they belonged to the corpses twitching at his feet.

There was the sound of footsteps to the rear of the marquis. The door across the corridor opened, and men leapt out with weapons in hand.

"Hold up!" Thomas cried, stopping them. Not a trace of drunkenness had remained on his face when he'd gotten up. "Marquis, what brings you here unannounced and uninvited?"

"I have no business with the likes of Quetzalcoatl's bandit chief. It is the woman and child you shelter here that I desire. Simply hand them over and I shall be on my way."

"And what'll you do if I won't?" Thomas inquired, holding his right arm out in front of him.

The sound of the projectile knifing through the air was even louder than that of it being fired in the first place. Swinging his upper body ever so slightly to the left to distribute its impact, Marquis Verenis stared down at the arrow sticking out of his chest.

"Nicely done. However, while even we Nobles cannot do much about the location of our hearts, it is possible to upgrade the muscle tissue around it."

Grabbing the arrow, he pulled it out. No sooner had he hauled back with it than Thomas shouted, "Brendon!"

As the Nobleman turned to look at the butler behind him, a stark flash of light mowed through his bull neck. Still holding a severed head in one hand, the decapitated Nobleman's body sprayed a powerful geyser of blood as it thudded forward.

Glaring at the butler with an awful look, the marquis's head groaned, "Bastard . . . What was your price . . . to betray your master?"

The color swiftly drained from the Noble's complexion.

"My apologies, Master. However, this was always to be your fate someday. And I received fifty million dalas in financing from Mr. Thomas through an intermediary."

"Why?"

One of them was a severed head. And terrifying as this was, the exchange between master and servant was bizarrely comical.

"In the beginning, I did it for you," the butler replied. "When we encountered setbacks due to the difficulty of funding the conversion process for soldiers to conquer the Frontier, I decided to lend a hand."

"And yet . . ." Marquis Verenis groaned, cataracts beginning to form on his eyes.

"And yet, you insisted that even Lady Matilda must be added to the ranks of your soldiers, Master. I—I was in love with her. Master, did you know how your decision pained Lady Matilda?"

"I never knew . . . She was such . . . such a tomboy . . ."

"But she is a woman, all the same. And your own flesh and blood at that, is she not? Lady Matilda's sorrow eventually melted my heart. And then I came to hate you, Master."

The marquis closed his eyes.

Nevertheless, Brendon continued, saying, "Do not go into that sleep yet. The main question is yet to come. Though Lady Matilda accepted her fate, that isn't to say that that was the end of it. For she sought cooperation from me, who sympathized with her, in her revenge against you, Master, who had reduced her to those circumstances."

The severed head moved no longer. But the faithful butler continued to direct his eloquence at it.

"Undoubtedly Lady Matilda had thought about killing you herself. I was opposed to it. I knew how powerful you were, and I would not allow her to commit patricide of all things. You say she was a tomboy, Master, but there is no one more feminine than Lady Matilda. You should know as much. And yet, you sold Lady Matilda to get your money. You explained that the money was only to turn Lady Matilda into something else—but that merely left me dumbfounded as well. It was then that I decided to kill you. Though I wondered when the time would be right, today is truly that day. You cannot stay the hand of fate. But as my last act in service to you, I shall bring the woman and the child back to the castle."

And reciting a quiet prayer, Brendon then got to his feet again. His body was pierced by iron spears and arrows from all sides. He coughed, bloody foam spilling from his mouth. An unsettling smile rose on the butler's lips.

"You know that I cannot die unless run through the heart, don't you?" he said. "I didn't mention it to my master, but I, too, underwent enhancement procedures. You cannot kill me!"

Brendon's entire frame became a blur. It became apparent he was spinning with terrific impetus when the weapons stuck in him came free, impaling his Quetzalcoatl attackers.

Dodging one by a hair, Thomas hung in midair. On his back was a huge pair of wings—his flight pack was open. Punching through ceiling boards that were thin by design, he disappeared into the hole.

"Oh, where are you going?" Brendon called out amiably. "I still owe you that money. I am prepared to pay you back. Look, is this not a fine, fat diamond?"

Bending down, the butler took the glittering jewel from Marquis Verenis's left ring finger and held it up to the hole in the ceiling.

"Not coming? Don't trust me either, do you? Well, you leave me no choice, then."

Quickly abandoning that plan, Brendon put the ring in his pocket, then grabbed the door knob to Lydia and Didi's room. Giving it two or three twists, he said, "I say, open up. No harm shall come to you. I shall simply bring you back down to the surface."

After waiting several seconds, Brendon then pulled on the door for all he was worth. Hinges went flying, and he threw the entire door he'd pulled free across the corridor and entered the room.

There was no one there. Looking up at the hole that'd been knocked in the ceiling, the butler clucked his tongue.

"Damnation! Where could they have gone?"

From behind him, a voice said, "Shall I join you in the search?"

Brendon turned and looked, bowing respectfully just scant seconds later.

"Oh, my good marquis. You are the very picture of health."

A heartbeat later, he was enveloped by flames.

As he made his rapid descent, Thomas let the pair of passengers he carried see the orange flower that bloomed in the night sky.

"Yay!" Didi cried out, eyes wide. He was terribly excited. For a little boy, death and destruction were attractions that made the heart beat faster. "But—are you sure it's okay? You just destroyed your airship."

Thomas looked all around him. A dozen or so figures were in flight.

"I've still got my men, and the ship was one we'd taken. We'll just have to do it again. But forget the ship—look at that," the bandit chief said, pointing at a certain spot.

"I can't see anything, can you?" Didi complained.

Thomas told the boy, "We've undergone procedures to give us night vision. Looks like Marquis Verenis didn't kick the bucket after all. Those bastards got flight units of their own on."

"Where are we going?" asked Lydia.

"To be honest, I'm not sure I can protect you from the marquis. We'll take you to another region."

"Boss—we've got incoming!" one of his men shouted.

"We've been made—so down we go! Fly nape of the earth and split up. We'll meet up at that hill at dawn."

"Roger that."

"Let's go!" Thomas told the pair in his arms, giving them a grin. But in the darkness they couldn't see it.

The three of them touched down in a square about three-quarters of a mile from the castle.

"Run for it!" said Thomas. There was blood mixed with his words.

"But you're—" Lydia began, hesitating.

"Never mind me. Hurry up! And if you see D, tell him something. I'm sorry I couldn't keep my promise. That, and to squeeze that fifty million dalas out of that bastard Brendon, okay?"

"Yes, sir," Didi replied in a tearful tone.

He and the girl squatted down and were scampering away when the sound of iron-shod hooves came from up ahead. As they were frozen in their tracks, the sounds gave way to a figure astride a black steed. The moonlight revealed his beauty.

"D?!" Lydia exclaimed, so relieved she nearly fell flat on her face. Holding herself up, she turned and called back, "Don't worry, it's D."

There was no reply.

The hoarse voice said, "We were looking out the window and saw this humongous fiery blossom in the night sky, then a figure with wings coming down—was that Thomas?"

"Yeah. While we were on the way down, the marquis and his servant caught up with us, and they killed all of Thomas's men. Even he got stabbed in the chest—"

D started walking over to where the winged man had fallen. He stood there for a few seconds, then came back.

Didi started to cry. After a little while, he managed to say, "He said he was sorry he couldn't keep his promise."

D stood there, saying nothing.

"And then he said—get his fifty million dalas out of Brendon."

"I see," D replied. "Apparently he's come to pay up."

The two of them turned and looked over their shoulders—in the same direction D was looking.

Bathed in moonlight, a pair of figures were headed their way with flapping wings.

D advanced on his cyborg horse, heading right at the pair. The winged figures halted about five yards shy of him. However, they were also about five yards off the ground.

"Strange, the number of times we've bumped into each other in a single night," the marquis said gleefully.

"You weren't supposed to raise a hand against anyone," D said, his voice wiping the smile from the Nobleman's face.

"I have kept that promise. It is my faithful servant who has broken it. I went out to stop him, you see."

D's voice reverberated in the ears of the shaken Brendon, saying, "I'll take that fifty million dalas you owed him."

Catching his breath, Brendon replied, "I don't have it."

"Then your life will serve as collateral."

With those words, Brendon knew his fate was sealed. The only way to survive would be to slay the Hunter below him.

I cannot be destroyed yet, he thought. *I mustn't leave Lady Matilda alone.*

"Whatever is the matter, Brendon? You said you would be the one to do away with D, or had you forgotten?" Marquis Verenis said mockingly.

Perhaps it was D who took that as a signal. From the back of his steed, the figure in black leapt into the air without showing the slightest signs of preparation. With a sense of security being up in the air and a sense of superiority looking down at D on his horse, Brendon never would have imagined that. Moreover—the Hunter was so fast!

Before the butler could beat his wings, D was right in front of him, moonlight trailing from his naked blade as it split the top of the man's head in two. It was a second later that the forms of the pair were distorted.

"Oh, is that a gravitational field generator?" the marquis groaned as he moved further away.

Accounts Settled in Fresh Blood

CHAPTER 6

I

T he gravitational field generator sealed off an area even as it completely compressed matter. Matter compacted on an atomic level would be broken down to its elementary particles, then "vanish." Nobles alone were immune to this through supernatural means. But did that extend to dhampirs?

Oh, look! D's outline was collapsing, peeling away, turning into something that's true form was unknown. When it was compacted to the point that not even light could escape, would he still be able to be revived?

D spread his hands.

"Is he signaling his surrender, or is it merely his death spasms?" Marquis Verenis mused, his face etched with curiosity. There was nothing snide about it, because he knew of D's true power. "It can't be!" the marquis exclaimed, having noticed something. But what?

D swung both his hands downward.

"He's cut through it," the Nobleman groaned.

D fell to the ground, white smoke wafting from every inch of his body. Remnants of the battle between the gravitational field and his atomic structure.

"Cutting his way out of a gravitational field—truly such a thing would be impossible for any man save D." The marquis then added, "Brendon, my faithful servant! Where shall you go?"

The subject of his speculation struggled in midair. But it was no longer Brendon. Rather, it was undoubtedly the flesh of something else being squashed down to nothingness by the gravitational field he'd created in hopes of taking his opponent with him.

"We're going back to the castle!" D called from the back of his cyborg horse.

"As you please," Marquis Verenis replied with a shrug of his shoulders. A sense of defeat made the action seem sluggish.

With Lydia on the back of the saddle and Didi set on his lap, D quietly advanced on his cyborg horse.

Seeing the smoke that continued to rise from the Hunter, Didi exclaimed, "You're incredible, mister!" And in true childlike fashion, he batted the puffs of smoke away.

"Three hours till dawn," Lydia murmured.

"Still a long way off, isn't it?"

Both she and the boy nodded at D's words. So many lives had been lost in the span of less than an hour. Human emotion had finally begun welling up in them.

They'd gone about five hundred yards when a cyborg horse appeared from the cover of the forest.

"Oh, it's the geezer," Didi said with childlike scorn.

"I'll give you 'geezer,' you lousy punk," Old El snarled through clenched teeth from high in the saddle.

"What the hell were you doing?" Lydia asked, not even attempting to hide her anger.

"Had to come see how pretty boy here made out, and I managed to follow him this far. No way was I gonna hang around that castle without my bodyguard. That idiot Tupperman's with the old lady, so he should probably be okay, though."

"So, why were you in there, then?"

"I couldn't keep up."

"That's a lie. You hid because you were scared. Sackless geezer."

Children were merciless.

Old El's face flushed and he was about to say something back when D delivered a kick to his steed's flanks, and the cyborg horse immediately tore across the ground.

On returning to the castle, they were greeted by Tupperman. He looked utterly exhausted, drawing a grin from the old man as he said to the puppet master, "Oh, looks like you had a hard time of it, stud."

"Say what you like, just trade off with me for a while. You wouldn't believe what a slave driver that old lady is."

"Just have one of them gimmicks you're so fond of rub her shoulders and back," Old El told him.

"I've already tried that. And she knew in a flash that's what it was. In the end, she caught hold of me. Broke all my gadgets, too."

"That's too bad, eh?"

Clutching his head in his hands, Tupperman said, "All hope is lost now. I'm finished."

"Still got your town, don't you?" the old man said coldly. "And another thing—you still got a duty to repay me. So relax, you got plenty to live for yet!"

Crying out, Tupperman raced back to his own room.

"Poor baby," the hoarse voice said pensively.

Since it was nearly dawn, Lydia and the boy moved into Old El's room, too. But dawn was only near in the physical sense. Imagining what was yet to come made the darkness as deep as hell, and the dawn someplace at the end of time.

"I wonder if the damn marquis's given up on making any more moves against us," Old El mused to himself.

"You really think he would?" asked the hoarse voice.

"Nope."

"Well, at least you know the boat you're in."

"Him and his daughter are probably up to something—and I don't wanna wait to find out what. Let's have Tupperman go snoop around."

And having said that, the old man left, coming back almost immediately to report that the puppet master was suddenly among the missing.

"Maybe he was so far from hope he made a break for it?" the old man suggested, even though he didn't believe a word of it.

"Then we have need of a replacement for Brendon, do we not?" Matilda remarked nonchalantly after hearing Marquis Verenis sullenly explain what'd happened. "I shall go search for one."

"Could you do that?"

"More or less."

"But we cannot push your power any further!" the marquis said wearily.

"I never thought I would hear such words from you, Father."

"D—he slew Brendon and escaped from the gravitational field as if it were nothing. There are things in this world to be truly feared."

"If we cannot triumph through power, what do you suggest, then? Our foe's ranks have diminished by one, but we also lost Brendon. You have no choice but to do as they say and pay them back. To wit, you can only offer me to them as collateral."

Marquis Verenis said nothing.

"We could enlist new allies."

"We have none." Having said that, the marquis looked at his daughter's face, and his expression changed. "Or do you mean to tell me we do?"

"Who can say? However, I do have someone in mind. And the means to sway them."

The marquis was left breathless. "Matilda, are you truly my daughter? When did you acquire these means?"

"After you enhanced me, Father."

The marquis fell into silence.

At that point, Matilda headed toward the door. "Here he is," she said. "Brendon's potential replacement."

The door opened gravely.

A figure entered.

"Welcome," said Matilda, curtseying.

That put a smile on Tupperman's lips.

Tupperman returned less than ten minutes after he'd gone.

First, the old lady asked, "Where have you been, you useless wretch?"

"I'm sorry, my emotions got the better of me. But I'm much better now."

"In that case, get right to massaging my shoulders. They're stiff as hell from worrying about your safety."

"Yes, ma'am," he replied exasperatedly.

At that point Old El and D came in, with the old man insisting the puppet master had to submit to an inspection. There was no telling what might've happened to him in the ten minutes he was missing. That was more than enough time for him to be turned into a servant of the Nobility.

"Do as you like," Duchess Marlingen said, making it a point to avoid looking at D. "He's human, I tell you. From when I first met him until just now, he hasn't changed at all."

"Sorry for the intrusion," D said, turning right around.

"Hey!" Old El exclaimed, repeating it twice more as he followed the Hunter into the corridor. "You sure it's all right? The guy went missing for ten whole minutes in a Noble castle!"

"The duchess recognizes him as human. No need for me to get involved."

"Yeah? B-but what if the two of 'em are in cahoots?"

"Then I'll leave it to you."

"H-hey?!"

D went back to their room.

Didi was sleeping. And in a chair beside the bed Lydia was also in dreamland, though when the old man came in after D she quickly woke up.

"Go back to sleep," D told her.

"Thanks. I feel better, somehow."

"Isn't that grand! Must be nice being a pretty boy, eh?" Old El spat bitterly as he settled himself on the sofa.

"You've got it all wrong," she told the old man.

"Huh?"

"Sure, part of it's due to D—but mostly, I'd have to say it's on account of you, I suppose."

An enormous question mark seemed to hang over the financier's head.

A voice from the vicinity of D's left hand could be heard to say, "Hmmm."

Staring at that for a minute, the old man then turned in Lydia's direction and sort of smirked. "What do you mean by that?" he asked, and the look on his face said he was being serious.

"The Frontier is no place for humans to live. What with the wild wastes, forests that are one big nest of monsters, bogs of boiling sulfur, vicious storms and lightning—they'd change even the kindest person. Then there's the Nobles."

Catching her breath there, Lydia blinked her eyes.

"The Frontier is theirs. I don't care how much you say they're in decline, their presence is in the very air we breathe. It swirls with that weird aura of theirs. And we'll never be rid of it. All of us live with this stuff in terror of the Nobility. I'm no different there. So does this kid, and Tupperman—hell, even you do!"

Old El turned away indignantly at that. The look in Lydia's eye was a little too earnest.

"So, what are you trying to say, then?"

"That I'm okay with that now. I've come to think maybe Nobles and humans are exactly the same."

"Whaaat?!" Old El replied, her remark something he never could've imagined.

"It's money," Lydia said brightly, as if she were laying down a winning hand. "I've broken my back since I was a kid for money. All four of my brothers and sisters died of malnutrition because we didn't have enough to eat. Even when just me and Papa were left, we were always sick as dogs. So I really envied the Nobility. I thought human suffering was nothing to them, that they were like gods. To look at their castles and mansions towering on the hills, anybody'd think that. But the Nobles in this castle are so poor. When I heard they'd borrowed money from you, to be honest, it kind of knocked me for a loop. I'd never heard of Nobles like that. At that moment, Nobles were like humans—something just like you and me!"

II

"I see. I suppose that's one way of looking at it," the Hunter's left hand murmured, though no one else's ears caught its words.

Nobles were like humans—that was how it felt to an ordinary girl of seventeen.

"Nobles strapped for money, bowing and scraping to the person who comes to collect from them, Nobles who think about killing those same people . . . It's all so stingy and scummy, just like the stuff we do. Don't you think so? So, I'm not scared anymore. I'm gonna work like hell and save a bunch of money so someday I can go to a Noble's castle and tell him, 'Okay, I'll loan you some money!' before slapping his face with a big wad of bills. Of course, I'll probably be that old lady's age before that happens."

"That's a hell of a plan," said D. There was something soft about his words.

"Give 'em hell," the hoarse voice from his left hand added.

"Thanks," Lydia replied, though it was unclear where her words were directed.

A calmness filled the air.

"Somebody's here," said the Hunter's left hand.

Tupperman was just coming in through the door they'd left open. They soon realized the reason for his morose expression. He was carrying the old lady on his back.

"Oh, headed out for an evening stroll now, are we? Nice going, puppet boy. Lady, you should make him your husband one of these days, you know?"

"Don't even joke about that," Tupperman groaned.

"Oh, and why's that?" asked the old lady. "I'm quite fond of you. And you've got a real knack for massages. It's not very nice the way you try to weasel out of it from time to time, but I'll break that out of you sooner or later."

"What'd you come here for, anyway?" Old El inquired rather unsociably. "There's just over two hours till daybreak. Keep messing around out here and you'll wind up a pile of ashes!"

"Well, I was lonesome all by myself, you see. Say, wouldn't it be nice if we all went on a sightseeing tour?" the duchess suggested.

"What's that supposed to mean?"

"It goes without saying. I'm talking about taking in the sights inside the castle."

"I wouldn't do that. Isn't that what you were doing earlier when you wound up in such rough shape? A tour, my ass. Don't get any dumb ideas, you damned pest."

"That's why I'm saying we should all go. Let's just call it 'The Tour to See What the Castle Has of Value.'"

Dumbfounded by this, it came as little surprise that Lydia, Tupperman, and D all looked at the old lady.

Old El waved the idea aside with one hand, saying, "I wouldn't. You can see they're practically paupers. How could they have anything of value?"

"How have you managed to live as long as you have and still not learn anything?" the duchess snapped at Old El. "Every time you got a little money in your pocket, you probably blew it on cheap booze and chasing saloon girl tails. That's why you've got a face like a soggy sea sponge. If you consider yourself a man, you'd best remember your personal history is written all over your face."

"Y-you've got your nerve saying that, you old biddy!" Old El sputtered, stepping forward with fists clenched.

"Stop it."

He was stopped by Lydia's words and D's left hand. For the instant the Hunter touched his shoulder, the old man couldn't move.

"Humans are pretty damned rough to begin with, but he's got them all beat in that department. I'll rid us of him now," the old lady said, reaching one arm over Tupperman's shoulder to grab the front of Old El's shirt.

"Stop it," Lydia cried out again, and D pulled the old man back.

"Lemme go!" the old man shouted.

"How about it? Why don't we join her tour for the time being?" suggested the flustered Tupperman. "Couldn't hurt to have at look around, at least."

"Are you a complete idiot?" said Old El. "What's this castle got besides dust and junk? On top of which, the lord of the castle wants us dead so he can skip out on his loan. If he's gonna kill us, it'll be before daybreak."

"Then I wouldn't be able to take part, either, would I? You ever consider that, you dimwit?"

"Y-you bitch!" the old man replied, and they were about to go at it again when D stepped between them.

Foam flying from her mouth, the old lady cried, "For a loan shark, you don't know a damned thing about anything, do you? No matter what happened, no Noble would end up that poor. This castle might look it on the surface, but if we check underground there's got to be some treasure socked away somewhere. You know, gold or silver, or some Noble inventions. And you're a lousy piker if you don't know that much."

"I'll kill you, you bitch!"

"Get going," D ordered Tupperman. Apparently he'd grown tired of the exchange.

"Don't you dare move. I'll kill you," the old lady shouted.

No sooner had she vanished through the doorway than the old man also headed for the door, saying, "Hey, I'm going, too!"

That made Lydia's eyes go wide.

"Why the look of surprise? Ain't about to let an opportunity like this pass me by. Treasure hidden underground? Oh, that makes my blood run hot. Let's go, D. You're coming with me. Hey, missy—if you're afraid to be left behind, grab the kid and come with us."

"Okay, we're going," Lydia replied with a nod, not even hesitating for a moment.

And so the pre-dawn investigative tour was launched.

When they'd all come out into the corridor, they found the old lady at the top of the stairs.

"Oh, had a change of heart, have you?" she said. "Well, I don't feel like bringing you along with me anymore. Follow along if you like, and it'll serve you right if you get lost in some maze and starve to death."

"Don't recollect nobody asking you to take us along, you old bag of bones. If you start giving up the ghost along the way, bitch, we ain't gonna lift a finger to help you!"

Tupperman and the old lady went down the stairs first, with Old El's group following after them. Riding piggyback on the puppet master, the old lady turned and looked back at the others. Pointing her cane at them, she said, "For all your big talk, you're still following along after me. If we find anything, you'll probably sneak up behind us to steal it. Well, I'm not about to let that happen. We'll take the corridor to the right. The rest of you can go left."

"Yeah, well, we were gonna do that before you even mentioned it," Old El said, indignantly advancing down the corridor.

After they'd gone about ten yards, he halted and said, "We're heading back."

This time the financier was tiptoeing as he began tracing along behind the old lady.

"Just a minute. Have you no shame at all?" Lydia asked, making no effort to mask the look of scorn in her eyes.

"What do you mean? It's the rational viewpoint to have here. She might be old and decrepit, but she's still a card-carrying member of the Nobility. Meaning she'd have a pretty good idea where the treasure'd be stashed in the castle. All we've gotta do then is swipe it from her, like the old bat said. Now, with somebody who knows where the treasure is right under their nose, what kind of idiot would intentionally go search anyplace else?"

"You're the lowest of the low."

"Shut up. Let's get going!" said Old El, and he started walking.

"Since you came, stick with us," D said.

There was no fighting the young man. Lydia nodded.

"Here they come!" the marquis, who was peering at an image of the group projected in midair, called over to the far side of the room.

"I expected as much—well, off I go," Matilda could be heard to say.

"And I, as well," said someone else—and it sounded like none other than Tupperman.

"I leave them to you!" Marquis Verenis exclaimed, but when he turned and looked, he saw nothing save an iron door that was closing.

As they advanced with light steps down corridors where flames danced atop candelabras, Matilda said, "So, is the one who accompanies them the real you?"

"Indeed, milady," Tupperman replied, touching the fingers of his left hand to his right shoulder. Beneath them were a pair of fang marks.

"In that case, *he* must be the first you dispose of!"

"As you wish."

Turning the next corner, the puppet master vanished. Operating independently, he'd gone to seek out the tour group.

Not surprisingly, Duchess Marlingen's directions were right on the mark.

"That's a trick corridor over there. It leads to a dead end or a pitfall. The real one's this way."

And saying that, she struck the wall with her cane, and it slid off to the right, exposing a hidden door. Once inside, she struck the interior wall with her cane again to shut the door, saying, "That should keep the riffraff out. To hell with them, I say."

"Great," Tupperman remarked, unable to conceal his fright. The old lady didn't seem to weigh anything at all, so that was no problem, but he got the impression that just being around her would cause one danger after another to rain down upon them.

Clinging to his neck, the duchess said, "Come to think of it, I said you were human, but was I wrong?"

"W-w-what do you mean by that, all of a sudden?" he stammered.

"Well, I'm getting a bit senile, and to be honest, I'm not too sure of myself anymore. Would it be okay if I had a drink of your blood?"

"N-no, it most certainly wouldn't!"

"Yes, well, you're not really my type, so that doesn't really bother me, and you're the genuine article, at any rate."

"Of course I am."

"Yes, I see."

The two of them continued down a long staircase for what seemed like forever, finally coming to a wide corridor.

"Which way do we go?" asked Tupperman.

"Left!"

"Pardon my asking, but could we wait till the rest of them get here? I'd feel more reassured that way."

"As if they're coming!" the duchess exclaimed.

"Why don't you think they are?"

"Oh, the old-timer certainly wants to, but the young fella would nix that. You think he's the sort of man swayed by riches?"

"Then what's he doing with us?"

"How on earth should I know? Don't ask me such nonsense! He's probably the only one who could open the door up top by sheer brute force. But there, he'd turn back. The young fella wouldn't accompany them any further."

Ultimately, it was unclear how the puppet master felt about the old lady's opinion. There was the sound of footsteps approaching from the depths of the corridor they were facing.

"D?" Tupperman ventured gleefully.

"Not on your life."

"Who is it?"

"Maybe it's you?" said the duchess.

Laughing, Tupperman said, "If anything happens, I'll be counting on you." The puppet master was quaking.

"Leave it to me. Now, onward!" the old lady said, her finger pointed straight ahead.

"I'd really rather not."

"Here they come!"

The footsteps took on a human form.

"Brendon?!"

"Well, I'll be damned," the duchess remarked. "According to what the old timer said, aren't you supposed to be dead?"

Absorbing the suspicion-filled words of the pair, the butler who'd been reduced to subatomic particles in a gravitational field gave them an unsettling smile, saying, "I shall serve as your guide from this point on."

"Not interested," the old lady replied without a second's delay. "You're an organic robot. Step aside. We have no use for someone who's truly dead!"

"I am afraid I cannot do that. There is but a single condition on you continuing beyond this point, my lady. And that is, you must void your essentially baseless loan agreement."

"Who'd ever agree to that? I wager there's treasure hidden up ahead. In which case it can be used to clear those past debts. And if it won't, it's because your master doesn't want to spend his money for his daughter's sake! I'm surprised the two of them haven't destroyed each other yet, you know?"

"I know nothing about that."

"In that case, don't give us any trouble and get out of the way. And just so you know, a lousy little gravitational field is nothing compared to my Qi powers!"

"I am fully aware of that."

"Gaah!" Tupperman shrieked. His outline had begun to blur, and then there was a dull thud as he rolled to one side of the corridor. The old lady had slid down off his back and kicked him out of the way.

"Okay, you're out of my hair now. Well, come get a taste of this," said Duchess Marlingen, the latter part directed at Brendon. Her deadly cane was already pointed at the butler.

His form distorted. At the same time, Brendon touched his chest and was sent flying.

"Are you okay?" Tupperman asked her, rushing over.

"More or less," she replied. But she undoubtedly clambered limply onto his back because the gravitational field had in fact affected her.

"Shouldn't we make a run for it?" Tupperman inquired confusedly. "We have no idea what awaits us up ahead!"

"Oh, I know. Nothing awaits us. Let's go."

"But, you've been knocked senseless, haven't you?"

"Over the last four millennia, I've been knocked around like this hundreds of thousands of times. Are you saying I should've cried over each and every one of them?"

"You don't say. Well, I'll wait here, then."

"Don't give me any of your smart talk! Get a move on!" she cried from his back in a tone so lively she seemed like another person entirely.

Heaving a single sigh, Tupperman slowly plodded forward.

The corridor was a good twenty feet wide. It was also a good twenty feet to the ceiling. Yet the air seemed terribly heavy due to the overwhelming mass of the stone walls to either side of them.

After walking for perhaps ten minutes, Tupperman was wheezing for breath when the old lady cried, "It's over there," and pointed with her cane.

A small, black door was visible off in the distance.

"Is that the treasure vault?"

"Without a doubt."

The fright faded from Tupperman's face, and desire welled up. He broke into a jog.

When it was right in front of them, the door was immense, towering over them.

Tupperman quivered at the thought of what might be stored inside. "What'll we do about the lock?" he asked.

"I'm on it!" said the duchess, pointing her cane at it.

There was no change.

No sooner did Tupperman give the old lady a quizzical look than a grave creaking sound could be heard. The door was opening.

"You did it!" the man exclaimed as he started to dash forward, but Duchess Marlingen's fingers dug into his shoulders.

"Ouch!"

"Stand back!" the old lady cried.

"Huh?"

"I don't know what I was thinking. I forgot the treasure'd have a guardian spirit."

"A-are you senile?" the man sputtered.

"Shut your mouth—because here it comes!"

Something resembling black smoke gushed out through the opening, which was still less than a foot wide.

"Oh shit. Let's run for it!" cried the puppet master.

"You want to see what's inside, don't you?"

"Not anymore."

"Coward. This is why all you're good for is borrowing money."

"Th-that's not true at all!"

"At any rate, keep your eyes shut and do as I tell you."

"I don't know . . ."

Both were frightening prospects.

Tupperman froze in his tracks. What gushed out wasn't black smoke, but rather could be described as a gaseous lifeform. Because what the man and old lady saw quite clearly was an enormous eyeless and noseless head and a pair of arms.

"Didn't you say you were some kind of puppet master? Do you have anything with you? Some robotic arm or leg gadget or something?"

"No, I don't have anything."

"Oh, what good are you?! Set me down."

Climbing down to stand on the floor, the duchess then tugged Tupperman's coat off.

"H-hey!" he protested.

"Shut up," she replied without a glance at the shaken man, balling his coat up and throwing.

A cavern that appeared to be a mouth opened on the lower half of the enormous face, swallowing the coat. A split second later, it spit it out. Black ash eddied, but before it could fall to the floor, it broke into even smaller fragments and faded from view.

"Not bad," said the old lady.

"I'll thank you not to waste time admiring it—hurry up and kill it!"

"Take that!" Duchess Marlingen shouted, making Tupperman stand bolt upright just as he was about to collapse.

The black head was scattered in all directions—or rather, it disappeared. And that disappearance extended to the gaseous lifeform's entire body.

Tupperman gazed dumbfoundedly as the enormous creature that'd been there just a second earlier suddenly vanished. *That's some old lady*, he thought to himself.

However—he then sagged under the weight of the old lady's body as she took it upon herself to climb onto his back again.

"Um, excuse me—"

"Well, I've really burned through a lot of energy tonight. I'm not surprised I'm tuckered out. But on we go!"

"We can't," said Tupperman.

"What?"

The door was in the process of discharging a black gas again. Was it the original guardian spirit weakened by her Qi, or was it a new one?

"Flee!" Tupperman groaned as he turned around.

He may have turned a little too hard. The old lady's hands slipped free and she fell to the floor, but not before the man bearing her had run another dozen paces. And then he squealed.

The black mass was closing on the writhing form of the duchess, who was clutching her lower back. Hands like colossal trees reached out for her.

"Die!" Duchess Marlingen cried, pointing her cane at it.

"Huh?"

Her hands were empty. The cane lay on the floor to her right.

"Oh damn."

Eyes wide with fear were filled by the mass of blackness, and then there was a flash of light at the center of it—a stark glint that shot right through it. A groan that fell short of words echoed across the corridor.

An arm like black steel wrapped around the old lady's waist.

"Y-you—how on earth?!"

As the knight in black stood there with the duchess under one arm, the gaseous lifeform seemed to be staring at him, forgetting the pain of its hewn limbs. Such was D's beauty that even fiends were mesmerized by it.

"Old El," D called out, staring back at the enemy.

"Right here!"

"Take care of her!"

And no sooner had he said that than the old lady was in midair.

"Gotcha," Old El said as he caught her. Lydia and Didi were right behind him.

And they all saw it happen. The black smoke that menaced D, though lacking both arms and subsequently getting its head split in two by a blow from the leaping Hunter, still managed to swallow the Hunter whole. And then the massive black form was sucked back through the doorway with terrific speed. And D with it.

The door was closing.

"W-wait!" Old El shouted, running even though he still had the old lady in his arms. None of his plans could move forward without confirming the existence of a treasure.

"Aaah!"

However, the door shut completely before he'd gone ten paces.

Old El dropped to his knees dejectedly, old lady and all, and didn't move another inch. Undoubtedly his soul left him for a while.

"Let's go," Tupperman called out, his voice fading in the distance, but for a while the old man made no attempt to move, as if swaddled in despair.

After Duchess Marlingen had been set down on her bed, her care was left to Lydia and Didi. But even then, there was only so much they could do. They gave her a shot of nutrients meant for humans and some water to drink, and let her rest—that was all.

Still, true to her Noble nature, just lying down for less than ten minutes was enough to calm her breathing and put the light back in her eyes. She pressed them to tell her what'd happened after her fall, and when they finished telling her she said, "Well, that young fella could fall straight to hell and you still needn't worry about him. But how did you folks make it down to the treasure vault, anyway? The way in should've been locked."

"Mister D—he cut a way in."

"Through that steel lock?"

"Yep."

"I'm sure that geezer told him to keep going, but you mean to tell me the young fella didn't try to stop him?"

"No, he cut through the lock before Old El could say anything about going in."

"Why?"

"Beats me," Lydia said, a troubled look on her face. That was only natural.

Apparently the duchess hadn't really expected an answer, and heaving a sigh, she looked up at the ceiling. "Beats me, too. It well and truly does."

"Get some sleep already. Soon, it'll—"

There, Lydia hemmed and hawed.

"—be dawn, right? You needn't worry yourself on my account. I'll go below ground to rest. If you like, why don't you follow along after me and pound a stake through my heart?"

"I'd never!"

"You're a human, and I'm a Noble—and that's the natural order of things, you know? Don't go feeling sorry for me just because I look this way."

"I—I know that."

"Then why did you bother patching me up?"

"You might be a Noble, but you look like an old lady. I couldn't just leave you be."

"If it were me, I'd leave a human child be, or drink their blood. Humans sure are strange creatures. I knew a Noble who was as rough as they come, yet he was oddly committed to humans. When I pressed him on it, he snapped back that he himself didn't know why, but I finally get the feeling I understand how he felt."

Lydia didn't know what to say to that.

"Well, I guess I should be going," Duchess Marlingen said, and as she got up, she looked over at Didi sleeping on the sofa. "Now that I look at him, there's really no difference between human kids and Noble ones. Pretty cute, isn't he?"

Lydia nodded. "Yep."

"Well, I'm going below ground. I'll see you again if the fates allow."

Cane in hand, the old lady walked to the door with an astonishingly steady gait. She was just about to reach for the door knob when she stumbled. Lydia raced over and was about to lay her hands on the woman's shoulders when she was knocked back.

"I'll thank you not to try touching me so casually, human," the duchess said, righting herself indignantly.

When she straightened her back, Lydia's eyes went wide at the beautiful old lady full of dignity who stood before her. Is that what it was to be a Noble?

Opening the door, the old lady turned just slightly in the girl's direction as she stepped through it, then quickly departed. Lydia tilted her head quizzically. She was trying to correctly replay the words that now lingered in her ears. Ultimately, she couldn't be sure, but they might've been "Thank you."

A Tale of Puppets

CHAPTER 7

I

D wasn't there. Not a single one of them could've imagined how uneasy that left them. Old El and Tupperman, as well as Lydia and Didi, were all people of the Frontier. These were humans who'd lived till now by overcoming their cruel way of life. And both Old El and Tupperman had, in fact, had dealings with Nobles. To be honest, they'd been left feeling the Nobility weren't the fearsome creatures that they'd previously thought.

But the men had been mistaken. The terror that was oozing from the marrow of their bones now told them as much. D's presence had been the only reason they'd been able to maintain a peaceful state of mind in the heart of a Noble's castle. Once he'd vanished, every passing second was horrifying. What if Marquis Verenis got it into his head to kill them now? What if that gaseous lifeform from earlier slipped in through the gap in the doorframe? Or if the marquis himself bared his fangs? They couldn't do anything. There was no way to stop any of that. Not with D gone.

A deep nihilism held sway over the room. They were in the midst of death, and could do nothing—and when they acknowledged that, they no longer even remembered to be afraid. Still, Didi was sleeping, and Lydia had begun to doze on the sofa because they, at least, had Old El and Tupperman. The shamelessly bold won out in the end. The less fortunate pair was sunken in the depths of gloom, but the old man finally got to his feet and headed for the door. He could no longer sit there doing nothing.

"Don't give in to despair," Tupperman said to him in a low voice, stopping him. "It'll be dawn soon—less than two hours to go. Let's try to keep it together until then."

"Them two hours are the problem. Ah, if only D was here," Old El said. The feet that'd stopped once quickly went into action again, and he opened the door and went out.

"Oh, there's just no making that man listen!" Tupperman said with a cluck of his tongue, checking on the two sleepers before following after the old man. From behind the financier aimlessly continuing down the corridor, he said, "You shouldn't be wandering around out here all alone."

Old El turned around and glared at him. "Like I need advice from you. Beat your feet back to the room and figure out a way to pay me back, why don't you?"

"Funny you should mention that," Tupperman said gleefully. "I've finally come up with a prospect for repaying you."

"Seriously?" the old man replied, his expression tending toward doubt rather than joy. Such was the nature of a debt collector.

"Yeah," said Tupperman, gazing intently into Old El's eyes.

A look of surprise rose on the old man's face, but it quickly became a vague, sleepy expression.

"It can't be . . . You're—"

"That's right. I changed places with the other Tupperman in the underground passages earlier. By now, Lady Matilda has probably either given him the kiss, or done away with him." The puppet master's lips twisted into a grin, exposing trenchant fangs. "Now, tell me something—what's the name of the person you entrusted with the deed to the marquis's debts? And where do they live?"

Tupperman's eyes—or rather, the eyes of this newly made pseudo Noble—burned with a vermilion light. And they would burn into some part of the old man's brain, as well.

The financier's lips trembled, spitting out words like air bubbles. "In the southern Frontier . . . city of Ecatelina . . . North 18 Ward . . . Serge Pattaya . . . is the name."

"No mistake about it?"

". . . None."

"Thank you—and now, we have no further need for you. We'd normally kill you at this point, but Lady Matilda is very circumspect. We'll keep you alive until we've disposed of this Pattaya fellow and have that document in hand. Actually, I'll head out now, and I should be back before dawn. If you're not lying, that is."

Once again, Tupperman's eyes blazed. Old El shook his head and blinked his eyes.

"When you say prospects for paying me back, what kind of prospects are we talking about?" asked the old man.

Scratching the back of his head sheepishly, Tupperman replied, "Uh, it's not really to the point where I can tell you about it."

"Then don't say things that'd make me think otherwise, you jackass."

"Um, okay."

"Well, forget this. Turns out coming out here alone is kinda creepy after all. Let's head back."

Old El went back to his room. But no matter how long he waited, Tupperman didn't come in again.

Two pairs of eyes watched Tupperman come in. One was Matilda's—and the second belonged to the other Tupperman, who was sitting on the floor.

"Nicely done," said Matilda. She'd been informed of the results by Tupperman on his way there.

"It is my pleasure to serve you."

"Set out immediately. A rotodyne has been prepared for you in the rear garden."

"Understood."

Picking up his baggage from the floor, Tupperman left.

"Stop . . . Don't do it!" said the Tupperman on the floor, but there was no way the other one would hear him, and even if he did, the other Tupperman never would've done what he said.

"How cheeky," Matilda said with a haughty laugh, approaching him with gliding steps and catching hold of his chin to make him look up at her. "However, Mr. Tupperman, you were clever enough with your words to get Father to loan you valuables, and your skill at your profession is considerable. Perhaps I shall allow you to work under me."

"That would be . . . great," said Tupperman.

Down in the subterranean passages, the duchess had kicked him aside to a spot where the other Tupperman had forced him to inhale a drug that rendered him unconscious, and Matilda had carried him off. That was before D and the others had charged in. Even now the drugs still had an effect on him.

"I do have a request, however," he said.

"What is that?"

"Would you be so kind as to drink my blood, traitor?"

Matilda's brow furrowed deeply. "Drink your blood? Why?"

"You plan on killing me, most likely. In that case, I've decided I'd rather be one of your kind."

Matilda narrowed her eyes. "Curiouser and curiouser . . . However, I certainly may be a traitor."

Their exchange up to this point had been possible because Tupperman was fighting the effects of the drug, but his head drooped, and he lost consciousness.

"Oh, this is such foolishness. At any rate, I shall let the matter rest until you awaken." And then, turning to the door through which Tupperman had disappeared, Matilda said, "Though you mistakenly believed it to be love, I did indeed once feel something for you. When you came to borrow money from Father."

Her gaze dropped to the floor.

"I gave your imposter the rank of servant. Very well, then—you shall be the same."

And then the ghostly beautiful princess made a throaty growl like a beast and strode over to the sleeping Tupperman.

What D found at the bottom of the hole was an enormous mountain of bones. Without exception, they were the bones of humans or supernatural beasts. Undoubtedly these others had come below the surface in search of treasure, just like Old El and his companions.

"Well, it's a vertical drop of a good eleven hundred feet—which would be kind of a pain to climb," said the Hunter's left hand. "So, the force of impact is enough to smash most to pieces, which is pretty cautious given how the Nobility always make light of humans. There are also traps set up in case there were any survivors. Look at that."

D was already facing that way before the hoarse voice even mentioned it. There was another yawning hole. And D detected a presence that an ordinary person—or even the average Noble—would never perceive. The bottom of the hole—it was already moving. Not angry, not clamorous, but rather it was slowly coming his way.

"It's coming. You hear that?"

The Hunter nodded at his left hand's query.

From the far reaches of the earth, or from its deepest depths, there came voices. Voices of men and of women. In less than a few seconds' time, they became screams that anyone might've heard.

Help me!
The pain!
Kill me, please!

It was a chorus of those three refrains. The voices echoing in the dark passageway had now become a black mass that spilled from a hole in the wall. This was a kind of soft-bodied creature that differed from the gaseous lifeform that had brought D there. In an instant, accursed screams echoed across the cramped bottom of the hole.

"Please forgive me for being tempted by the treasure!"

"I'll never come back here again. Please, just let me return to the surface. I've been this way for five hundred years already."

"Ah, my flesh melts away. And then it comes back again. Please, just kill me and get it over with."

"Mommy! Mommy! Mommy!"

This last voice came from a tiny face. The faces of those tormented by a hellish pain that humans, or even Nobles, couldn't even imagine covered every inch of the creature's enormous body.

"This is awful," the Hunter's left hand groaned. "Can you kill them? There are kids in there, too!"

D knew that as well. From the time it'd come down the passageway, a number of youthful voices had rung in his ears incessantly.

Between the agonized, pleading faces of adults, there appeared other faces that still retained their innocence for all their pain, sinking back into the gigantic body as if it were muck and then rising again on it.

"Mama! Kill me . . . Mama!"

"Kill me . . . Put me to rest!"

They had probably wandered into the castle, or were targeted when they came close to it.

"There's kids begging their parents to kill 'em! D, can you put that thing down?" his left hand asked, its voice trembling with anger.

However, it might as well have asked D if his sword could take the thousands of lives trapped in that creature. Could you do that, D?

The monstrous creature turned in his direction. And it was clearly the monster's face that stared at D. A strange growl issued from its mouth that was something between a choked groan and a dry heave.

At the same time, the countless faces turned in D's direction pursed their lips. When the transparent streams that shot from them struck the walls or floor, white smoke gushed from these spots, and everything dissolved. It was a strong acid—or rather, it would be more correct to say it was a poison that would corrupt anything it touched. Streams of it shot to the Hunter's left and his

right, toward the heavens and the stone floor, and no one could possibly escape their deadly net.

But the monster saw. The solvent net its captive humans cast was dissolving even the bones of the creatures left in its surroundings. Coming through them, the figure in black had a sword in his right hand, and every time it flashed out, a stream of solvent was cut down, so that not a drop ever touched him.

And then—the thing screamed. Along with every face on its body, it let loose its pain, its fear. It was a cry that would make even the most callous foe hesitate.

No sooner did the thing realize it was its own cry than its body was split in two.

II

D's path ran right down the boundary his sword carved between life and death. Now, his blade made that split once again. Life for D. Death for his enemy. Even if that enemy was a thousand faces?

However, this young man had no use for powerful emotions.

Flicking off drops of gore with a curt shake of his sword, he then climbed into the hole in the wall. As if to say it didn't really matter what awaited him there.

D's ears caught a number of children's voices saying, "Thank you."

The side cave presently led to a wider space. The terrible stench that had become evident during his battle was at its worst there. Up ahead of D, the bleached bones scattered across the stone floor formed a mountain. This was probably the lair of the monstrous creature he'd just faced. D's eyes were drawn ninety degrees to the right of the mountain of bones.

"A metabolism tuner, eh?" said his left hand. "But not for that monster just now. That gadget's for adjusting the metabolism of the lair itself. You know, so it always offers the best possible environment." Pausing for the span of a breath, it continued, "There's gotta be some passage down here for delivering meals to the occupant. It couldn't have lasted centuries down here just off what wandered in. Hold on, just hold everything—oh, there's a breeze."

D was looking up at the ceiling.

The face on his left hand followed suit, saying, "There's a stone door set in the floor. Distance-wise, it's roughly a hundred feet—should be an easy enough climb."

In lieu of a reply, D turned his hand to the left side.

"What in the world?!"

Part of the stone wall had been massively gouged. Wait. Was that a passageway? It seemed to go on for more than twenty yards.

"Melted, eh?" remarked the hoarse voice. "Judging by the state of things—that'd be digestive juices."

D went over with swift steps, and suddenly thrust his sword into that area. It immediately sank in all the way to the hilt.

"Hmm," his left hand remarked, not at all surprised since it had guessed both D's purpose and the consistency of the rock wall.

Around the spot he'd stabbed, D limned a rectangle with the blade of his sword. One that was more than large enough for him to fit through. Pulling his sword back out of it, he pushed his hand against the rock wall. The part he'd cut around easily fell back into the area beyond, exposing a new passageway.

Heaving a sigh, his left hand said, "Always gotta find the crazy way out of everything, don't you? Well, it's certainly faster than scaling the wall. That monster wanted out of here—must've been making a way out like that, if only it'd kept at it for another three feet!"

As if unfazed by that earnest remark, D threw himself into the black hole.

A short time later, the hoarse voice rang out, saying, "What is this place?"

In less than three minutes' time, the rotodyne's magnetic field engine had the man over the border, and he set it down in a grassy plain near his destination. The Nobles who occupied this domain still maintained a tight control over it. This operation required absolute stealth. Activating the "self-propelled suit" he wore, the man headed toward North 18 Ward. He was there in less than two minutes.

A blacksmith sign hung from the shop, and there was a residence out back. There was no problem disabling the lock with his electron knife.

The man was sleeping in his bedroom. He lived alone.

"Serge Pattaya," a voice called out to him. Perhaps his very tone alone was enough to stir some instinctive fear, because the blacksmith who'd clearly been sound asleep opened his eyes wide and trained a terrified gaze on the speaker.

It was a common enough reaction among people who lived on the Frontier. There was no telling when a Noble might be standing beside their bed like a ghost.

"My name is Tupperman. I was originally a puppet master, but now I'm a poor excuse for a Noble. And I've come for something Old El entrusted to you."

"What the hell would that be?" the blacksmith said, head tilted in puzzlement not after some consideration but as a reflexive response. "I don't know anything about that."

That was the reaction Tupperman had expected.

The puppet master's eyes began to give off a reddish glow. When the same glow spread to his own eyes, Serge lost consciousness.

"Your conscious mind doesn't know. However, as this is something to be delivered to a Noble, you have undoubtedly been ordered to do so. It's surely in the deepest levels of your psyche—your unconscious mind. So, where is the deed?"

The red glow grew more blinding.

Several seconds passed.

Serge nodded and got out of bed. Lighting a lamp, he left his room and walked down the corridor that led to his workshop.

"I see, chose a place no one but you would know, did you?"

For a while, Tupperman looked around wistfully at the stone forge, blacksmith's anvil, the hammer and other smithing tools left lying around as they were picked out by the lamp's flame. Having worked to produce gadgets himself, this was a familiar place in the first stage of their production process.

Serge's destination was the forge. Opening an iron lid, he dug down into the cold coals, then pulled an iron box from their depths. It contained the document that would determine the marquis's fate.

He handed the box to Tupperman.

"Well done. Forget everything that happened today. Actually, you don't have to do that—I'll give you your reward now. You, too, shall have the power of a Noble."

He brought his face closer to the blacksmith's throat.

The act of drinking someone's blood had a magical power to it that for an instant plunged even the ultra-keen senses of a Noble into the depths of oblivion. However, that only applied to their own kind. The breathing of a human coming up behind them, their footsteps, their presence—try as they might to hide them all, there was absolutely no way they could go unnoticed. However, Tupperman sensed nothing until a voice told him, "Stop."

When he turned to look, an expression of astonishment had risen on his face.

"Y-you . . . What the hell are you doing here?"

"Come with me," said the shadowy figure behind him. "You can still prove useful."

"Don't make me laugh. Why would I ever take orders from you? My master is—"

Tupperman's breath caught in his throat. The person he was speaking to had brought a hand out from behind their back. And Tupperman's eyes were riveted to the longsword it held.

"Come," said the shadowy figure.

Sensing the inescapable power in that word, Tupperman exclaimed, "I'm getting out of here!"

His right hand reached for what looked to be a longsword test piece work-in-progress leaning against the forge. With a cry he swung it, and his opponent deftly dodged it, driving the other longsword into Tupperman's chest. The only reason it had narrowly missed his heart was because of the Noble agility his body had acquired.

"Too bad," he said as he made a thrust with his longsword.

Sparks flew. His opponent had also parried.

†

It was several minutes later that Tupperman hurriedly exited the house.

There was only an hour until dawn. If there were to be a battle, it would probably be the final one. This much everyone understood. Therefore, when Tupperman returned, everyone but the old lady wore looks of suspicion on their faces.

"Where have you been out dillydallying?" Duchess Marlingen inquired crossly.

"My apologies. A number of things came up," he replied.

"Hmm," she said, giving his throat a long, hard look. "Well, it doesn't much matter what happened. So long as you haven't lost your talent for massages, that is."

"I thought you'd never ask," the puppet master replied, a beaming smile rising on his face, but then his expression looked like he wanted to vomit.

They went to Old El's room. To Lydia and Old El, who held stake-firing guns at the ready, he said, "Please, rest assured. I'm my usual self."

"Shut up," the old man told him, adding, "And beat it. Think we'd trust anyone who'd gone missing so long in a place like this?"

"That's understandable. You can't trust anyone. And that goes double for verbal agreements. But worst of all is probably the people who say they love you. Especially if they're Nobility. I was almost taken in myself once," he laughed.

"Daybreak'll be here in an hour. Just gotta be patient until then. And given the circumstances, we've gotta cut loose anybody that seems even a little bit suspect. So go on back to your old lady. Get going!" Old El told him.

"What a truly regrettable turn of events, when you no longer trust a friend who's accompanied you on your journey this far. Is there no love here?"

"Shut your trap and get out!"

And so the puppet master was expelled from their room.

"One more hour to go," Old El murmured, his face a mask of tension.

"One more hour," Tupperman remarked in a carefree manner.

"Just an hour," the duchess groaned, sounding far from amused.

And there was one more person who donned a disturbing smile, saying, "One more hour. That rascal Tupperman has done us a great service." It was the marquis. Smiling even more broadly, he continued, "Just as you instructed him to do."

Matilda nodded silently. "Yes, very good. However, would it not be best to confirm the contents of the box just to be certain, Father?"

"Yes, such goes without saying."

The marquis touched the iron box sitting in front of him—the one that contained a deed ceding rights to all his debts. Lifting the lid, he found a row of small keys. He'd been given the combination by the puppet master.

When he'd entered the seven-digit number, a bass male voice from within the box said, *So nice of you to come.* Its tone was almost threatening. *I will now open up for you. Consider yourself fortunate.*

"What is the meaning of all this?" snarled the marquis, baring his teeth.

"It must be some form of jest," said the equally amazed Matilda.

The lid opened. There was, indeed, a letter inside it.

"Rather cheeky for a lowly box," said Marquis Verenis, extending his hand.

The instant his fingertips touched the letter, it burst into flames. Not surprisingly, father and daughter alike were astounded, and at that point the box let out a shrill laugh.

I was constructed by Elias Sodom, the world's greatest gadgeteer. I will not reveal my secrets so easily—would you care to play with me some more? You needn't worry. That letter just now was a fake.

"Damn you," the marquis growled, grinding his fangs together. "Give me the document immediately. If not, I shall burn it, box and all! And then we shall have no further need of you."

Oh, you could go without being sure of my contents? the box said with a mocking laugh. *It may be that all my contents are fake, and the real one has been hidden somewhere else. Could you rest easily after destroying me without first confirming this? Perhaps I contain the location of the real one in writing!*

"Matilda—summon Tupperman for me!"

No point in that, no point at all, the box said condescendingly. *Unfortunately, Sodom is a master of gadgetry on a whole different level than Tupperman. Tupperman himself will admit it. Call him in if you like, but you won't see my contents until I consent or succumb, regardless. So, will you throw in the towel or give it your best shot? Hmm?*

Pale fingers touched the box.

Oh, trying to charm me with feminine wiles now, are we?

"I would never think to do such a thing," Matilda said with a sweet smile. "The modifications Father had done to my body can be applied in a variety of situations. See if I don't unravel your mechanisms."

The box was left speechless. For it had seen the way Matilda smiled.

Eventually, the room was filled by an indignant cry that seemed to freeze the very air.

"Damn that bastard for tricking me, of all people!"

It was unclear whether the Nobleman's indignation was due to the reason stated, or because it had taken an hour to open the box.

III

Dawn came without incident. Ironically, the Nobles were not the only ones who then went to sleep. The sunlight invited both Old El and Lydia to slumber as well. Nevertheless, Lydia tried her best to stay awake. For Didi's sake.

"No, you can't go outside," she kept telling him, and Didi understood. However, as soon as Lydia drifted off, the boyish frustration that'd been bottled up so long began whispering to him. *It'll be okay if it's just for a little while. Why not step outside?* The conflict within him lasted less than ten seconds.

A few minutes after Lydia set off for dreamland, the boy stepped out into the corridor with muted footsteps. He didn't intend to do anything rash. He just wanted to hang around for a while in the room's immediate surroundings.

It had never occurred to Didi it might be this bright inside a Noble's castle.

"Wow, it ain't all that different from our house," he remarked.

Walking without particular purpose, he headed toward the great staircase. Peering down it from the top, he found the bottom of it not-surprisingly swathed in darkness. A figure in crimson was on the bottom step and headed up the stairs.

Didi stopped in his tracks. He was a child of the Frontier. He'd heard more than enough about the Nobility and their way of life. However, the young lady in a crimson dress who stood before him seemed nothing except beautiful.

"You were awake?" the young lady said with a smile. "In that case, I suppose one could say you and I are the only humans."

The boy was at a loss for words.

Looking over Didi's head at the row of doors down the corridor, the young lady said, "Wait a moment. Then we can play."

And having said that, she walked down to the door to the old lady's room. A push was enough to open the door. She immediately came out again.

"Where has she gone?" the young lady mused. Coming over to Didi, she inquired gently, "Do you know?"

"Uh-uh."

"I see. Well, would you care to help me search for her?"

The boy didn't know what to say.

"I shan't do anything to her. I simply wish to discuss the repayment of a debt."

Matilda's smiling face suffused Didi's brain. The boy nodded.

"Here, then."

Didi sheepishly took hold of the left hand Matilda offered him. His cheeks were flushed.

The two of them slowly descended the stairs.

"Why are you bringing me along?" the boy asked.

"Besides the two of us, there is someone else walking about this morning. Just being on guard against that."

"Oh."

"Father has told me to strike down this man named El, but I choose to do what is in my own best interest."

"I see."

"Such is the state between Father and I."

"Hmm," the boy said. "Ma and Pa were always fighting. Pa called her a 'lousy house pig,' and Ma said he was her 'worse half.'"

"You don't say?" Matilda remarked, a strange look on her face. These were terms unknown to the Noble's language.

"But when there wasn't enough to eat, Pa would say he was full and let Ma and me eat. The next day, Ma would give Pa her share."

"So, your mother and father were liars."

"No!" the boy snapped, pulling his hand from Matilda's.

"I see. Then it seems they were merely reticent."

"Huh?"

"Worry not, someday you will understand. When you're older."

On descending the stairs, Matilda raised her right hand and a three-dimensional image was projected in midair. It was a floor plan of the castle.

Gazing at it intently, she said, "She's not there. Where could she be hiding? Of course, despite being the place I was born and raised, this castle still has many places I know not. This will take some time. Child, where do you think she is?"

Didi stared at Matilda. The look in his eyes said he still didn't trust her completely.

Matilda smiled.

"Around here," he said, pointing to a room near the top of the northern tower.

"Why do you think that?"

"Just a hunch."

Matilda nodded. "Let's go look, shall we?" she said.

"So, what do I get if I'm right?"

"What do you desire?"

"I wanna be a Noble."

"Why is that?"

"Because then I can eat my fill."

"You shouldn't ask for that."

"Why not?"

"You are ill-suited for Noble life. You lack class."

"What's class?"

"Class is not asking that question."

"Huh. Sounds pretty interesting."

As they walked down a corridor with no end in sight, Didi looked all around and remarked in an impressed tone, "Noble castles are so cool. They're so big and fancy. Bet it'd take the rest of my life to go around and see the whole works."

"The rest of your life?"

"Yeah."

"This isn't much of a castle. The lord has sold off everything. Even treasures and pieces of art passed down from our ancestors."

"For booze?" asked the boy.

"No."

"Women?"

Clapping a hand over her mouth, Matilda laughed. "Is that how one comes to be destitute where you live?"

"For the most part. Our neighbor Old Man Burgundy ran off with a bar girl, and Mr. Yojirico who lived across the street from us was an alcoholic who ended up splashing booze all over his house and setting it on fire."

"How dramatic."

"You think so?"

"And what became of the old man who ran off with a girl?"

"She dumped him and he hanged himself. Lots of stuff like that happens."

"I dare say it does."

"What about your father, miss?"

"He used me for a transformation."

"A transformation?"

"Yes, into a tool to satisfy his own greed."

"Satisfy his greed? Do Nobles loan out money, too?"

"No, we were borrowers."

"From humans?"

"Yes."

"Wow! Nobles are just like humans."

Matilda grinned wryly. "Perhaps we are."

In no time, the pair had arrived at the tower room Didi had pointed out.

"When did she manage this?" Matilda murmured, her eyes invested with a red glow and fangs peeking from the corners of her lips. Her hand reached for the door knob. It didn't budge.

"Damn you," she said, pulling with all her might, but it wouldn't move an inch.

Didi's eyes went wide at the scene, which was the polar opposite of what'd happened at the old lady's room.

Drawing a breath, Matilda took a step back. It seemed she might've given up, but plucking a strand of hair from her head with her left hand, she wrapped it around the bar that tied the door to the stone wall.

"Back away ten paces," she told Didi, and then her form quickly grew blurry.

A sharp pain shot through Didi's right cheek. Matilda's entire body right down to the molecular level was producing ultra-vibrations, and they traveled through the hair to be transmitted into the door the duchess had shut. There was a shrill ringing in his eardrums, and Didi covered his ears. It felt like sweat was gushing from every pore in his body. But it stopped.

Even as he reeled, Didi saw Matilda open the door. With a haughty laugh, she said, "As if the ancient powers were any match for those of the new age!"

The interior was choked with darkness.

Matilda took a step inside. A terrible nausea assailed her. Unable to stop herself, she retched. It was a stream of blood she expelled.

The blackness within was not the darkness. It was a vampiric dimension that sucked the blood from intruders.

"Damn you! My blood—"

The young lady's cries of pain reached Didi's ears.

"Miss?!" he exclaimed, feet pounding the floor as he raced toward her.

"Stay back!" Matilda shouted at him, dropping limply to her knees.

Her hair all stood on end. And the boy heard a different cry of pain. The cry of the darkness that'd been pierced by her hair. The hair wasn't hair at all. It was thousands of needles. Not only that, but when they started to hum, they gave off tens of thousands of degrees of blistering heat.

The darkness writhed, trying to absorb Matilda's blood. Something resembling ash fell all over the Noblewoman.

When she stepped unsteadily through the doorway again, Didi raced over to her. Her dress had been crimson from the start, but now her head was stained red as well. The boy didn't recoil, but rather grabbed Matilda by the shoulders and dragged her away from the door. A thick trail of blood followed her.

"Flee . . ."

Didi didn't understand the meaning of the single word Matilda groaned. Only after dragging her more than six feet did he look at the doorway and notice something.

Was that something like a black cloud roiling out of it?

"It's coming after us," she said.

His blood froze. Still, he didn't give up. Didi put even more power into his little arms and legs.

"Flee!"

"No!"

The cloud enveloped Matilda's feet.

"I'll show you!" Didi snarled, standing up and raising his fist before charging at the cloud.

"Don't!"

Matilda's cry was split by a stark light.

About to swallow up Didi, the cloud ripped in two, turning to black dust that covered the floor. As the boy stared in amazement in the direction the flash had originated, his eyes were filled by a youthful face brimming with a dreadful beauty.

"D!" Matilda cried out, all the while trying desperately to conceal her weakened state.

Repayment Complete

CHAPTER 8

I

"W e were supposed to be underground, but we came out on the highest floor of the castle. Pretty weird place."

Looking back and forth between the left hand that'd said that in a hoarse voice and D's beautiful countenance, Didi said in a tone that bordered on tears, "Mister, the lady's gonna die." Relief had calmed his emotions.

D came over, running his eyes over Matilda from head to toe, then placing his left hand on the swell of her left breast.

"Oh, that's naughty!" the boy exclaimed, eyes going wide.

With the slightest trace of a wry grin, the Hunter waited for his left hand to remark, "That should fix 'er."

It didn't look that way at all to Didi, who was still flustered.

"She's okay," D said, and the boy's shoulders finally came down at the sound of the Hunter's voice. At the same time, there was a noise behind him. That of the door closing.

Looking that way uneasily, Didi then turned his eyes toward Matilda.

"Miss, are you okay?"

"I am . . . fine."

"Great," the boy said, and something glittering ran down his cheeks.

"Why do you cry?" asked the Noblewoman.

"Because he's happy," D replied in place of the sobbing Didi.

Looking over at him, Matilda quickly turned her eyes back to the Hunter and asked, "Why did you save me?"

"Why did you save the boy?"

An angry expression graced her face for an instant, then Matilda let out a long breath. "Kill me," she said. "I will comply with Father's commands. Not a single one of you shall be allowed to leave here alive. If you would not die—kill me."

"Miss, don't," Didi begged Matilda. "Don't say that. You're scaring me, okay? Just quit it!"

Matilda fell silent.

D said softly, "I haven't been hired to kill you. Not as long as you don't make an attempt on Old El's life."

"Take that child away from here," Matilda said.

Saying nothing, D took hold of the Noblewoman's arm and pulled her up. The Hunter laid her over his shoulder as if she didn't weigh anything at all.

"Set me down! Will you not set me down again?!"

"Save your breath," the hoarse voice said mockingly. "Left to your own devices, you'd probably go after that old lady again. And it seems he wants to stop that from happening. For somebody with a face like that, he's actually a big softie when—"

There was a choked cry, and the hoarse voice said no more.

Not unclenching the fist he'd made, D began to descend the staircase.

Once they were outside the tower, Matilda climbed off his shoulder on her own.

"Are you going back?" D inquired, staring coolly at the lovely princess.

"Miss, what're those?" Didi asked, suddenly pointing at something.

Beyond the overgrown garden, a fairly large pond was visible. There were swans floating in it.

"Those are boats."

"I wanna ride in one," said the boy. "Let's go for a ride."

Matilda didn't know what to say.

The hoarse voice prodded her, saying, "Why not? For folks not good around water, the Nobility sure must've wanted to hide it, since they always built their resorts by the water's edge or put ponds in them. But you're not afraid of the water at all. Take him for a ride."

"But I—"

"You've never experienced the daytime, right? Go anyways. Should be real interesting!"

Didi took a firm grasp of the hand of Matilda, who was still just standing there. It was Matilda who first went into motion.

Tufts of cloud hung in the sky. The shadow that was cast on the marble-paved path was from one such tuft.

On seeing one of the gigantic swans stopped by the wharf, Didi pursed his lips and said, "It's sooo dirty. It's totally covered in dust!"

"That is because the power was shut down here nearly a thousand years ago," the Noblewoman replied.

"Really?"

"However, they should still run. Watch."

Matilda beckoned with one hand, and one of the boats glided closer, beating its wings. The dust flaked off, dirtying the surface of the water. Didi's eyes were open as wide as they could possibly go. The bird that could've passed for an enormous dirty dish was now gleaming and white.

"Climb aboard," Matilda told him.

Once she was also aboard, the swan glided toward the center of the pond without her needing to do anything.

"Wow, this is really great!"

Just watching Didi intently as he jumped up and down, Matilda asked, "Are you enjoying yourself?"

"Yeah."

"Would you like to fly through the air?"

"What? You can't be serious. This is a boat, isn't it?"

"It's a swan."

Matilda raised a hand, a motion that was recognized somewhere, and though it was unclear what kind of machinery went into operation, the swan beat its wings mightily and rose toward the sky with dozens of streams of water trailing behind it.

"Th-this is awesome!" the boy exclaimed.

"If we so desired, we could go to the moon. And the speed, well, that would be perhaps a tenth the speed of light."

"Higher—take us up a lot, lot, higher, please!"

Before his shout had even finished, the pond below had been reduced to about the size of Didi's fist.

"There's no wind. And it doesn't even make a sound!"

Up in the heavens, the boy was as excited as could be. But his expression suddenly clouded, and he asked, "What's wrong?"

Shaking her head, Matilda replied, "Nothing."

Though her eyes reflected the sky and clouds, a memory was now emblazoned in her brain as they climbed—a vivid image burned there of a figure headed toward the building where Old El and the others were sleeping.

D toured the castle's interior. He intended to learn the entire layout during the day. The only member of the living dead who could walk in the light of the sun was currently playing with the boy somewhere up in the skies above.

He came out into the courtyard. The rich, green area had marble paving stones running through it, and statues of all sizes were on display there.

A cold wind blew from somewhere beyond the sculptures. It had a sufficient chill for D to turn his eyes that way.

About ten minutes after heading in that direction, the Hunter came to a world of white. The ground was entirely frozen over in an area that must've been more than eight acres. The white rock towering before D was a cliff of ice.

"Somebody's got weird tastes," his left hand remarked. "There's a Noble who made a fiery hell underground, too. Fire and water are troublesome areas for the Nobility, but it's said this habit they have of keeping them close at hand is a manifestation of Nobles' self-destructive urges. In other words, they want to die."

D extended his left hand before him.

"Wow, that wind is two hundred and forty degrees below zero," the hoarse voice remarked. "That's cold enough to turn a human to ice right down to the marrow of their bones with just one gust. And the temperature at the source of that wind is minus four hundred and fifty-seven—just a hair above absolute zero. Nothing can exist in the middle of that iceberg. Okay, let's pull back. Pull it back, now!"

The moment D was about to change direction, he was struck from head to toe by a terrific gust of wind. His muscles froze in an instant, making his movements torpid. An arrow pierced the left side of the Hunter's chest. That he merely fell to one knee from that could only be described as being entirely true to form for him. However, when the white ground beneath his feet collapsed, D was unable to leap away. In his black raiment, he was held fast amid the glistening white, and he fell. Into minus four hundred and fifty-seven degrees—and the abyss of a truly frozen hell where no substance could exist.

From the top of a surveillance tower a good five hundred yards away, the figure that had achieved their aims with a crossbow sixteen feet wide set the two-hundred-twenty-pound weapon down at their feet, turned their face to the sun above, and let out a satisfied breath at their success in battle. The rest of the work would be easy.

Returning to the castle from partway up the tower, and slowly walking down the long corridor, they turned a number of corners to finally reach Old El's room. The door was locked, but the figure only had to touch one hand to it for it to open on its own.

Both the old man and Lydia were sleeping. The figure whispered into Old El's ear, telling him to wake up. When the old man got up, he was a puppet devoid of its own will. The figure whispered a question to him. When Old El replied, the shadowy figure was enveloped with rage. Under the circumstances, they would have to go to an additional location. However, going there right now would accomplish nothing.

Their anger was directed at the old man and Lydia, who were right there. The figure's hands reached for Old El's throat. The fingers pressed into the flesh, and the old man groaned. However, the fingers came away again. There was no longer any need to keep the old man alive. However, since the figure wasn't entirely sure about certain facts, it would've been reckless to kill him. And the same went for Lydia, too.

Daytime was the best time for the shadowy figure to recover. However, chance had foiled the figure at every turn. *Hurry up and sink, sun,* the figure thought, grinding their teeth together.

"This is not good," the hoarse voice said at an abnormally weak volume.

D lay at the bottom of the icy area with his left hand haphazardly extended out onto the ice—and the remark had come from the tiny face that'd formed on the palm of his hand. A flame burned in the depths of its throat.

"We've got the works—earth, wind, fire, and water. But the earth, wind, and water are all frozen," the hoarse voice continued. "Ummm, this is gonna be a toughie."

His left hand put its palm against the ground. There was a raspy sound like ice being scraped, and then the hand was quickly raised again. When the tiny mouth opened, it sucked in the wind with a howling whistle, and the flame in its depths blazed. And then feebly began to fade.

The four elements of earth, wind, fire, and water could be said to be the source of D's life—but three of those were frozen now, turning to ice and threatening to extinguish the fire of life.

The sun would be setting in no time. The time of the demons would come.

Can you make it out before that, D?

II

Darkness fell.

Tupperman awoke. His whole body was brimming with power. That was proof that he'd joined the family of the night.

A shadowy figure suddenly appeared before him. It was Marquis Verenis.

"What a surprise. And what may I do for you?" the puppet master inquired.

The Nobleman grabbed him by the front of his shirt and lifted him high over his head, saying, "The Elias Sodom box that you took from Serge Pattaya—where have you hidden its contents?"

"Its contents? I don't know anything about that. I did indeed take the box from him and give it to you, as you know."

"Yes. But the box had nothing in it."

"Th-that's news to me. The old man must've lied to—"

"Yes. I thought so, as well. You are an imposter of the real Tupperman, and were bitten by Matilda. You would not have the ability to prevaricate." The marquis gave the man an elegant smile, continuing, "However, I asked Old El about it. And he could not lie in answer to my query. The old man's response was the same as before—he said it was entrusted to Pattaya the blacksmith."

"Yes, and I got it from Pattaya—but we know nothing of the authenticity of its contents."

"No, we know. Why? Because Matilda opened the Elias Sodom box with her own hands. The box surrendered, and it confessed that the contents had been taken by someone else!"

"It—it wasn't me," Tupperman protested.

"No, it was. The box itself asserted that the only one besides Sodom who could open his box was a gadgeteer on par with him. You— Langen Tupperman."

"There must be some mistake. I'm not the real Tupperman. I am but a puppet Tupperman created—an imitation. And I now serve your daughter. How could I disobey her commands?"

Turbulence coursed across Marquis Verenis's face.

"An excellent point. The same thought occurred to me. And then, an idea came to me. Where is your former master, the real Tupperman?"

"Where? How should I know?"

As the marquis looked at the stupidly blinking puppet master, the Nobleman's expression changed. Verenis's eyes blazed with crimson, and his fangs were exposed—it was the face of the devil himself.

"I looked at a map of the castle," said the marquis. "There is no Tupperman here save you."

The man was at a loss for words.

"In other words, the other one has vanished. He has either fled or been killed. And he could not flee. Because he was bitten by Matilda. Meaning he was killed. But by whom? It could only be you."

"I-I'd never! When could I even do it in the first place? I retrieved the box as instructed and have been here ever since."

"Yes, you have—since returning from the blacksmith's house, at least. And up until you left for the blacksmith's house."

Not a word from Tupperman.

"What happened there? Can you not tell me? In that case, allow me to tell you. You went to Serge Pattaya's house and took the box. And then, you were killed and the box was taken from you."

"Th-that's the most preposterous story I—"

"But I think it more than just a story. When we dispatched you to the blacksmith's, neither I nor my daughter suspected anything. And you got into the rotodyne along with *the other you* that had concealed himself in it, and he killed you while you were out there. Or did you kill him? Tell me, the real Mr. Tupperman, which was it?"

"I'm merely a—"

"No, you are the real one. Therefore, you were able to slay your imposter. After all, you were his former master, were you not? However, when the imposter was bitten, Matilda became his master. There was only one way around that. You needed to be bitten, just as the imposter had been. Only then could you regain your control over the imposter. Therefore, you requested Matilda give you the kiss before the imposter got into the rotodyne, and Matilda granted your request. However, there is no reason to let the old man live any longer if you have the deed in hand. It would be greatly to your advantage for him to die. So, why did you stray from your course, then?"

"Because I didn't want to see the Frontier descend into war and utter chaos. That's where I draw the line," Tupperman replied.

"I see. Then something of your human heart yet remained, did it?" Marquis Verenis inquired, his crimson eyes open wide. "Good enough. If such is the case, there is no point in any further discussion. On occasion, a strange aberration like you is created. So, where is the deed?"

Tupperman said nothing.

The marquis's right hand grabbed hold of Tupperman's nose.

"It would be a simple matter to make you tell me. With but a single glare from me, you would not only divulge its hiding place, but kill yourself with your own two hands as well. I shan't do that, though. I am somewhat vexed. So I shall do this the old-fashioned way. A way known as torture."

In the next instant, Tupperman's nose was torn right off. Blood spilled out, thoroughly soaking the puppet master's chest.

"Does it hurt? Human hands and tools can do it without drawing blood, but when our hands do it the agony is tremendous. You mustn't tell me yet. Next is this."

Tupperman's left ear came off with a long tearing sound. His right ear was next. Discarding the bloody bit, Marquis Verenis extended a pair of fingers right in line with Tupperman's eyes.

"The eyes are even more painful! Would you care to tell me now?"

An answer came quickly enough.

"It's right here."

An unseen sword pierced the heart of the marquis, who'd just twisted halfway around.

"Gaaah!" Verenis exclaimed in a cry of agony unlike that of any other creature, and he stared at the assassin who'd struck from behind him.

The blood-spattered Tupperman fell to the floor.

"My . . . Duchess . . . what a strange way of saying hello you have," the marquis said, blood mixing with his words.

"You've gone and made a terrible mess of my personal masseur. I'll see to it you're more than repaid in kind!"

"Duchess—I am Matilda's father!"

"So what?" Duchess Marlingen replied. "The only one your death would inconvenience is that old man. I just need to get your daughter to pay me back. And if she can't, I'll have her use that strange power of hers to rob people or something and make enough to take care of me for the rest of my days."

"How . . . how incredibly pedestrian . . . I could weep," said the Nobleman.

"If you wanna cry, be my guest. I've suffered more than you have here when you hurt my precious masseur."

The air snapped like the crack of a whip.

The marquis's body was sent flying, crashing into a stone wall more than fifteen feet away. As he slid down it, the duchess told him, "I don't care whether you die or not, but the next time you do anything to one of my personal possessions, you'll sorely regret it!"

The old lady looked down at Tupperman at her feet, saying, "You're pathetic, too. No doubt you went and got yourself bitten, though probably not by him. So, how about you slap him around some?"

"I'm not really up to it," Tupperman replied, giving Duchess Marlingen a smile despite the fact that he was clutching a bleeding nose and ear.

"Off we go." Turning once again toward the marquis, the old lady pulled a document out of the front of her blouse and showed it to him, saying, "Look, here's the deed you were after. If you want it, come try and take it."

Chortling, she walked toward the door, while a flash of black flew at her back with a whine. The sound of wood meeting steel reverberated, and a longsword arced up to the ceiling, where it stuck.

"You coward. You're not even fit to be a member of the Nobility," the duchess said, looking the marquis right in the eye. However, her back was still turned to the Nobleman. Her head alone had turned a hundred and eighty degrees—but no, her arms were also facing his direction.

Still gripping the cane that had struck down Marquis Verenis's sword just now in her right hand, she said, "This should finish you!"

The duchess extended her cane.

Just as the tip of it was about to unleash her deadly Qigong, the marquis rolled his body to the right.

"Damnation!"

His body rolled like a fallen top, and the old woman's head and arms alone turned to follow him. Her final attack scored a direct hit on the wall by the doorway where Marquis Verenis had made his escape.

"Shit, I seem to be losing my touch in my old age, too." As she said that, the old lady turned her head and arms back to their proper positions. "Well, let's go," she said, but when she turned toward Tupperman, there was no sign of the noseless and earless puppet master, though there was the sound of footsteps passing once more through that doorway and fading down the corridor.

"Oh, this is not going well," a frozen voice groaned at the bottom of the white hole. It was D's left hand. "Damn, it's all I can do just to keep our body temperature up. I don't have enough power for more. We'll be stuck here for the rest of our lives!"

Its serious tone was swallowed up by the cold wind.

From the depths of that wind, a voice called out, "D!"

"Huh?!" his left hand exclaimed, moving in that direction. "Matilda, wasn't it? I'm surprised to see you here. Come to finish us off?"

"I suppose I could."

Snow clung to the face and body of the lovely princess, and every time she spoke it went flying. Was the lithe young woman able to operate in the depths of this brutal cold due to the modifications the marquis had had her undergo?

"Money makes the world go round," the hoarse voice said, sounding impressed.

The young lady grinned wryly at that, then came over by D's head and extended her left hand. Her right hand went across the opposite wrist, and a stream of red began dribbling down into D's mouth. It was fresh blood spilling from the wrist she'd just clawed open with her fingernail. The temperature was minus four hundred and fifty-seven degrees—cold enough to freeze the very molecules of anything. However, Matilda's blood was hot and red, and it rained sensuously onto D's lips.

Lowering her arm before long, she said, "I saw you from up in the sky. Before I could venture down here, though, it took some time to adjust my body."

The Noblewoman began to effortlessly climb the rock. Just before disappearing into the far reaches of the white air, she said, "The depths of earth are dark and cold. The sky is the complete opposite. The child and I enjoyed it!" At least, that was how it sounded between the gusts of wind.

As soon as she opened her eyes, Lydia was horrified. Didi was gone. Her mind went completely blank. She shook Old El awake, and the two of them flew out of the room. In the corridor they split up, one going left while the other went right, with Lydia dashing forward blindly. Old El said he'd get the marquis to look for the boy, but she didn't trust the Nobility at all. Didi might've been abducted.

Usually lit by lamps, the interior of the castle seemed far more expansive in the light of day, and that left Lydia feeling unsettled. The footsteps that echoed in the sunlight were all swallowed up, and no matter how much she ran and ran the distance never seemed to decrease. Why, when she called out Didi's name, her voice didn't even seem to reach her own ears.

Lydia was in the middle of a smallish hall, the exact location of which she didn't know, when she halted. Someone was watching. The walls and floor were illuminated by lamps on the walls—but someone was in the darkness left between them.

Eyes were trained on Lydia. It was a gaze of hatred and desire—and that desire was a hunger.

The strength drained from Lydia's body with alarming speed. Desperately holding herself in check all the while, she shouted, "Who's there?"

A voice right by her ear said, "How nice, meeting you here."

Fingers like iron clamped down on her shoulders, and cold breath fell on the nape of her neck. It was only for a second, and she had no time to think about what was happening. A sharp pain shot through the nape of her neck. Despair exploded through the girl's brain.

"Nooo!" Lydia cried out, her body quivering.

III

It was Old El that heard her scream. With only his instincts to rely on, it took him thirty minutes to race to the scene.

Lydia had given up the ghost. Her throat was torn open wide. And it went without saying there were teeth-marks on the nape of her neck.

Crouching down, the old man said to himself, "Rather kill you than make you one of 'em, eh?"

Humans who'd been fed upon turned into the pseudo-Nobles referred to as their "servants." Yet there were many among the Nobility who didn't care for them. Because it meant raising a lowly human up to their own level. They would tear open the victim's throat either before drinking their blood or once they'd finished, denying them the pathway to immortality.

Not a drop of blood flowed from the girl's torn throat. All of it had been consumed.

"A hell of a thing to do," Old El groaned. "Damn that Verenis!"

A terrible strength pressed into his shoulder.

"What in the—?!"

Perhaps it would've been better if it'd been Marquis Verenis.

Crimson eyes gleamed in Lydia's waxen face.

"B-but you—you got killed . . ." the old man stammered.

"I . . . died . . ." she said, working pale and bloodless lips. "But . . . I . . . got some licks in . . . Their wounds . . . will never heal."

Lydia's other hand rose in front of Old El's face. Her nails were stained with red.

"You done good," the old man told her, taking a tight grip on her fingers.

"The kid . . . Didi . . ." she said in what was nearly a sob, and her face had returned to that of Lydia. "I'm begging you . . ."

"Leave him to me," the old man replied with a vehement nod.

"Good . . . That's good . . . Thank . . . you . . . I was going to my uncle's . . . even though he's really poor . . . and told us we couldn't . . . but I was gonna go there . . . anyway . . . Since . . . there was nobody else . . . I could count on . . . But that doesn't matter anymore . . ."

"That's crazy talk," Old El said, gazing at her pale face. "If you'd just said the word, asked me to loan you some money—I could've set you up with all you needed."

". . . Interest-free?"

"That I couldn't do."

Lydia smiled. "I know, right? You're such a miser."

All the strength drained from Lydia's body.

Swinging his head from side to side once, Old El slipped his hand behind Lydia's back. However, he then laid down beside her and closed his eyes. In a low voice, he began to recite some words.

"O good person, tarry not in the town of grief. Thou goest to the town of the joyous dead. The requiem comes to the living. Nevertheless, rejoice! Rejoice!"

It was a prayer for the dead. The last time Old El had heard it, Lydia had been the one reciting it.

Even after finishing the prayer, the old man didn't move for some time.

Behind him, someone said, "Very nicely done."

As the old man stiffened, Marquis Verenis appeared before him, no longer even attempting to mask the naked hostility in his expression.

"You bastard . . . You've got your nerve . . ." Old El groaned, drawing the stake gun from his belt.

The marquis took a step forward, seizing the old man's wrist.

Seemingly turned to stone by the pain that pierced him to the very core of his brain, Old El groaned, "Do this . . . to me . . . and the collection papers . . . go to that Greater Noble . . . And things . . . will go badly . . . for you!"

"I was shown those papers by their current owner. Now I need not keep a swine of a man like you around any longer. But drinking your blood would be vile. I know not who did this to her, but I shall now tear your throat right open just as this woman's was."

"You son of a bitch!" the thrashing financier snarled, but then Old El's brow was furrowed by something other than agony. "Hold up. You didn't do this?"

A second later, the old man's body sailed through the air and crashed into the stone wall across from him.

The next thing the old man knew, he was lying on a stone altar. His arms and legs were bound to it by spring-loaded shackles. From the foot of the altar, a trio of figures were looking down at him. More than Marquis Verenis or Matilda, it was the third member that made Old El bug his eyes.

"Toba?!"

The beastmaster stood there with an emotionless face, while behind him a black shape let out a beastly growl.

"This man is still of use," said Verenis. "He has been stitched back together and given new organs, but there still weren't enough." The marquis raised his right hand, and a cylindrical surgery machine descended from the ceiling. "So, I have decided to take some of your parts. I have already checked them, and they are all I could hope for."

"Damn you—planning on skipping out on what you owe, Verenis?"

"I have heard it said that it is impossible to collect on a hundred percent of debts," he replied. "This is one of those cases. Toba, yank out his pancreas first."

"Y-yank it out? Don't do it, Toba. You still owe me money too, you bastard!"

"Yes, both I and Toba—we do want to be thorough."

Toba gave a toss of his chin. The black shape behind him stepped forward. Patting its head, the beastmaster walked over to the altar.

"Stop," Old El cried out. "Don't do this."

"Your mistake was in thinking you might burst in on a Nobleman where you are merely a lowly human loan shark," said Marquis Verenis. "With every organ of yours I remove, I shall give you a treatment to prolong your life. Living on until nothing remains of you will be interesting, but oh so painful!"

"Don't. I'll knock ten percent off."

The marquis leaned back and laughed heartily.

"Fifteen percent? How about twenty? If that ain't enough, just freaking kill me!"

"What a truly entertaining man you are. By all means, continue negotiating till the very end."

One of the black shape's forepaws reached for Old El's chest. Claws sprang from it.

"Don't do this, Toba. You're just gonna end up dead again!" the financier exclaimed.

"I know not what you could mean," said the marquis. And he told the beastmaster, "Do it."

Toba nodded.

The claws pressed against the old man's skin.

"Toba!"

A second later, the beastmaster exploded.

Liquid gunpowder had been introduced into Toba's body. And the trigger switch was implanted in one of Old El's molars. That was the natural outcome. The impact and flames enveloped his beast, and the altar fell on its side. The shackles were retracted.

Quickly taking stock of the state of the flames and the marquis's location, Old El chose a blind spot and dashed toward the door. Just when he thought he'd made it out, a voice suddenly called to him, "Hey, old guy!"

He knew who it was without even looking.

It was Didi who stood by the doorway.

"What are you doing?!" the old man snapped.

"Exploring."

"Are you soft in the head?"

Scooping the boy up without another word, Old El was about to start running again—but a hand as cold as ice grabbed him by the collar.

"Oh, that won't do!" Marquis Verenis howled. "I shall show you what becomes of loan sharks."

"I've got a kid to take care of. Let's make it thirty percent off."

"Enough!" the marquis said, taking Didi from the financier's arms. "Even a child can prove useful. Their bones, the internal organs—and the nervous system, in particular."

"Don't you dare!"

Marquis Verenis raised Didi high over his head.

"Quit it!" Didi cried.

"Be still," said the marquis, swinging his right hand around with all his might.

Didi should've been dashed against the floor, killing him instantly. However, while he was still hoisted high in the air, the boy was taken by a pair of delicate white hands.

"Matilda—you dare interfere with me?"

"Stop this, Father. Human or not, he is but a child."

Quickly backing away, the Noblewoman set Didi down on the far side of the corridor, then squared off against her father.

"Give me that child," said the marquis.

"Never. You are merciless with children, Father. Even with your very own daughter."

Perhaps the marquis felt something at that last remark, because turbulence streaked through his expression. But his eyes burned as if to atone for that, and both Matilda and Didi were blown some sixty feet down to the end of the corridor.

At the same time, the marquis dropped to his knees. For Matilda had expelled her breath at her father. The same poisonous breath that'd seared D's brain.

"You dare . . . disobey . . . your father?" Verenis said, his voice no longer really a voice.

"Yes. And I have always desired to do so."

As Matilda got back to her feet, somewhere in her body there was a sound like that of a motor.

"Go to your reward now, Father. But at least know that I will press on and realize your ambitions."

The marquis's body grew hazy, like a mirage. For Matilda was equipped with the same gravitational field generator as Brendon. Squeezed to conform to a place where mass increased infinitely and volume decreased infinitely, the space sank into the Dirac sea.

As Matilda dropped weakly to her knees, Didi threw his arms around her.

"Hey, what happened to your father?" Old El inquired.

"He faded away. We shall never see him again—or so I imagine, but I really know not."

"Faded away, you say? Hey, what the hell are we gonna do about that six hundred million dalas? This castle and his lands were collateral—and you were the damn interest on it!" Old El said to Matilda.

"Regretfully, I will not be an interest payment. Nor shall I cede this castle and lands to you."

"Huh?" Old El exclaimed, the air around him ringing with a high metallic sound.

The old man's body distorted.

"Y-you too? You plan on stiffing me? Even if I die, somebody's gonna collect!"

"Father converted me into a warrior. With the power I have, I need fear no one who comes to collect. Moreover, the deed of transfer is right there. It appears the results of Father's experiments were added to it as payment for the inconvenience. See now what those results were!"

As the Noblewoman said that, the old man fell to the floor.

Matilda was looking down the corridor. At the old lady and Tupperman, who were standing there.

"The deed of transfer—would you be so kind as to give it to me?" Matilda asked.

"I guess so. If you pay back what you owe me, that is," the duchess replied, her cane rising.

"I need not pay back money borrowed in a former life."

"I thought you'd say that!"

The two figures were connected by an unseen power. It changed direction three feet shy of Matilda, piercing the old woman.

Matilda's gravitational field could also be used as a defensive measure.

"Matilda, stop it!" Tupperman exclaimed, running out in front of the fallen duchess and shielding her.

"You said you loved me, but it was a lie," said Matilda. "Do you intend to break your promise to her, as well?"

It's said that on occasion, Nobles and humans wear exactly the same expressions. And it's also said that most of those expressions are sad ones. Such as the one Matilda now wore. However, the eyes of the lovely princess gave off beams of crimson light.

Tupperman twisted—and disappeared. But he wore a mournful look to the very last.

"Stop it! What the hell are you doing, psycho woman? He owes me fifty thousand dalas! And he borrowed another five million dalas from Verenis. Are you outta your mind?"

Matilda gave Old El no further reply. Her crimson eyes were trained on him—and on the old lady. Both of them had their bodies distorted by the gravitational field.

A brief scream split Matilda's lips. Lowering her chin ever so slightly, she looked down at the steel blade poking from between her breasts.

"Father . . . You live yet . . ."

"Indeed. I have returned, and it seems I must add the failure to be dutiful to your parents to your litany of sins."

"How . . . when my gravitational field was so . . ."

"Your power has ebbed terribly. You may have killed Tupperman, but you cannot kill me. Not even if you had a little blood to drink."

Marquis Verenis's right hand rose. Matilda's attire shredded, exposing a naked figure so alluring it might wake the dead. Five vermilion lines ran across it from her right breast down to her solar plexus.

Old El's eyes went wide.

"Lydia's fingernails—that was you?!"

"Judging from those wounds, I believe that girl was possessed by something not unlike ourselves. Most likely the ghost of some faux Noble. And that is why Matilda remains in that state despite drinking blood," the marquis declared.

Old El snapped at him, "S-s-stop it! She's my damn interest payment! Can you pay me back the whole six hundred million dalas, you bastard?!"

"I have just watched fifty million dalas of mine reduced to dust. There was yet some use to be had from that damnable Tupperman."

"Don't you lay a hand on that girl!" Duchess Marlingen fairly groaned from where she'd collapsed on the floor. "She hasn't paid me back yet, either."

"Silence, all of you!" the marquis howled, irritated. "Do you wretches think of naught save gold? You should be ashamed of yourselves!"

"That's rich coming from a deadbeat like you!" Old El shouted back.

"You think this is about shame or Nobility?" the duchess asked. "In this world, there's only coin. The sun, the moon, the stars—hell, they all move in accordance with the laws of money. Ignore that, and it'll be the end of you. Neither you nor your girl gets to die till you pay that money back. Don't die on us."

"Damn straight," Old El concurred. "Verenis—you oughta be ashamed of yourself for raising a hand to your daughter."

"You were the daughter I needed," the marquis said to the reeling Matilda. "But now, you are merely another obstacle. It cannot be helped. I shall accomplish the conquest of the Frontier by myself."

"Father . . . ?"

As Matilda looked at him with glassy eyes, the marquis thumped his chest and said, "In your case, I spent fifty billion dalas. But I was a hundred billion dalas. And my power is double, as well!" He laughed loudly. "There is no particular reason why I concealed this truth. I underwent the procedure after you did as I had become somewhat anxious about the prospects of you meekly following my lead. And I was correct in that, was I not? However, I find it difficult to believe how feeble you are now. What on earth happened?"

The answer came from the far end of the corridor.

"She donated some of her blood. To me."

A wind colder than the one that blew in that frozen hell chilled all present from head to toe.

"D," someone groaned.

A shadowy figure formed in the depths of the corridor, took human shape—and then, then, then, even his foes melted in rapture.

D!

"Your fight with your daughter is none of my concern," D said coldly, stopping about five yards shy of the marquis. "But I am indebted to your daughter. If you intend to harm her, I will slay you."

Somewhere on Marquis Verenis, there was the sound of a motor. D's form grew hazy.

"Not even Matilda could escape that!" the marquis laughed.

The effect quickly faded. He wasn't the least bit hazy. There was just D—and his gorgeous face.

As the marquis stood there rooted both by astonishment and ecstasy, D took a step forward, drawing his sword from his back and striking in a single fluid motion. Marquis Verenis was slashed open from the top of his head down to his solar plexus. His body sprayed fresh blood, but his flesh was reduced to dust before it could hit the floor, and then Old El let out a scream of unsurpassed sorrow and crossed the corridor.

On returning his blade to its scabbard, D looked around at the group and asked, "Where did she go?"

There was no sign of Matilda. Drops of blood led down the opposite end of the corridor from D.

"Well, I don't know," Duchess Marlingen said as she finally managed to pull herself up off the floor. "But with wounds like that, I don't care how much she'd been upgraded, she won't be doing any more fighting. She'd just be waiting to get staked. On the other hand, that'd probably be the best outcome in her eyes."

"Well, it ain't the best in mine!" Old El bellowed. "They made off with my six hundred million dalas, and the girl I figured was my best piece of collateral has gone missing. The castle and his lands are still here, but to be honest, there ain't nothing in the castle worth a damn, and it's gonna be a pain in the ass to unload. Ah, if this ain't just the worst possible way things coulda ended. Julas-Han Toba, Galkis Thomas, Langen Tupperman—they all stiffed me. Damn it, what a waste of a trip!"

"The job's finished," said D. "Now tell me what the Sacred Ancestor had to say."

The old man suddenly returned to normal. Licking his lips, after a few false starts he began to speak.

"It was in winter fifty years ago. I was mining sulfur in a hot spring area in the eastern Frontier. That day, I was walking around the hot spring closest to the volcano when the ground gave way, and I wound up falling into an underground cavern. This cave was freaking enormous. Large enough it coulda held a big ol' town.

There was an awful lotta sulfur smoke gushing up all over the place, choking the hell outta me. There were hot springs, too. Milky warm water gushing up here and there, bubbles coming to the surface and popping and crap. A little slice of hell. It must've been thirty feet up to the hole I'd fallen in. Knew I was lucky to have landed on my ass, but there was no way I was getting out that way again, so I set off in search of another exit.

"I walked for about ten minutes, I guess. And an old castle surrounded by massive crags caught my eye. He was in there. Saw him and his face, practically stared at them, even. That much I remember. When I try and ask myself what kind of clothes he was wearing or how his face looked, though, not a damn thing comes to me. Now, I know there's no way he could be, but he just seemed incredibly big, like a freaking mountain.

"While I'm standing there dumb as a post, he went and said something to me. I remember what sort of voice it was. Can't freaking put it in so many words, though. Pardon me if I just give you what he said. 'Tell the man called D this: I'll meet you in Jipa,' he said. That's it."

And then Old El collapsed.

"Jipa, eh?" the hoarse voice murmured.

"You know it?" D inquired.

"Vaguely. It's the name of a country that existed a long, long time ago—I think."

The Hunter said nothing.

"You'll meet there—meaning what, that's where you'll settle everything?"

"One other thing," said D. "What did you tell Lydia?"

Scratching his head sheepishly, the financier replied, "Oh, that? Um, it was just something I pulled out of my ass then and there. Told her you were the bastard son of the Sacred Ancestor!"

Everyone was left speechless.

"It was a joke! A joke!" Old El continued, laughing nervously. "But I'm gonna find her for sure!" he said, almost as if for his own benefit.

"That damn Matilda's gonna be my collateral, sure as I live and breathe."

"I'm going to sleep somewhere or other in the castle," Duchess Marlingen said with a great yawn. "For a thousand years or two. When I wake up, I really hope it's in a different world. Maybe I'll meet up with Matilda then." Drawing a breath there, she then gave D a strange look. "You saved me, and more than once. If it was what you owed me, you'd already paid that back. Tenfold, even. So, why'd you do it, then?"

D thought for a moment. "Call it interest." And then, leaving the speechless pair as they were, D offered a hand to the sobbing Didi. The boy clung to it, and D put him up on his shoulders and started walking down the corridor.

"Hey, wait a second!" Old El called out. Running after the Hunter, he pulled the boy away from him.

"This child wasn't part of anyone's debts," said D.

"Well, Lydia asked me to take care of him with her dying breath." Giving the boy a kind look, the old man said, "C'mon, you're coming with me. Being with me's a real adventure!"

Didi's reaction was an honest one. He clung to D's neck for dear life.

"Little bastard," Old El groused, but it was effaced by the sound of a door opening.

Everyone but D turned a puzzled face in that direction.

The woman who stood there was like a hot air balloon. Her sumptuous garments and jewels looked like they might burst at any moment. And the woman was missing one ear.

"Oh, yeah—there was *another girl* around here, wasn't there?" Old El said, eyes alight.

"You're a daughter of the marquis? I'll be damned," the duchess remarked, her expression becoming equally intrigued.

"Yes. Pudding is the name. Where has everyone gone?" she asked.

"Here and there," the old man replied, licking his chops. Not a whit of interest in Didi remained. "Sure, you're probably an organic robot or some nonsense, but I've gotta ask if you're really Verenis's daughter."

"Of course I am. And it shan't go well for you if you continue to harbor any odd suspicions!"

"Got any talents?" Old El asked.

"I consider myself a good singer," the woman replied as she inched backward, apparently guessing that this was a somewhat turbulent situation.

"Yeah, nobody cares about that. Could you scarf down as much human food as ten people in one sitting?"

"I believe I could manage that."

"Then it's settled. You've got an interesting look to you, and if we bill you as the Noble's daughter who can eat ten servings' worth of potatoes, you can earn me a small fortune as an attraction even if you can only work nights. Verenis, you went and left me a nice little memento, you bastard!"

"I'm in for a piece of this, too," the duchess declared.

"Sure, we split the profits eighty-twenty, though!"

"I'll thank you not to pull my leg. I lent them far more money than you did. Twenty-eighty is more like it."

"Screw you."

"Oh, you ready to fight over this?"

"Shit. Seventy-thirty."

"Thirty-seventy."

Ultimately settling on a fifty-fifty split, the old man and the duchess saw dalas signs when they looked at the dazed Pudding, but as they donned their phony smiles, they finally seemed to remember D and Didi and turned to face them. Naturally, no sign of either remained in that realm of filthy lucre.

END

Postscript

This past September, I turned 74. That same month marked 41 years since my debut novel, *Demon City Shinjuku*, was published in 1982. That means that my second novel published in January of the following year, *Vampire Hunter D*, had its 40th anniversary. Once my debut novel was published by Asahi Sonorama Bunko, which is no longer around, my first thought was that I'd like to do something with vampires next. I had a powerful urge to do the first Japanese novelization of the 1958 film *Horror of Dracula*, which had, in a manner of speaking, determined the course of my life.

If you'll allow me to write a bit about this masterpiece, my encounter with it during the summer when I was in the fifth grade could even be called a tad dramatic.

The port town where I lived at the time had a population of over 90,000, and there were seven movie theaters. (Now, there's just one). *Horror of Dracula* played at one of them as a local engagement (I guess?), but for some reason I missed out on seeing it. For starters, the previous year I'd actually had a hair-raising experience when I went to Tokyo. One of the movie billboards lining the streets of the Ginza had an image of a man who might pounce on someone at any second, blood dripping from his mouth. (In fact, it was so scary, I had to look away after a moment, and even now I'm not entirely certain whether or not it was for *Horror of Dracula*).

Even writing the kind of novels I do these days, I'm still innately a coward, and when *Horror of Dracula* finally came to my hometown, I didn't go to see it at the theater. It may have been because the tagline promoting it, "A beautiful woman leaves her teeth marks in a man's neck", was too frightening. The film's engagement ended, and *Horror of Dracula* was gone from my life forever . . . or it should've been, but perhaps fate wouldn't allow it. Actually, one of the theaters in town specialized in return engagements. One week they'd show a Japanese gangster movie, another it would be AIP's *The Hideous Sun Demon* or *The Spider*, and I was surprised by their interesting line-up.

And then one day during summer vacation, several friends and I were delighted to hear a woman who taught our class recount the movie she'd just seen. A dead beauty returns from her coffin, transformed into a vampire, and a cross is pressed against her forehead, while a wooden stake is hammered through her heart . . . it goes without saying that *Horror of Dracula*, which I was meant to encounter, had come to the second run theater next to the cemetery. A few days later, my friends and I saw *Horror of Dracula* for the first time. And the scene where a stake is hammered into the vampire's heart scared us so much we all got out of our seats and fled to the bathrooms.

You know how the rest of the story goes. Lucy gets turned into a vampire, and is granted the peace of death by Doctor Van Helsing in a ghastly manner, and after Mina is ultimately attacked as well, Dracula and Van Helsing square off in Castle Dracula, and Dracula is exposed to sunlight and reduced to dust, and while all this was going on I was completely captivated by this movie.

Actually, I wasn't in time to catch the beginning of the movie, missing the nearly ten minutes from Harker's arrival at Castle Dracula to his encounter with the female vampire in the study. As a result, I also missed seeing the famous scene where Dracula appears at the top of the stairs. Regretting that, I asked a friend who'd seen the whole thing how the movie had started. What'd happened while Harker was in the castle? And I continued in that way *ad nauseam* until he threw a fit. It's almost impossible for me to describe the impression this movie had on me. They speak of people being possessed by something or someone, and I was hopelessly possessed by the movie *Horror of Dracula*.

To be honest, *Horror of Dracula* is a fairly sloppy movie. Firstly, the depictions of the tavern in the village where the Holmwood house and Castle Dracula are located, as well as garb of the patrons, are purely eastern European. However, they don't say that the Holmwood house is in London, as it is in the original novel. The town's undertaker is located at 49 Friedrichstrassen, and Castle Dracula is a half-day's ride away by carriage. They may have initially intended it to be eastern Europe when they filmed it, or changed it for screening for the sake of the tempo of the movie as a whole. However, that desperate measure (?) is what raised *Horror of Dracula* to the level of a masterpiece. The sense of speed and tension in the final act is no trifling matter. Going off to find Dracula when he is about to bury Mina alive (why is that?), the carriage bearing Van Helsing and Holmwood races along. Van Helsing pursues the fleeing Dracula. And as a fifth-grader, I was breathless and my eyes were glued to the screen as candlesticks were put together in the shape of a cross, driving Dracula back into a pool of sunlight on the floor, destroying him. Looking at it now, there are other things, like the fact that there are several months discrepancy between the dates in Harker's journal and the date the wagon carrying Dracula's coffin passed through the checkpoint, the question of how Mina managed to get Dracula's coffin into her own basement without anyone noticing when she was Dracula's puppet, or how Dracula happened to have a carriage and driver ready to make his escape. The questions pile up, but the crucial point was what kind of blood flowed through the veins of the people who watched this. I saw this as an elementary school student, a blank slate that could accept it all, but others my age might see it and just find it scary, while some grown adults could fall under its spell.

In which case, it would be a matter of "blood." Those who were captivated by it, myself included, had "the blood of *Horror of Dracula*" in their veins. Depending on how thick that blood was, some of them would merely be fans, while others like my late friend Hajime Ishida became researchers. And I became a writer. When the chance to write a novel finally presented itself, the very first thing I thought was that I wanted to write something as scary and delightful as *Horror of Dracula*. And yet, my debut novel turned out to be *Demon City Shinjuku* because stupid old common sense kicked in and made me question whether readers would take to something like that right out of the gate.

On the heels of the publication of *Demon City Shinjuku* in September of 1982, *Vampire Hunter D* hit bookstores in January of 1983. As for the setting of the *Vampire Hunter D* series—why D is a dhampir, the reason it's set in the far distant future, his connection to the left hand, the reason it's praised for resembling the western *Shane*—that discussion will have to wait until a later volume.

Hideyuki Kikuchi
November 3, 2023
While watching *30 Days of Night*

Vampire Hunter D

WILL RETURN IN

Volume 31
Sylvia's Road Home

Written by
Hideyuki Kikuchi

Illustrations by
Yoshitaka Amano

English translation by
Kevin Leahy

Coming soon from Dark Horse Books

ABOUT THE AUTHOR

Hideyuki Kikuchi was born in Chiba, Japan in 1949. He attended the prestigious Aoyama University and wrote his first novel, *Demon City Shinjuku*, in 1982. Over the past two decades, Kikuchi has written numerous works of weird fiction, and is one of Japan's leading horror masters, working in the tradition of occidental horror writers like Fritz Leiber, Robert Bloch, H.P. Lovecraft, and Stephen King. Many live-action and anime works in 1980s and 1990s Japan were based on Kikuchi's novels.

ABOUT THE ILLUSTRATOR

Yoshitaka Amano was born in Shizuoka, Japan in 1952. Recruited as a character designer by the legendary anime studio Tatsunoko at age 15, he created the look of many notable anime, including *Gatchaman*, *Genesis Climber Mospeada* (which in the US became the third part of *Robotech*), and *The Angel's Egg*, an experimental film by future *Ghost in the Shell* director Mamoru Oshii. An independent commercial illustrator since the 1980s, Amano became world famous through his design of the first ten *Final Fantasy* games. Having entered the fine arts world in the preceding decade, in 1997 Amano had his first exhibition in New York, bringing him into contact with American comics through collaborations with Neil Gaiman (*Sandman: The Dream Hunters*) and Greg Rucka (*Elektra and Wolverine: The Redeemer*). Dark Horse has published over 40 books illustrated by Amano, including his first original novel *Deva Zan*, *Shinjuku*, written by Christopher "Mink" Morrison, as well as the Eisner-nominated *Yoshitaka Amano: Beyond the Fantasy–The Illustrated Biography* by Florent Gorges.